Trace

— ♘ Coral Canyon Cowboys —

LIZ ISAACSON

ISBN-13: 978-1-63876-179-2

1

Trace Young stood third in line, behind Momma
and Daddy in the first row, and Tex, Abby,
Bryce, and Melissa in the second. His son stood
next to him, both of them with their hands clasped in front
of them, both wearing an identical suit and cowboy hat,
and both smiling as Morris, Leigh, and Eric walked down
the aisle.

"He's a character, isn't he, Dad?" Harry whispered as
Eric did a hop-skip step, and Trace nodded. He sure was.
Trace knew the effort it had taken Morris and Leigh to get
to this point. Ten months of hard work, forgiveness, therapy, and who knew what else. Trace didn't, though he'd
spoken to Morris several times about his relationship with
Leigh.

His brother was far more open to conversations of the
heart than Trace was. He'd refused to ask Everly to the

wedding, though he'd kept in contact with her for the past few months. Harry had acted like he didn't care about the dancing at Christmas, but Trace had quickly realized that was a public front.

Harry still very much cared who Trace went out with —as long as it was anyone but Everly. Trace had prayed about it, and the Lord had told him to choose his son. So as difficult as that had been, Trace had done it.

His heart hurt inside his chest, but the Lord had also whispered one more word to Trace while he'd been on his knees, alone in his dark, cold bedroom last winter.

Patience.

Patience, Trace felt like he did not possess enough of. He wasn't getting any younger, and every time he looked at Melissa, the tiny girl Tex and Abby had welcomed into their family only six weeks ago, he was consumed with jealousy.

At least that was all he had to repent for these days. He'd told the boy how very much he liked Everly, though he hadn't gone into many specifics of the random-not-random "meet-ups" last year. He'd left the other four-letter L-word out of the conversation, too, though Trace had definitely started to fall in love with her.

Harry was fourteen now, and Trace had been telling himself that he could be patient for four years, and then the boy would be on his own. Everly would be thirty-nine by then, as she'd turned thirty-five in March. Trace had sent her a text with seven words and a heart emoji.

She'd responded with the same heart emoji. Nothing more.

Happy birthday, my Ev. I miss you. <3

As far as he knew, she hadn't gone out with anyone else, but he didn't watch or participate in social media, and she certainly didn't have to report to him. He'd told her everything that Harry had said, and when he'd shared his impressions from God, Everly had wept quiet tears and nodded.

"All right, Trace," she'd said, sliding her slim, cool fingers down the side of his face. "Let's see what the future holds, all right?"

That was the last time he'd seen her in person, almost five months ago now. He could still feel the ghost of her hand on his face. Still hear the agony in her voice. He'd never kissed her, but he thought about it constantly.

He shook his head as Morris passed by him, fist-bumping Harry as he approached. Trace patted him on the back, but Tex took the man fully into a hug. Of course. Tex was larger than life in everything he did, and he could never allow Morris to simply walk past him to the altar.

Trace had been zoned out for what the other brothers had done, and once Morris, Leigh, and Eric reached the altar, everyone started taking their seats. Her sister and fiancée sat across the aisle from him and Harry, and Sheri took Eric onto her lap so his parents could get remarried.

He'd watched this couple pledge themselves to each other once before, and it hadn't felt quite this joyous. He knew God loved marriage and weddings, and Trace patted his son's knee, hoping the boy knew how much he loved him.

Harry looked at him, but Trace just returned his attention to the altar. Harry was slighter in the shoulder than Trace, but he was quickly becoming a man. He'd grown about six inches this year, and he'd started dancing lessons, advanced guitar lessons, and tennis lessons. He liked being active, and he played his guitar every single day. His lessons were done over the Internet, from a professor at UNLV—a contact of Blaze's that Trace had utilized.

The boy had plenty of friends, and a specific girl who called and texted him constantly. Trace had implemented the rule that the boy couldn't erase anything she sent him, and he had to talk to her out in the living room where Trace could hear. Harry hadn't liked that, but Trace had been firm.

"Then don't talk to her," he'd said.

"I talk to her at school without you there."

"Yeah, well, I don't worry about you sneaking into the bathroom to have sex with her at school. Do I need to? Because I can come over to the school if I need to."

Harry had turned the color of a deep, purple beet, sputtered something about not doing that, and gone to his room for the evening. Trace didn't regret the conversation, because he knew fourteen-year-old boys and what their hormones drove them to do.

"Leighann has her vows ready to read," the pastor said,

and Trace reminded himself to be present. Be in the now. Right here, not inside his head. Not living in the past, and not imagining what the future could hold.

She stepped slightly away from Morris, and as she stood facing the Young side of the tent, Trace could see her perfectly. She wore bright red lipstick to match her fingernails and her heels, and he liked how unconventional her attire was. He liked the quirkiness of it, and he liked that they hadn't allowed tradition to dictate their second round of nuptials.

"Morris," she said. "I have loved you since the moment I met you. I know our road here has been jagged, with steep inclines and sharp drop-offs. I'm sure it'll continue to be that way, because life isn't easy just because you're married. I've learned over the past year, however, that there is no one on this planet meant more for me than you. There is no one I trust more; there is no one I feel safer with; there is no one I love more than you."

She whispered the last couple of words and reached to swipe at the corner of her eye. "I don't want to be on the jagged, winding, terrifying road of life with anyone but you, and I will do my best to be a strong, capable, safe co-pilot for you, as well as the one driving when you're tired or stressed or need a break. Together, I know we can arrive at our final destination safely and happily. Together, we'll fill our own family book of life with amazing things. I want to be together with you forever."

Trace had to swipe at his own eyes after that, and

nothing his brother said could top what she'd just pledged to him. Trace also wanted that. He wanted a life partner. He wanted a copilot. He wanted a best friend, in whom he could confide his deepest cares and worries. Someone to carry his stress and hold his hand when things got hard.

"Wow," Harry whispered. "She loves him so much."

Trace put his arm around his son's shoulders and dipped his head closer to Harry's. "She sure does," he whispered back. "That's the kind of love you want, Harry. Don't settle for anything less."

His son looked at him, and Trace nodded. "Did you feel like that about Mom?" he asked.

Trace shook his head. "Not quite."

"What about Everly?" Harry asked.

Trace swallowed, suddenly praying for the right words to say. "I don't know, son. I need time with her to know." He hadn't truly had any time with her. He'd met her almost eighteen months ago now, but the actual time they'd spent together, getting to know one another had been very little of that.

He looked at Harry again. "You need time with her too. I won't bring anyone into my life that is bad for you, Harry. Not again." He set his jaw and nodded like that was that. Because it was.

Morris had been speaking his vows, and Trace listened as he said, "I love you with my whole heart and soul, Leigh. We'll build an amazing life for each other, and for our family, because we're two halves of the same whole."

They looked back at the pastor, who went through the legalities of marrying them, and then Morris gathered her into his arms and kissed her, his new wife. Trace got to his feet and clapped, his voice silent while many of his brothers whooped and hollered. Harry applauded too, and then he joined Bryce in the row in front of them. Trace took the few steps down the aisle to Morris and Leigh and waited his turn to give them a big hug.

"Well done, brother," he said to Morris, who clapped him on the back. He got out of the way so others could congratulate the couple, and he grabbed Harry and Bryce to go get the tables ready for lunch.

Immediately following that, Morris and Leigh were leaving on a short second honeymoon, and then they'd be back in Coral Canyon, ready to start their new chapter together.

Trace felt ready to do that too, but he'd been stuck grinding his wheels in muddy snow for months. The album was going extremely slow, and the future was wide open after that. No new contract had been signed yet, no tour dates for the album they still had to finish had been scheduled. Everything felt like it had been tossed up into the air and was taking its sweet Southern time to fall to the ground.

Sweet Southern time, he thought. *That's it!*

He spun back to the wedding, looking for Otis. "Sweet Southern time," he said aloud. "Otis?" He couldn't find him anywhere, as this wedding was full of tall, hatted men in black suits.

"Dad, he's over here," Harry called, and Trace surveyed the tables and chairs before him. They'd agreed to get everything set up so Leigh and Morris wouldn't need a wedding planner. Whiskey Mountain Lodge didn't do a lot of events, so they didn't have staff for such a thing. Leigh had rented the tent, the tables, and the chairs, and the Youngs were providing the manpower.

Otis looked up from where he'd just put two chairs at a table near the buffet. They'd catered the meal too, and Trace's sure step toward his brother stuttered as he saw a familiar face come out from behind the drape separating the food prep area and the service table.

Everly's brother. Shawn owned Pork and Beans, and while Trace had never been formally introduced to the man, he'd stopped by his new retail location in downtown Coral Canyon a time or two. He told himself it was because he liked the food—as Morris and Leigh obviously did too—but it was more than that. He just wouldn't admit to himself that he'd hoped to see Everly.

He looked away from Shawn Avery and his stilted step and grabbed a couple of chairs on his way to Otis. "Sweet Southern time," he said as he unfolded them.

Otis didn't need more introduction that that. His eyes rounded, and he paused in pulling the bright red bow over the back of the chair. "That's genius," he said. "Sweet Southern time."

"That's the song title," Trace said, his voice picking up speed. "We can switch out that line at the end of the first verse where it says 'he takes her to the five and dime' and put 'he kisses her on sweet Southern time.' Or something."

Otis started to laugh. "This is incredible. How could we not see this before now?"

Trace shrugged, his own grin wider than he thought possible. He continued setting up chairs and pulling on bows. Momma flitted around, putting huge vases of red and white roses in the middle of each table, and even Luke and Jem set out white napkins and red charger plates, which sat under the white plates they'd eat off of.

"Ladies and gentlemen," Gabe yelled from the back of the tent. "May I present, Mister and Missus Morris Young, and their beautiful son, Eric." He stepped out of the way, and the three of them entered the tent as if they'd recently been crowned royalty. Trace threw down the last bow, pushed it into place, and started clapping along with everyone else. Tex whistled, and Luke's booming voice filled the air.

Morris and Leigh walked to the front of the tent, where they'd sit with her parents and Momma and Daddy at the head table. He finally raised his hand to get everyone to calm down. "Thanks," Morris said into a handheld microphone. "Thank you for being here. I know how badly some of you dislike weddings, so right after you eat, you're free to leave."

He grinned at Leigh, handed her the mic, and she

swept her hand toward the buffet. "Hopefully, the food will be worth sitting through that terribly long ceremony." Several people laughed, because it had taken all of ten minutes. "We have Pork and Beans here with us today, and I'm going to let Shawn Avery talk about the food so y'all know what it is."

But it wasn't Shawn who ducked out of the tent this time.

It was Everly.

She wore a beautiful blue dress the color of the perfect summer sky over the Tetons. The fabric slipped and swayed around her, and Trace wanted to feel it slide between his fingers. He had to run his hands through her hair and hold her face and kiss her while she wore that dress.

That subtle makeup. That white flower tucked right over her ear.

She was female perfection, and Trace had to have her in his life.

He swallowed and looked around for Harry. His son wasn't looking at him, praise the heavens, and Trace's gaze darted back to the front of the tent as Everly's angelic voice spoke into the mic.

"Welcome Young family," she said, and her gaze swept the room—and landed on him.

2

Everly Avery lost her train of thought the moment her eyes met Trace's. He stood about halfway back in the tent, on her right side, and everything about him called to her. It always had, like he was the North pole and she the South.

In truth, they were separated by the entire world too, and Everly had no idea how to get closer to him. His son had put every barrier between them, and Trace had let him. She didn't doubt the things he'd told her a few months ago, but the attraction between them also couldn't be denied.

The food sat on her left, and she drew in a breath that shook in her mouth, throat, and lungs. Shawn was going to pay her double for getting out here and talking to this family. "Shawn's prepared brisket today, because he knows how much cowboys love a good piece of beef."

She grinned, her speech coming back to her now. She went over the country-style food, mentioned the drinks on the side table, and said, "Come get us if y'all need anything."

She looked back to Morris and Leigh, the two of them glowing with joy. "Congratulations to the happy couple. I believe they're going to have someone pray first." She handed the mic back to Leigh, nodded curtly, and got the heck out of the spotlight.

Once behind the white curtain, she sighed and ran her hand through her hair—or she tried. She'd pulled her long, blonde hair into a ponytail and set a white flower behind her ear, so she only succeeded in dislodging that.

"I'm not doing that again," she said to Shawn.

"You do it at every wedding," he said back. She hadn't told him about her insane on-again, off-again, secret relationship with Trace. She could still feel his big, warm hands on her waist from their dance at Christmastime.

Coming back to this lodge had been a mistake. The memories here were too fresh. Too real. Too wanted.

Her stomach growled and swooped, and she wished she was out there in the tent, settling down to eat with Trace and Harry. She wanted to hold Abigail's new baby girl, and give Leigh a hug as a fellow Young significant other. She felt cheated and robbed of such an experience, and she had no idea why.

She and Trace had never truly gotten serious. He'd whispered sexy things about falling in love with her in her ear, but he'd never kissed her. Even now, she reached up to her lips, as if they had tasted his and forgotten to tell her.

"Everly," someone said. "I need you over here."

She went toward the woman on wooden legs. She hated feeling like this. She'd walked and danced in a shell for a month after Trace had told her about the fight he'd had with his son. The world had been cold, blanketed in snow, and Everly's heart still was. It had been frozen in time from that day in January, and she didn't know how to thaw it out.

"Is this the spiced mayo we use for the potato-ham salad? Because they went through that first bowl like madmen." Keely laughed, and Everly managed to smile.

"That's it," she said. "Two cups. I pre-measured it, so all of it."

"More cowboy caviar," one of the food runners called, and Everly got to work. The Youngs had ordered food for seventy-five people, but they'd only set up tables and chairs for sixty. She figured men like the ones related to Trace could eat a lot, and the time in the prep row passed quickly.

"All served," Shawn finally said. "Now we just watch for seconds."

Everly started to stack used containers and pile them in the bins that had once held bowls full of food. She kept her head down and her hands busy, as she had for the past couple of years since moving here to Coral Canyon. She couldn't get in trouble that way, and by trouble, she meant she didn't let her thoughts wander to the gorgeous Trace Young.

A new scent entered her personal bubble, and Everly looked up as her brain tried to process it. Woodsy, spicy, and crisp—all belonging to the man now standing five feet from her.

Trace Young.

He gazed at her with an intent expression, his jaw, which sometimes jumped, perfectly still. "Everly," he said, his voice smooth and velvety. She'd listened to every single Country Quad song since meeting him, always searching for his voice. She could find it easily now, through all the harmonies, the guitars, and the drums.

It connected to her, infused inside her, and haunted her in her dreams.

"Can I talk to you for a second?" he asked, his eyes finally moving to the activity and people around them.

She wiped her hands on a dish towel and tossed it into a bin. "All right."

He nodded and turned around. After leading her out of the prep row and behind it, he just kept going. Everly wore a dress and wedged sandals, and they'd left the flatter part of the yard. "Where are we going?" she asked, struggling to walk at all. She definitely couldn't keep up with his long, determined stride.

"Just over here," he said. He reached a sidewalk and started down it. Everly went after him, not sure why she was tagging along like a lovesick puppy. Probably because that's what she was.

A barn came into view, along with a paddock with a couple of horses in it. Trace stepped off the sidewalk again and went over to the biggest, brownest one. Everly wasn't familiar with horses, so she had no idea what kind it was. It seemed gentle enough, and she moved to stand only an arm's length from him.

He stood there and bent his head toward the horse's. He stroked the side of its neck and said nothing, which only irritated her now. "Trace," she said crisply.

He looked at her. "I'm sorry," he said.

She folded her arms. "We've had this conversation."

"I know, but I hate how you look at me."

Everly tilted her head at him, trying to find the true meaning behind his words. Trace didn't always say what he meant, and that had taken some getting used to. He was a puzzle she was desperate to figure out. "How do I look at you?"

"Like you're nervous." His feet shifted. "I'm nervous too. Remember I told you how you make me nervous on our first date?"

"Our *only* date, Trace." She looked at the horse too and lifted her hand as an enormous black one plodded over to her. "I don't mean to look at you like that."

"I hate it," he said. "I want you to light up when you see me, not be scared of what might happen."

Everly didn't know how to answer. She wasn't scared,

exactly. It was more like...just nerves. Anxious. She wasn't sure if he'd come talk to her or ignore her. Both weren't great options. They had no options right now.

"Has anything changed, Trace?" she asked.

The two of them stood there at the fence, each stroking a horse, not looking at one another. Anyone walking by wouldn't know her heartbeat thrashed in her chest, or that she'd already started wondering if she could ask him to meet her at the ice cream shoppe later that night, after his son had gone to bed.

No, she told herself. *You won't ask him to sneak around again.*

It had been fun for her. Exciting. A thrilling, almost forbidden relationship. It had been torture for him, and Everly didn't want to make his life harder. She wasn't the one who had to justify where she went and when to a teenager, and she still didn't know why Harry's opinion of who Trace dated trumped his own.

"Not much," he said. "That's the point, Ev. I want you to know nothing's changed."

"Then why are we here?"

"I...my feelings for you haven't changed." He did look at her then. "Are you seeing someone else? Dating?"

She couldn't hold his gaze, deep, dark, and delicious as it was. She looked back at the horse, whose eyes had gone semi-closed. "No," she whispered.

"Have your feelings for me changed?" he asked.

She shook her head this time.

He finally removed the weight of his gaze from her, and she nearly sagged into the fence in relief.

"I love your dress," he whispered. "That flower in your hair."

"Thank you, sir," she said, a playful smile coming to her face. She glanced over to him. "I like your hat."

A smile touched his lips for a moment, then drifted away. "Thank you, ma'am." He tipped the cowboy hat at her and then moved back from the horse. He faced her fully now, ignoring the equine as it nosed his shoulder. "I am lost without you," he said, pure regret in his voice and his eyes. "Do you think I should try talking to Harry again?"

"What good would it do?" she asked. "Has he changed?"

Trace ducked his head. "I don't know."

"You're the only one who can decide that," Everly said. "I don't want to put you in a tight spot with him again." She shook her head. "I really don't, Trace."

He took a step toward her. "I want to play for you," he said.

"Mm." She focused on her horse again, her adrenaline buzzing with his nearness. "I'd like that, cowboy. I've already danced for you."

"It was incredible," he whispered. His hand floated along her waist, and Everly pulled in a breath and closed her eyes. She felt him all around her, the scent of his skin, the warmth of his breath, the way he held her so close, so close as they danced inside the lodge up the hill.

He took hold of her waist and turned her toward him, and Everly only had time to open her eyes and look up at him before he said, "I'm going to kiss you now," in that slow, sweet, sexy voice he possessed.

He swiped his cowboy hat off his head, looked straight into her eyes, and leaned toward her.

Surprise left Everly speechless, but her eyes fluttered closed again, her pulse beating with rapid wings in her throat. Trace hadn't kissed her, and she'd never imagined it would happen at Whiskey Mountain Lodge beside two horses at his brother's wedding.

But as he touched his lips to hers, their first kiss exploded into all of the repressed feelings she'd kept caged for so long.

They breathed in together, and then Trace matched his mouth to hers again, and Everly found the ability to kiss him back, stroke for stroke, her hands wandering along his shoulders, his neck, and into his hair as if they had a mind of their own.

Oh, he was trouble with a capital T, and Everly only wanted more, more, more of him. So she kept kissing him, praying they could deal with the fallout later.

3

Trace could stroke his mouth against Everly's for a good, long while. He'd fantasized about this moment, these long, tender moments between them, with her fingernails tracing a pattern along the back of his neck, sending fiery shivers down his spine.

She tasted like salt and apples, and he'd never need anything but those two things for the rest of his life.

Everly pulled away, and Trace's lips smoked and tingled at the same time. "Hey," he whispered, wanting her touch again.

"Your phone." She reached into his inside jacket pocket for him, eliciting another tremor to move through his whole body. She plucked it out just as it started to ring.

His mind fired at him—this had happened while he'd been kissing her. He'd just been so deep into the kiss, he'd managed to ignore the irritating ringtone.

"It's Harry." She handed him the phone and backed up a step at the same time.

Trace wanted to draw her right back into his chest and lace his fingers together on the small of her back while she pressed into him. Instead, he swiped on the call from his son. His eyes caught on the number of missed calls as he lifted his phone.

Six. And not just from Harry.

Trace's pulse danced beneath his ribs. "Hey," he said as brightly as he could as Everly turned away from him.

"Where are you?" Harry hissed. "Uncle Morris is waiting for you to do the send-off, and no one can find you."

"Uh, yeah." Trace reached for Everly's hand, took it, and headed back to the sidewalk at a decent clip. "I'm on my way back right now. Just went for a walk."

"Went for a walk?" an angry voice demanded. "And lost service somehow?" Luke. He'd obviously grabbed the phone from Harry. "Wow, this luxury lodge—where you've never lost service before—must really be on the decline."

Trace rolled his eyes as his feet met cement. "I'm literally two seconds down the path. I just needed a minute."

"Well, hurry up." Scuffles filled the line, and Harry sighed into the phone.

"He just grabbed the phone, Dad."

"It's fine," Trace said. "I can handle Luke." He glanced over to Everly. Could he handle her? Or Harry?

She gave him a small smile that didn't broadcast any nerves, or embarrassment, or anything out of the ordinary other than it wasn't full of her usual wattage.

"See you in a second," he said to Harry, and he hung up and shoved the phone back into his breast pocket without counting how many calls he'd missed from others.

His pulse picked up speed, and not because of the incline of the sidewalk that went back to the flat ground where the tents had been set up.

He couldn't be seen walking back to the wedding—late—hand-in-hand with Everly Avery. She seemed to sense his rising emotion, because she slipped her hand away from him and ducked behind him. "I'm going to run inside the lodge for a minute," she said.

"Ev," he said, but he wasn't sure what to add to it.

"It's okay, Trace," she said. Her lovely smile didn't appear. "Go be with your family and son. I'm sure I'll see you again really soon, okay?"

She stretched up and brushed her lips along his cheek, and Trace couldn't help leaning into the touch, his eyelids falling softly closed. Then she left, and Trace took precious seconds that Luke would be livid about to watch her slip inside the lodge.

He faced the hill again, and he'd taken a couple of steps when Tex and Otis arrived. Trace's relief swept through him, and he hated it.

Still, he raised his hand and called, "I'm sorry. I'm comin'." He hurried now, drinking in Tex's frown and

Otis's open curiosity. Trace trusted these two brothers the very most, but he didn't know how to open his mouth and tell them the truth.

So many knots curled inside him, and he knew he'd never be able to sleep deep enough to get true rest until he unraveled all of the secrets in his life, laid them flat, and spilled them all.

He knew it, and yet he said, "Sorry. I just needed a minute away."

"Fair enough," Tex said. "But you answer your phone."

"Sorry," Trace said again. He knew Morris was on a tight schedule to get out of Coral Canyon and on the road for his honeymoon, and guilt tightened the knots in Trace's throat.

Thankfully, Tex and Otis absorbed some of the tension as the three of them stepped into the tent, and he took the punching balloon his son held for him.

Morris and Leighann had been married before, in a much more formal affair, with more press, and bigger celebrities in attendance. Morris had just been drafted into the NFL at the time, and the differences between this wedding and that one stood out in Trace's mind.

This was mostly family and very close friends from Coral Canyon and the lodge, and Trace felt the weight of every single eye as he took his place in line.

Eric started skipping down the created aisle, and the punching balloons had been his idea. The almost-four-year-old loved balloons, and he'd said in an off-hand comment that they sounded like fists clapping, and Morris and Leigh had decided then to use them for their send-off.

Trace managed to smile as his nephew, whom he hadn't known about a year ago, pranced by him, and he found a rhythm with his balloon. The sound crescendoed as Eric moved down the aisle, and then Morris and Leigh came through the tent.

Trace whooped with his voice too, and the noise his family of nine men could make was unbelievable. Morris held Leigh's hand as he paused in front of Trace, and Trace put his arms around both of them simultaneously.

He should apologize, but instead, he said, "I love you guys."

"Love you, brother," Morris practically yelled.

Trace nodded and released them so they could go down the rest of the line of well-wishers. Trace got his balloon going again, if only so as to not draw more attention to himself than he already had.

He grinned at Harry, and the two of them beat their balloons at one another until they couldn't anymore due to how hard they were laughing.

Trace finally bopped his balloon high into the air and let it drift away from him, the rubber band dragging it back to the ground.

Harry kept his, and Trace slung his arm around his son.

"You going to Grandma's tonight with the other cousins?"

Harry turned and looked at Trace, and he didn't have to tilt his head back as far as he once had.

"I was hopin' to," he said. "After I meet up with Sarah and Mal and Brady at Casper's."

"Mm." Trace didn't think his son could hear his guttural hum of displeasure, and Harry kept searching his face.

"Can I?" Harry asked. "I helped Uncle Tex with the horses already, and Bryce is takin' all the younger cousins bowling first. Grams said she's getting pizza at eight." Harry'd gone real serious, and Trace saw so much of himself in his son.

He'd been the boy's sole caregiver for a couple of years now, and neither of them had heard from Val, except for a single birthday card in January which came near enough to Harry's big day to remind them both that Val remembered she had a son.

The last communication had been three months ago now, and the return address had been absent.

The stamps had been foreign, European, and Trace honestly didn't care where his ex-wife currently lived. He and Harry had carved out a solid, stable life here in Coral Canyon, and Trace prayed every day that whatever was best for Harry and the forthcoming album and tour of Country Quad would come to fruition.

Trace played lead guitar and sang back-up for Tex for

Country Quad. He helped Otis write a lot of the music. He kept Luke calm and grounded. Together, the four of them had enjoyed a fabulous country music career in Country Quad, and Morris—their band manager— currently had another contract from their record label that they hadn't signed.

Trace wouldn't be opposed to putting his signature on another dotted line, but he didn't think Tex would. Even traveling for the tour of this last album on their contract would not be his first choice.

"If I can't go," Harry said next. "I need to text and let them know." He let his balloon droop to his side as he lifted his phone. His eyebrows raised too, and Trace hated this part of parenting.

He honestly didn't mind if his son went out with friends. Every time Harry asked if they could come back to the house and watch movies, Trace said yes. He ordered burgers and fries, popped popcorn, and spent the evening in his bedroom so Harry could have the living room.

He knew Harry's friends by name, and they knew him. He knew the boy's girlfriend, even if Harry said they hadn't put labels on their relationship. He'd asked his son over and over if he'd kissed Sarah, and Harry never had— at least that was the report Trace got.

His lips tingled, the memory of kissing Everly as physical as it was mental and emotional. "Yeah," he said. "You can go. How are you going to get there?"

His son couldn't drive yet, and Trace spent a large

portion of his time arranging transportation for his teenager too.

"Brady's mom is driving us," he said. "Since we're on the way, he said they'd stop by and get me."

"All right," Trace drawled. "And you're sleeping at Grandma's?"

"Yep." He pocketed his device. "What are you gonna do?"

Trace swallowed, the lump in his throat too big to get down all the way. "I don't know." That was true, of course. He knew what he *wanted* to do, but he didn't know if Everly would be available.

Blaze laughed loudly, and Trace let himself get distracted over to another group of family. Here, he could stand quietly without the focus on him, as Blaze was a big rodeo star, and he loved the spotlight though he'd retired last year.

Trace pulled out his own phone, and he started typing out a message to Everly. *Harry's going to spend the evening with friends and then his grandparents. I was thinking you could come over and I'll try not to burn the pancakes this time.*

He smiled to his device, as he'd cooked once for Everly, and it hadn't gone well. They'd carried on an under-the-radar relationship last year, and Trace hadn't been able to stomach it for very long. The sneaking around, the secrets, the half-truths. They still ate at his conscience, and he didn't want anything between him and Harry.

Talk to him again. The words ran through his head, and Trace looked up from his phone. He could find Harry right now and talk to him about going out with Everly that night.

His son was getting older now, and he understood more, and he had a solid footing of friends and relationships here in Coral Canyon now. Things weren't what they'd been eighteen months ago when Trace and Everly had first gone out.

Upon the first scan of the remaining guests, Trace didn't see Harry. His phone chimed, and he glanced down at it, some insane part of his mind imagined it would be Everly, suggesting a romantic dinner date for the two of them that evening.

It wasn't Everly, but a group message that took a moment to download to all the parties.

From Luke, to all the brothers, even Gabe. *Cards tonight? My place. It's been a while...*

Warmth spread through Trace's chest, because Luke really was trying to establish or re-establish his brotherly connections.

He didn't want to be the first to say no, because then he'd have to say he'd rather go out with Everly, and no one knew about Everly Avery and his obsession with the woman. Except maybe Morris.

"And Luke," Trace murmured. Luke had conspired

with Everly last Christmas to stage a dance with Trace, right here at this lodge.

He looked up from his phone and found Luke's eyes, as the man stood only a few feet from him. "I don't know about anyone else," he said. "But I'm in."

Luke nodded and leaned toward Trace. He leaned in too, Luke's hand landing on his shoulder. "If it's just me and you, you can tell me what happened with you and Everly after you snuck away from the wedding together."

Trace's heartbeat stopped completely, and he jerked back from Luke. His brother grinned at him, his deep, dark eyes glittering like fool's gold.

His phone chimed, and Luke looked down at his phone. "Oh, Mav's in." Another buzz. "So is Otis." He looked up again. "Guess you're off the hook...for now."

"Luke," Trace said, the name full of warning.

"Don't worry," his brother said. "I won't say anything to anyone."

Trace nodded, because he trusted Luke too. "Thank you."

"What are you going to do?" Luke asked.

Trace only shook his head as Blaze's attention swung toward the pair of them. "I used to live in Vegas, boys," he said. "I don't think you really want me to play cards with you." He wore his wide, nearly-manic smile, which meant Blaze had something that grin was covering up.

"We don't play with money," Luke said.

"Where's the fun in that?" Blaze asked, his eyebrows

drawing down. He focused on Trace. "Where'd you disappear to earlier?"

A flash of a blue dress caught in his peripheral vision, and Trace employed every ounce of willpower he possessed not to look for Everly. "Nowhere," he said. "Is Jem coming to card night?" He looked around innocently, as Jem had surely been invited. "I hear he's quite the shark when it comes to cards...."

Blaze scowled, and that made Trace and Luke start to laugh. A twinge of guilt cut through Trace that he'd used Blaze's jealousy of Jem against him just to get out of an awkward question, but he met Luke's eye, and his younger brother nodded. So maybe it was okay to deflect for the time being.

"Eight-thirty," Luke said as he turned toward his daughter. He scooped her into his arms. "Come on, baby. Let's get on home and get you out of this dress so you can go to Grammy's."

"I'll bring the cards," Trace said, to which Luke nodded before he walked away. Trace looped his arm around Blaze's shoulders. "You should come. It's fun, even without the stakes."

Blaze looked doubtful, and he cocked one eyebrow. "Does anyone throw punches?"

"Nah," Trace said. "Now, elbows...I can't guarantee that Tex won't throw those. He really likes the Special Dark Milky Way bars."

4

Everly seemed to be tuned into Trace's DNA. She could look up from wrapping a full pan of left-over mini cheesecakes and find him in less time than it took her to inhale. She wondered if that was because he'd finally kissed her. Like that missing piece between them had fallen into place and couldn't be denied, no matter the time, space, or distance between them.

Their eyes met, but Trace tipped his head back and laughed at something Blaze had said. The other man chuckled too, and Everly ducked her head and picked up the tin of desserts. Earlier, Trace's kiss had revived her weary muscles, but without him, her exhaustion quickly marched through her again.

Behind the curtain, she slid the tin into the rack.

"That's it," she told Shawn, who glanced over to her from the table he scrubbed.

"Thanks, Ev," he said. "We'll load, and I'll take you to dinner." He gave her smile, and Everly returned it.

"Okay," she said. "But it better be somewhere you're sure you'll like. I'm not listening to you complain about the food somewhere and how yours is *so* much better." She patted her brother's chest while he tried to protest, but he so did that. All the time.

Dining with him was a nightmare, honestly.

"Should I call Reg?" she asked. "Maybe we can get him to give us a report on that Nancy girl he's dating."

Shawn's right eyebrow quirked. "Sure," he said. "He's not going to do that...unless you start talking about a certain cowboy-hatted man." The other eyebrow went up, and Everly stepped away from her oldest brother.

"Nothing to tell there," she said, swallowing the lie. "I've told you guys that."

"The way your eyes turn sad suggests otherwise," Shawn said. He went back to the table, where he'd spilled something jammy and red. "I'm telling you; you've got to give that singer an ultimatum."

Everly turned away from the advice. She'd heard it before, and she didn't agree with him. Trace's situation wasn't as simple as Shawn would like it to be. Or as Everly would like it to be.

She'd tried to be patient, but now that she knew what it felt like to kiss Trace, to be kissed by such a giant of a man like him, she was utterly ruined. She wanted more, and she wanted it now.

"Everly," someone said, and she turned toward one of the waitresses she'd been working with. "Can I get your help out here?"

"Sure." Everly went back out into the main area of the tent, where a lot of the guests had left. She caught sight of Harry talking to Trace, their father-son hug, and then Harry left with his uncle Luke. Everly's pulse pounded in the vein in her neck, no matter how she tried to deep-breathe it away.

"Should we empty these drink containers?" Keely asked. "They're pretty heavy."

"We separate them," Everly said, her words the result of working events with Shawn for the past several months. "I'll get the smaller barrels."

"Need some help?"

She shivered at the nearness of that delectable, smooth-as-velvet voice which could sing the most romantic lyrics. Heat shot from her head to her toes and rebounded back as Everly turned to face Trace.

He stood there with Gabe, who looked identical to the groom, who'd already left with his bride. Both Youngs smiled, and Everly swore she heard Keely sigh.

"Yes," she said, a giggle following the word. Everly did her best not to melt, but the memory of Trace's mouth against hers had her practically on her knees.

"Show me what you do," Gabe said, and he went off with Keely.

"Boss me, Everly," Trace said, and she gestured for him to follow her behind the curtain.

"We need this out at the van," she said. "We have a built-in rack there, and it'll go twice as fast if I don't have to climb in and out to load them."

Trace put his hands on the rack and started to push. Everly led the way, glancing over her shoulder. "The wedding sure was nice."

"Yeah," he said. "They're real happy." He smiled too, all the harsher lines in his handsome face evening out and smoothing away with the gesture.

"How's the album going?" she asked. "Last time we talked, you and Otis were almost ready to start over on... something. *How the woman won?*" Her eyebrows went up, and his mirrored her.

"You remember the name of the song?"

"Did I get it right?"

"Yes." The wheels on the cart caught as he tried to push it up onto the sidewalk, but he man-handled it, added some oomph, and got the job done.

They walked along the narrower sidewalk there, a house to the right and the enormous lodge to the right. The silence between them had never bothered her, because Trace said the important things out loud. He showed her the other things, and Everly really wanted to see him more often.

"The song is going okay," he said. "We might've made a break-through on it a month or so ago, but Tex is still butchering it."

She smiled and nodded. "You said he always does that."

"I had a break-through on a different song tonight, actually."

"One of your real-life moments?" she asked. He'd told her how sometimes, when he was just living his regular life, his mind could relax enough to find the way through the music to the right emotion. From him, she'd learned that writing music, playing the guitar, and singing the things he wrote wasn't just about words. It was about a feeling. It was about conveying something with just the right note, with a very small number of words—just the *right* words, he'd told her.

"Yeah," he said. "Weddings are stuffed full of emotion."

Her stomach swooped as she indicated the van. She opened the back of it and splayed the doors wide before she faced him. "Is that why you kissed me? You were just overcome with the emotions here?"

"No," he said quickly. His throat bobbed as he swallowed. "I kissed you, because I had to know if we still had something to fantasize over, or if I was torturing myself for no reason."

Oh, this man. He always knew exactly what to say.

She ducked her head and tucked her hair. As she climbed into the van, she asked, "And?"

He slid a tin out of the cart and handed it to her. With both of their fingers on it, hers on one end and his on the other, he met her eyes and said, "And my fantasies weren't even close to how good the real thing was."

He released the tin, and Everly had to hold it herself. She quickly slid it into the top slot of the built-in rack in the van. By the time she turned back to Trace, he had another tray ready for her.

"What are you doing tonight?" she asked as she took the chilled tin of desserts. "Do you want—?"

"Everly," he said quietly, but with plenty of power. "You don't get to ask me out, remember?"

"I just saw Harry leave with Luke," she said, her eyebrows up. She made no move to turn and slide the tray into a slot. "And you're just standin' there like you didn't kiss me an hour ago." He'd kissed her like he was a drowning man, and she was his last breath of air.

"My brothers are playin' cards tonight," he said in a near-growl. "I can't...beg out of that without some major explanations."

She took the tray and turned away from him. "Fine, Mister Young," she said. "But I'm not feeling very patient right now." And Lord knew she'd been nothing but patient with this cowboy. More than she'd been with anyone before, ever.

There was a good reason why, and his kiss had spun

her world on its axis too. Before that, she'd wondered if she could walk away; now she knew she couldn't. At least not without her heart torn right in two.

She turned back to him, and Trace had crowded right into the back bumper of the van without gathering another tin for her. His hands slid along her waist, which sent flames licking down her legs and ice straight up her spine.

She put her hands on his broad shoulders and refused to look into those eyes. They undid her completely every time, and he seemed to know it.

"Tomorrow?" he asked. "Harry will be back at school tomorrow. You don't dance until two." He ran the tip of his nose along her throat, his lips at her ear when he whispered, "Plenty of time for breakfast or lunch...or both."

She smiled against the side of his face. "Seems like it," she said.

"Is that a yes?"

She pulled back and met his eye now, a measure of seriousness pulling through her. She'd always been the playful one in the relationship, because Trace was always so serious, so quiet, so down-to-earth.

"It's only a yes if we can talk about how this time is going to be different than the last two."

A hint of frustration filled his expression, and plenty of it poured out in his sigh. "I don't know the answer to that."

"You don't have to know the answer to talk about something," she said. She searched his face, trying to place his emotion. "That was the single best kiss of my life, and I don't want to...." She trailed off, because the cowboy already had an ego the size of Greenland. Sort of. Only on stage, he said. He'd never treated her with anything but kindness, tenderness, and respect. A pure country gentleman, the best kind of man, and someone Everly had always wanted to be with.

"We can talk about anything you want, Miss Everly."

"All right," she said. "Now, hand me something else before Shawn comes out and says he won't pay me for flirting when I should be working."

He chuckled, stepped back, and had just picked up another tin when Shawn said, "Oh, good, you roped some muscle into helping."

"Shawn," Trace said, moving to shake her brother's hand. "The food was fantastic, as always."

"Thanks," he said, shaking Trace's hand quickly, his smile professional and quick. "Ev, how about Boulders? Reg says he's in, but only if we go there."

Everly took another tin from Trace, their eyes skidding past one another. "Shawn, you *hated* Boulders last time we went."

"Do you two have plans?" Shawn looked between the two of them, and even Everly saw the flush crawl up Trace's neck.

"No," Everly said. "But my rule was that we go somewhere where you won't complain about the food."

"Reggie won't come if it's not Boulders."

Everly sighed, because she was constantly stuck between her brothers. She and Shawn were closer in age, but Reggie had been a caboose baby, coming along when Everly was twelve years old. When their parents had died three years ago, Everly had immediately uprooted herself to come to Wyoming, only to be near Reggie, who was attending college here.

She moved twice as fast as Shawn started handing in tins too. "Fine," she said. "But I'm ordering five courses."

Trace chuckled and shook his head. "Boulders is fast casual, Ev. The best you'll get is a rice crispy treat as dessert."

Shawn stopped working and stared at Trace as he handed her the last tin. She slid it into the rack and said, "Go put that in the other van, would you?"

"Sure thing." He trundled away with the cart, it rumbling and tossing metallic sounds into the quiet mountain air.

"Stop it," Everly hissed at Shawn.

He turned back to her, his own blonde hair too long right now. "What?"

"You're staring at him like he's got three heads."

"He called you *Ev*." He leaned forward and took Everly's hand as she jumped down out of the back of the van. In her wedges, that was a feat. "You're *so* seeing him."

"He asked me out for tomorrow." She cut a glance over to Trace, but the second van had been parked several spaces away. "I like him, okay?"

The fire in Shawn's eyes softened. "I know you do. What will this be? Try three?" Together, they faced Trace as he wrestled with the rack and finally got it in the back of the van.

He turned back toward them, and Everly waved to him. He tipped his hat at her, ducked his head, and walked away. "The third time's the charm, right?"

5

Trace shook the pan with the sausage links, the satisfying sizzling making him smile. Truth be told, the fact that Everly would be arriving soon was responsible for his grin. She'd texted fifteen minutes ago to say she just had to stop by her brother's house and then she'd be on her way to his place.

Harry had been at school for an hour, and Trace wasn't bad in the kitchen. He'd gotten better and better in the past couple of years, since he'd been responsible for feeding another human being besides himself. He'd even taken a class at the community center, though that had been short-lived.

He didn't like getting hit on when he should be tending to his bacon bits, that was for sure. Plus, no other woman in town interested him in the slightest—only Everly.

His mind whirred as he thought about his forthcoming conversation with the woman. He lidded the pan and turned his attention to the Belgian waffle batter. He'd made these several times for himself and Harry over the past year since he'd asked his momma for the recipe, and the batter looked light and ready, with the bubbles big and open along the top of it.

The iron beeped, and he opened the top lid to scoop in the batter. He did that on both sides of the iron, two waffles now baking. He poured a pint of whipped cream into the mixing bowl, tossed in a handful of sugar and a splash of vanilla, and got that rotating on the stand mixer.

The doorbell rang, and Trace spun toward the front door. His heartbeat leapfrogged over itself, and he blew out his breath. "Calm down," he told himself. "It's Everly."

He wasn't nervous around her anymore, but at the same time, he was. He couldn't lose her, and it honestly felt like they'd been dangling over the edge of a cliff for months and months.

Could he kiss her?

His mind buzzed around that as he walked to the front door, wiped his hands on the apron around his waist, and then twisted the doorknob. He'd just thought that if she was wearing pink, he'd kiss her when she came into view.

A dumb criteria, but Trace honestly felt himself at a loss when it came to the gorgeous blonde standing on his front stoop—not a stitch of pink in sight.

He so should've gone with white, as the angel in front

of him wore a flowing, white dress that had fluttery and billowy sleeves along her shoulders and then fell to her ankles. He couldn't tell if she was wearing shoes or not, but Trace honestly wouldn't be surprised if she wasn't. Everly had told him once that as a dancer, she spent a lot of time in her bare feet.

"I think someone might be lost," he said, leaning into the doorjamb and kicking a smile in her direction.

She peered past him in mock confusion. "It's not me," she said. "So unless this isn't your house...." She grinned back at him and held up a container of freshly squeezed orange juice. "Shawn's offering for our date."

Trace's surprise rose, but he stepped back into the house, giving her room to enter. "Did you tell him about us?"

"Yes." Everly entered, and it was the first time she'd been to his house, a fact that Trace became painfully aware of as she surveyed the living room. He hadn't gone crazy cleaning it up—he'd literally just remembered she'd never been here before—but thankfully, it was fairly put together.

The blanket Harry had used last night still sat wadded up on the couch, and Trace resisted the urge to go fold it and drape it over the back of the sofa. He'd been cooking, so the kitchen couldn't be expected to be clean, and he didn't have small children or pets, so there weren't finger-prints or noseprints on the sliding glass door or any of his furniture.

"This is nice," she said, turning to him. "I can see where that painting would go." She nodded over to the fireplace. "I could do one for you." Her perfectly sculpted eyebrows lifted in a silent question.

"Sure," he said easily. "Then, when you're rich and famous, I'll have an original."

She laughed, the sound light and airy like wind moving gently through chimes. "I'll never be rich and famous, Trace. Not like you."

"Yeah, well, there are pros and cons." He didn't deny he was rich and famous. He had more money than he could ever spend, and he did get recognized from time to time, especially on tour. The people of Coral Canyon treated him like a normal person, because he was a normal person.

"I love your couch," she said. "Is it microfiber?"

"Yeah," Trace said. "I have my nieces and nephews sometimes, and some of them are pretty little." He went into the kitchen, hurrying now to get back to the things he'd left cooking. The waffle iron steamed, and he pulled open the lid to a golden, crisp waffle.

"Yum," Everly said as she followed him and slid onto a bench.

"It's waffles and sausage," he said over the sound of the mixer. The cream was practically butter, so he flipped it off quickly and went back to getting the heat off the sausage and waffles. He couldn't afford to burn breakfast, because he wanted everything about this morning date to be perfect.

He slid the waffle onto a plate and put it in front of her. "There's butter and syrup, and that's my momma's buttermilk syrup, not maple. I have that too." He turned and opened the microwave, where he'd been warming the syrup.

He grabbed the sausage on the turn back to the island and put it all down in the line he'd created before she'd arrived. "And fruit and cream." A rubber spatula quickly brought the overwhipped cream down a little, and he looked at her. "Do you want to say grace?"

Her face shone with a light Trace hadn't seen before. Or maybe he hadn't noticed because a new door had opened between them the moment he'd touched his lips to hers. "I'll say grace." She shook her hair over her shoulders, and he noticed she'd clipped back the sides with golden barrettes. He wanted to carefully pull those out as he kissed her, but that fantasy would have to wait.

She wasn't wearing pink, and he wasn't going to lunge at her and kiss her. Not again. He told himself he hadn't lunged yesterday as she folded her hands and said, "Lord, we're grateful we could find a time for us to get together, to get to know each other better, and to talk about things that are important to us."

Everly paused, and Trace wanted to peek and see what she was doing. See what her face looked like. He kept his eyes closed and his hands clasped in front of him.

Contrary to popular belief, he didn't wear his cowboy hat twenty-four-seven, so he hadn't had to remove that.

"Bless Trace's son, Harry, that he can have a good day at school. Bless my brother Shawn that his meeting with his beef supplier will go well this morning, and bless Reg that he'll get back to campus safely."

Another pause, and Trace couldn't resist the urge to take a peek at Everly this time. She sat ramrod straight, her arms folded under her chest and her eyes squinched shut in concentration.

"Bless Trace and I to trust how we feel, talk about hard things, and get along. Oh, and bless the food. We're real grateful for it, and I'm glad Trace was willing to feed me this morning. Amen."

She opened her eyes so fast, Trace didn't have a chance to close his again or look away. Their gazes locked, and Trace couldn't keep his lips straight.

"You didn't have your eyes closed, Mister," she teased.

"You're too pretty not to look at," he quipped back.

She rolled her eyes, but Trace suspected Everly liked the compliments. She started spooning sliced strawberries onto her waffle, and Trace double-checked that the stove and the waffle iron were off before joining her at the bar.

"Thank you for praying for my son," he said quietly.

Everly turned her attention to him, her blue-as-the-sky eyes wide. "Of...course," she said. "I need people to pray for, and Harry's a good kid."

He nodded. "I'll take any help with him I can get,

from you or God or otherwise." He picked up the spoon after she finished, though his second waffle would be drenched in his mother's buttermilk syrup.

"He's not a good kid?" Everly asked.

"He's the best," Trace said. "But he's still fourteen, and all fourteen-year-olds have their moments." He gave her a smile, which she returned.

"I still can't believe you have a fourteen-year-old," she said, a coy elbow darting out to barely touch his ribs. "You make me feel so behind."

"I got married young," he said. "All of us boys did." He shook his head and scooped on a generous helping of whipped cream. "My momma wouldn't think it was a good idea, trust me."

She nodded and cut into her waffle. "I'm old enough for a fourteen-year-old, at least."

"Ever been married?" he asked, cutting her a look out of the corner of his eye before slicing off a bite of his own waffle.

"Nope." She shook her head and took her bite. A moan came out of her mouth, and Trace had to pause and watch her eat. She suddenly moved in slow-motion, the fork coming out from between her lips so slowly, Trace had enough time to be jealous of the utensil and relive their kiss from yesterday.

Then she smiled at him, and time rushed forward again. "You obviously have been," she said.

"Yes," he said. "Briefly."

"How briefly?"

"Oh, Val and I were married for…almost a year. Something like that."

Everly nodded, and he couldn't tell if more or less surprise had entered her expression before she looked away. "Where is she now?"

"Europe." He shifted in his seat. They hadn't spent much time talking about his past in their previous attempts at a relationship. Trace knew why—he didn't want to talk about it. "Reggie's going back to school today?"

"Yes," she said, and if she noticed the rapid conversation topic change, she didn't mention it. "Only a couple more weeks for him, and then he'll graduate." She smiled wider and wider, almost like she was the one who'd finally finished college. "My parents would be so proud."

Trace noticed the use of her verbs, and he took a moment to search his memory about her parents. She had never said anything about them. Her brothers, yes. Her cat, sure. Her mom and dad?

No.

"So you—" he started.

"What are you thinking about Harry?" she asked. She turned fully toward him. "Sorry, go ahead."

"No, uh, Harry's…." He took another bite, trying to get his thoughts lined up. "Here's what I've been thinking. Yesterday, at the wedding, he asked me if I was in love with Val the way Morris obviously loves Leigh. I told him no. He asked if I felt like that about you."

He cleared his throat and cut another, huge bite of waffle. He couldn't take it though, not until he said all of this. "I told him I needed more time with you."

"That's awesome," she said, and Trace couldn't remember the last time he'd used that word. Everly was only five or six years younger than him, but she spent a lot of time with kids and teenagers, so she existed on a different wavelength than he did. "And? Did you tell him about us?"

"This was all before I came to talk to you," he said. "Before, we, uh, before I kissed you."

Everly only shone brighter, and she wasn't embarrassed about kissing him in the slightest. Just like that, Trace's hesitation to talk about it disappeared too.

"So I was thinking," he said. "We should just tell him. Tonight. I can stop and pick you up after band practice, and we'll all go to dinner." His throat felt like he was sucking air through a straw. "Or another night if tonight doesn't work, but it's Monday, and I know you do your teen classes later in the week." He shrugged and pushed his food around his plate. "I want to do it as soon as possible. Just see what he says."

"What if he says he still doesn't want you to see me?"

Trace shook his head. "I don't know." He reached out and stabbed a sausage link. "I told him he needs time with whoever I'm dating, because he's the most important thing to me." He couldn't stop himself from looking at her again, desperate for her to understand. "I'm sorry, Ev. I want you to be the most important thing, and I hope to be like Mav, and Otis, and Tex, where I can find that balance between my kid and my girlfriend, but I'm not there yet."

She leaned into his bicep, having paused in eating her breakfast too. "I know you'll get there, Trace." She straightened, took a deep breath, and sighed. "I'd love to come over tonight."

"Great," he said, and he finally took another bite of breakfast. The sausage was salty and full of maple, and as he ate it, he knew he had more to tell her. After he swallowed, he said, "Harry has been through a lot, Ev. He has to be first, because his mother abandoned him at my momma's house and called me while she was in New York City, saying she wasn't going to come back, and that it was 'my turn' to take care of him."

His chest stormed again, and Trace knew he still had a lot of work to do to forgive Val for what she'd done to their sweet boy. "I won't do that to him. I was gone a lot for the band, on tour, all of that, but he came with me whenever possible. I came back for science fairs and performances and graduations. I had him every summer, for months and months. And I took the first flight I could after Val's message, and he hasn't left my side since."

"Trace," Everly said, her voice full of compassion and concern. "I'm...I don't even know what to say."

"Nothing to say," he said, his voice almost a growl again. He told himself not to do that. He could talk about this stuff; he had to if he wanted Everly to give him time and tenderness—and he did. "I just want you to understand. It's more than my son being embarrassed in front of his friends. It's about me making sure he knows I'm not going to drop him at my momma's, so I have the freedom to go live my life the way I want."

He shook his head. "It isn't about what *I* want anymore."

She nodded and leaned forward to chastely touch her lips to his. "I understand, Trace," she whispered.

He only got the faint hint of cream on her lips, and he wanted so much more. He focused on his breakfast instead. After one more big breath, he said, "I—those are my ideas. Dinner with the three of us tonight, where we tell him. He's a person, Ev. He has feelings and thoughts that are valid, and I want to hear them as much as you do."

"Tonight," she said. "If I remember right, band practice ends when it ends. Right?"

"Yeah," he said. "It's a bit unpredictable. I can text you. We're out at Tex's, and it's a good twenty minutes just to get back to town."

"I can meet you somewhere too," she said.

"Nope," Trace said, a smile finally popping onto his face. "Remember, I'm—"

"Oh, I remember," she said, the teasing lilt back in her voice. "You're old-fashioned when it comes to dating. You want to pick me up at the door, flowers and compliments in hand. You want to ask me out, not the other way around. You want to call me the day after." She flushed now, and Trace found her the most beautiful woman in the world.

"If it's a problem for you," he said. "I'm sure there's plenty of fish on Christian Pool who'd be willing to let you meet them somewhere for dinner—where you're going to meet their teenage son."

She burst out laughing, and she looped her arm through his and leaned into his bicep again. Trace chuckled with her and pressed his cheek to her temple, the moment between them joyful and soft and oh-so-meaningful. At least for him.

Everly seemed to feel it too, because she sobered fairly quickly and stayed right where she was. "I'd rather eat glass than get on that dating app again," she whispered.

"Is that right?" he asked. "*We* met on that app."

"Yeah," she said. "And lightning only strikes the same place once."

Trace closed his eyes and let her words pour through him. She definitely felt the way he did, and he silently begged the Lord to help him keep her in his life. Because she was right—lightning only struck the same spot once, and he wanted the time he'd told Harry he needed to know if it was the good kind of lightning...or the kind that charred hearts.

6

"It went really good, Reg," Everly said later that day. "He wants me to go to dinner with him and his son tonight."

Her younger brother whistled. "Wow, Ev. This has accelerated quickly in two days."

"Yeah." Everly picked up the ledger on her desk at the dance studio and dropped it just as quickly. "I like him too much, Reg." She slumped into her desk chair. "I mean, he has a *fourteen-year-old*. With a woman he didn't love but married anyway. I mean, I want someone to love me so much, he hurts when I come visit you."

She shook her head and looked up at the ceiling. *Mama*, she thought. *I'm ridiculous, I know.*

"Everly," Reggie said. "You don't have to apologize for wanting someone to love you like that."

Everly blinked back her tears. "Mama would say I'm

being too romantic. That life isn't all these big gestures of love and romance. That it has to be real too. That sometimes babies get sick and dogs die."

Reggie started to laugh, but it wasn't at her. "Even I've heard Mama say that to you, Ev, and she's right. But so what? You still deserve a man to love you so much it hurts when he's not with you."

Everly wiped at her eyes, where one tear had started to slide down her face. She had a class of five-year-olds in ten minutes, and she couldn't be weeping when they started showing up. "Do you want to love someone like that, Reg?"

"Maybe," he said.

"There's going to be someone like that for you," she said. "It wasn't Claudia, but I just know God has someone for you."

He didn't argue with her immediately. He was only twenty-three, and he had plenty of time to find his soulmate. Everly felt like she was running out of time. No, what she felt was that she'd found Trace eighteen months ago, and God had played some terrible trick on them by not allowing the two of them to be together.

"I'm almost over Claudia," he whispered.

"It's okay if you aren't," she said.

"I just wish...." He didn't finish the sentence, but Everly didn't need him to. She knew what came after it, because her heart had been broken in the past too.

"Mama wouldn't have liked her," she said.

"No," Reg said, some of the sadness in his voice covered over with happiness now. "She wouldn't have, you're right about that."

"So...Nancy?"

"Nah," Reg said. "She's not it either, Ev."

"Shoot. I'm sorry."

"It's okay. Maybe I'll get on an app like you."

"Maybe you'll meet someone in Seattle," she said.

"I don't even want to think about Seattle," he said. "I'm so nervous."

"Don't be. Shawn and I are going to be there to help you move. They love you." Reggie had been drafted by the Mariners, and while yes, he wouldn't play much his first year, he had a great contract and would have more money than any of them.

"I've got to make it through this stupid stats class first," Reg said. "I better go. I have a study group in a few minutes, and you have to teach."

"Yeah, I'll talk to you later."

"Call me after tonight. I want to know how it goes."

"No," Everly said. "I'm not doing that. I'll call you and Shawn together on Thursday, like we normally do."

"Oh, fine," Reg said, and they both knew that if things went really well or really bad, Everly would call him whenever she wanted. She needed his support and advice. Without her mom and dad around, she felt lost and like she couldn't make her own decisions. She had to get second and third opinions, and her brothers had been her best friends and biggest champions even before the terrible accident that had claimed both of her parents.

Trace had started to ask about them that morning, and she'd cut him off with questions about his son. She wasn't sure why, but she wasn't ready to tell him about her orphan status quite yet. He'd comfort her in the best way possible—at least in her imagination, he would—and she didn't want his pity. She wanted him to think she was strong and beautiful and capable, and not a broken woman who still spoke to her deceased parents when she needed to work through a problem in her life.

Later that evening, Everly picked up her phone as it rang. "Oh, it's Muenster Mash." She swiped on the call and chirped, "Tell me you're coming on Friday, Syd."

The man on the other end of the line chuckled, and Everly sank into her desk chair. Her lessons for the day were done, and she once again thanked herself for giving herself a light schedule on Mondays. Her teen and adult classes were on Wednesdays and Thursdays, and she reserved Fridays for her line dancing classes and events, with a few scattered classes on Saturdays, usually before competitions.

"We're coming on Friday," Syd said.

"Praise the heavens." Everly shifted some papers on her desk to find her calendar. "The Stomp won't be the same unless we have grilled cheese bites outside for those ready to sneak away from the dancing."

"Please," Syd said. "No one sneaks away from your dance events."

Everly grinned and put a checkmark next to Muenster Mash on her list. "Well, you're the fourth food truck, and I have two hundred confirmed for Friday. So bring your *gouda* game."

They laughed together, and Syd promised he'd be there with a special menu especially for her line dancing shindig. "Oh?" she asked. "What does that look like?"

"You'll have to come out and see for yourself," he teased back, and Everly promised she would. She did events at The Stomp, her dance studio, every few months, and they'd become bigger than she'd ever imagined they would.

Families came. Couples. Teens. For this one happening on Friday night, Everly had sold tickets, as she had a limit for the number of people who could be in her building at any given time. She'd do twenty minutes of instruction at the beginning of the event, and she'd emcee the dance-off. After that, come nine-thirty, anyone could show up at The Stomp without a ticket, and the dance would spill from the studio and into the parking lot.

Food trucks would be present for the entire event, and she'd carefully chosen the vendors who could provide teen-friendly food once darkness fell.

She'd been praying for good weather, and now that it was mid-April, almost all of the snow had melted, especially down here in the valley.

She consulted her list and saw she still hadn't heard from Hole in One, which was a popular doughnut hole dessert truck, and she lifted her phone to make another phone call. She'd love to post a final list of the food that would be in attendance, as she'd seen several questions about it on her other social media posts.

Once she knew, then she could update the event website too, and a wave of overwhelm hit her. Everly took a deep breath as the line rang, wondering how band practice was going for Trace and Harry. She hadn't heard from them yet, and she didn't want to crowd him while he worked.

"Everly," Faith said by way of hello.

Her eyes popped open. "Faith," she said. "I'm just checking on you for this Friday. I'd love to have you at The Stomp, because everyone in Coral Canyon loves your doughnuts, myself included."

She sighed, and Everly had her answer. She still listened as she said, "You're not going to like this. We've had two trucks break down over the weekend, and we're already booked for a wedding this Friday."

"Shoot." Everly sighed too, her pen scratching Hole in One off her list. "You don't think you can get one repaired by Friday?"

"I'm trying," Faith said. "When's the very last moment I can tell you?"

"You can show up on Friday night," she said. "I just won't be able to publicize it for you."

"You'll have a spot for us?"

"I always have a spot for you," she said. "We're sold out for the dance-off, and after that, it'll be the 'it' place to be for anyone in town, but the families generally head home by nine-thirty, and it's a more teen crowd."

"Gotta hook 'em while they're young."

Everly found herself laughing with someone again, and she told Faith to let her know as soon as she could, and the call ended. With her phone still in her hand, she fired off a quick text to Trace, noting the time.

It was half-past seven. He'd said they wouldn't be much later than eight, and he'd asked if she could stand to wait to eat dinner that late. She'd waited later to eat with him, and she once again recognized the fact that she'd waited for Trace Young in ways she'd never done for anyone else.

He's worth it.

She wasn't sure where the words came from, but they sounded in her head in her own voice. After a quick read-through of the text, she sent it. *All done at the studio. I really can meet you somewhere for dinner. Just let me know when you're on your way.*

She tapped out a couple more words without thinking too hard about them and stood from her desk. Trace wasn't going to let her meet him for dinner, so she needed to get home and get ready for a dinner-date with her boyfriend and his teenage son.

The words she'd sent echoed in her mind as she drove

home, dusk falling into night rapidly.

Miss you, my Trace.

She'd seen him that morning. They'd spent a few hours together over waffles, strawberries, and sausage. He'd taken her out to the police dog academy and they'd talked about dogs and her cat and their lives. They'd separated about lunchtime, and Everly had come to her studio, where she'd been for the past several hours.

As she pulled into her driveway, her cute little white brick house welcoming her home, her phone sounded with the twang of a country guitar, the sound she'd assigned to Trace.

She couldn't get her phone out of the holder fast enough, and the device sang again as she lifted it up to read. *Practice is not going well,* he'd said. *I'm sorry, my Ev, but dinner might not happen tonight.*

One more message popped up as her heart fell to the soles of her feet.

Miss you too.

Everly quickly told him it was fine. They could reschedule. Good luck with things over there in the barn-slash-studio. Her disappointment cut through her, but she wouldn't make life harder for Trace because of it.

She went inside, where Mutant, her fluffy white cat with gray markings and ears, rushed toward her the way dogs did for their masters. Mutant had eyes the same bright blue as Everly's, and she grinned at the feline as she slung her dance bag over the back of the couch.

"Well, you're in luck," she said to the Birman. She loved this breed of cat, as her mother had always had one in the house while Everly was growing up. Seeing Mutant reminded Everly of her mother, and she bent down and scooped her cat into her arms. "Trace had to cancel for tonight, so I won't be going out again."

Mutant meowed and cuddled into Everly's chest. She was very expressive and could be vocal sometimes, especially when she didn't like something. When she did, her purring could rumble through Everly's body, and she loved to curl into her back at night. Otherwise, she put up with a cuddle when Everly got home from the studio, and then she'd jump down and trot expectantly over to her food dish.

Mutant did just that, and Everly set about getting her dinner for her. Her thoughts never moved far from Trace, and she'd made herself a bowl of beef pho and eaten it before her phone twanged at her again.

It was after nine, and he said, *Just leaving. I'm so sorry. What does Wednesday look like for you?*

I have a late class, she typed back to him. *It's my last line class before the dance on Friday. Can you still make that?* Her event had sold out for long before he'd kissed her at yesterday's wedding, but she'd mentioned it to him that morning, and she was willing to break the occupancy rule to have Trace there.

Friday's fine, he said. *What about Thursday for us and*

61

Harry? Abby doesn't drive the Bookmobile on Thursdays, so we always end early.

Her heart stabbed a beat through her whole body. She couldn't believe Trace was finally going to bring their relationship into the light. She'd been waiting and hoping and praying for this, but now that it was here, her nerves screamed through her body.

Thursday is great, she said. *I have my last teen class that ends at eight. So if you don't mind a later dinner...*

She smiled as she sent the text.

Eight it is, he confirmed. *I can pick you up at the studio. Harry has a guitar lesson that goes until eight-fifteen, and we can then go get him. Or I can wait for him and then come to your house. Whatever works.*

Where does he do his lessons?

Online, Trace said. *Depending on when we end at the studio, he sometimes does them there and then we drive home. If that's the case, I could have Luke or Otis bring him to us.*

Whatever works, she said, mimicking him. *We have phones. So tell me why tonight didn't go well.*

He didn't answer, and Everly couldn't tear her eyes from her phone. It took her a few minutes to realize he'd probably silenced his phone and stuck it under his leg so he could drive home. That was a twenty-five-minute drive, he'd said, and she sighed as she set her phone down and settled in to wait for him to get home and be alone again so they could keep talking.

7

Trace's impatience felt near an all-time high. The drive from the recording studio in Tex's backyard seemed to take all night, the cab of his truck stuffed with silence. He'd finally stopped texting Everly—right in the middle of a conversation, mind you—when Harry had griped at him that he still had homework to do.

In all honesty, Trace couldn't wait for school to get out. He couldn't wait for his son to be able to drive himself places. He couldn't wait until Bryce got home from college, because then Harry wouldn't be so glued to Trace's side.

Then all of those thoughts made Trace feel like the worst father on the planet. His grip on the steering wheel tightened and loosened with every moment that passed, and because he'd silenced his phone all the way, he had no way of knowing if Everly had texted him again.

She most likely had, as the woman loved to talk, and texting was just fine with her. His own disappointment at not being able to take her to dinner and tell Harry about them cut deep inside him, and he stole a glance at his son.

"Harry," he said.

His son swung his attention toward Trace instead of out the passenger window. "Yeah?"

Trace's courage failed him. "Uh, what are you and Bryce planning this summer?"

The atmosphere in the truck softened as some of the tension leaked away. "He's getting another horse," Harry said. "He'll have four then, and we've been talkin' about doing lessons—guitar lessons and horseback riding lessons."

Trace nodded. He'd talked to Tex plenty over the past few months about Bryce. The boy had graduated last year and gone to Montana State University for two semesters. He claimed to like college, but Trace wouldn't be surprised if he didn't go back. Tex had only gone for a year, and Bryce had other options outside of higher education.

"He wants to run a horse rescue ranch," Trace said.

"He's mentioned it," Harry said.

"And you? What do you want to do with your life?"

"Music," Harry said without any hesitation.

"Yeah?" Trace's voice didn't hold a lick of surprise. His

son had talent in droves, and he could make it huge in the country music industry. "You don't think you'll be the next tennis phenomenon?"

They chuckled together, and Harry shook his head as Trace went under an orange streetlamp. They'd finally made it back to the more populated parts of town, and their house waited only five more minutes away. "My shoulders are too big," Harry said.

"Girls like shoulders like yours," Trace said.

"I wouldn't know," Harry said dryly. "My father never leaves me alone with any girls."

Trace grinned at him. "Sarah's mother thanked me for that, I'll have you know. So it's not just me tryin' to put a wet rag on your relationship with her."

Harry didn't smile back, and Trace wished he had gotten some of Val's more sociable personality traits. The producers at King Country always wanted Trace to look one step away from committing a felony on the album covers for Country Quad. He hadn't even had to try, and Harry could throw the same look in under a second.

"There's a summer dance comin' up," Harry said, and he cleared his throat immediately afterward. "The Park Prance or something lame like that. It has a stupid name."

"I think I've seen posters for it at Georgia's shop," Trace said, knowing exactly where this conversation was headed.

"I was thinkin' you could drive me and Sarah there, and her momma could come pick us up at the end."

Trace made the final turn that led onto their quiet, small-town street. "Have you asked Sarah to the dance?" His memory told him it was a fifties affair, with poodle skirts and such. He suddenly had a vision of him and Everly at the dance, a big, puffy, pink skirt poofing out from her petite body, a bright white cat sewn into the bottom third of it.

"Not yet," Harry said. "It's not until the end of June. Everyone knows we're kinda goin' together, so...."

"Everyone knows, huh?"

"I mean, yeah."

"You takin' her to The Stomp this weekend?" Just saying the name of Everly's dance studio almost had him choking. He should just tell Harry now. For some reason, he wanted Everly there with him. He wanted Harry to see the chemistry between them. To *feel* it. To know that there was something special there, the way there was between Morris and Leighann. He'd seen it at their wedding, and Trace wanted—no, he *needed*—Harry to see it between him and Everly.

"Not taking her," Harry said. "Our whole friend group is going."

"But you'll dance with her," Trace insisted. "During the slow songs." He pulled into the driveway while Harry grunted in agreement. "I'm going to the line dancing part."

Harry whipped his attention to Trace then. "You are? Since when?"

"Since...I got a ticket."

"You don't line dance."

"That's why you go," Trace said. He put the truck in park and looked at his son. The garage lights had brightened upon their arrival, and he could see his son's face clearly. "Listen, Harry, I—" He cut off as Harry's phone rang.

They both looked at it, and Harry lunged for it when Sarah's name shone there in bright white letters. He swiped the call on, unbuckled his seatbelt, and slid from the truck all in one swift, fluid movement.

"Hey," he said brightly as the door swung closed.

Trace flinched with the resulting slam of it. He pressed his eyes closed and took a deep breath. "Lord," he prayed. "How come he gets to drop me at the mention of a girl, and I can't do the same?"

He knew why, but the frustration of his situation still filled him from top to bottom. So he stayed in the truck and pulled his phone out from underneath his leg. Everly had texted again, and Trace's fingers flew as he responded to her.

He became aware of the goofy smile on his face as they flirted back and forth, but he couldn't erase it. He also couldn't sit in the truck and text all night. He had to arrange things for Thursday evening, and he had to make sure his son got his homework done for his finals.

I better go, he finally told her. *I'll see you soon?*

She didn't answer right away, and Trace got out of the truck and went inside too. Harry sat at the bar, a monster-sized bowl of cereal in front of him and his algebra book spread open before him. "I hate this stuff," he complained.

"How's Sarah?" he asked.

Harry looked up and took a bite of cereal with a spoon made for and by cavemen. They didn't use any small utensils in this house, that was for sure. He shrugged one shoulder, which only made Trace sigh heavily.

"Fine," he said. "Get your homework done. We have a dinner on Thursday at eight, and you don't get done with your lesson until eight-fifteen. So we need to work that out."

Harry finished chewing and he swallowed. "A dinner? With who?"

"Maybe Luke or Otis can bring you in from band practice," he said. "If we're still out there when I need to go meet them. Or I can come back here and get you." He knocked on the countertop. "I'm going to go shower."

He'd showered that morning, but Trace's routine was to shower after band practice. Harry didn't know about that morning's breakfast date, and he was already waist-deep in keeping him and Everly off the boy's radar until Thursday.

"Help me make it three more days," he muttered to the Lord, and then he switched on the shower spray and sat on the closed toilet seat so he could talk to his girlfriend some more.

THE FOLLOWING EVENING, TRACE LEANED INTO HIS microphone and sang the new lyrics for *Sweet Southern Time*. The song had come together beautifully this afternoon after yesterday's semi-disaster.

Tex got his boxers in a bunch when Otis and Trace changed things on him, and Luke had been in a foul mood too. With Morris out of town, and so many things either wrapping up or starting again—summer, Bryce coming home, Blaze's forthcoming back surgery—tensions in the studio had been high.

Not today, and Trace wished he'd talked to Everly about meeting tonight. His schedule was unpredictable at best, and he'd felt sure Thursday would work out.

His fingers ran along the strings of his guitar effortlessly, and the song held on a pretty chord that would leave plenty of time for their fans to scream and hoot and holler during their live concerts.

They all held there, perfectly still and quiet until Mav said, "I think I got it." He'd been coming out to the studio for the past two days to help with recording while Morris was on his honeymoon. He currently had his sleeping thirteen-month-old strapped to his chest as Trace lifted his eyes and met Mav's through the glass.

Only then did the mood break. Luke whooped and threw his drumsticks into the air. They clattered back to the studio floor as he yelled, "That was insanely perfect."

"Pretty amazing," Tex said, his grin the size of the state of Texas. Trace couldn't stop his smile from spreading either, and Otis nodded as he grinned and made notes on the music stand a few feet from his recording mic. "Let's take ten. I've got to run next door and check on Wade." He hung his guitar on the rack and strode out of the studio.

Trace envied his older brother on a lot of levels. Tex had seemingly everything now that he'd moved back here to Coral Canyon. Their family land. Amazing next-door neighbors. A pretty, loving wife. A new baby. A great relationship with his older son. Everything.

Trace felt like every step happened in the thickest, swiftest-moving quicksand, and his laughter and euphoria over a near-perfect recording of *Sweet Southern Time* faded quickly.

"Be right back," Mav said into the mic, and he left too. Trace turned away from the glass and set his guitar in the rack too. His voice would stay warm for ten minutes, and he plucked his phone from his pocket and sat on the black leather couch where his son usually did his homework during practice. Today, Harry had stayed at school for an algebraic study group, and Trace had checked his pin only a few minutes before they'd started playing.

Everly had dance classes in the afternoons, and she didn't text while she taught. Still, he hoped to see something from her, perhaps from before she'd begun. But he had nothing.

The couch moved as Luke settled in beside him. "Texting Everly?"

Trace looked up and found Luke unabashedly peering

at his phone. He tilted it away from the prying eyes of his brother. He said nothing, because it was obvious he was texting Everly.

"I know something happened with you two on Sunday," Luke said next. His voice held plenty of forced casualness, which Trace did not appreciate.

Especially as Otis—ever the hawk about hearing things he shouldn't—migrated closer. "You're texting Everly again?"

Trace saw no point in trying to deny it. Luke knew so much already. Everly had set up the dancing at Christmastime through him, and Trace had sat right here and confessed his strong feelings for the woman several months ago. They hadn't changed, and he looked first at Otis.

"I don't need this getting around to everyone until I've had a chance to talk to Harry."

"Who am I gonna tell?" Otis asked, the affronted look on his face sort of funny.

"Georgia," Trace bit out. "And she knows Ev, okay? They have businesses in the same small town. They run in the same circles."

"I'm—she's my wife," Otis said.

"Which is why I'm asking you not to tell her. Or go take your break in the house while I talk to Luke."

Otis grumbled something about how he'd rather gargle with sand, and he stayed right where he was. He folded his arms and sat on a nearby stool. "I won't tell Georgia until you've had a chance to talk to Harry."

Trace exchanged a glance with Luke. His younger brother had some warped opinions about women, but he'd been more and more supportive over the past couple of years as Mav, Tex, Otis, and Morris had fallen in love and gotten married.

"I kissed her at Morris's wedding," Trace said. That stupid smile came to his face again. "I was thinkin'—what if I was torturing myself for no reason? What if I'd been imagining this inferno between us all this time?"

Silence pressed upon the studio until Luke asked, "And?"

"And I wasn't imagining it," Trace said.

"So you're going to tell Harry this time," Luke said, and it wasn't phrased as a question.

"Wait," Otis said. "There was a last time? Where you didn't tell Harry?" He looked between Luke and Trace. "Man, I miss so much sometimes."

"It was the night everyone left because of the snow," Trace said. "And yes, I sort of snuck around with her last year, and it was horrible. Fun for me, but horrible for me too."

"You danced with her at Christmastime," Otis said. "Anyone with eyes could've seen that you were enamored with her then."

"Yeah," Trace said. He looked back at his phone. "Harry doesn't want me to see her, but he said something at the wedding, and I don't know. I think if Ev and I come clean and come out and just tell him straight-up, and he can *see* us...and see how much we like each other.... I don't know. It's the best plan I've got."

"What do you need help with?" Luke asked.

"It's happening Thursday," Trace said. "I might need help getting Harry there. Ev's done at the dance studio at eight, and he's not done with his lesson until eight-fifteen."

"I can bring him," Luke said.

Trace lifted his fist for Luke to bump. "Thanks, brother."

Otis said nothing, his eyebrows drawn down for some reason. His focus had centered on his phone, and his expression became more troubled. Trace had noticed him being a touch more distant lately, but he'd thought it was the music. Maybe there was more, though, and he said, "Otis?"

He looked up, almost startled to see Luke and Trace there. "Yeah. Yep."

"You okay?"

He looked at his phone again. "Yeah. I have to go make a call." He got up and walked away without another word, leaving Luke and Trace to stare after him.

"What's goin' on with him?" Trace asked.

"I don't know," Luke said thoughtfully. Otis left, and the strange awkwardness went with him.

"How's the shoulder?" Trace asked.

Luke rotated it. "Good. Seeing that massage therapist helps a lot."

"Good."

"You're taking Blaze in for his surgery, right?" Luke asked. "And then keeping Cash for the first couple of days?"

"Right," Trace said. "Bryce will be back to help with everything too, and it should go fine."

Neither of them said anything else, because major spinal surgery was anything but fine. Blaze was worried about it. Jem had said he'd move in with Blaze for a while, but he had two young kids. With Tex's baby, and Luke's young child, and Mav's busy family, Trace had emerged as the most stable and able to help Blaze.

He and Harry would be moving in with Blaze and Cash for a couple of weeks, or as needed, and Momma would be helping a lot too.

The door to the studio opened and Mav and Tex walked in. Trace exhaled and braced his palms against his knees. "All right," he said. "Not a word from you to anyone either, please."

"Who am I going to tell?" Luke said with a laugh. "Corrine? She doesn't stop talking for more than five seconds about what her teacher is going to do with Mister Whiskers for the summer, and the only other person I see is Sterling."

He got to his feet and turned back to Trace to offer his hand. He pulled him to a stand and embraced him. "Good for you, brother. I've seen you with her, and honestly, you look made for each other."

With that, Luke walked over to Mav and Tex, his loud voice filling the studio and keeping the attention off of Trace while he wondered what Luke had seen when he saw Trace and Everly together...and if Harry would be able to reconcile their relationship as well.

8

Everly pulled up to the well-kept house about in the middle of Coral Canyon. It wasn't new by any means, but Trace had money and knew how to use it to keep the grounds and exterior in immaculate shape.

She'd suggested another day-date, since Harry had another week and a half of school, and they both seemed to be so busy in the evenings. She couldn't believe she hadn't thought of stopping by his place with breakfast every day; they hadn't had to sneak around at night, while he told half-truths to his son so they could meet up in random places like the grocery store or the post office.

She could've been bringing him breakfast sandwiches all this time. As it was, she reached over to the passenger seat of her sedan and picked up the casserole dish. Everly loved anything she could make pretty with her hands. Crafts, paintings, cookies, home décor, all of it.

This morning, she'd spent a couple of hours lovingly tying long strips of dough into beautiful knots laced with butter and cinnamon-sugar. They'd risen perfectly, and her icing looked like a crown for the best of baked goods, if she did say so herself.

She smiled at the pan of pastries and got out of the car. Trace opened the front door before she'd taken a full stride down the sidewalk, and his smile brightened the day though the sun had been up for a couple of hours and glinted merrily over Wyoming.

"I told you we could order in," he said as he came down the steps.

"Oh, I was up early." She returned his smile, glad when he reached her and swept one hand along her waist, drawing her straight into his body, while the other deftly took the pan of cinnamon buns from her.

"Mm, smells good." He pressed his lips to her temple and pulled back. She wanted a taste of his lips again, but he had not kissed her since the wedding. Not even on Monday after their time together.

Everly tamped down her impatience and secured her hand in Trace's as they went up the walk together. "Your lawn is coming in far better than mine," she said. "Do you have some magic trick?"

"Yeah," he said. "It's called paying a lawn company."

He chuckled and glanced across the yard toward the drive-way. "They've come to do the spring fertilizing already."

"See?" she teased. "I didn't even know you needed to fertilize grass. I thought it just grew up every year."

"If there's somewhere you don't want it, it'll grow there," he said.

They went inside, where the scent of coffee and sugar lingered with the delectable smell of his cologne, his skin. Everly's hormones sang at her, but she'd been playing such a high-flirt game with Trace, she wasn't sure where else to go.

He took the cinnamon rolls to the island and then went around it to get out plates and forks. "Coffee?" he asked.

Everly noted the six-string guitar sitting on the stand near the sliding glass door, and she moved her eyes to his. "Yes to the coffee." She nodded to the guitar. "Is that yours?"

"That's Harry's," Trace said, glancing over to it. "He's not coming to the studio tonight either—he's got your dance class, and he's decided to do his lesson here tomorrow. Something about his final project in home economics."

He set the plates on the counter and turned to get the mugs down. "He's going over to the Endmans to finish that, because I don't have a sewing machine, and he lost time in the lab...or something."

When Trace faced her, he wore a frown between his eyes. "It made sense when he told me."

"Sarah's his girlfriend." Everly wasn't asking.

"Well, don't let him hear you say that." Trace gave her a wry smile. "I guess teenagers don't like labels." He turned back to pick up the coffee pot, and then he poured two cups of coffee and pushed one closer to her.

"Mm." She picked up a spoon and began to stir sugar into her brew. "And what about their fathers?" she teased. "Do they like labels?" She sipped her coffee and looked up at him over the lip of the mug.

Trace blinked at her, his expression somewhat blank. "Yeah," he said. "I think their fathers—who are going to be forty years old in a few months—like labels just fine."

"I see." Everly delicately set down her mug. "What label would you like?"

"Boyfriend," he said immediately. "I'm your boyfriend."

Oh, Everly liked this man. "Okay," she said. "Because Shawn *was* asking last night, and I wasn't *quite* sure what to tell him."

Trace caught up to her game and shook his head as he came around the island. "Who's asking about us?" he asked. "Besides your brothers, I mean." He cut her a look out of the corner of his eye. "Your momma?"

Everly froze, her heartbeat the only thing still moving, and boy, it moved fast. Her eyes opened wider than normal before she could stop them, and she couldn't look away from Trace.

"You've said nothing of your parents," he said gently. "Is there a reason why?" He tore his gaze from hers and poured cream into his coffee, giving her a break from his scrutiny. And he wasn't really scrutinizing her at all.

Everly's muscles softened, and she pushed her hair over her shoulder. She'd worn it down again today, and she'd draped her body in another dress, this one cream with lots of colorful butterflies on it.

Trace had not commented on it, nor her hair, which she'd added a wave to while the dough had risen that morning.

Why did her chest pinch so hard? Why couldn't she force the truth from her lips? Tears burned behind her eyes, and she got up to put some distance between her and Trace. She disguised her feelings behind getting out a serving spatula and pulling the tin foil from the casserole dish.

Her cinnamon rolls made her smile, and she found the strength and courage to look at Trace across his kitchen island. He wore compassion in his dark eyes, but Everly knew he wasn't going to let the topic of her parents go. He hadn't exactly asked about them via text last night, but in some ways, he had.

She slid the squat spatula under the corner roll and asked, "Do you want an edge one or a middle one?"

"The gooier the better," he said.

She served herself the corner roll and him the one from right in the middle of the nine she'd made. Only when she sat next to him on her barstool, their breakfast in front of them, did she say, "My parents died." She cleared her throat, though she had the very distinct impression she could cry in front of this man and he wouldn't find her weak. "In a thirteen-car pile-up down in the Dallas-Fort-Worth area. They were on vacation there, and...." She exhaled and traced the lines of cinnamon in the browned dough along the edge of her roll.

"And that was that," she said. "Reggie was going to school near here, and so I moved here to be closer to him. When Shawn got discharged, he came here."

"Ev." Trace didn't have to say anything more. He turned toward her and wrapped her up in both of his strong arms. "I'm so sorry." His whispered words broke the dam of strength, and Everly let her tears slide down her face.

Silently.

She'd had plenty of times where she'd wept and wailed, and she could cry in a much less dramatic way now. "I don't know why saying it still gets me choked up every time," she said. She tried to straighten, and Trace finally released her enough to let her. "It's been three years."

"Hardly any time at all, then." He covered her hand with his. "I'm sorry. I didn't know. I didn't...." He shook his head, his mouth pressing into a tight, fine line.

"How could you know?" she said. "I never told you. I... don't talk about them much. I think I'm still trying to find a way to do it that doesn't make me feel so...lost."

"It's okay to be lost," Trace said. "With something like this." He got up and added, "I'll be right back."

"Where are you going?" She twisted as he jogged away from her, past the dining room table and down the hallway that branched into the other half of the house.

She took a bite of her cinnamon roll, her taste buds rejoicing at the perfection of the frosting, both in texture and the amount of sweetness. She hoped Trace would like the bit of orange juice she'd put in, just the way her mother always had.

As his footsteps returned, Everly twisted on her barstool and crossed her legs. Surprise darted through her as he adjusted the shoulder strap attached to another guitar. "You're going to play for me."

Delight filled her, and had Everly known she'd get a show with her breakfast this morning, she'd have arrived an hour ago.

He looked up, still adjusting his shirt, his belt, his guitar. His eyes now harbored all the anxiety she'd felt firing through her when he'd asked about her parents. "Yeah." He cleared his throat. "I think I...well, you'll see."

His fingers started to move then, and the guitar became a natural part of his appendages. He could coax the most beautiful sound from it, seemingly without even trying if the effortless way he stood there and made gorgeous music by barely moving his fingertips told her anything.

Everly could sit here and watch this man play the guitar all day and all night. It was no wonder Country Quad sold out across the globe when they toured, or that their next album was already being talked about on the country music online forums. Everly could admit she'd looked them up—more than once. She'd watched Trace play in concert snippets and online videos.

It was nothing like being ten feet from him, in his element, his talent so obvious and so...perfect.

"There's nothing like coming home," he started to sing, and Everly honestly had no idea why he wasn't the lead singer for Country Quad. He'd told her once, on their very first date many, many months ago, that he didn't have the personality to be the lead. Tex did.

"It's fresh cookies after school,

And old friends who know your heart,

And that tree where you carved your initials...with hers."

Everly reached up and wiped a tear from her eye. She hadn't told Trace that she'd watched his videos online. He didn't know that she streamed Country Quad at home or in the studio when she was alone. He had no idea that she knew the lyrics to this song, and that *Goin' Home to Her* was one of her favorites.

She may or may not have fantasized that he'd sing it for her one day. For her...and about her.

She's the same – in your memory, he sang.
But she's older now.
Wiser and better and more pure.
You wish you could tell her where you've been,
And why you didn't come home to her
Why you couldn't come home to her
Why you finally came home to her
Right now.

Everly wept through the rest of the song, not bothering to hide her tears. Trace watched her, his emotions swelling with the chorus and dropping on the verse. He was a gorgeous man on the outside, but as the last chord hung in the air, infusing the walls and ceiling and windows in his house, Everly realized how very beautiful he was inside.

She slid from her barstool and walked toward him. He slipped his guitar around to his back and received her, his big hands moving seamlessly from the strings to her face. "I'm sorry," he whispered. "I thought that would help. It could be about your momma."

"It helped," she whispered right before she tipped up and touched her lips to his. He kept the kiss slow, even, and pure, never taking it further though Everly wanted him to. She marveled at his control and his maturity, when everything inside her felt wild and out of her ability to control.

They breathed in together, and Trace broke the kiss. "Your momma and daddy are just waitin' for you at home," he whispered. "That's what the song was meant to be."

"I thought it was about your One True Love," she whispered back.

"Not every country song is a love song," he said with a smile. "Though most people think that it's about the cowboy's wife. To me, it's about anyone you're missing. Anyone at all. I wrote it when I'd just gotten divorced, though I didn't really miss Val. I missed my momma the most, and how easy it was to be in her house, because she loves me just how I am."

Everly studied his face, trying to find the man he'd been back then. Scared. Alone. Probably lost.

Lost.

"I don't see why she wouldn't," Everly said. "You're perfect."

Trace shook his head. "No, I'm not." He stepped away from her, his warm hands dropping from her face. "If I was, I'd be able to tell my fourteen-year-old about my girl-friend. I wouldn't have made such a mess of things between us for so long. I wouldn't still be scared out of my mind about how he'll react."

He frowned again and removed his guitar. He laid it carefully on the dining room table and indicated the bar. "There. I've played for you now. You've danced—and baked—for me. Let's...talk about something easier."

"Easier sounds good," Everly said.

He took a big bite of his gooey cinnamon bun and groaned. "Oh, I have to have this in my life every single day."

Everly giggled, because that sounded very much like he needed *her* in his life every single day. He hadn't said that, though, and Everly would need to keep praying they could find their way through the maze of their individual lives to a joint path, if only so she wouldn't have to ever tell another boyfriend of hers about her parents.

Because if she did, no reaction would ever be as perfect as the one Trace Young had just given her.

9

He *was normal.* Trace read Everly's text about Harry and his dance class the previous evening. *I didn't notice him acting any differently.*

All right, he said. *I'm outside whenever your class is done.* He looked up at The Stomp from where he'd parked around the corner from the building. Harry hadn't been acting strangely, per se, but Trace definitely felt like something was off.

Luke was bringing Harry to The Bayou, which was a relatively new restaurant in Coral Canyon that served Cajun food. Harry loved the spicy stuff, and Trace could tolerate it well enough every now and then to satisfy his son's craving for spicy shrimp and grits.

Everly came jogging out of her studio a few minutes past eight, and Trace shifted in his seat. She locked the

89

door behind her, tucked her keys in her huge dance bag, and looked both ways before crossing the sleepy Main Street to his truck.

Her grin widened with every step, and his did too. She wore a pair of dark blue bicycle shorts that shone like gasoline in sunshine, with a light blue tank top that showed off the muscles in her arms and shoulders. She hefted her bag into the back seat as she said, "Hey, Trace," and then she climbed into the front passenger seat.

Trace said, "I should've gotten out and helped you with that."

"It's fine," she said. "I'm just gonna grab a skirt...." She climbed up on her knees and reached into the back seat, and Trace marveled at how lithe and flexible she was. She unzipped her bag and pulled out a skirt.

She faced the front again and shimmied into the skirt, then beamed at him. "Ready."

He chuckled, because she'd gone from dance teacher to his pretty little date by pulling a skirt over her shorts. He'd been pacing at his place for a solid hour, had changed his shirt four times, and had half a mind even now to drive them south until they ran out of gas.

Instead, he headed for The Bayou as he asked, "How was class tonight?"

"Good," she said. "You're actually never going to believe who showed up to my adult open class." Her eyes shone like sapphires, and Trace grinned.

"I never will," he agreed. "Just tell me."

"Mav," she said. "He grumbled something about his wife wanting him to learn to dance."

Trace's heartbeat stuttered over itself. "The class that just got out?" He hadn't seen Mav's truck, nor his brother as the class had let out.

"Yep," she said. "He's not bad, actually."

"We all took dance lessons for Country Quad," Trace said. "It was part of our PR training."

"Even Mav?"

"Mav set it all up, and he said he'd better do it too, so he knew what he was askin' us to do." Trace chuckled at the memory. "I was a much younger man then, and I just did it."

"You wouldn't now?"

"No, ma'am," he said. "I don't reckon I would. I don't need lessons to do my job on stage."

"You do a good job up there."

Trace looked over to her, because the streets on Thursday past eight weren't that busy. "What does that mean, Miss Everly? Have you been watching my videos online?"

Her cheeks turned a pretty shade of pink, and she giggled as she looked away from him. "Just a few," she said. "You and Otis...I don't know who to watch more."

"Me," Trace said. "You watch *me* more, Miss Everly. You let Georgia ogle Otis."

She burst out laughing then, and Trace sure liked the banter between them. "He has a big personality on stage," she said. "You're more...I don't know the word. You're so good, Trace, and it's like you don't even know it. It's like you're having *so* much fun up there, and then you sort of realize it, and you pull back."

Trace thought about what she'd described, and he found it fit. "I'm almost a different person up there," he admitted. "The lights are bright, so it's easy to block out the crowd. Tex is the front man, so I don't have to be on all the time. I don't have to worry about Harry, or if I'm doing the right thing, or if it'll be too cold in my trailer by the time the concert ends." He shook his head, feeling like he wasn't making any sense. "I can't explain it."

"You love performing, though," she said.

"Yeah," he said. "I do. When Tex came to me and said we should try to put together a band, that he had a contact in Nashville, I didn't even hesitate."

"Where were you?" she asked.

"Val and I were living in LA," he said. "She was modeling there. Well, all over, but she was based in LA." He reached up and ran his hand along the back of his neck. "Man, I hated LA." He gave a nervous laugh. "I wasn't upset to leave that city, I can say that."

"Harry must've come along later," she said.

"Yeah," Trace said. "Yep. Val and I weren't married when Tex and I went to Nashville the first time. We got married right after I signed our first contract. Harry came along only ten months after that, and we were divorced in another two months." He glanced over to her, trying to see that time of his life through her eyes. "It was a crazy year, to be honest."

"I've had some of those," she said simply, and Trace appreciated Everly so much in that moment.

They arrived at the restaurant, and Trace took her hand and went inside with her. "Three, please," he said to the woman at the hostess podium. "My son is on his way."

"Sure," the woman said. "Do you want to go back now, Mister Young? Or wait?" Her eyes flickered over to Everly and back to Trace. He wasn't always recognized and called by name, but he and Harry had eaten here several times.

"We can go back, Tina," he said with a smile.

"Trace?"

He turned at the sound of the familiar voice, and he came face-to-face with Mav. Trace's heart sank all the way to the soles of his boots. His brother stood there with his entire family, Dani holding their one-year-old on her hip.

"Hey, brother." He stepped into Mav and gave him a one-armed hug, deftly dropping Everly's hand. He wasn't sure why, and he disliked himself for doing it. So after he hugged Dani and gave Boston a high-five, he stepped back to Everly's side and re-took her hand in his.

"Ev, do you know my brother, Mav?" His eyebrows went up. "His wife, Dani. Their boy, Lars and Boston, and Beth." Trace smiled at Beth and reached out to boop her nose. "Are you living with your daddy this summer, Bethy?"

"Yes, sir," she said, always a bit more formal than Trace thought a seven-year-old should be.

"School's out early for you," Everly said, her smile perfect for children.

"You teach the dance lessons." She looked at Dani. "She teaches the dance lessons."

Dani smiled at Beth. "Yes, Bethy, she does." She stepped over to Everly and with the baby on her hip, gave her a quick hug. "Howdy, Everly. It's good to see you again."

"Too soon for me," Mav said, stretching his back. "I'm too old for the line dancing." He chuckled and quickly swept a kiss across her cheek. He looked at Tina and said, "We can sit together, maybe?"

"Mav," Dani said, but her voice got drowned out by baby Lars as the baby squabbled and dang near jumped out of her arms.

Trace wanted to yell at Mav that no, they could not sit together. Instead, he bit back the growl and glanced over to Everly. They had an entire conversation in two seconds, and she turned back to Mav and said, "Sure. We're just waiting for—"

"Uncle Mav," Harry said, and Trace switched his gaze to his son. His first instinct was to pull his hand away from Everly, and he stopped himself even as he started moving. "What are you guys doing here?"

"Eating dinner with you," Mav said, and Trace wanted to throttle him. Dani met his eye, pure compassion in hers.

The fact was, this train was off the rails now, and Trace couldn't stop it. No one could stop it.

Harry made Boston laugh, and then he stepped over to Trace. "Dad, you should've seen me at my lesson tonight. It was so sick!" He didn't even glance at Everly, and Trace wondered how a person could overlook her. Everything inside him felt called to her.

"Yeah?" he asked. "Why's that?"

"How many do you have now, Mister Young?" Tina asked.

"Fine, there he is," Luke griped, and Trace nearly got whiplashed from looking at the hostess to where Luke had just arrived, Corrine on his hip. She hiccuped as she cried, and she squirmed to get down.

She ran over to Harry, and Trace could only watch as his son scooped her up into his arms. "Hey, it's okay," he said. "I told you I'd ask my dad, and I am." He smiled at his cousin and looked at Trace. "Uncle Luke and Corrine can eat with us, right, Dad?"

Luke met Trace's eyes and then he took in the circus in the lobby of The Bayou. His eyebrows went up, and Trace had no doubt that Luke would start turning over tables to clear the restaurant so Trace could have his "intervention dinner" with Everly and Harry.

Trace shook his head, because nothing good would come from Luke getting loud. It would only cause a brighter light to be cast onto Trace and Everly, and by the way her arm slipped through his and rested there firmly told him that she didn't want that spotlight.

He bent his head toward her and whispered, "I'm sorry, Ev. This is my family. You best get out now if it bothers you."

"I can take you back," Tina said. "I think we have a table that will fit you all."

"Great," Trace said, and he let Harry lead the way with Corrine's hand in his. He still hadn't looked at Everly once, and Trace wanted to shove her in front of him so Harry would *see her*. Was he deliberately ignoring her?

They reached the long table, with a bench seat along half of it and chairs on the other half, and Trace managed to snag a seat across from Everly by the time all the kids claimed who they wanted to sit by.

"I'll sit here by Trace," Dani said. "Then I can put Lars on the end."

"You sure?" Mav asked. "Boston and Beth are down here." He stood a few places down, with Luke already pulling a chair out beside Beth, who wanted to sit by him and her father.

"It's fine," Dani said, exchanging a glance with Everly. "It'll give me a chance to talk to Everly about your dance lessons."

"Oh, brother." Mav rolled his eyes and sat down, and Trace smiled at Everly as she gave a grin back to Dani.

Once everyone had settled and had menus, Trace couldn't stand the weight of Luke's gaze. So he looked over to him and frowned. That alone got his brother to back off, and he looked down to find Harry sitting basically on the opposite corner of the table.

He held a crayon and was coloring with Corrine, who sat beside Mav and across from Boston. He still hadn't told him why his guitar lesson was "sick," and Trace found he missed his son.

"So," Dani said. "How long have you two been seeing one another?"

Trace yanked his attention to her, catching the startled look on Everly's face too. "Not long," Trace said, going for vague. "And Dani, we haven't told Harry yet. We were going to do that tonight." He leaned closer to her, his voice dropping in volume.

"My husband can be dim sometimes," Dani whispered back. "I'm blaming it on him being overly tired from the dancing tonight."

"He's actually very good," Everly said as she reached for her glass of water.

Dani turned her eyes on her and blinked. "Well, that's good to know." They started to laugh, but Trace didn't get the joke. She patted Trace's hand. "I'm sorry, Trace. I'll loop Mav in for next time."

"It's fine," Trace muttered. "The whole family is going to know before my son." He looked helplessly at Everly, because he honestly didn't know what to do. He cast a glance down the table to his son, and their eyes met.

Harry raised his eyebrows, and Trace lifted his. Then

they grinned at one another, both of them acknowledging that tonight wasn't going the way either of them had thought it would.

"Are you coming to The Stomp tomorrow?" Everly asked, and Trace tuned in to the conversation in front of him. He'd talk to Harry later, and he pressed his eyes closed and said a silent prayer as Dani said their whole family would be there for the line dance-off.

Lord, he prayed. *I need to get my son on board with this relationship. If it's not the right thing to do, tell me. Please, tell me.*

God had told Trace to be patient in the past. He'd told him to choose Harry—more than once. Tonight, as Trace sat in the noisy restaurant, and told Beth that she could order whatever she wanted, and he fed Lars pieces of cereal from a baggie Dani had brought along, Trace didn't hear anything from the Lord.

He only felt peace, and he took that to mean that his current course of action should and could continue. Now, if God could only provide for him an easier path to getting the truth out there, Trace would really appreciate it.

10

Everly smoothed her hair back into a tight ponytail. She wore the matching leggings and long-sleeved workout top she'd ordered specifically for this line dance-off. They were done in denim, and she'd already tried on everything with her dancing cowgirl boots. She secured her ponytail and then prettied it up with a denim scrunchie.

She worked on her makeup next, only evening out her skin tone with a touch of foundation. With everything the same color now, she swept on a ruby red blush, a bright red lipstick, and a quick sweep of black eyeliner. She already had dyed and curled eyelashes, and ten minutes later, she waltzed out into the kitchen.

Mutant sat on the counter, her bright blue eyes drinking in Everly. "Well?" She put one hand on her hip. "What do you think?" She turned in a full circle, wishing she'd seen the leggings with fringe in time to order them for this event. She hadn't, though, and she'd consoled herself by saying there'd always be another dance at The Stomp.

"Meow," Mutant said, and Everly took that as a compliment.

"Thanks," she said. Trace had offered to pick her up and take her to the dance, but Everly had said she needed to be there early. She needed to put out her email signup list, turn on the outdoor tea lights, and go through her routine one—last—time.

She'd tested the music this morning while she'd been in the studio to make sure her hired cleaning crew had done a good job last night after her classes had ended. Everything had been perfect, and her speakers could handle the crowd—all of whom would likely be wearing cowboy boots. Or the ladies in their heels.

Her head hurt a little right now, imagining that sound, but it also brought a smile to her face.

She picked up her phone to take a selfie for Trace, and once she'd sent that, she quickly put together her early dinner for the evening—a spinach-strawberry protein smoothie.

Her phone rang while the blender worked, and she swiped on the call from Trace. "Howdy, cowboy," she teased.

"I'm on my way," he said.

Alarm rang through her. "Now?" She reached to push

the button to shut down the blender. "I have to set up tables and do lame things like put out flowers."

Scuffling came through the line, and he practically growled under his breath, "I want to dance with you—alone—in that outfit."

Everly's whole body warmed, and she smiled at her smoothie. "Oh, I see. You want a private lesson. Those aren't cheap, cowboy."

"Name the price," he said.

"Don't you have band practice right now?"

"We're on a break."

"Trace!" someone yelled on his end of the line, and Everly didn't think he was on a break at all.

"What about Harry?" she asked. "He's not out there with you tonight?"

"He's occupied with Bryce," Trace said. "I'm coming, Luke. Chill." He sighed, and Everly could just see him glaring at his younger brother. "I have to go."

"So you're not on your way."

"I'll be there as soon as I can." The call ended, and Everly didn't even mind the abrupt good-bye. She laughed as she set her phone on the island, then turned to get her smoothie in her travel thermos. It would keep it icy cold until she could sip it all.

She'd known the first time Trace had shown up on her doorstep that they'd be good together. She wasn't sure how good, or if there would be some flaw that would irritate her too much, or so many differences that they couldn't make things work. But she'd known they'd be good together—and they were.

"So far," she told herself. "His son still doesn't know you're dating." That alone could break them—again—and Everly reached up to pull her ponytail tighter though it couldn't actually get tighter.

She placed both palms against the counter and closed her eyes. "Lord," she said. Then she just held still. She listened for anything she could. She'd done some meditation classes after her parents' deaths, and her focus naturally went to her breath. Then her pulse.

She tried to hear something from her heart, but all it beat was *Trace. Trace-Trace.*

With her eyes closed, her awareness seemed to zoom out, until she was one very small part of a much bigger picture. Was this how God saw her? One minuscule piece among so many?

And yet, she thought. *He loves you and knows you.*

That thought rang so true in her heart that her bottom lip trembled with the sudden rush of emotion moving through her. She didn't have to say anything else in her prayer. The Lord knew she wanted things to work out between her and Trace. He knew she needed this dance event tonight to go well. He *knew* her, her thoughts, her heart, her desires, and everything about her.

Everly drew in a deep breath and opened her eyes. "Okay," she said. "Then, here I go. Guide me. Help me. Bless Trace and Harry." She turned and found Mutant still eyeing her. "Help Mutant not to be lonely tonight." She picked up her fluffy white cat and buried her face in her fur.

Mutant put up with it for a moment, and then she jumped to the ground. Everly smiled at her feline, shouldered her packed and ready bag, and hit the road.

She had the tea lights bright and ready, the welcome table set with the book, a few pens, the sign telling people to sign up for her newsletter for class information and future dance events, and the tin milk can that held fake flowers, by the time the bell on the front door chimed.

She turned from the corner of the large room in the studio where the dance-off would take place, expecting to see the first guests. The light in the studio had started to shift, which meant seven o'clock was approaching.

Trace Young entered, wearing his dark-wash jeans and a bright blue and yellow plaid shirt. The short sleeves almost couldn't contain his biceps, and Everly had never asked him if he worked out, but he obviously did.

He wore a brown belt to go with his dark brown cowboy hat and his matching cowboy boots. He was pure male country music star perfection in one package, and Everly dang near fell off the mini-ladder she stood on to hide the wires for the speaker system.

Trace licked his lips and stayed very statuesque in the doorway.

"Are you gonna stand there and stare?" she asked.

"It's a beautiful sight," he said.

She appreciated the compliment—and his quick wit. "Come help me with this, please."

"Yes, ma'am." His boots sounded on her hard floor as he approached, and he didn't need the ladder to do the job. He pressed in close to her, tucked the wires away, and then used those magnificent hands that could play beautiful music to wrap her in his embrace.

"Mm," he whispered. "You smell amazing."

"It's awesome what a shower can do," she joked.

He smiled up at her. "I missed our morning together."

They'd only done that twice, but Everly could admit she'd missed him that morning too. She realized in that moment that she wanted to see him all the time. Morning, noon, night. Instead of taking things into the flirtatious zone, she traced her fingernails along the side of his neck with one hand and held onto one gorgeous broad shoulder with the other.

"I did too," she said. "Would you say that makes us pretty serious?"

"I've always been serious about you, Ev."

She nodded, her throat suddenly too narrow. Everly knew she was a cute little package. She knew she could flirt with anything with a heartbeat and make them fall in love with her. She didn't want someone who only liked her on the outside, or for the entire relationship to be teasing and flirting.

"Are you dating to get married again?" she asked.

"Yes, ma'am." He closed his eyes and tucked his head

into the hollow of her throat. There was no skin-to-skin contact, but the way his cheek was positioned very nearly above her pulse felt intimate and special.

"Do you want more kids?" she whispered.

Trace took a moment to answer. Then another. "Tex just had a baby," he said. "He seems to be doing okay with it, so yeah, I'd probably be okay with having more kids." He lifted his head and looked at her. "What about you, my Ev? Do you want children? Maybe with your bright blue eyes?" He smiled, but it was slow and small, and that made it once again feel oh-so-intimate. Like this was a smile he'd never used before, and that he'd only ever given to her.

"I think I'd be okay as a mother," she said, returning his small smile. "I mean, I don't know. I'm good with the little kids who come for dance lessons."

"Everyone loves you," he said. "Teens, adults, and everyone in between."

"I'm at work when I'm here," she said. "I'm not the same at home."

His eyebrows went up. "No?"

She shook her head and moved to get off the ladder. "The dance starts soon. If you want that private lesson, we better get started."

His smile broadened, and there was that country music star quality. She took his hand and led him into the smaller back room, where she did her three-year-old classes. More importantly, this room wasn't visible from the entrance, and anyone who came in while they were back here wouldn't be able to see them without crossing the large studio. She'd hear the bell anyway.

Trace seemed to get the message, because he closed the door between the big studio and the small one, and when Everly turned back to him, he took her effortlessly into his arms. He pressed her right against him, giving her barely an inch to breathe as he swayed back and forth, taking them in an easy, slow circle, his head ducked so the side of his face touched hers.

"You are a good dancer," she whispered.

He shifted slightly, pulling back, and when he came near again, he matched his lips to hers and kissed her. Everly had never been kissed the way Trace kissed her, not when he did it with such passion.

His stroke said more than his voice ever could, and Everly got the message from him. He wanted to see her morning, noon, and night too. He was falling in love with her too.

She did her best to kiss him back with all the same messages, and when he pulled away, Everly felt the loss of him keenly. "Don't stop," she whispered.

"The bell rang out front," he whispered back. "Your event is about to start."

Everly opened her eyes then and found Trace's dark, dangerous, vibrant ones watching her. He looked like he wanted to say something else, but he didn't. He moved back to give her some room, and Everly stepped out of his arms.

Her muscles felt like they'd been melted, and she walked over to the bench against the back wall where some parents sat to watch the toddler classes. She picked up the sign she'd made for the back door and turned to give it to Trace. "Will you hang this in the window in the back door, please?"

"Yes, ma'am." He took the sign, tipped his hat at her, and went in the opposite direction of her.

Everly opened the door between the two studios and smiled at the couple who'd arrived. "Welcome," she chirped. "We should have cookies and lemonade here any moment." She looked out the huge front window to check for the food cart she'd hired to do refreshments. In that moment, Karla from Dough Good rolled up and relief moved through Everly.

"You're welcome to stay in here," she said. "But the good stuff is outside." She indicated the handcart Karla had turned into a cookie and beverage cart. "And it's all free with your tickets." She held out her hand. "Can I see those?"

She dealt with the couple and then she managed to move outside so she could greet her customers and take their tickets before Karla served them. Trace came through the line and handed her his ticket.

"Evening, Mister Young," she said with a bright smile. "I can't wait to see you dance tonight."

He gave her his plastic, professional smile and went to get a cookie. Soon enough, Everly found herself standing in front of almost two hundred people, teaching them a line dance combination. After she'd gone through it three times, she said, "Okay, let's put it to the music." She picked up the remote for the stereo system, her pulse suddenly picking up speed. Mav and Dani and their family had come tonight. Trace was obviously in the audience. Other than that, the only other Young in attendance was Blaze and his son, Cash.

None of them had taken a spot near the front of the crowd for the lesson, and she hadn't seen Trace since taking his ticket.

"It's a little faster with the music," she said, and she clicked to turn on her mic. "Remember, you get sixteen rolling counts to get out on the dance floor. Here we go!" She pushed play, and a popular Country Quad rock song filled the studio. A cheer rose into the air, and Everly faced the crowd and smiled.

"Feel the beat? One, two, three, four, five, six, seven, eight!"

The crowd didn't exactly part, but plenty of them turned to look behind them, presumably at Trace. She'd chosen *Take the Long Road* for her dance-off tonight, because it had a great beat and she'd always wanted to put the Electric Slide to it. She'd modified the dance slightly—making it more country—and she yelled into her mic, "Here's your cue. We go on one! Five, six, seven, eight, one!"

She spun on eight and started the dance steps on one,

just like everyone should have behind her. With the full wall of mirrors, she could see everyone, and she laughed as some stumbled, as some took off, and as some laughed and smiled too.

Joy filled her studio, and Everly never felt more alive than when she did her events here at The Stomp. Well, maybe when Trace kissed her....

She thought of her mother, then her father, then Trace and Harry as she completed the combo, and she turned back to the crowd and lifted both hands above her head as she clapped for them.

"That's it," she said into the mic. "We'll go through it a few more times, then you'll get a number for the dance-off."

While they did that, a natural break ensued. Not everyone would participate in the dance-off; they'd only watch. Once it finished, Everly would host a couples dance class for a few minutes, and then the party would move outside.

She chatted with people, announced the food truck arrivals, and sent families to get dinner. Then, she started looking for Blaze. She found him standing with some other famous cowboys in town—the Hammonds. They weren't country music famous, but they had truckloads of money and had donated for schools, the library, the building of the theater, and more. So much that the new downtown events center would be named the Hammond Center once the construction on it finished.

"Howdy, boys," she said, moving right into their conversation. Ames and Cy had come tonight, and she assumed they'd brought their families. "Can I steal Blaze for two seconds?"

He was darker and even more menacing than Trace, but since she knew Trace, she also knew Blaze's front was exactly that—a front. "Me?" he drawled. "I think Trace went outside for a drink."

She smiled at him and said, "You, Blaze. I need a dance partner for the couples' class. Will you do it?"

His eyebrows went even higher. "Again, *Trace* is just outside."

Trace had obviously not clued all of his brothers in on his relationship...issues. For some reason, she found that surprising.

"He's comin' back," Blaze said. "I'll get him."

"No," Everly said. "I...." She cut a look over to Ames and Cy, who weren't going anywhere. She suddenly felt super self-conscious in her skin-tight denim clothes, but she leaned closer to Blaze all the same. "Trace and I...we're not exactly public." She lifted her eyebrows too. "You hear what I'm saying?"

Blaze heard, and he nodded. "All right," he said. "But you better tell him, so he doesn't slit my throat on the dance floor." He wore a wicked grin, and Everly thought he was Trouble with a capital T too.

"I'll text him," she said. As she turned, she saw no less than six women loitering far too close to Blaze to be casual. One of them even lifted one hand and waggled her fingers at him. She knew he was having back surgery next week, that Trace and Harry would be staying with him up the canyon for a bit to help out, and that he was a huge name on the rodeo circuit.

The evening progressed, and there was no spilling of blood, no tripping, and only good, family fun as the dance-off ended with a winner—Burke Ewing, a single cowboy Everly had actually gone out with a time or two—and then the couples' lesson.

By the time she spilled out into the cooler night air, Everly was ready for the event to be over. But the food trucks had the parking lot lit up, and lines had formed. Lines full of teenagers.

"Speakers out here now, my Ev?" Trace's voice landed warm and soft in her ears, and she shivered.

"Yes, please."

The party moved outside, and while a lot of people left, a fair number stayed. She didn't have a DJ or an emcee, but when a slower ballad came on, people automatically paired up and started to slow dance.

Trace hadn't moved far from her once they'd come outside, and he offered her his hand. She took it, because she'd go anywhere with him, and he led her off the sidelines. Not far, but enough that they wouldn't be bumping into those who needed a breather and a drink.

She hadn't spoken to Shawn. She hadn't gone around

to any of the food trucks to taste their food yet. She had a long night of clean-up in front of her.

But standing in the circle of Trace's arms, none of that mattered. There was only him, and her, and the two of them together, and everything was absolutely perfect.

Until an angry voice said, "Dad? What are you *doing?*" and Trace practically dropped her where she stood.

11

Trace took in the anger on his son's face. Slightly behind him, Sarah Endman stood with a shocked look on her face. Two or three other boys—not including Bryce—hovered nearby.

"You're practically swallowing her," Harry said. "I thought you guys weren't dating." He looked past Trace to Everly, and Trace's first reaction was to protect her. Hide her behind him. He did step in front of her, but she quickly came to his side, her hand in his strong and sure.

"I wasn't swallowing her," Trace said, all of his defenses in place. "We were dancing."

"You'd never let me dance with a girl like that."

"You're fourteen."

Harry's fists clenched, and his face already shone red in the bright lights. Trace glanced around to his friends. "Hey, guys," he said as jovially as he could. "Could you give us a minute?" He didn't need permission from a group of teenagers to talk to his son, and he took Harry by the shoulder and turned him around.

"Let's talk inside," he said.

"I don't want to go inside," Harry threw over his shoulder. "I don't want you dating her either."

"Yeah, well, we're goin' inside," Trace growled. He marched his son past everyone else still dancing, past the lemonade stand, and right inside Everly's studio. He wasn't sure who saw him; his vision had tunneled. He wasn't sure where Everly had gotten to, as he'd released her hand in order to get Harry to go with him.

Instead of going into the big studio room, he detoured into Everly's office. He'd just closed the door when the bell chimed outside. Everly opened the door and entered, her eyes those of a scared rabbit facing down a wolf for the first time.

Trace didn't know what to do or say. This wasn't how this was supposed to go at all. Not even a little bit. Harry retreated to the far corner and faced the two of them, everything about him tense and angry and upset.

"Son," Trace said.

"I asked you to date anyone but her," Harry said.

"I know that." Trace took off his cowboy hat, because it felt imposing to wear it inside. Harry kept his on, and he was so handsome and so good and so...smart.

Be honest with him.

"I haven't been honest with you," Trace said. "Let me

start with that, up front. I need to apologize for it, and say how much I hated not telling you things. I hate that I put this wall between us, but I did, and now I have to figure out how to knock it all down and rebuild it."

Harry softened slightly, but only to look confused.

Trace took another breath. "I like this woman, Harry. A lot. From the moment I met her. I thought I could break it off with her, and I did. After that first date, I did. But it was real hard, and I think about her day and night." He swallowed, because he wasn't one to talk about his emotions much as it was. Not with his son, and not with Everly either. And now he was saying all the intimate things of his heart right out loud for both of them to hear.

"Last fall, we ran into each other again." He sighed and moved to take a seat in one of the chairs in front of Everly's desk. "We started sneaking around. Sort of. I didn't want to lie to you, so I'd say I was gonna go pick up pizza, and then Ev would plan to be there, and we'd 'run into each other.'" He made air quotes around the last few words.

Harry's mouth dropped open. "You were *sneaking around* with a girl?"

"First, she's not a girl," Trace said darkly. "She's of-age, as am I."

He pointed a finger at Trace. "You would kill me and chain me in my room if I snuck around with a girl."

Trace glowered at him. "You make me sound like a

terrible father. I'm protecting you from the dangers of a fourteen-year-old mind riddled with hormones."

"Yeah, well, it seems like a forty-year-old mind isn't that much different," he grumbled.

To Trace's surprise, Everly started to laugh. Neither he nor Harry joined in, and she cut the sound off quickly. "Sorry." She cleared her throat. "That was pretty funny though." She tried to flatten her smile and couldn't.

Trace watched her, realizing how differently she handled things. "I couldn't handle the sneaking around for long. I broke things off again."

"You danced with her at Christmas," Harry accused.

"You were there, honey," Everly said. "That was all my idea. I was hoping you'd see me and your dad together and see how much we like each other. How good we are together." She wrung her hands around one another. "So I'll take the blame for that one."

"The truth is," Trace said. "I've been prayin' and prayin' for over a year to know what to do about Miss Everly. And you." He rose to his feet again and went around the desk. He put both hands on Harry's shoulders and they looked at one another openly.

"I love you to the stars and back," he whispered. "I will do anything for you. Anything at all."

Harry's face crumbled, but he held strong and still. He took a breath and put everything back together. Trace wasn't sure if that was a good thing or not.

"I know your mother walking out on you was very

painful," he said. "Beyond hard. No kid should ever have to deal with that, but you did. You are. I will not do that to you. Me dating Ev doesn't mean you're second."

Everly came to his side. "He even told me he can't put me first, Harry. I'm okay with you being the top priority."

Trace thought she was for now, but he knew women. She wouldn't stay second and happy forever.

"We're adults," Trace said. "It's not embarrassing for me to date her. If you have friends teasing you about that... well, maybe they're not your friends."

Harry still didn't budge, and lecturing him about his friends wasn't the tactic Trace wanted to use. He took a big breath, desperate for some help.

"I thought maybe I could try again with Ev." He dropped his hands and gave Harry some breathing space. He and Everly backed up, and he took her hand in his again. He loved her soft, smooth skin. The delicate way her hand fit in his much larger one.

He studied the way their hands looked together as he spoke. "At Uncle Morris's wedding, you said you could see and feel how much he and Aunt Leigh love one another." He looked up at Harry then. "Remember?"

His son swiped at his right eye and nodded, just once.

"You asked me if I felt like that about your mother."

"You didn't," Harry said.

Trace shook his head. "And then you asked me if I felt like that about Everly."

Harry dropped his head then, his chin practically

touching his chest as he showed Trace and Everly the top of his cowboy hat. "You said you needed more time with her."

"I do," Trace said. "And then what did I say?"

Harry looked up, and he was so strong, and so bright, and so good. Trace prayed he'd stay that way, that Val's abandonment would not hurt him terribly forever. "You said I needed time with her."

Trace lifted one shoulder in a sort-of shrug, asking Harry if he wanted that. "I mean, whoever I'm with will be your step-mom," he said. "And son, I'm ready to be with someone again. There's a reason it takes two people to have a baby. Raising kids is hard, and I know I'm failing you each and every day."

"You're not failing me, Dad."

"I am, though," Trace said, his voice taking on a new level of agony he hadn't anticipated. "I can't be a woman. I can't love you the way a mother does. I'm on you about girls all the time, and I can't remember the last time we had a meal with vegetables in it, and there's nothing like hugging your mother." His voice broke, and he did the same thing Harry had done earlier.

He took a deep breath and caged it all away for later.

He glanced over to Everly, who had unshed tears brimming in her eyes. "I'm not dating just to find you a mother." He looked back at Harry. "I'm lonely too. I want a partner. Someone to talk to after a good band practice and a bad one, and someone to ask if I'm bein' too harsh on you about Sarah, and someone to hug me good-night too."

"I hug you good-night," Harry said, his voice tinny.

"Yeah." Trace smiled at him, his own eyes burning now. "And it's awesome. I love it, and I love you. I'm just askin' that we try and see if we can love Everly too."

His mind relaxed, and that was how Trace knew he'd said all he needed to. Silence filled the small office, and it was hotter in here than Trace would like. Still, he didn't move a muscle.

Harry watched him for several long moments, then looked over to Everly. She rushed at him in true Everly Avery style and wrapped him up in a tight hug. "We can just try," she said. "If you hate me, then I'll leave you and your dad alone."

"I don't hate you," Harry grumbled, and he sounded so much like Trace that Trace found himself smiling. His eyes burned as Harry closed his eyes and sank into Everly's hug, because he'd been right. His boy needed the feminine touch of a mother more than Trace had even known.

Not more than God had known, though, and Trace regretted taking so long to get this third try with Everly out of the darkness.

Everly stepped back and held Harry's face in her hands. "Okay, then. This doesn't change anything. I'm still going to make you lift that arm higher in class."

Harry gave her a small smile. "Yes, Miss Everly."

"And your daddy is right. If you have friends giving

you a hard time, I want you to send them to me. I'll have a little chat with them."

Trace couldn't see her face, but the strength and whip in her voice told him she wasn't kidding around. He would not want to be on the receiving end of that "chat."

Harry's face blanked, and he nodded. "Yes, ma'am."

She nodded, backed up, and turned toward Trace. She wore a fierce look on her face that Trace could only describe as a Mama Bear look, and she returned to his side. They once again faced Harry, and Trace opened his free arm.

Harry moved into him for a hug, and Trace held him right against his chest, his hand palming the back of his son's head. He leaned down so his mouth was right at Harry's ear. "I am not your mother," he said. "I will not abandon you. Not for anything or anyone."

Harry's shoulders shook as he cried, and Trace simply held him there, both of Harry's arms gripping his torso tightly.

Everly slipped away from them, and Trace wrapped his son in both of his arms too. She left the office, and still they stood together, father and son.

"I love you, son," he finally managed to say.

"I love you too, Dad." Harry pulled back and wiped his face. They breathed in together, which made Trace chuckle.

He sobered quickly though. "Be real with me, Harry. Do I need to get you in with a counselor?" He'd asked his son this question before, and Harry had put him off. Said no. He was fine.

This time, pure vulnerability lingered in his son's expression. He didn't duck away, but he did swallow nervously.

"It's not a big deal," Trace said. "Cash sees a therapist. You can tell them anything you want, even all the things about me that drive you bonkers." He gave Harry a smile that only lasted for a moment. "Anything you want. Stuff you don't want me to know, though I hope you know you can tell me anything, about anyone, even me."

Harry nodded. "I...I want to see someone."

Trace nodded too, his heart withering right there in his chest. "Okay," he said with as much control as he could. In the end, he dropped the façade, and he shook his head. "I'm so sorry you have to go through this. I really am."

"It's not your fault, Dad."

He nodded, but he didn't really believe his son. "I will do anything I can to help you."

"I know you will."

"So I'll ask Blaze who he sends Cash to."

"Okay."

"Doesn't have to be the same therapist."

"Okay."

Trace let the silence back in as he watched his son. Then he said, "Okay. Then let's get back to the dance. It's a big event for Miss Everly, and I don't want to ruin it for her."

"Me either," Harry said.

Trace slung his arm around his son's shoulders as they moved toward the closed door. "Have you danced with Sarah? I'd maybe like to see how you do it to make sure it's appropriate."

"Oh, my gosh, you're insane," Harry said. The two of them laughed together, and that cleansed Trace's soul more than he knew it could. His heart grew a few sizes, though it still hurt that Harry's mother had damaged their son so badly.

"In fact, you should head on home," Harry said. "You're always complaining about how you can't stay up late. I'm fine here."

"Yeah, I noticed Bryce isn't here," Trace said.

"He just dropped me off," Harry said. "He said—he's acting kind of weird."

"Weird how?"

"I don't know."

"He's probably just adjusting to being home for the summer."

"Yeah."

"Is he coming back for you tonight?" Trace opened the door to leave the studio, and he let Harry go first.

"He said he would. I'm sleeping out there tonight so we can work with the horses tomorrow."

"That's what I thought. If you need a ride, you call me."

"Yes, sir."

They reached the parking lot, where they both paused on the fringes. Everything looked the same as it had when they left, and Trace marveled that the world could go on as simply as it had while he experienced such a monumental moment with his son.

He spotted Sarah as she moved through the crowd toward them, and he gave Harry a nudge. "There she is, son. Go on."

Harry looked up at him, and they shared another meaningful moment. "I'm sorry I've kept you from Everly," he said. "I didn't realize how much you liked her."

"Yeah, well, I lied to you about how much I liked her. How would you have known?"

Harry's features hardened, and then he said, "I really like Sarah, Dad. I don't want to get in trouble with her." He threw his arms around Trace. "Thanks for always being on me about her. You're a great dad."

Surprised, Trace barely had time to pat his son on the back before the embrace ended and Harry walked away. He swallowed hard as Harry took Sarah's hand, as he saw the concern in her fourteen-year-old face, and as they moved back into the crowd.

He stayed where he was, not too eager to submerge himself back into all those people. Everly was the people-person between them, and he looked for her blonde pony-tail among all the cowboy hats.

He found her dancing with Old Mister Shoemaker, her face vibrant with a smile. The dance ended, and she immediately cast her eyes toward the edge of the lot where he stood. She came his way, and Trace ducked back along the front of the building. The lemonade stand waited unmanned, and he picked up a can of strawberry as he passed by.

Everly caught up to him easily, but she didn't say anything. They walked to the corner and crossed the street. "I know you can't stay away for long," he said. "Let's go back."

He looked at her as he turned, and time froze. "I'm sorry, Ev. That didn't go the way I imagined, but at least it's done."

"It was perfect," she said. She put one hand over his heart, and she wore the most earnest expression on her face. "You have a heart of gold, Mister Young. I am lucky to know you and privileged to have witnessed you talk to your son as openly as you did."

He shook his head, because he didn't need her accolades. "It was a mess."

"A beautiful mess."

"I spoke true," he said. "I'm not *just* looking for a mother for my son, though that's part of it."

She gave him a kind smile. "Let's see how things go now that he knows, okay?"

He wrapped one arm around her waist. "He's sleeping at Tex's tonight. Breakfast at my place? Or yours? I'd love to come try to win over Mutant after that last pancake disaster." He gave her a smile he hoped was sexy and soft and enough to get her to say yes.

"My place, cowboy," she said. "But you better not show up before ten."

"Let's make it lunch, then," he said, his memory firing at him. "Tex is having breakfast at his place."

12

Blaze Young watched Trace disappear past the corner of the building, and he threw back the last of his lemonade. His son had gone to Tex's tonight, as had most of the Young cousins. Bryce had returned from Montana State University that day, and he'd invited all of his cousins for a sleepover.

Blaze had let Luke drive his son out to the ranch that their oldest brother now owned, and he'd go out in the morning for a welcome home breakfast Tex was hosting.

Tonight, he'd come to the dance with Trace, and he'd already seen him grab his son and haul him into the dance studio. Everly, who Trace had been all over on the dance floor, had scampered after the two of them.

She'd come out first—and alone—and while Blaze didn't usually care at all about who his brothers dated or didn't date, he'd seen Trace and Everly with one another. The chemistry between them sizzled, and a romance wouldn't really be worth it if there wasn't some drama.

At least in his opinion.

Trace didn't talk to Blaze about his love life, and Blaze was still getting to know his brothers again. Trace especially, as the man wasn't particularly loquacious. He would be coming to stay with Blaze next week when he went in for his back surgery, because Harry was close in age to Cash, and Trace didn't have little children to deal with.

He tossed his empty can of lemonade into the recycling bin, half-wishing it was something harder. At the same time, he never wanted to go back to the nights where he drank too much. Or drank at all.

He'd lived every kind of life, and he rather liked the one where he didn't wake up with fur on his tongue and a headache so severe he couldn't even see. A twinge of guilt stole through him as he thought about his younger, wilder days. He'd certainly come a long way, though he still hadn't gone back to church.

Something stewed inside him, though, and he had half a mind to talk to his father about having a family prayer before his surgery. Daddy hadn't offered yet, and the surgery was on Monday morning.

Blaze swallowed as he started over to the doughnut truck. The line had finally dwindled enough where he wouldn't be standing there with fifteen-year-old girls, and he gave Harry a glance as he went by him standing with his friends.

Harry stuck out his fist, and Blaze bumped it with a grin. He was a good kid, and whatever Trace had going on with him would surely be worked out, probably with cotton candy and unicorns.

Blaze chastised himself for thinking his brothers' lives and children were perfect. The scene he'd witnessed twenty minutes ago told him Trace's life wasn't perfect. *But he doesn't need back surgery*, Blaze thought.

Trace had simply chosen a different path to stardom, and he had plenty of burdens to carry. Lots of demons to face. Everyone did, Blaze knew.

The scent of smoke met his nose, and he jerked his attention to the food truck in front of him. An auburn-haired woman scrambled past the window, and Blaze leapt into action. He hurried over to the end of the truck, went right up the steps, and entered the cramped, galley kitchen space.

"Tell me what you need," he barked at the woman. The oil where she fried her doughnuts bubbled like someone had poured baking soda into a vat of vinegar, and Blaze's memory blitzed at him about how to deal with an oil fire.

Was he supposed to smother it or throw water on it?

The woman looked at him with wide, emerald eyes.

Dark emerald. Blaze was a man, and even in a tense, harried situation, he had the distinct thought that she was gorgeous.

"Give me that lid," she yelled above the furious bubbling and sizzling of the oil. She nodded to the glass lid on the counter, and Blaze picked it up.

He took the few steps to her, but he really didn't know how this round lid was going to cover the long, rectangular baskets. He gave it to her, and she covered up the boiling oil.

Nothing changed. A spark of a flame leapt into the air, and they both cried out. "This has to be unplugged," he said.

"You think I didn't already do that?" she yelled back at him.

"Why is it so dang hot?" he asked. He crouched down —so not good for his back—and opened the front panel on the fryer. "It's not off, genius." He snuffed out the pilot light on the fryer with his thumb and forefinger, and then did the same with the one beside it.

"Don't do that," she said. "They take forever to get going again."

"You're not getting these going again."

"Yes, I am," she said. "This is a minor mishap."

"Sweetheart, your truck is on fire." Blaze put out the third fryer, noting that the boiling had not gone down, not even a little bit.

"It is not," she bit out. "This is just a little too hot."

He straightened as she fished out a completely black piece of fried dough. He raised his eyebrows at her as she faced him from the trash can. Something sparked, and then the lights above them flickered.

She cried out, but Blaze just looked up to the ceiling. "I hate to be right, but...."

"I didn't ask for your help."

"You didn't need to," he said. "I'm chivalrous and saw a lady in need. I jumped on my white steed and came to the rescue." He gave her the smile that had brought many women to their knees.

Not this one.

She glared at him and folded her arms. "I have orders to put out."

He leaned a little closer to her, feeling dangerous now that he knew she wasn't going to back down from him. "Unless you plan on running down to the grocer to pick up the doughnuts they have on their half-price sale this late at night, you're not serving any more doughnuts."

"Who are you?" she demanded.

"Blaze Young," he said as if she should know who he was. "You know? Of all the famous Youngs here in town? My brothers have that band."

"Yeah, I've heard of 'em," she said. She scanned him down to the cowboy boots he wore. Her gaze took longer to come back up, and he'd like to think she was impressed by the sizable belt buckle he wore.

The displeasure in her eyes suggested otherwise.

Though, Blaze could've sworn he saw a hint of attraction in the depths of those dark green eyes. Did she know he had a soft spot in his heart for women with green eyes?

No, he told himself. *You don't.*

He wasn't dating right now. Strictly female-free, he was.

"Never heard of you, though," she said. "You're not in the band."

"No, sweetheart, I'm not." Blaze did his best not to sound upset about it. He wasn't upset about it. That ship had sailed a long time ago, and he'd had the life and career he wanted.

Sort of.

The career, yes.

The life?

Blaze wasn't so sure about that. It had been harder than he'd thought just to get a house set up. His condo in Vegas had been the definition of a bachelor pad, and he'd paid a cleaning service to deal with his mess. He hadn't even owned a toaster before picking up Cash and making the move north.

He didn't cook, so he didn't need a toaster. Or a stove. Or a microwave. His life had changed dramatically in the past ten months, and while Blaze had wanted the changes, they hadn't been easy.

"Faith?" someone asked, and both he and the woman looked to the end of the food truck where the door was. "Everything okay?"

A man Blaze recognized came up the last step.

"I'm fine, Shawn," Faith said, and Blaze wanted to repeat it. Send Shawn Avery on his way.

The force of his glare seemed to get the point across, because Shawn actually raised both hands and backed out of the food truck. Impressive, given the fact that the steps weren't that easy to navigate as narrow and steep as they were.

Faith faced him again, and Blaze had the inexplicable urge to ask her for her number. They stood there in minimal light, the sound of the boiling oil finally settling down.

"I don't think anything's on fire anymore," he said.

"I also can't serve doughnuts anymore," she said. "And I just got this truck fixed."

"Apparently not."

She folded her arms again, and she wouldn't do that if she knew it only made her more attractive in Blaze's opinion. "I'm sending you the bill to fix this truck."

"Great," he said easily. "Do you want to take my number so you can call me and let me know how much it is?" He had so much money, he could buy her a fleet of the best doughnut trucks that existed.

Her mouth dropped open, her threat clearly not hitting its mark. He gave her half a grin. "Did you not see my belt buckle?"

Her eyes flickered down but came right back to his again. "Uh, no?"

"I'm a National Championship winning bull rider. I've won lots of money in the rodeo. Now, get out your phone and put in my number. I'll pay to fix your truck...if you'll go to dinner with me once I'm all recovered from my back surgery."

Her eyes opened a little wider with every word he said until she stared at him with the most stricken expression he'd ever seen a woman wear.

"I'm—I—I'm not going to dinner with you."

"Why not?" he asked.

"Because you're arrogant," she said. "And assuming. And you turned off my fryers."

"I'm not arrogant," he shot back. "It's called confidence. I never assume; I read people. And I *saved* your truck from certain flame."

Faith backed up a step. "You did assume. How do you know I'm not seeing someone?"

Blaze settled his weight on his left leg, as his right side was starting to feel weak. He needed to get home, get ice on his hip, and go to bed. Such an exciting Friday night.

"I've been here all night," he said. "There hasn't been anyone hanging around this truck. You never check your phone to let someone know when you'll be done—and it's Friday night. You're not wearing any jewelry to indicate the token of someone important to you needs to be close to you at all times."

He looked out the window as someone approached it.

"I'm so sorry," Faith said, immediately tending to them. "My truck is clearly not operational. Have you already ordered?"

They said they had, and Faith quickly refunded their money. When she turned back to him, he said, "I'll cover that too."

"Arrogant," she said as she covered the word in a cough.

He grinned at her. "Having money doesn't make me arrogant."

"Throwing it around doesn't make you likable," she shot back.

Blaze was the one who folded his arms this time. He told himself his Vegas ways wouldn't win over the women here. He honestly didn't know what would—that was part of why he'd put himself on a strictly female-free diet. That, and he was still learning how to use a toaster and parent his son.

He honestly had no idea how he could manage a girl-friend too.

"Really," he said, his voice much softer. "Send me a bill for everything. I don't mind paying for it." He nodded at her and squeezed past her in the small space. She hadn't taken out her phone and typed in his number, so she had no way to contact him.

Again, he reminded himself he wasn't in the big city. He lived in small-town Coral Canyon now, and he wouldn't be hard to find should she really want to track him down.

He half-expected the lovely Faith, owner of Hole in One, to call him back. But she didn't, and Blaze limped down the steps and back to the parking lot, now without the promise of a sugary, fried piece of dough.

13

Faith Cromwell could only stare after Blaze Young. Boy, that man had a mouth on him, and strangely enough, all Faith could think about was how those lips might taste against hers.

She gave herself a little shake and surveyed the interior of her food truck. Coming here tonight had been a mistake. She'd been praying for the past three hours that the truck would hold up, and of course it hadn't.

She couldn't believe she hadn't scooped out all of the doughnut holes. Under normal circumstances, it wasn't that big of a deal. In this truck, hanging on by a thread as it was, it had definitely caused a problem.

Sighing, she looked up, the reality of her situation crashing down on her. The truck had no light. No electricity. She wondered if it would start.

Panic poured through her, and Faith reached up and

wiped her hands down her face. She felt oily and sweaty, and she couldn't believe a man like Blaze Young found her even remotely attractive right now.

But he had to have, right? He'd asked her out.

"He was too arrogant," she told herself as she started to go through her closing procedures. She first went outside and closed the front of her truck, taking a good, long look around the parking lot. She didn't see Blaze, but he'd obviously been watching her and the truck tonight.

No, a man hadn't been hanging around, making sure she had what she needed to get through the night. No, she didn't have a boyfriend texting her to find out how the event was going and when she'd be done. No, she'd never received a special piece of jewelry from a special someone.

Well, not one she'd kept, at least.

She tore her gaze from the lot, where mostly teenagers still hung out in groups or couples, and went back inside her truck. She closed the door behind her and started cleaning up. Oil seemed to cover every surface, and the scent of cleaner didn't mix well with the hot, fried smell permeating the interior of the truck.

But Faith was used to it, so she dug in to get the job done. She couldn't stop thinking about Blaze Young, and her mind got away from her so much that she paused and pulled out her phone.

A quick internet search would solve this. Surely he wouldn't be that famous. Yes, he'd been wearing a ridiculously oversized belt buckle. That honestly wasn't that uncommon here in cowboy country, Wyoming.

Her search for "Blaze Young" pulled up dozens of links in less than a second, and his stunningly handsome face smiled at her from her screen. He wore a huge cowboy hat, his teeth white and straight, and she swiped down to see a different version of the same man.

The next photo was Blaze again, all right, but in this one, he wore black leather chaps over his jeans, and a blue, black, and dark red striped shirt with long sleeves. He wore his rodeo bibs over that, his arms folded across his chest, and the most sinister look on his face.

Faith actually shivered looking at him. There was no way she could go to dinner with him, and yet, she couldn't stop fantasizing about what that might be like. He'd softened there near the end of their conversation, and she tapped on the picture.

It took her to the National Rodeo Association webpage, where Blaze had a whole feature to himself. Things like "highest prize winner," and "record-breaking ride" stuck out to her. Everything he'd said was true.

The man was rich. Talented. Powerful. Devilishly handsome.

"Why in the world would he be interested in you?" she wondered aloud. "And why is he living in Coral Canyon?"

She stuck her phone in her back pocket and returned to work. Blaze refused to leave her mind, and she finally gave up trying to think about something else. When the kitchen was clean, she stepped into the cab of the truck and took a deep breath.

The dance raged on, though another food truck had already started to close. Everly would wrap things up in the next half-hour, and Faith would have to explain later. Or she wouldn't. Everly knew her trucks had been having problems.

Faith put her elbows on the enormous steering wheel and cradled her head in her hands. "Lord," she whispered. "I need my trucks to function. Can I really ask Blaze to pay to repair this one?"

The malfunction wasn't his fault. Not even close. But he had money, and she did not. He probably didn't work, and Faith put in fifteen-hour days just to make ends meet.

The Lord always seemed just out of reach for Faith, but she definitely felt like she shouldn't dismiss Blaze so quickly. He certainly wouldn't be dismissed easily, if the past forty minutes told her anything.

She stuck the key in the ignition and added more to her prayer. "Bless me that this truck will start." She twisted the key, but the engine didn't even sputter. The truck clicked, and that was it.

Not that unusual, actually. Faith sometimes had to sit behind the wheel and try to start this truck dozens of times before it would actually connect. She tried again, and then again. Over and over, she tried to start the truck, each moment adding another brick to her frustration and desperation.

Her forehead wrinkled as her emotions overcame her. She whimpered, though her eyes stayed dry. After trying for another five minutes, Faith slammed her palms against the steering wheel.

The truck wasn't going to start.

She reached for the door handle and caught sight of a man standing just beyond the window. She yelped and threw her hands up as if to ward off an unwanted attack.

Blaze likewise held up one hand as he backed up.

Faith opened the door and flew from the truck. "You scared me." She swatted at his chest with both hands. "You don't do that. It's dark out here, you heathen. And I'm a single woman, alone in my truck!"

He grabbed onto her wrists and pinned them against his chest. "Okay, I'm sorry. I'm sorry."

They both panted, her with increased adrenaline, and him probably because he'd been getting hit. The moment lengthened, and on this side of the truck, the bright lights from the parking lot dance were getting blocked a bit.

His eyes were nearly black to begin with, and standing there in the dim light with him felt...forbidden. Danger-ous. Exciting.

"I noticed you get behind the wheel," he said.

"You stalking my every move is kind of creepy," she said.

Blaze gave her that sexy smile. "I thought your truck

might not start, what with it being out of power and all. That's all. So I got an order of fried cheese curds—have you had those from Muenster Mash? Delicious, if not."

"I've had them," she murmured.

"Then you know." His smile widened, and it was a glorious sight.

Faith told herself she just hadn't been out with anyone in a while. A long while. Years. She told herself she wouldn't be going out with this cowboy either. For one, he was out of her league. For another, they existed on opposite ends of the spectrum. For a third, his observations of her were far too accurate, and she didn't want to admit it.

"I came to see if you needed a ride home," he said. "No strings attached." He tucked his hands into his jeans pockets, and he had to know how adorable that made him. A tall, dark, handsome, delicious, absolutely stunningly *adorable* man.

Faith had a weakness inside her for men like him, and she reminded herself that she'd been walked on by one too many. The rodeo champion wasn't going to be the next to dust his boots on her back.

She glanced over her shoulder to buy herself some time, just to make him think she was leery of him. She *was* leery of Blaze Young. Everly would likely be able to give her a ride home. Shawn, her brother, would too. But his truck was still open, and Everly would have to stay until everyone left the dance.

Exhaustion pulled at Faith, and she turned back to

Blaze. She gave him the best smile she could muster, when only five minutes ago she'd been on the brink of tears. "I'd love a ride home."

"Perfect." He reached for her easily and, with the practice of a man who'd done so many times, slid his hand along her arm to the small of her back. "I'm parked just over there." He nodded with that wide-brimmed hat across the street, and Faith went with him.

She wore thick-soled shoes to work, but her feet still ached. They said nothing as they left the dance party, the bright lights, and her decrepit food truck behind. He unlocked the truck with the fob, the clicks sounding like shots in the quieter night over here.

He went all the way around to the passenger side of the truck with her, and he kept his hand on her back as she boosted herself up and into the seat. He closed the door and rounded the hood, all while Faith watched him.

"He's not new to this," she muttered. And he wasn't. Someone who'd lived the life he'd lived? Someone who had to pose for pictures? Had scads of information pages on the Internet? Had traveled all over the world? Had interviews, reporters in his face, sponsors?

He'd likely had a lot of women too.

She turned toward him as he climbed into the truck, finally realizing what was physically off about him. "Are you okay?" she asked. "Did you hurt yourself dancing tonight?"

Blaze swung that powerful persona toward her, and

Faith dang near scrambled out of the truck to get away from the intensity in his eyes. "No," he said.

"You were limping," she said, not sure where her bravery to say such things came from.

"I rode bulls and broncs for decades," he said. "I have back issues." He started the truck and gave her a quick smile. "In fact, I'm having major back surgery on Monday morning."

Concern dove through her, and his words from when he'd asked her out a half-hour ago sang in her ears. She hadn't really heard them, because he'd been so...big in the small kitchen.

"I hope it helps," she said, and she meant it. Just because he was larger than life and intimidating didn't mean she wanted him to be in pain.

He eased away from the curb. "I don't know where you live, Faith."

"Oh, sure." She rattled off her address, and at the stop sign, he idled there while he typed it into his navigation system.

"You're close to me," he said. "So it's on the way."

"Where do you live?" she asked.

"I'm up on Mountain Lake Drive."

Of course he was. There wasn't a house up the canyon that didn't cost over a million dollars, and Faith shouldn't be surprised. She *wasn't* surprised. "Do you have a lakefront property, or are you on the hill side?"

"Lakefront," he said, throwing her another look. "You?"

She laughed, half expecting him to join her. When he didn't, she quieted quickly. "Uh, no." She sat on her hands, suddenly feeling greasy and gross again. "I'm not up the canyon. It just looks close. The highway up to Dog Valley separates the town from the canyon communities."

"I thought it was all one town," he said coolly.

"I mean, sure." She wasn't sure what she was trying to say. He'd already boasted about how much money he had. She didn't have to tell him how little she did. "It's just... when you've lived here a long time like I have, when the town's expanded over the years, we have different names for different areas. The canyon community is newer."

"Ah."

Faith's nerves rattled, and that was never good for her. She said too much when she got shook. "I live in an older part of town. Nothing like Mountain Lake Drive."

He said nothing, the drive easy for him. Faith felt one moment away from losing the little dinner she'd eaten before she'd coaxed her truck over to the dance studio. "What do you do now?" she asked.

He looked at her again, the shadows on his face making his rugged features more severe. "I'm retired."

"How old are you?"

"Would you like it if I asked you that?"

"It just seems odd to be like, thirty and retired."

"I'm older than thirty."

"Good," she said. "So am I."

She thought she caught the barest of a smile before he looked out his window and turned left according to the navigational directions. A few seconds later, he pulled into her driveway, and from her seat high up in his luxury truck, she could suddenly see how small and pathetic her house was.

His truck could've swallowed it and still been hungry for more.

Faith had to get out of here. Away from him. "Thank you, Blaze," she said, his name burning her throat as it came out. Oh, she shouldn't have said his name. Now all she could hear was the shape of it in her voice. The way it felt leaving her mouth. How much she wanted to say it again.

"Let me come help you down," he said, already opening his door.

She didn't need help down, but she sure did like being taken care of. No one had concerned themselves with her for a long time—at least not romantically. Faith had a lot of friends in town, and her sister and her husband and family lived here too.

But someone like Blaze Young? Men like him didn't see her. They didn't even know she existed.

As Blaze opened her door and then stepped into the small space between the truck and the gaping door, it was clear he saw her. He was looking, and she couldn't escape his gaze.

"I was serious about takin' you out," he said. "Even if I said it all wrong." That hint of a smile returned. "Maybe you can think about it?" He extended his hand to her, and she put her skin against his.

Her blood suddenly boiled the same way the hot oil had been in her doughnut truck. Could he feel that too? Her mind clouded with what she could only describe as smoke as she slipped from the truck.

Blaze gave her hardly any room at all, and he kept his hand in hers as he backed up and then started up her front sidewalk with her. "The surgery takes months to recover from," he said. "I won't be in any shape for going out for a long time. So you can take all the time you need to think it over."

They reached her stoop, which was three steps up, no railing, and no porch. Just an ugly slab of cement. He paused there, her automatic lights now bathing them in plenty of wattage. "I'll give you my number, and you can use it if you want." His eyebrows went up, a silent question mark at the end of his statement.

Faith studied him for several long moments. He didn't fidget or fuss with his clothes. He didn't clear his throat or sigh at her lengthy staring. He simply looked back at her, something sharp and filled with desire in those deep, dark, nearly black eyes.

She had no idea what she was looking for. An excuse not to give him her phone? Every cell in her body urged her to give him her phone.

A reason to turn him away? His first impression hadn't been great, but his second was spectacular.

She didn't know what she was trying to find. She finally blinked, not knowing how long she'd stood there drinking him in.

Then she reached into her back pocket and handed Blaze Young her phone.

14

Tex Young stood at the big back window and watched his son lead the horse back to the barn. There was something...not quite right with Bryce, but Tex hadn't been able to get him to say anything.

He'd arrived back on the farm yesterday afternoon, during band practice, and his welcome party had spanned the ages from three to seventy. Everyone in the Young family adored Bryce, Tex included.

But he'd been quiet. His smile hadn't been as quick to arrive, though when it did, it was just as bright and just as playful. He adored his cousins—and they all adored him— so they'd all piled into the basement here at the farmhouse for a sleepover last night.

Only Bryce and Harry were up this early in the morning, and Tex lifted his coffee mug to his lips for another sip. The baby girl in his arms grunted, and he looked down at his precious daughter.

Melissa was about two and a half months old now, and Tex loved her with all he had. He'd worried he wouldn't, what with everything he felt he had already going to Bryce. But he hadn't needed to worry. The Lord somehow expanded his heart and made room for Melissa too.

He leaned down and pressed his lips to her forehead and whispered, "Shh, baby. Keep sleepin'. Mama's not up yet." He tried to give Abby any extra sleep he could. She still worked at the library, though she'd finally decided to give up her position there in favor of being a full-time mom.

But she hadn't felt right about abandoning them right before all the summer reading programs, so her last day wasn't until September first. At that point, she'd only drive the Bookmobile three times a week, and occasionally on Saturdays. She'd told Tex she didn't want to give that up yet, and if she wanted to drive the bucket of rust to Rusk once a week, he was fine with it.

He was fine with whatever she wanted to do. His schedule in the band was ultra-flexible—at least right now.

Worry ate at him, and he tried to swallow it down with another mouthful of coffee. Country Quad would have to tour for this album, and once Morris got back from his honeymoon and could get to Nashville, they were going to try for a summer-only tour next year.

Tex could bring his family then. All of them, if Bryce wanted to come as he had in years past.

"Think he'll go back to school, Mel?" he asked the sleeping baby. Of course she didn't answer, and Tex had his doubts about Bryce returning to Montana State, despite his claims to have loved his college classes.

He'd changed in the past nine months since he'd been gone, and Tex's heart worried and worried for his son. He didn't know how to make it stop, so he watched from the window as Harry led the second horse into the stable.

Bryce came out a few moments later, and he paused, his eyes closed. He ran his hands over his face and then tilted his head back to look into the sky. Tex wondered what plagued him, and how he could draw it out of his son. They'd had plenty of difficult conversations over the years—about Bryce's mother, about Tex's shortcomings, about girls, about school, about life—and Bryce didn't usually hold back.

Give him time, Tex told himself as Bryce's attention moved to the property next door. His face split into a grin, and he jogged toward Wade and Cheryl's place. Tex shifted from his spot at the window to be able to see further north, and sure enough, he found Wade standing there.

Bryce practically crashed into the man, who wrapped him up in both arms and held him tight. Tex's heart warmed and a smile sprang to his face. It sure was good to have good neighbors and men Bryce could lean on.

Not that Tex didn't have a plethora of brothers for that. Wade was Abby's brother, but not a Young, and he and Bryce did have a special relationship.

"She's still sleeping?" Abby asked quietly.

Tex ducked his head and inched over to make room for his beautiful wife at the window. "Yeah."

"You're spying on your son."

"I'm just watchin' him."

She did the same, her arm sliding around his waist. "He'll be okay."

"He's different." Tex didn't know how to express his fears other than that. He didn't want to lose Bryce, and he didn't want Bryce to lose himself.

"He's still him," Abby said. "He's a good kid." She looked up at him, compassion and concern in her eyes. "I can try talking to him, if you'd like."

"I think we should have everyone try talking to him," Tex said. "He'll open up eventually, to the right person."

"Could be Wade," Abby said as she went back to watching the two of them. They talked and laughed, and when Harry came out of the barn, the three of them went out onto Wade's farm.

"Could be," Tex said.

"Aunt Abby?" a little girl said, and she turned to Corrine.

"Yes, baby?" Abby bent and scooped the little girl into her arms. "Are you hungry?"

Corrine nodded, and Abby set her on the countertop. "Well, let's get breakfast going. You can help with the waffle batter, okay?" She set about doing that, and an hour later, the scent of bacon had woken all the kids in the basement.

Bryce and Harry came in off the farm with Wade and Cheryl, and Tex's brothers started showing up for breakfast. He'd given Melissa to Abby to feed and then taken over the preparations for feeding a massive group of people.

The noise level in the farmhouse grew with every body who walked through the door, and Tex simply kept making waffle after waffle. Some people ate at the dining room table. Some took their food outside to the back deck. Some did that and then went downstairs to the covered patio.

Tex smiled and laughed and talked with all of them, until Otis came back for a third waffle. "How many are you gonna eat?" Tex slid the perfectly crisp pastry onto his brother's plate.

Normally, Otis joked and laughed with everyone too. He could eat a lot, and he usually took the ribbing just fine. Today, there was no smile in sight. "As many as I want," he said.

"Hey." Tex reached out with the hand that didn't hold the large serving fork he used to bump the waffles out of the iron. "What's wrong?"

Otis gazed back at him with as much of a glare on his face as Tex had seen outside the recording studio. In there, Otis could be a bear. But in real life? He was all *teddy* bear. As Tex stood in front of him, trying to find the source of contention for Otis, he realized how...off he'd been in the past few months.

"Is everything okay with Lauren?" Tex asked. Otis's ex-wife had been sick for the past few years. So much so, that Otis had taken full custody of their daughter.

"She's fine."

"Joey?" Tex asked. "Georgia?"

Something flickered in Otis's eyes. His whole face collapsed, and Tex had his answer. He looked past Otis to the commotion in the dining room. Eric and Liesl knelt on kitchen chairs and looked at a gaming console Cash held in his hands. Bryce and Harry sat on the other end, both of them looking at a music book and then talking about whatever was in it.

Trace had just gone outside, and Mav was just coming in.

Tex leaned closer. "What's wrong with Georgia?"

"Are you making more waffles?" Mav asked.

Otis flinched and backed away. He looked over to Mav, put a tight smile on his face and said, "He's got lots, Mav." He left, and both Mav and Tex watched him go.

"What's with Otis?" Mav asked.

"I don't know," Tex murmured. He quickly ladled

more waffle batter into his hot iron and put a winning smile on for Mav. "How are the kids? Dani?"

"Good," Mav said with a sigh. "I'm annoyed no one asked me to help with Blaze's surgery." His expression darkened, and Tex actually felt bad for him. Mav had been the glue that had kept them all together, even when some of the brothers didn't get along. Even now, there were certain pairings that made Tex nervous, though Luke had calmed a lot of his anger, and Gabe had learned to silence his tongue.

Morris had come home, and a lot of bridges had been rebuilt and old wounds soothed. All of that had started and continued to happen because of Maverik, the middle brother of nine, and he hated being left out.

"I don't have a job," he said. "I can literally be anywhere or do anything." He glared out the big windows to the deck beyond. "And Trace is goin' over there?" He shook his head.

"Trace doesn't really have a job either," Tex pointed out. "You have little kids. Your daughter is already here for the summer. Blaze eliminated anyone with kids under age ten."

"That makes no sense," he said. "I know how to handle Cash. In fact, Cash *likes* coming to play with Boston and Beth."

Tex chuckled and shook his head. "No, brother. Cash likes coming to play with your drum set."

"Same thing."

Tex nodded over to the table where the five kids sat. "Who's Cash with right now?" The twelve-year-old had gotten up from his chair and now stood with Harry and Bryce, the three of them looking at the handheld game machine. "Where are Boston and Beth?"

"We would've been fine," Mav griped.

The waffle iron beeped, and Tex opened the lid to check it. The more waffles he made, the longer it took to truly get them crispy, but this one looked good. He forked it onto Mav's plate.

"There are others of us who need opportunities to serve too," Tex said.

Mav's eyes widened as he looked from his waffle to Tex's face. "I know that."

"Do you?" Tex started putting more batter into the iron. "Because this isn't about you. This is about Blaze and Trace, and you know what? Maybe they need this time together."

"I...." Mav didn't finish, and Tex only smiled at him. He closed the waffle iron and reached for Mav. He curled his fingers around the back of his brother's head and leaned forward until their foreheads touched.

"You're the best of all of us, Mav," he whispered. "Everyone knows it. We all know we can call you or Dani day or night, and you'll be there, no questions asked."

Mav drew in a long breath and then started to release it slowly.

Tex loved his brothers so much, but he hadn't been the

uniting force. He hadn't been the leader. Mav had, and Mav was. "Let them have this time." He stepped back and released Mav. "Besides, you need to keep working on Gabe, not Blaze."

"What about Gabe?" Mav turned around as if the man would be standing there.

"I think he might like coming to Coral Canyon more than he'll ever admit," Tex said.

Loud laughter broke out at the table, and that ended the conversation between Mav and Tex. No one else had queued up for a waffle, so Tex took out the last one and unplugged the iron for now.

He went over to the table. "What are you boys doing?"

"I have this cool skateboarding game," Cash said with plenty of enthusiasm in his voice. "Bryce just did the most epic crash."

Tex smiled and looked at his son. Bryce seemed his old self now, with everyone here and surrounded by the family he loved—and who loved him. "Bryce is good at everything," he said. "Even the stuff he messes up."

Bryce's face fell for only a moment, and then he formed his expression back into that smile that Tex knew so well. Still, Tex had seen the fall, and he had no idea what to make of it.

"Tex," Abby said, her voice on the upper registers of what a human ear could hear. "Get out here, baby." She gestured to him wildly from the sliding door that led onto the deck, and his pulse pounced up into the back of his throat.

"What?" he asked, already moving that way. "Do I need a first aid kit?" He tried to keep the back yard clear of dangers, because the band went out to the white barn recording studio every day, and they brought their kids.

Though the farm sat on the outskirts of town, and it was a good drive to get here, his brothers and their children came all the time. The last thing he needed on his conscience was an injured toddler that was his fault.

"No," Abby said. "Wade and Cheryl just said they have an announcement." She squealed and dashed down the steps to the covered patio, Tex hot on her heels.

He'd just reached the bottom step when Cheryl, who glowed from head to toe, said, "We're expecting a baby in October!"

The whole Young clan—at least those downstairs—started to cheer. Tex joined in, whooping and hollering and clapping with the others.

His eyes caught on Georgia, who sat on a bench on the edge of the patio. She wore a smile, but tears streamed down her face. Tex elbowed Abby, who stood right in front of him. Shockingly, she wasn't all up in Cheryl's face, hugging her.

She spun back to him, the fire already in her eyes. "What was that for?"

He nodded over to her best friend, and Abby turned back to her. "Oh, no." She hurried away from Tex and to

Georgia, who collapsed into Abby's side. She wrapped her arm around Georgia and held her, and when she looked up at Tex, Abby only wore bewilderment in her face.

The two women were best friends, and Tex and Otis went out a lot with their wives. They had them over for dinner, and they went to Otis's house often. So for Abby to not know why Georgia was sobbing on the patio?

This was something serious.

Tex honestly wasn't sure how he could deal with everything in his life right now. Being a new father who didn't get enough sleep felt hard enough. Add on his adult son coming home and having...something on his mind, and Tex felt out of his element. And now something wasn't right with Georgia?

He looked around for Otis and found him standing on the fringes of the group. He held his half-eaten waffle, but he wasn't cutting it to take another bite. He wasn't congratulating Wade and Cheryl.

He simply stood there, watching his poor wife cry into Abby's side.

Tex purposely didn't move too fast as he walked over to his brother. "We're here to help," he said quietly. Otis once again flinched, as if he hadn't realized there was anyone else on the planet besides the two women he watched.

Tex met his eyes and saw pure agony in Otis's. "With whatever you need, even if that's just a hug or a prayer or...." Tex's emotions overcame his voice, and he couldn't continue.

Otis's agony turned to anger, and Tex didn't like that look on his brother's face. It was Luke's MO to get angry. Blaze was a pro at it. But Otis? Otis took life by the horns, wrestled it to the ground, and then got up laughing.

At least the Otis Tex had known before today.

15

Otis Young couldn't quite get his voice to work. A huge family breakfast on his brother's back patio wasn't where he'd ever choose to talk about his personal problems, so he simply nodded.

"You and Abby should come to dinner tomorrow night," he managed to say.

"All right," Tex said. "Kids? No kids?"

"You can bring the kids." Otis couldn't meet his brother's eye. A thread of fury wove through him, the way it had been since he and Georgia had gotten the news of her health troubles.

Life wasn't fair, and Otis had never felt it so keenly until this past week. Yes, he'd dealt with his ex-wife's problems, but he'd been removed from it. He couldn't run from Georgia.

He didn't even want to.

Her grief only added to his, and he didn't know how to shoulder anything less than both of their emotions. Maybe if they told someone else, they could share the burden.

Otis had wanted to the moment his wife had called him at band practice a few days ago. Trace was in the middle of his relationship issues, but Georgia came first.

Otis felt like an island. One that had broken off from the motherland and currently drifted far from home. He didn't know everything going on in the Young family anymore, where he felt like he once had. He barely kept up with the happenings of the band, and with Morris gone, he knew he wasn't the only one who felt discombobulated.

But this was worse.

Otis had wanted to call his parents and then Georgia's, but she simply operated differently than him. She needed time to absorb and think and come to terms with things. That took time, and Otis had said he'd follow her lead for when they'd tell everyone what was happening with them.

In the meantime, Otis felt like he got shorter and shorter each day from the weight pressing him closer to the ground. And now, with his gorgeous wife still crying and sniffling, she'd have to tell Abby something.

Georgia looked up, and their eyes met. Otis handed his plate with the waffle on it to Tex and said, "Come by anytime in the afternoon. I'll grill something, okay?"

"Okay."

Otis went to sit beside Georgia, and Abby got to her feet to vacate the spot for him. "Otis," she said.

"It's okay, Abby," he said. He sat beside his wife and let her curl into his chest instead of her best friend's. "Hon, do you want to go home?"

"No." Georgia wiped her face. "Let's go ride the horses." She took a long breath in and looked up at Abby, who hadn't walked away. "Really, Abs. I'm okay."

"You guys are coming over for dinner tomorrow," Otis said. "Five or six. I told Tex y'all could come anytime."

Abby still wore anxiety on her face. "Okay," she said. "I'll get Bryce, and he'll tell you which horses need a walk." She turned and left, and Georgia got to her feet.

She immediately turned her back on the group on the patio, and only Tex remained looking at them. As Otis got to his feet, his oldest brother nodded and turned back to the table where Blaze sat with Jem, Jem's kids, and Trace.

Mav's family laughed with them, and Wade and Cheryl looked like they'd been to the moon and back and had so many amazing tales to tell about it.

Otis swallowed the bitterness in his throat. He was okay with the family he had, even if it never got any bigger. Not everyone had to have nine children. Or even two. He adored Georgia, though, and she wanted babies.

Babies she couldn't have.

Otis started to turn just as Gabe called his name, and he found him walking down the sidewalk from the side of the house. Gabe practiced family law, specifically fighting for the parental rights of fathers, in Jackson Hole, and he'd built a big practice and a strong network for dads. When Otis had learned of Georgia's issues, he had texted Gabe.

He hadn't told his wife yet, because Georgia still needed to mourn her infertility. Otis, on the other hand, wanted to give his wife options.

One of which was adoption. Gabe dealt with unmarried parents who put their babies up for adoption, sometimes the woman doing it without the father's knowledge, so he knew people in the adoption industry.

His keen eyes took in Otis and Georgia facing away from the group, and his brow furrowed. "Are you two leaving already?"

"Just going horseback riding," Otis said. "Tex is making waffles upstairs."

"Perfect." Gabe arrived and gave Georgia a light hug. "Good to see you, Georgia."

"You too, Gabe." She started down the sidewalk, her steps slow and even.

Otis hugged his brother, who slipped him a regularly sized envelope. "A few people to talk to," he said quietly. "You haven't told her yet?"

"Did you see her?" Otis stepped away and stuffed the envelope in his back pocket. "She's not ready to hear about adoption yet."

Gabe surveyed the rest of the crowd. "No one else knows?"

"We invited Tex and Abby for dinner tomorrow," Otis

said. "I mean, Cheryl just announced that she and Wade are expecting a baby, and Georgia...."

Broke.

The truth was, she'd broken down instantly. She'd assured him and reassured him she was okay, or would be, but anyone with eyes could see she wasn't.

"Then we'll see how she is," he said. "I hope to loop everyone in soon."

Gabe nodded, his jaw jumping with emotion. "Well, I love you guys."

"Love you too." Otis stepped past him and then turned back. "Will you ask Momma to keep an eye on Joey while we're gone? She's usually fine, but just so I know someone's watching her."

"Sure," Gabe said. "My daughter must be upstairs."

"Yep." Otis followed Georgia, catching her hand quickly.

She squeezed his fingers and said, "I'm so sorry, Otis. I don't know what happened."

"I really think you'd be happier if we told some people."

"We will," she said. "Tomorrow, okay? Can we just enjoy one more day today?"

Bryce's footsteps came down the steps, and he said, "Uncle Otis, hey."

"Heya, buddy." Otis put a smile on his face and clapped Bryce on the back. Harry and Cash came down the steps too, and Otis gave them both a hug too. "Are you all going to come riding with us?"

He wanted to tell Georgia they'd have so many kids around them, they wouldn't be able to get rid of them.

"Nah," Bryce said. "We only have four horses, and two have been out already."

"Oh, got it."

"This way." Bryce led them toward the barn and then down to the stalls. Georgia ducked her head and ran her hands along a pretty toasted-golden-brown horse's neck, and he sure hoped she could find some measure of peace.

She was the woman who liked to go watch the cows graze after Sunday services, and she went to visit her sister's grave when she had something huge on her mind. His whole family would know she couldn't have children —probably for days—before she'd even think about telling her parents.

Otis didn't want to change her; he simply wanted to give her the support and love she needed. *Help me give her the love and support she needs.*

She looked up, and he offered her the kindest smile he possessed. He reached up and touched two fingers to his lips and pressed them to his pulse, and Georgia smiled too.

That was something, he supposed, and Otis went back to where she stood with the horse. "You want this one, baby?" he asked.

"Yeah," she said. "I want to ride this one."

THE FOLLOWING AFTERNOON, OTIS STIRRED THE mayo and mustard into the potatoes and cubed eggs to make the salad. It needed to chill in the fridge for a couple of hours, and then he'd serve it with an easy meal of hamburgers and grilled corn on the cob.

Church had been out for hours, and he'd taken Joey to Lauren's afterward. Georgia hadn't come, as she worked at her bookshop on Sundays until three.

It was about that time now, and he expected to see Abby and Tex at any moment. Tex had texted to say that they weren't bringing the kids, and that Bryce had wanted a break from all the socializing and had agreed to stay home and take an afternoon nap with Melissa.

He'd barely put the huge bowl of potato salad in the fridge when Tex called, "Hey-o, we're here."

"In the kitchen," Otis called back.

Abby entered first, her face full of concern and her arms full of cookies.

He grinned at her. "You've been baking."

"Nervous habit," she said.

Otis wanted to drop his head, as it was suddenly too heavy for his neck to hold up. "You didn't need to be nervous."

"My best friend was sobbing yesterday morning," she said, coming forward. She slid the towering plates of cookies onto the counter. "What's wrong with her?"

"Abby," Tex said gently.

"She's not even here," Otis said. "Do you want me to tell you without her here?"

"Is she working?" Abby's eyebrows went up.

"I'm sure you've texted her," Otis said, his eyebrows mirroring hers. "Has she responded?"

Abby snapped her mouth shut, which meant no. "Georgia goes quiet sometimes," she said.

"You don't have to tell me, honey," Otis said with a smile. He went around the island and took his sister-in-law into a hug. "I love you guys. I love how much you love Georgia. I really do."

Abby gripped him tightly, and he realized she needed some reassurance of her friend's well-being too. Otis took another few moments to hug Tex, and then he figured he'd be the one to tell them anyway, and he could deal with Georgia's displeasure if she didn't like it.

"We've been tryin' to have a baby," he said. "It hasn't been going well. I mean, she got pregnant earlier this year, but she was so sick. Like, beyond sick, and we ended up going to the hospital, and she miscarried."

"Oh, no," Abby said. Her eyes couldn't get any wider.

"We started some tests," Otis said, his voice going dim. He hated how easy it was to disappear inside himself, his voice hardly sounding like his own. If he didn't, though, he got mad, and he hated feeling like punching something hard enough to break his hand.

"It's been a rough few months, ruling things out, trying

another test, all of that. This past week, we learned that she can't carry a baby." He swallowed, because he wasn't sure he'd said it out loud exactly like that before. "There's nowhere for the baby to implant and grow inside her uterus. So any potential embryo dies or it could implant in her fallopian tube, which is obviously bad."

He shrugged and lifted one hand, like, *That's that.*

"Georgia needs a long time to process and accept things," he said. "She's very private, and I think Cheryl and Wade's announcement yesterday just...."

"Broke me," she said from behind him.

They all spun toward the sound of her voice, and Otis hurried to her. "Hey, baby." He swept a kiss along her forehead. "They wanted to know."

"I'm not upset," she said. "I'm glad I didn't have to say it." She looked up at him, more hope and life in her eyes today than he'd seen in months.

Otis smiled at her, kissed her again, and together, they faced Tex and Abby. Together, he and Georgia could get through anything, even this.

"It's just so disappointing," Georgia said. Her voice did shake slightly. "It's like, you know how you have a story for your life, and then you find out that you can't turn the page? It's like that."

"Oh, honey." Abby flew into her arms, and Otis noted the confused look on Tex's face.

Otis moved over to his brother. "I don't have a story for my life," he said.

"Thank goodness," Tex said with an exhale. "I wasn't sure what that meant."

Otis watched Abby hug Georgia and start talking to her. "Women do, though, I think."

"Yeah," Tex said. "I think they do."

"So." Otis breathed deeply, his chest expanding until it was almost painful. "We'll tell Momma and Daddy soon, I think. But don't say anything yet."

"I won't," Tex said. "I'm real sorry, Otis." He faced him. "How are you doing?"

Otis's emotions shook through him. "I'm trying to be strong," he admitted.

"You're the strongest man I know." Tex drew him into a hug and held him tightly. "If there's anything I can do, you let me know, you hear?"

"I will," Otis said.

"Protect yourself," Tex said. He pulled away, and he looked straight at Otis. "Protect her. If it's too much to come to family stuff for a while, then don't come. No one is going to think anything of it."

Otis nodded. "That's a fair point. Sometimes our family is...."

"Oppressive?" Tex supplied.

Otis chuckled and slung his arm around his brother's shoulders. "I was going to say *intense*, but oppressive sort of works."

Tex laughed too. "Right? I love 'em, but even I want to stay home sometimes."

"So," Otis said, ready for the topic to be on something besides him. "How's Bryce? Are you glad to have him home?"

"Yeah," Tex said, his voice perhaps a bit too bright. Too false. "It's great."

Otis didn't press the issue, because he didn't have a lot of mental bandwidth to take on more problems than his own. Maybe tomorrow he'd call Tex on his half-truth, but today, he simply grabbed the fire starter and went into the backyard with his brother to light the grill.

They talked about Mav, and Blaze, and Trace, and Otis was able to find some relief from his grief for a few hours, and he thanked the Good Lord for a good brother who could help him do that.

16

Everly pulled up to Trace's house, unsure if she should get out of the car to ring the bell, or if she should honk for Harry to come out.

Trace had asked her to pick him up that morning and drive him to school, and while that had been a surprise, she'd readily agreed. She didn't have the fourteen-year-old's phone number though.

Her fingers shook as she put the car in park, and thankfully, the door swung inward. Harry came out first, with his father right behind him. Everly could see why the teenager had a girlfriend, because he wasn't hard to look at. He wasn't quite as tall as Trace yet, but getting there, and she'd learned over the weekend that his mother was a supermodel.

He had the good looks on both ends of the gene pool, and Everly smiled at him as she stood from her car.

Harry looked one breath away from going postal, and Everly's smile vanished. He said, "Thank you for taking me to school today, Miss Everly."

"You're welcome." She watched him go by her and get in the passenger seat before she turned to face Trace. "He looks like he might kill me on the way to the junior high."

Trace frowned at his son. "The boy thinks he's older than he is."

Everly had no idea what that meant, but Trace's hand landed on her hip, his touch burning into her bloodstream. "I'll call you later, okay? Once they take him back."

"Yes, sir," she said. "You better. I can bring breakfast over to the hospital just as easily as I can here."

"My parents will be there," Trace said, his eyebrows going up.

"We nearly got mauled by your son in my office not two nights ago," she said. "I think I can handle meeting your momma and daddy."

"I don't know," he teased. "My daddy's a real tough nut to crack." He grinned at her and leaned down to kiss her. Everly wanted to stand out in front of his house and kiss him back forever, but she broke it off after only a couple of strokes.

His son was waiting in the car only five feet away, and she thought they ought to be more respectful than that. "Call me," she whispered as she stepped out of his arms.

Behind the wheel, she looked over to Harry. He sat straight and tall, his backpack on his lap and his arms clenched around it like it carried an atomic bomb that might go off if he didn't.

She backed out of the driveway, her mind buzzing like someone had shoved a hive of bees in there. Everly didn't know how to talk to this boy.

This *boy*.

She reminded herself that Harry wasn't an enormous spider. He wasn't an adult. She didn't need to be afraid of him.

"What finals do you have today?" she asked him.

He didn't even look at her. "History," he said. "Earth science."

"Ew," Everly said. "I don't like either of those." She glanced over to him. "Do you?"

He shrugged, and Everly felt herself crashing and burning. "Does your dad ever let you drive through the McDonald's on the way to school?"

That got him to unclench his arms and glance over to him. "No. Dad's real...scheduled."

She smiled. "Yeah, I can see that about your daddy." She threw her grin over to Harry, who softened even more. "Are you worried about your uncle?"

"We had a family prayer last night," he said.

"Oh?" she asked. "What does that mean?"

"It means my grandpa had us all over to his condo, and he prayed for Uncle Blaze." He sighed and dropped his arms completely. "I don't think Uncle Blaze appreciated it a whole lot—he doesn't like the God stuff much."

"No?" Everly asked. "Do you, Harry? Like the 'God stuff'?"

He dropped his chin to his chest, almost like he was embarrassed. "I mean, yeah," he said.

"Is that why you're not worried about your uncle Blaze?" she asked. "Because your grandpa said a family prayer." She wasn't asking. She'd asked him if he was worried about Blaze, and his response was that they'd had a family prayer. So that was it. Done. Nothing to worry about anymore. The surgery and the outcome of it was in God's hands.

It was actually beautiful, and Everly marveled at Harry's maturity. "You know," she said, making the turn that would take them to Mickie-D's instead of the junior high. "My momma and daddy aren't alive anymore."

That brought his head up, his eyes wide.

Everly's chest stormed. The last time she'd spoken of her parents, she'd ended up weeping into Trace's chest. His strength seemed fused to her bones, and she was able to continue with, "So it sounds real nice to have a family prayer with everyone in your family. I think I'd like that." She squeezed the steering wheel tightly. "It's just me and my two brothers now. Nothing like what you've got."

Harry let a few seconds go by, where the tires whispered to the road. She turned into the drive-thru lane at McDonald's and looked at Harry. He watched her too, his eyes wide and innocent. "I'd pray for you, Miss Everly," he said with all the innocence of a fourteen-year-old who believed in God.

She gave him a shaky smile. "Thanks, Harry. I'd like that." She reached over and squeezed his hand. "Don't go feelin' bad for me, okay? No one wants someone to feel bad for them because they don't have a momma and daddy anymore."

"Do you miss them?" Harry asked.

"Yes," she whispered. Tears rushed into her eyes, and she looked away, feigning the need to study the menu though she came to McDonald's plenty and already knew what she wanted. "I miss them every single day."

The girl chirped through the speaker about their order and she got the pineapple mango smoothie and looked at Harry. "Diet Coke," he said.

She put in the order, and pulled around to the window.

Harry said, "I miss my mom, sometimes." He let another second go by. "Don't tell my dad, though, okay? I don't want him to know."

Everly handed her debit card to the girl in the window and looked at Harry. "Why don't you want him to know?"

"It makes him hurt," Harry said simply. "My mom left me here, at my grandparents' house, a couple of years ago." He looked away, his voice turning a shade or two lower. "I shouldn't miss her. I should hate her. My dad hates her for what she did to me. So I don't tell him, because I don't want him to hurt."

"Oh, honey." Everly covered his hand again, and then had to take her card. She shoved it back in her purse and moved forward. "I'm sure your daddy doesn't hate your mom. I don't know him super well yet, but a little, and I don't think he has any bones in his body that can hate another person."

"Maybe not," Harry said.

She handed him his Diet Coke, and she sipped on her smoothie. They didn't converse on the way to the junior high, and just before she needed to make the turn, Everly pulled to the side of the road instead. "Do you want to get out here?"

He looked over at her. "Really?"

"I don't want to embarrass you, Harry." She really didn't. She wanted to connect with him; she wanted him to know how smart he was, and how valuable, and how much Trace loved him.

"You don't embarrass me," he said. "You can drop me off at the school." His jaw jutted out, and he took another sip of his soda as he faced forward.

Everly did just that, and while Harry didn't turn around and wave at her after he'd gotten out of the car, he did say, "Thank you, Miss Everly," before slamming the door and walking away.

She took a deep breath and blew it all the way out. "Thank you, Mama," she said. "He is the nicest boy, don't you think?" She smiled at Harry's retreating back and got the car moving again. "Did you like him? I think you'd like him so much. He's so much like Trace, what with the silent brooding, and then the vulnerability...."

Everly continued to chat with her mother as she made her way home. She got everything out before she went inside to feed Mutant, and it was mid-morning before she realized that Trace had not called or texted.

Surely Blaze had gone into surgery by now, and he should've had a moment to do one or the other. She had the feeling that she should let Trace come to her that day, so she checked her lip gloss and then headed back out.

The weather was too nice in Coral Canyon now that it was almost June, and Everly needed a project that would get her out of the studio and out of the house. She drove over to the furniture store, hoping her friend Hilde would have something new in the secondhand section she ran out of the back of her shop.

On a Monday morning, with school still in, the parking lot didn't hold too many cars. Everly took a front spot and headed into the store. The air conditioning kissed her cheeks and welcomed her to the store, where Hilde's finest living room set was staged just inside the entrance.

The woman herself didn't linger too close to the door, but she was never too far away either. Everly looked over to the armchair section, but she already owned too many as it was. She wasn't here for a new piece of furniture anyway.

She went to her right, sticking to the front of the store,

where Hilde made sure the window displays showed off all the latest products she'd gotten in.

"Everly," the woman said, and Everly smiled at her friend. "What are you doing here so soon after your dance-off?"

Everly smiled at her and stepped into the brunette for a hug. "I need something to keep my hands busy and get me out of the house in the mornings." She didn't want to tell Hilde if she didn't have a project, she'd head over to Trace's every blasted morning, desperate to see him.

"I've got just the thing." Hilde beamed at her. "I didn't even put it in the shop; I knew you'd want it."

"And you didn't text me right away?" Everly followed Hilde down the aisle toward the back of the store. She accepted used pieces in excellent condition, poor condition, and everywhere in between, and she ran a yard sale every third Saturday of the month for anything in the secondhand shop.

Everly had discovered the event her first weekend in Coral Canyon, and the dresser she'd gotten for forty dollars now stood proudly in her bedroom, sanded, re-stained, and now shining beautifully in a cherry finish. Her mother loved to repurpose things, and Everly had grown up watching her mother turn a bicycle wheel into a chandelier.

They reached the entrance to the shop, and the air conditioning wasn't quite as good back here. Everly paused to take in the new items Hilde had collected, but nothing caught her creativity and wouldn't let go.

Sure, she could take that old dining table and chairs and have days of work ahead of her. The old wingback needed more than she could give it, so she went past that too.

Hilde had walked by all of it, and she fitted a key into a door Everly had never seen her open before. "It's in here," she said, and she gave Everly a smile over her shoulder. "You're going to freak out."

"I am?" Everly's excitement grew, and she tried to peer past the taller woman. That didn't work, and she switched her gaze back to Hilde's to find her beaming. "Show me already." She bounced up onto the balls of her feet, but she still couldn't see anything.

Hilden entered the room and flipped on the light. Everly followed her, finding only three items in the room. An old coffee table with clawed feet, a nightstand that looked close to dust, and a tall, five-drawer cabinet that captured all of Everly's attention.

"I want that," she said. The wood a dark red, almost brown, and the knobs perfectly round. "I need this." She hurried over to it, the top of the cabinet almost to her shoulder. "My mother had a cabinet almost exactly like this."

She turned to Hilde, excitement flowing from her. "She brought it with her from Toronto when she moved to the States."

"You showed me that picture of her," Hilde said. "When I saw this, I knew it had to go to you."

"Yes." Everly ran her hand along the top of the cabinet, almost able to hear her mother's voice, though she hadn't had the luxury of that for just over three years now. "How much?"

"Name the price," Hilde said.

"A hundred?" The cabinet was in decent shape, and Everly started opening the drawers. The first three moved smoothly, but the fourth one hitched, and the fifth one didn't open at all. It didn't matter. She could fix it.

She even had the perfect place to put this cabinet—right next to the door in her office at The Stomp. She'd put treats for the little kids in the top drawer and extra shoes in the second. Her mother would be with her in the studio, and Everly smiled at the cabinet.

"You can just have it," Hilde said.

Everly turned toward her and wrapped her in a hug. "Thank you."

Hilde laughed lightly as she gripped Everly back. "You're welcome, Ev." She pulled away. "I'll have Malcolm get it in your car, okay?"

"Yes, thank you." Everly looked at it and smiled. "You're the best, Hilde." She turned back to her. "Now, what can I bring you for lunch?"

Her eyes lit up. "I'll take the berry citrus salad from The Bar." She got a glint in her eye Everly wasn't sure about. "When you get back, you can tell me about your new boyfriend."

Everly's eyes popped open. "Who says I have a new boyfriend?"

Hilde only laughed. "It's funny you think the whole town doesn't know. You're dating a celebrity, Ev—and not just the small-town type. Trust me, everyone knows about you and the dreamy Trace Young."

17

Trace hadn't looked at his phone in a while, and he had no desire to do so now. He'd promised to call Ev, but he was rather enjoying his device-free time with his family.

His momma and daddy hadn't shown up yet, but Mav had arrived with apple strudel muffins only ten minutes after the physicians had taken Blaze back to start the procedure.

Jem had come with coffee in another ten minutes, and the three of them had been sitting together, talking sometimes, and just being brothers.

Trace loved his brothers best in small groups, and even better one-on-one. He and Tex were especially close, and his oldest brother had probably texted him a half-dozen times by now. Or more.

Trace had been designated the Young family

spokesman, and he was doing a poor job. They'd all learn not to elect him to disseminate information again, that was for sure. Perhaps that was why Trace kept his phone under his thigh, silent, while he listened to Mav talk about his wife and kids.

Jem had plenty to say about his move to Coral Canyon a few months ago, and eventually, they both looked at Trace. He'd said very little, though he'd smiled, nodded, and laughed with his brothers.

That was what Trace did. He'd never been the one to step into the spotlight and take it for himself. If it got thrust upon him, he endured it well enough, he supposed, but he didn't crave it. Not the way Tex did, or Luke, or even Blaze.

Jem too, for it took a special type of man to want the world to watch him try to tame a bucking bull.

Trace looked from Mav's rounder face to Jem's more chiseled one. They looked like Momma and Daddy respectively, and Trace himself took after his father. "Where are your kids?" he asked.

"Momma's," he said. "She said she'd bring them by later, with Cash, once Blaze is out of surgery."

He hadn't enrolled his kids in school for this year, though he'd been here for a few months. Rosie wasn't old enough for school anyway, but Cole was. Trace had sent Harry with Everly that morning so he could get Cash to school and then Blaze here for his surgery.

"They doin' okay?" Trace asked.

"Great," Jem said, his voice a touch false. His face fell slightly. "It's a big adjustment for all of us. Basically, I feed them cold cereal for breakfast and then take them hiking in the morning. That gets us all out of the house and into nature. They get to run and throw rocks, and then in the afternoon, they'll watch TV while I nap."

He shrugged, and Trace thought that sounded like a great day. Mav wore a slightly horrified face, though his days couldn't be much different than that.

"What about you and Everly?" Mav asked. "You two looked really cozy over the weekend."

"Yeah," Trace said, seeing no point in denying it. "We're dating, and I told Harry."

He tugged his phone free. "I should text her and find out if she's still alive. I asked her to drive Harry to school, and he thought he could drive himself."

"He's fourteen," Jem said.

"That's exactly what I said." Trace rolled his eyes. "He's tall, and I guess Bryce lets him drive out on the farm sometimes."

"Farm driving is different than street driving," Mav said.

"You're preachin' to the choir," Trace said. "Anyway, I sent him off with Ev—for the first time—mad as a hornet."

"She's good with kids," Mav said. "I'm sure she was fine."

"Yeah." Trace sighed and wiped his hand through his hair. Out of the three of them, only Jem wore his cowboy

187

hat, and he'd paired that with one of his huge rodeo buckles. He'd retired, but Trace figured it was easier for the man to leave the rodeo than for the rodeo to leave the man.

"Do I really need to come stay with Blaze?" He leveled his gaze at Jem. "You're there."

"I'm useless," Jem said. "And I'm leaving tomorrow to take the kids to their mother."

"You're picking up Morris and Leigh on the way back, right?" Mav asked.

"Yes," Jem said. "Not really picking them up. We're arriving at the airport within an hour of each other, and I'm driving us all back to Coral Canyon."

"I forgot you were going back to Vegas." Trace sighed. He'd put off packing, half-hoping he wouldn't have to go stay with Blaze for the next couple of weeks. His brother didn't want him there anyway.

At the same time, Trace couldn't wait to pack a bag and join his brother in the mountain mansion so he could help.

Blaze was the third-oldest Young, and Trace had been close to him growing up. He'd always had a temper, and he'd always been the dare-devil of the family. But he'd also asked Daddy to do a family prayer last night, and Trace had seen the fear on his face that morning too.

He met Mav's eye. "You're the only one who can handle Blaze," he said.

"Seriously," Jem said. "He's a bear, and he's only ever listened to you."

"That is the furthest thing from the truth I've ever heard."

"It is not," Mav said. "Who else does Blaze listen to?"

"You," Trace shot back.

"No, he tolerates me," Mav said. "He barely answers me, just like Gabe and Morris for a lot of years."

"And you brought them back," Trace said. "I mean, look at Morris now. We can't get rid of him."

They all smiled, and Jem hung his hands between his knees. "I always appreciated the texts, Mav, even when I didn't respond."

Mav said nothing, and Trace gave him a *so-there* look.

"I appreciate y'all welcoming me and the kids so well," Jem said next. "I wasn't sure what it would be like coming home, and you guys made it feel like, well, coming home."

Trace reached out and patted Jem's leg. "I felt the same way when I came back to Coral Canyon."

"I'm kind of jealous of Tex." Jem looked up at Trace and then Mav. "He's got the farm, and I sure loved that place."

"You did?" Trace asked.

"Oh yeah," Jem said with a smile. "Me and Blaze and Otis got into so much trouble. Stealing the Ingalls' peas in the summer, and smashing pumpkins up and down the road every fall." He chuckled, and Trace's mind and memory threw him back to his teenage years too.

He'd always been more sober than Tex older than him and calmer than Blaze younger than him. Sometimes

Momma would call him Gabe, then Luke, then Tex until she finally shook herself and got his name right.

She told him it was because he didn't get in trouble often, and he hadn't had the heart to tell her that he did plenty of questionable things. He was just *quiet* about it, unlike Blaze, Luke, and Jem.

"Tex has a pretty sweet set-up," Trace agreed. "It took him a while to get where he is, though."

"For all of us," Mav said. He cocked one eyebrow at Trace. "I mean, look at you. Finally dating someone without a title or a Wikipedia page."

Trace rolled his eyes, but he didn't argue with Mav. He also didn't tell him that Harry had asked him not to date Everly because all the teen boys in town knew her.

"He's gonna be okay, right?" Jem asked, looking over to the door where Blaze had gone with the nurses.

Trace followed his gaze, his own worries doubling. "Yeah," he said anyway. "He's gonna be okay."

And he'd be there to help Blaze, even if he didn't want it.

Trace finally checked his phone, but Everly hadn't called or texted. His stomach growled when he realized what time his phone showed him, and he was surprised she hadn't asked him if he wanted her to bring him something to eat.

She'd probably assumed he needed some space, and she'd given it to him. A soft hum moved through him and lodged in his heart, and it felt a little bit like love.

Trace couldn't be sure, because he'd never been in love before. He'd been married. He'd thought he'd understood what romantic love was.

He hadn't. He didn't.

He loved Harry; he loved his momma and daddy; he loved his brothers.

But a woman? Everly?

He wasn't sure what that precisely felt like, and he took a long moment to recognize the hum and name it as something like love. Something soft at the very least.

You must've found a project to keep you busy, he sent to Everly. They were still getting familiar with one another, but she'd told him once in the past that she liked to create with her hands. Painting. Crafts. Furniture refinishing. Painting a room or a door for a refresh. Choreographing a new dance. Anything that would employ her creativity and keep her hands busy.

We're just sitting here waiting. No word from the doctors yet, but it's only been a few hours. Hopefully more soon.

He backed out of their thread and checked his other messages. Sure enough, Tex had messaged a few times, and Trace quickly answered his questions. He had nothing to report, so he gave short responses, and then said, *No, Momma and Daddy aren't here yet.*

He tapped to text Harry, because while his son was at school, he could still get messages. Some classes, he sat there for most of it doing nothing, and there was only four days of school left.

Nothing on Uncle Blaze yet. You got to school okay? Was it the worst thing in the world having Miss Everly take you? I hope you said thank you.

His son had some raging hormones that blurred his judgment sometimes and sent his temper to the top of his head in under a second flat. But once he cooled, he usually went back to his normal, human self.

It went fine, Harry said. *I said thank you. Bryce wants to know if he can pick me up and take me to Uncle Blaze's. Can he?*

Trace hadn't made any arrangements for Harry's pick-up. He wasn't sure why. He didn't have so much going on that he couldn't make some texts or phone calls, and Blaze would be in the hospital for at least three days. Maybe longer, depending on how well the surgery went.

Sure, Trace said. *That would be awesome. Ask him if he can get Cash too.*

Band practice for the next couple of days had been canceled—until Morris returned—and Trace was grateful for the break.

He can get Cash. He says he'll be in charge of dinner, so you and Jem can do whatever you need to with Uncle Blaze.

Trace's heart swelled with love for Bryce. He was such a good example for Harry, showing him how to step in and help when those around him needed it. Trace made a mental note to tell Tex what an amazing son he had, because he liked it when people told him that about Harry.

He then remembered he needed to find a counselor for Harry, and he really should've packed a bag so he could go to Blaze's tonight and take care of the kids, and he really wanted to see Everly today too.

As if summoned by his thoughts, her name popped up on his screen. *I went to get a new refurbishing piece, and I found the cutest little cabinet! Now I'm getting lunch for my friend and I from The Bar. I can bring you guys something?*

He looked up from his phone. "Do we want Everly to bring us some lunch from The Bar?'

"Is that a real question?" Jem asked. "I've never even met this woman, and I'll take anything with potatoes, cheese, and bacon."

"You've met her," Mav said. "She was the one who told us about the food at Morris's wedding."

"Oh, that pretty little blonde?" He swung his attention to Trace. "Dang, brother." He grinned and held out his fist for Trace to bump.

He looked at it for a moment, and then decided that Jem meant no harm by his warm grin and assessment of Everly. There was so much more to her than her beauty, Trace knew, and he decided it didn't matter if Jem did or not.

So Trace bumped his brother's fist and looked at Mav.

"I could eat," he said.

Trace grinned at the inside joke from their time on the road with Country Quad. Once, when they'd literally just eaten a mess of pizza, a fan had delivered an enormous box of ice cream sandwiches. And in the south, those didn't stay hard for long.

So Otis had taken the box and brought it into Tex's trailer. He'd put it on the table and stood there while they all looked at him.

"What?" he'd asked. "I could eat. Couldn't you?" Then he'd proceeded to eat not just one ice cream sandwich, but three.

Trace hadn't said no either. No one had.

Trace smiled and started typing. He knew what his brothers liked, and he could give Everly some decent instructions for what they'd like to order.

He finished that, and both Jem and Mav watched him when he looked up. "What?"

"Do you realize how you smile when you text her?" Mav asked, his own smile growing.

Trace flattened his mouth, because no, he hadn't realized that. "I'm sure I don't."

"It's okay to like her," Mav said.

"You've been alone for a long time, brother," Jem said. "Don't be embarrassed."

"I'm not," Trace said. "I just...I don't know how to feel about her."

"What does that mean?"

"It means I'm not sure I know how to love a woman," Trace said, completely surprised by the words—and how true they were.

Both Jem and Mav stared at him; they were clearly shocked by what he'd said too.

Thankfully, his phone rang, and Otis's name sat on the screen. Trace got to his feet and answered with, "Otis, hey, brother," as he walked away.

He could deal with his feelings and his brother's reaction to them later.

18

Everly put another bite of her salad in her mouth and shook her head. Hilde kept saying ridiculous things about her and Trace, and Everly had defended herself in the beginning. The conversation had moved on to something else, and then she'd ordered food for Trace and two of his brothers, and Hilde had started in again.

She giggled and took a bite of her salad too. Everly couldn't help glancing at her phone to check the time. She had to zip across town to the hospital, and then she had to get to the dance studio for her toddler classes.

"Don't let me keep you," Hilde said. "I see you checking your phone every other second now that he's texted."

"I do not," Everly said. She looked at Hilde. "He's exciting, I can admit that. If I don't see him this afternoon, I won't get to see him today." She shrugged with one shoulder. "I almost took him breakfast, but he hadn't texted me yet, so I came to the secondhand store instead."

"It's awesome that you're excited to see him." Hilde gave her a brilliant smile. "And I know he has brothers." She lifted her eyebrows. "I'm just saying, you could help your friend out."

Everly laughed with her, and she said, "I have to count them on my fingers. Let's see...Tex is the only one older than Trace. He's married, Hilde, so he's out."

"He's handsome, though, so keep talking."

"Then there's Trace, and you can't have him."

"Darn," Hilde teased.

"Blaze is third," she said. "I hate to say it, but he's a little scary. But I bet that means he has the softest side out of all of them." She raised her eyebrows.

"He's having back surgery," Hilde said. "We'll save him for later."

"Otis is next," Everly said. "He's married too, so out. Mav, also married." Everly paused while she thought about Trace's brothers.

"Uh...I think Jem is next. I haven't actually met him yet. He's single, but I think just recently, so you might not be interested in him."

Hilde finished chewing and looked at Everly. "I'm interested in anyone who treats me like a queen."

Everly grinned back at her. "Fair enough." She pushed

her lettuce around, having eaten her last strawberry. She decided she didn't want any more greens. "Then there's—"

"Wait," Hilde interrupted. "Did you say Jem?"

"Yes." Everly watched her friend turn from sweet to sour. "What?"

"Tall, dark, big belt buckle?"

"I mean, he's a rodeo guy, so the belt buckle would make sense."

Hilde folded her arms. "I'm not interested in him. He was in the store for *hours* one day a few weeks ago, and he had me writing up all these receipts for special orders, and then—" She smacked her lips. "He walked right out. Got a phone call and left. Just like that." She shook her head. "Not interested in Jem."

Everly smiled, because Hilde made snap judgments sometimes and later had to eat crow. "Okay," she said. "No Jem. After that, there's Luke and then the twins. Gabe is single, but he's a lawyer in Jackson Hole. Morris is married."

"You skipped over Luke pretty fast."

"Luke is probably great," Everly said. "I mean, I've met him in a crowd and that's all. I don't know him at all."

"So we've got a cowboy having back surgery," Hilde said, holding up one finger. "An arrogant rodeo guy, a lawyer who doesn't live here, and a brother who's *probably* great." She held up four fingers by the end. "These aren't great options."

"Maybe you shouldn't let your first impression of Jem

guide your whole life." Everly grinned at Hilde, who rolled her eyes. "Or." She stood and started cleaning up her leftover lunch. "Tex has a son who's an adult."

"I'm gonna stop you right there." Hilde glared up at her. "I'm thirty-four, Everly. I'm not dating someone half my age."

"He's almost nineteen, I'm sure." Everly giggled as Hilde looked scandalized.

"You should go," she said. "Take your hot boyfriend his lunch." She stood too and started tossing her napkins over her mostly empty tin of salad. "Too bad I have to go back to work." She looked out the big glass window that showed her the showroom floor from her office. "We're pretty dead today."

"Then you'll go stage a master bedroom," Everly said with a smile. "You love doing that."

"Yeah." Hilde sighed. "Call me when you start stripping the dresser. I want to see if there's anything under that lacquer."

"You think there will be?" Everly's interest piqued.

"Maybe," Hilde said. "It came from the Beverly estate up in Dog Valley, and Wilma was one hundred and one years old. You never know what people from a different generation did with their things."

Excitement built within Everly. "I can't wait to get started." She stepped over to Hilde and hugged her. "If you really want me to help you find a boyfriend, I will. I'm so good at that."

"Yeah, that's why you haven't dated anyone in almost two years," Hilde said, her voice as dry as a desert.

Everly didn't say why she'd deleted the Christian Pool app from her phone, or why she'd hung her hat on the Trace Young rack for the past year and a half. "I'm so good at Christian Pool," she said as she stepped back. "I can swipe left and right and get you matched with the right cowboy in like, two days. Maybe faster."

Hilde smiled and shook her head. "No, I'm not ready for an app yet."

"All right." Everly noted the word "yet," but she filed it away for later. She picked up the other to-go bags of food and headed for the exit.

A quick drive from the furniture store to the hospital had her heartbeat pulsing in the back of her throat as she carried the plastic bag toward the visitor's entrance. Trace had texted to say he and his brothers were waiting on the second floor outside of orthopedics, which was apparently where someone went to get back surgery.

Everly got on the elevator and moved to the back, then turned to face the front. Two more people got on, and she knew instantly who they were. She'd seen them at Morris's wedding, but it wouldn't have been hard for her to pick out Trace's mother and father.

"Oh, hello," she said, her voice sounding just a tiny bit chipmunk-y. They both looked at her, and the light of recognition flared in his momma's eyes first. Why couldn't

Everly remember the woman's name? Had Trace ever told her?

"Hello, Everly, dear." His momma moved right into her, jostling the plastic sack as she gave Everly a quick hug. "Jerry, it's Everly Avery." She stood back and let her husband shake Everly's hand. She leaned over toward him and said in a very non-whisper whisper, "She's his new girlfriend."

Everly didn't really like the word "new" on the front of her label, but she supposed it did fit. No one but her and Trace really knew how long they'd had eyes for each other.

"It's good to meet you," Jerry said. "You catered Morris's wedding."

"Not me," Everly said. "My brother owns Pork and Beans. He makes me get up in front of guests, because he says I'm a natural at talking to people." She smiled at both of them and looked back at Trace's momma. "I'm so sorry, ma'am, but I can't remember your name."

"Oh, it's Cecily." She touched her palm to her chest. "Are you taking the boys lunch?"

"Yes." Everly lifted the plastic bag. "Trace didn't say y'all would be coming."

"It's fine," Cecily said. "We're not staying long. We've got a whole condo full of kids to look after." She seemed pleased as punch to be doing that. "We left them with a neighbor just to run out and get a bag of marshmallows and to check on the boys here."

The elevator came to a stop, and Everly got off first.

Jerry held his hand over the doors while his wife exited, and Everly scanned for the signs that would lead her to the right place. In the end, she simply fell into step with Cecily and Jerry, who seemed to know where to go. "How was your dance the other night?" Cecily asked.

"Good," Everly said, brightening. Her pulse had settled slightly, but every step she took reminded her that she hadn't really met Trace's family as his significant other. Moving into that new role would definitely shed a different kind of light on her. "Whose kids do you have right now?"

"We've got Eric for Morris," Cecily said. "And Jem's kids today, while he's here. They're all so close in age, so it works out really well."

"Ran out of marshmallows, though," Jerry said. "So we underestimated there."

"Well, someone shouldn't have gotten out the mouth-guns," Cecily said, giving him a swat on the bicep. Jerry only laughed, and Everly felt the love and joy they had for their grandchildren.

"There they are," Cecily said next, and Everly moved her attention from the two people she walked with to the three men seated in the waiting area ahead. No one else sat there, and Mav looked up and saw them first.

He said something to his brothers, and then Trace and Jem looked their way too. Trace bolted to his feet as he took in Everly approaching with his parents, anxiety on his face. "Momma," he said as she slowed and let them move ahead of her. "Daddy." He gave them both a hug at the same time, his eyes stuck on hers as she smiled at him.

He really was the best-looking man she'd ever dated. Ever met, period. He radiated tension and apprehension, and when his momma stepped back, she said, "We ran into Everly on the elevator. She introduced herself."

"Great," he said, moving between them to her. He didn't take her into his arms or kiss her, but simply faced his parents with her at his side. "We've been seein' each other for a bit."

That could mean a day or a week or a year in Trace-terms, and his parents didn't question him. "I heard," Cecily said, something sharp flowing through her eyes for only a moment.

"From who?" Trace demanded.

"Seemingly everyone knew before me," she said. Then she turned and hugged Mav and then Jem.

Trace slid his hand into Everly's free one and looked at her. "You look amazing," he whispered, and Everly tilted her head back to let him kiss her. He only touched his lips to hers for a microsecond before he straightened again, and he lifted their joined hands slightly.

"Mav," he said. "This is my girlfriend, Everly. Ev, this is Mav. I think you know him from the studio and all that."

"I sure do," she said. "You looked pretty good on Friday night, even if you didn't win."

Mav grinned that trademarked Young smile. "My back is still killing me." He stretched it as if to prove his point.

"And just younger than Mav is Jem," Trace said. "He rode in the rodeo with Blaze for a long time. He's just barely back in Coral Canyon."

Jem wore a smile full of white teeth and charm, and he reached up and tipped his cowboy hat at Everly. "Aren't you a pretty little picture?"

"Jem," Trace warned. "She's not single."

Jem kept grinning at Everly, then moved his gaze to Trace, where it finally slipped. "She is pretty, though."

"Thank you," Everly said, and she could see why women would get transfixed by this man. He was gorgeous —even she could admit it—and she thought if Hilde would just look past the small indiscretion of filling out orders that didn't get paid for, she'd like Jem.

He had big hands and a big personality, but he wasn't loud. He shook her hand and thanked her for the food, and they all sat down in the waiting area. True to their word, Trace's parents only stayed for a few minutes, and when Trace finished his roast beef sandwich, he tossed the wrapper in the trash and said, "Ev and I are gonna go for a walk. We won't be gone long."

Their eyes met, and Everly got to her feet and took his hand in hers. They walked away from his brothers, and Everly decided that things had gone as well as they had because of Trace. He was calm in the face of any storm, and Everly sure did like his steadiness.

"Where are we going?" she asked as he led her past the elevators.

"Just over here." That so wasn't very informational, but Everly didn't really mind.

"I don't have much time either," she said. "I have to get over to the studio soon."

"Mm, I know." He took her around a corner and the hallway here didn't go much further. No one seemed to be coming this way at all, and Trace's goal became crystal clear when he stepped in front of her, swept his hands through her hair and said, "You *are* a pretty little picture."

He grinned at her and added, "A balm to my weary soul today," just before he matched his mouth to hers and kissed her. She felt something urgent in his touch this time, something he tamed and held back after only a few strokes. She couldn't get close enough to him, and he seemed to crave more of her too as he continued to kiss her, and kiss her, and kiss her.

Everly wasn't sure, but behind her closed eyelids, she certainly felt like she was falling. She was falling fast, and it was wild, and terrifying, and exhilarating all at the same time.

She was falling, and the only person who could save her was the one currently making everything in her body swimmy and soft, the one and only Trace Young.

A couple of hours later, Everly stood at the back door and said goodbye to her four-year-old ballet students. When the last one had gone, she reached for her phone. She'd put it on the shelf next to the speaker, and she checked it between classes. Right now, she didn't have to teach again for another hour, and she headed toward her office as she swiped on the device.

Her heartbeat crashed against the roof of her mouth when she saw that Harry had called her. "When?" She came to a complete stop in the middle of the small studio and checked the timestamp. Only five minutes ago.

She hurried to dial him back, and he picked up on the second ring. "Harry?" she asked. "What's wrong?"

"I was just wondering if you'd been in touch with my dad," he said. "I've called him like a bajillion times, and he's not picking up."

"Not for a couple of hours," she said. "I've been teaching."

He sighed, and Everly wanted to drop everything and run to his rescue. "What do you need?" she asked.

"Bryce and I were supposed to pick up Cash after school," he said. "But Bryce got to the junior high to get me, and his truck started making this knocking noise. So we figured out it's his tire, and we're getting it fixed now, but we couldn't get Cash. I texted him, and he said he's fine to wait, but it's already been twenty minutes. I thought maybe my dad could go grab him."

"I said we should call Mav," Bryce said on the other end of the line.

"I can get him," Everly said. "He's at the elementary school, right?"

"Yeah," Harry said.

"I'm only two blocks from the elementary school." She started walking again. "I can get him in like, two minutes and bring him to you."

"Could you?" Harry said. "If you're teaching, then he can just walk down to the studio and wait for us there."

"I don't have a class for a bit," she said, channeling her inner Trace. "Tell me where you are, and I'll bring him." Everly grabbed her keys from her office while Harry said they were at The Tire Spot. She said she'd see him in fifteen minutes, and she hurried into the parking lot.

Getting Cash would be easy, and Everly wanted to do it. With the Young family as big as it was, and their network so huge, she wanted to feel like she could contribute to it somehow. Silly, she was sure, but still how she felt.

Trace had everything in the world, and Everly somehow wanted to let him know that she was valuable, even if all she could do was drive his son or his nephew to and from school.

"He values you," she told herself, because Trace had never made her feel anything but amazing about herself. But she couldn't help feeling like she had to show him that she was more than a pretty face, and if that meant running down to the elementary school between classes, she'd do it.

19

T race noticed the way Blaze gripped the handle above the passenger window, but he didn't know how to drive any more gingerly. He felt every pebble that went beneath the tires, and each one added more tension to the cab of the truck.

His anxiety shot through the sky, but he said, "Almost there."

Blaze grunted, and honestly, the storm currently raging across his face wasn't new. It had been there for the past three days, and Trace knew he wasn't really the one Blaze wanted to scream at.

A keen sense of tiredness pulled through Trace's shoulders too. He'd been sleeping part of the night at the hospital, and part of the night at Blaze's house. Bryce had become instrumental in helping get Harry and Cash to and from school, and Trace was grateful for his nephew's help.

Everly hadn't been coming around as much, though she had brought Blaze one of his favorite pink-iced sugar cookies last night. Trace hadn't been able to spend the time with her he wanted, but that honestly wasn't anything new. He could tamp down his emotions and his hormones for a while, but he was anxious to see her.

Bryce's golden pick-up sat in the driveway, but Blaze had told Trace to take him around the back of the house to the garage. That meant more bumps, and more grunts, and increased white knuckles from Blaze.

But Trace got them there and put the truck in park before killing the ignition. "Hold there," he said as if Blaze would try to get out of the truck himself. Every time one of the nurses entered his hospital room, he gave them the blackest look, and last night, while Everly was there, he'd flat-out refused to get out of bed and do his walking.

Trace was amazed that the single best thing Blaze could do to continue and speed his healing was to walk. And how cruel that the one thing that hurt him the most was...walking.

He made it around the truck and opened Blaze's door. "Move your legs, but don't get out." He'd been schooled in how to help Blaze the best, and as Blaze worked on moving his legs so he wouldn't be twisting his hips or spine to get out, Trace got the walker from the back seat.

The garage door opened, and Trace glanced over to it.

He couldn't really see, but he knew who it would be. Cash. The boy had been concerned about his father, and he'd been reluctant to leave the hospital each evening since his dad's surgery.

The first night, Bryce had brought him only for a few minutes, and he, Harry, and Cash hadn't stayed long. Long enough for Trace to learn that Everly had gone to get Cash when Bryce's truck had broken down, and long enough for Trace to witness the powerful love between Blaze and Cash.

He'd been glad for that, because Blaze had been largely absent from his son's life for the first eleven years, and they'd been slowly figuring out how they fit together.

"Dad?" Cash asked.

"Yep," Blaze said. "Just give me a second, Cash." He hadn't tried to get down, and Trace flipped out the sides of the walker and set the brakes with his heel.

"All right." He met his brother's eye and held out both hands, palms up. "Do you want me to make you walk now, or do you want to see if dinner's here?"

"Dinner's not here yet," Cash said as he came around the front of the truck. "Can I take him, Uncle Trace?" He wore such open vulnerability on his face, those dark eyes so much like Blaze's. As he continued to grow up, he'd break so many hearts, Trace was sure.

He looked back at Blaze, his eyebrows up. "The path is fairly even," he said. "I checked it, and I can follow behind if you'd be more comfortable with that."

Blaze nodded a single time, and then he put his hands in Trace's. He steadied him and backed up a step. "Slow. Put down one foot and wait if you need to."

Blaze's sigh told Trace that he was insufferable, but suffer it he would. He put his left foot down first, the rest of his body sliding along the seat and following. His right knee bent as far as it would, and then he put that foot down.

Trace and Blaze practically stood chest-to-chest, and only Blaze breathed like he'd just ridden the toughest bull on the rodeo circuit and beaten it. All he'd done was get out of the truck. The road in front of him was long, and it wouldn't be pleasant, but if Trace had learned one thing this week, it was that Blaze was tough and vulnerable at the same time. He could do this, and he could cry about it later.

"Dad, you're doing so good," Cash said, and that lit Blaze's face with a partial smile.

"Walker," Trace said, and he released Blaze's left hand and kept ahold of him on the right until his brother had a good grip on the handle of the walker. He then released his other hand, and Blaze transferred his weight to the walker.

"He can't go very fast, Cash," Trace said. "He has to stay on the road, and he can't go past the Hillier's. Then it's too steep for him."

"Yes, sir."

"He's gonna follow behind us," Blaze said. "Just in

case, okay? I'd hate to fall and put you in a position where you can't help me."

"I can help you, Dad."

"I know you can, bud, but I'm like three times as big as you, and it's simply safer if we let Uncle Trace shadow us. Understand?"

"Yes, sir."

"Okay, now take me into the house first. I've gotta use the bathroom."

Trace was certain he didn't, because they'd only taken the catheter out an hour ago, but he said nothing. The nurse had said that Blaze might feel like he needed to go when he didn't for the next day or so.

Every step Blaze took seemed to take an agonizingly long time, and Trace employed every ounce of patience he had. By the time the three of them arrived in the kitchen, Trace was glad he had more avenues to walk around the house.

Harry and Bryce sat at the enormous dining room table for eight, a laptop open in front of them. "This looks like trouble," Trace said with a grin. "School's out for both of you, so what's so interesting on that thing?"

"Come listen to this single," Harry said. "Conrad Conchran just released it." He stood from his computer as if Trace would take his seat. He moved past him and said, "Wow, Uncle Blaze. Look at you."

Trace did take his son's seat, and he slung his arm around Bryce's shoulders. He looked at him, something...

off about his nephew. Then he brightened and said, "Hey, Uncle Trace."

"Thank you so much for all you've done this week," Trace said. "I thought I could manage two kids who went to school all day, and I failed mightily." He smiled at his nephew, whose grin widened.

"Yeah, of course."

"I can fill up your truck for you." He raised his eyebrows. "For how much you've driven around this week."

"It's no problem," Bryce said. "I like it on this side of town."

Trace grinned at him. "Yeah, I bet. Bailey lives over here, doesn't she? Did she come home for the summer too?"

Bryce's smile dropped from his face instantly, and he shook his head. "She's got an internship in Butte," he said.

"Oh." Trace foot might as well be halfway to his stomach for how hard he'd jammed it down his throat. "Uh, I'm sorry."

"It's fine." Bryce got to his feet, leaving Trace in front of the laptop alone. So it totally wasn't fine. Trace watched his nephew go around the table and over to where Cash stood guard outside the half-bath concealed around the corner.

Trace looked at the computer, decided he didn't want to hear Cochran's new song. They weren't exactly in competition, but he and Otis didn't listen to new country music coming out while they wrote and worked on their own album. Trace's near photographic memory with chords and notes could bleed into a revision of one of their songs, and that was the last thing he wanted or needed.

"Ready," Blaze announced, and Trace noted how sunny and eager he was to walk when his son would be his companion. They started for the front door, and Trace let them get ahead. He closed the laptop and met his son's eyes.

"You ordered pizza, right?"

"No," Harry said.

Trace's eyebrows furrowed. "No? I thought you were ordering pizza so we'd have dinner." Blaze didn't cook, Trace knew that, and since he'd been here all week, he also knew there weren't many groceries in the fridge. He didn't have patience for this, and he growled as he pulled out his phone. "I'll do it."

"Calm down, Dad," Harry said, and oh, how Trace hated those words. They brought his head up sharply, and he glared at his son. Harry held up one hand, realizing what he'd said. "Everly texted and said she'd bring dinner."

"She's teaching until eight," Trace said. "It's too late." He'd already told her this.

"She said she'd bring dinner," Harry said. "That's what I know."

"Uncle Trace!" Cash yelled, and Trace shoved his phone in his back pocket and dashed after Blaze and Cash.

He found them at the top of the steps, both of them looking down. Trace dang near skidded to a stop, expecting them to be further away than they were. His chest heaved. "They're just stairs," he said. "The nurses showed you how to go down them."

"I can't do it," Blaze said.

Trace moved down one step and directly in front of him. "Yes, you can. So Cash, you come stand here. He shouldn't go down steps very much, but he can do these if you stand in front of him." Trace put both hands on the walker. "He can lower this, and then you hold it really still and steady for him."

Trace pulled the walker down to the step in front of him. "I showed these to your dad's doctor, and he said they're okay since they're so big and wide." He looked at Blaze. "Remember that?"

"No."

Maybe he didn't, but Trace did. He set the walker and then the brakes. "Ready." He held up one hand, and Blaze took that and then reached for the walker. Down they went like that, in stuttering, stilted steps—one, two, three—until they reached the sidewalk. Trace grinned at Blaze and then Cash.

"That's it."

"Okay," Cash said. "Good job, Dad."

If Trace had praised Blaze as much as Cash had, he'd have lost his head by now. But Blaze only moved his walker and kept going when his son complimented him.

Trace waited until they'd gone past Bryce's truck, and then he tugged his phone out of his pocket and followed at a snail's pace.

He walked so slowly, he could easily text Everly too, and he asked her when she might be arriving with dinner. *If it's too much, just say the word,* he typed out. *I can order pizza with a few taps.*

Are you there? she asked.

We're at Blaze's, yes, he said. *Been here about ten minutes.*

She didn't answer again, and Trace didn't know what was happening. She hadn't said when she'd be there, and he really didn't want to wait until eight-thirty to eat. If that, as she usually cleaned up after her last class, would have to pick up dinner, and then drive to the west side of town.

He quickly sent a text to the family string that said: *Blaze is at home, and Cash is walking with him down the street.* He took a picture of the two of them from behind, capturing Blaze with his head turned toward his son, and part of a smile showing there.

Trace had no idea what they were talking about. The important thing was that they were talking.

His brothers and their spouses started responding, and Trace kept up with the congratulations and well wishes Blaze would have to read later. He hoped he'd be able to feel the love and prayers his family had for him, and that they'd help him heal.

Trace's faith strengthened, and he whispered, "Thank you, Lord, for bringing him home where we can watch over him during this time." He'd given up praying for Blaze's own heart to be open to the gospel or to religious things, but his brother had changed so much in the past year since moving here, Trace thought the Lord had been working on him all this time anyway.

The sound of a car engine came toward him, and Trace automatically moved to the side of the road. He glanced up as the car eased to a stop, and his own smile probably blinded Everly as the beautiful sight of her face filled his vision.

"Hey." Surprise cut through him as he crossed to her car. He leaned down and kissed her through her open window. "What are you doin' here? You're not teaching?" It was barely five-thirty, and she should have hours of classes in front of her.

"I'm not teaching today." Her smile reminded him of crisp apples and cotton candy. It was flirty and fun and made just for him. "Surprise. I brought dinner and a puppy."

Trace leaned his elbows on her doorframe. "A puppy? What?"

"It's scientifically shown that puppies help surgery patients heal faster," she said. "Don't worry; I only rented him, and he's house trained already."

Trace looked across the car and then into the back seat. "Where is he?"

She grinned. "See? You didn't even know your son has been tending him for the past couple of hours." She nodded down the road in the direction he'd come. "He's already at Blaze's, so hurry up and finish your walk. I made chicken cordon bleu casserole, and it's best eaten piping hot."

She drove off then, and Trace could only stare after her. "She brought a puppy to my brother's house, and we didn't notice?"

He really wasn't the best option for helping Blaze through the next several weeks, and yet, he couldn't walk away now.

20

Everly didn't bother knocking at Blaze's house. The front door sat ajar about two inches anyway, and she toed it open with her foot as she didn't have hands to spare. She carried a rack of two casserole dishes, both of them filled with chicken, ham, and cheese, plus the creamy, delicious sauce on the chicken cordon bleu casserole.

Her grandmother had been making this to feed a crowd for decades, and Everly smiled as she called, "Dinner's here. Some help, please?"

The sound of cowboy boots hitting tile came toward her, and both Harry and Bryce Young appeared in the wide, arched doorway that led from the foyer into the rest of the house.

"Everly," Harry said. "You should've texted me." He sounded so much like Trace that Everly's heartbeat warmed toward him. She'd always had a soft spot for children, and while Harry wasn't a child, but a teen, she still felt an easy connection to him.

"Don't try to take these," she said as he reached for them. "They're hot. I have salad and dessert in the car."

"On it," Bryce said, and the two boys went to get the rest of dinner from her back seat. She slid the rack of dishes onto the countertop and pushed it further onto the granite, which could withstand the heat.

She started getting out plates and utensils, not caring that she'd have to do dishes later. She'd gladly do them in order to serve Trace and Harry, and making dinner and bringing it had the added bonus of her being able to spend time with both of them too.

She'd just opened the bottom cupboard when Harry returned with the three family-sized bags of salad. "This is too much, Miss Everly," he said. "Not sure if you've noticed, but we're all boys."

Everly abandoned her search for a big bowl for the salad. "Does that mean you don't eat salad?"

"I mean, I only eat it when my dad makes me." Harry grinned. "And he never makes me."

Bryce slid the sheet tray of caramel popcorn onto the counter. "I can't remember the last time I ate a salad willingly." He beamed at her, and because he was a Young, and so good-looking and charming, he laughed and then took her into a big-chested hug. "But thanks for bringing it."

"I'll only make one bag," she said as she stepped back, a bit surprised at Bryce's hug. She met Harry's eyes, and the tension between them bumped up a little. Did he want to hug her? Could she hug him? She suddenly wanted to but swallowed instead.

"I'll leave the rest for you guys. You'll have salad for three meals instead of one."

"Sure," Bryce said easily. He glanced down at the dessert. "Now, this, I'd love to eat all of."

She swatted his hand away from the caramel popcorn. "Nope," she said. "That's only for boys who eat their salad."

The three of them laughed, and Everly moved the dessert tray further from both Bryce and Harry anyway. "How'd it go getting Blaze home?" she asked. "Oh, and where's Steve?"

"Oh, he's in Cash's room," Bryce said. "I'll go grab him."

"Good, I think," Harry said.

She nodded and finally located a big wooden bowl. As she set it on the counter, she asked, "How was the last day of school?"

Harry sat down across the expansive island and laid his forearms on the granite. "Good," he said. "It was yearbook day, and they let us out before lunch. So great."

Bryce returned with a very excited golden retriever—Steve—and the eight-month-old puppy wore a huge smile on his face. He'd surely heal Blaze with a single look.

"Yearbook day, huh?" She gave Harry a twinkling smile. "Did you get a lot of 'stay cool this summer,' and 'call me, Harry.'" She giggled, but Harry looked like she'd spoken another language.

Bryce sat next to him at the bar, and they exchanged a glance.

"No," Harry finally said. "I had a couple of my good friends sign it by their picture, and then Bryce came to get me."

Everly blinked at him. "What? You didn't pass it down the hall and then wonder if you'd get it back, and then when you did, who'd have signed it?" She looked between Bryce and Harry.

"I hate to break it to you, Everly," Bryce said with a chuckle. "But we have phones." He held his up as if Everly had never seen a cellphone before. "I can literally talk to anyone I want, pretty much any time."

Harry nodded and showed her his phone too. "Same."

She cocked her hip, feeling very old and out of touch—and she didn't like it. "You're telling me Sarah didn't sign your yearbook?" she challenged. "And that you haven't read it fifteen times since lunch?"

Harry's face turned the color of a beet in less time than it took for her to reach for a bag of salad. He dove under the counter for the dog, and see? Puppies were good for more than healing spirits. Harry had just used the retriever as a distraction for his embarrassment.

"Mm hm," she hummed. "That's what I thought." She

ripped open the bag. "I bet she did more than just sign her name next to her picture." As he emerged from below the bar, she gave him a look complete with lifted eyebrows, but Harry only shrugged one shoulder.

She'd seen his father do that same thing when he didn't want to admit something, and Everly grinned at their similarities and how she could read Harry the same way she did Trace. "You boys like chicken and ham and cheese, right?"

"Yes, ma'am," he and Bryce said together.

"All right, then," she said. "Help me set the table. I heard that Uncle Blaze should sit at the table to eat."

Both boys jumped to attention and did what she said, taking the plates, cups, and silverware she passed across the island to them. She wasn't sure how long Blaze would walk, and he had been moving at the speed of a tortoise. The table had been set, and Everly had put a casserole dish in the middle of it and one at the end of it, then turned back to the island to get her salad before the door opened. Steve walked around them all, obviously happy to be out of the bedroom.

Scuffling steps entered, and she continued about her business, going over to the fridge to get ice cubes from the dispenser for their drinks.

"Harry," she said. "I brought lemonade. Can you find a pitcher and mix it up, please?"

"Sure thing," he said. He returned to the kitchen to do

that, and Bryce went to see if Blaze or Trace needed anything.

"Somethin' smells good," Blaze said, and Everly finally abandoned her tasks in the kitchen to meet his eye. He was a fierce man, with some of the more chiseled features in the Young family. Everly had interacted with him a couple of times now, and she'd picked up his son at school in an emergency, so the man looked at her without any edges in his eyes.

He radiated gratitude, and a flash of pain also stole across his face. Everly motioned to Bryce and handed him the serrated knife she'd just picked up. "Cut the rolls, please," she said. "Your uncle needs his pain meds."

She went toward Blaze, easily putting one arm around Cash as she said, "Hey, baby. How was your last day of school?"

"Great," he said as if it really was. "Free for the summer!"

She laughed with him, and then she told him to go wash up. She met Blaze's eyes just as he asked, "Why is there a dog in my house?"

"I brought him for you," she said. "He's so amazing. He'll lay right by you and make you feel like the best person in the world."

He simply looked at her with a semi-bewildered look on his face. He'd abandoned the walker in favor of the couch, and she looked from him to Trace as her boyfriend entered the house and started to close the door. "When's the last time you took your meds?"

"Uh." Blaze looked over to Trace too, and he suddenly realized he was on the hot seat.

"What?" he asked. "Sorry, I was talkin' to my momma." He stowed his phone in his back pocket, and Everly wanted to kiss him so completely that she could steal it from that pocket and he wouldn't know.

"He looks like he's in pain," she said. "When can he take more pills?"

Trace looked startled, and then he studied his brother. "Uh, let me get the sheets from the truck."

He bustled off to do that, slowing briefly to bend down and pat the nearly golden dog. She smiled at his back and then said, "Come sit down, Blaze. You can eat and take more meds, and then I'll even let you go to bed."

"Thank God for you, Everly," he said with a sigh, and she had the very real feeling that he meant exactly what he'd just said.

She accompanied him to the head of the table; Bryce put the sliced rolls on the table; Trace re-entered with a fistful of papers and a plastic bag hanging off his forearm. The sound of pills rattling met her ears, and Everly wanted to tell him he needed a pill case for this.

Honestly, what was he thinking? Would he read that wad of instructions every time Blaze needed to swallow something? It would be easier to do it once, divide up all the pills as he did, and then simply text his brother to take his meds.

Everly knew, because that was what she did for Shawn —and he only took a handful of supplements and then the major one: his anti-depressant. With it, he functioned really well. Without it...Everly filled the pill box for him each week, so she didn't have to deal with days where Shawn didn't take his medication.

Trace met Everly's eyes, and she said, "Let's do it after we eat, okay? Dinner's ready."

Harry put the pitcher of lemonade in the middle of the table, and Bryce finished filling the last of the glasses with ice. They both sat, and Trace got the hint. He tossed the meds and the pages onto the counter and joined them at the table.

"Will you say grace?" Blaze asked, and it took Everly a moment to see that everyone was looking at her.

Cash had sat next to his father, and Trace pulled out the chair beside his son. He sank into that seat, a sigh pulling from his mouth, leaving Everly as the only one still standing.

Sudden emotion clogged her throat for these good men. From twelve to forty, they all looked to her for something. They *needed* her, and more than that—she needed them.

"I will if you don't want to, Miss Everly." Harry looked up at her, his dark eyes so full of light and goodness. She hoped he never let anything dim the vibrancy inside him, but she knew something would. The Lord always sent the hardest of challenges to the best of men, and Harry emanated goodness.

He was strong, and God would surely try him and his faith, the way He did for everyone. Everly simply hoped she could shield him from the worst of it, and she'd barely started to get to know him.

"I can," she whispered. "I just...." She didn't finish. Instead, she clasped her hands together and closed her eyes. Without the sight of the five of them waiting for her, she was able to more easily find her center, her core, the very essence of her that knew and loved the Lord.

"Heavenly Father," she said, her voice barely more than a whisper. This cavernous kitchen should've swallowed the sound of it, but her words somehow boomed throughout the house. "We love Thee so very much."

Emotion swept through her again, but she could feel the love in this house. Brotherly love between Trace and Blaze. Father to son love between Cash and Blaze, Trace and Harry. Cousinly love between Bryce and everyone.

Friendly love between her and all of them, and of course, the love of God prevailed over everything.

"We're grateful Blaze was able to get the surgery he needed this week. Bless him to be as pain-free as possible, and for his physical body to heal quickly. Bless him—" She cut off, because while she'd met Blaze several times now, she didn't know him very well, and she didn't want to make him uncomfortable in his own home.

A warm hand touched hers, and she knew instinctively that it was Trace's. His fingers threaded through hers, and she clutched his hand between both of hers. "Bless him to learn whatever lessons he needs to from this experience. Bless him to be kind to his brothers, and bless his family to anticipate his needs and act quickly to fulfill them. Bless Cash to have the comfort and knowledge that his father loves him, and that Thou loves him, and...."

Everly knew this prayer was off the rails, and she needed to wrap it up quickly. A phrase her mother had always used filled her mind, and she said, "Bless anyone here who's in need of something to have it, to have their prayers answered, and to know that You are watching over us all."

She took a deep breath, because that covered everyone. She didn't want to go around the table and pronounce blessings on each of them, because she figured she might break down bawling if she did that.

So she simply added, "Bless this food to make us healthy and strong, and help us to do Thy will with our health and strength. Amen."

No one said a single thing, and Everly quickly opened her eyes. Blaze's head was still hanging down as he reached up and wiped his right eye. Harry stared at her with wide eyes, and Bryce sniffled and covered his whole face with both hands.

Surprise filled Everly as she swept her gaze past Cash,

who watched his father weep, and looked at Trace. "Sorry," she murmured.

She hurried to sit down too, and she wished Blaze had asked someone else to pray.

"Nothin' to be sorry about," Trace said, his voice too loud in the resulting silence of her prayer. "That was the most beautiful prayer I've heard in a long time."

Blaze finally looked up, his eyes so wide and so watery. "Yeah," he said gruffly. "Thank you, Everly."

"All right," Harry said in an even louder voice. "I'm starving, so let's eat." He reached for the serving spoon for the casserole closest to him, and he scooped a big portion onto his plate. "Cash? Hand me your plate, bud. I'll dish it up for you."

Without another word, Trace picked up Everly's plate and started to serve her too, and Bryce stood and poured lemonade for everyone while he continued to let tears roll down his face. Everly looked at Trace with questions in her high eyebrows, but he simply shook his head and watched his nephew.

Everyone waited until Trace had tonged salad onto her plate, buttered her roll for her, and spooned chicken and ham and cheese sauce onto half the dish. When he set it in front of her, Harry finally lifted his fork and took a bite of dinner.

"Wow," he said with his mouth full. Delight filled his eyes. "Miss Everly, this is fantastic."

She smiled, but she couldn't speak. Not right now.

She'd just bonded to these men, and she loved them each in many different ways.

Trace leaned toward her, and she naturally inclined her head toward him too. "Thank you," he whispered again, and after a quick sweep of his lips across her temple, he picked up his plate and started getting food for himself.

Everly couldn't help but wonder if she'd just fallen a little bit in love with Trace—and if he'd done the same with her. The thought scared her, but also brought a quiet excitement to her soul that allowed her softer emotions to harden to the point that she could say, "Bryce, tell me about this horse rescue ranch I've heard Trace talk about."

The boy looked at her, and he'd stopped crying now. "Well, it's not really a ranch. I have four horses is all."

"How many horses does it take to be a ranch?" she asked.

He smiled, though the action didn't quite reach his eyes. "I don't rightly know, Miss Everly, but I think more than four."

Trace chuckled, and his hand landed on Everly's knee under the table. She had the urge to ask another question, to fill this silence with conversation, but she refrained. After several long seconds, Blaze finally said, "I'm real glad to be home." He cleared his throat and looked around at everyone seated at the table. "Thank you for all being here to help me." He looked as scared as a jackrabbit meeting a wolf in the dead of night. "I really appreciate it."

Trace only nodded, as did Harry and Bryce. Cash said,

"I'm glad too." He smiled around at everyone there. "This is way more people than I knew in Utah." And with that, he burst into tears too.

Blaze's mouth trembled, and he cuffed his son's shoulders and dragged the boy, chair and all, closer to him. He leaned down and said something to Cash, who nodded.

Everly loved the tenderness here, and she'd never felt more included outside of her own parents and siblings. She leaned into Trace, and he put his arm around her too, pulled her close, and took another bite of his food.

This was the perfect life, and Everly couldn't help thinking this soft, strong, quiet cowboy could provide a whole new world of experiences and people for her to belong with, and belong to.

A COUPLE OF WEEKS LATER, EVERLY SCRUBBED AND scrubbed at the lacquer on the cabinet she'd purchased. She hadn't had as much time to work on it as she'd originally planned, because Trace had needed quite a bit of help with the kids as he took care of Blaze.

She went to Blaze's mountain mansion almost every evening now, and while she didn't cook the way she had the first time, she'd pick something up or eat whatever Trace or Blaze had ordered. Trace had made breakfast once, and that had been Everly's favorite meal over there.

Moving into summertime, Everly had redone her

dance class schedule, and now she worked from eight to noon four days a week. She attended a teacher's class online, and that lasted ninety minutes every Tuesday and Thursday, and on this spare Friday morning, she found herself with a piece of sandpaper and her biceps burning with every stroke.

She should use a circular sander, but she liked the physical nature of getting the wood shavings on her hands, the feel of the paper against the grain of the plank, the way it sounded in her ears.

She'd finished all the drawer fronts before she stopped, and her back ached and ached and ached. Stretching it backward, she rolled her neck left and right, trying to work out the tension there.

An engine rumbled through the neighborhood, and Everly turned toward the shiny black truck as Trace brought it against the curb. She smiled at her boyfriend and tossed the sandpaper on top of the cabinet.

Trace got out of the truck, and he didn't have anyone younger than him with him. Everly reached the end of the driveway. "Where is everyone else?"

"The Whittakers are having a party up at Whiskey Mountain Lodge," he said. "They invited all of our kids, and Luke took everyone up there." He grinned at her and swept her into his arms. "Workin' on your cabinet?"

"Yes, sir." She grinned up at him. "That cherry lacquer is stubborn, and it's taking a lot to get it off."

"Mm, do you have time for lunch?" He didn't wait for

her to answer before he leaned down and kissed her. Everly felt like she was standing next to the paddock at the lodge, having snuck away with this man during his brother's wedding.

The passion poured from him, and Everly let it rush straight to her head. He pulled back after several long seconds and murmured, "I'm falling in love with you, Miss Everly Avery."

She smiled with everything she had and giggled as she pressed her forehead to his breastbone. Summoning her bravery, she looked up at him, enjoying the protection from the summer sun as the shadow from his cowboy hat fell on her face. "The feeling's mutual, Mister Young."

His smile touched her heart, and Everly could stand here in front of her house, with him, for a good, long while. "I have time for lunch," she said. "If you're done staring at me."

He kept gazing at her for another few moments. "All right," he drawled. "Now I'm done." He laughed with her, and she'd gotten in his passenger seat and he'd gotten behind the wheel when his phone rang.

A name flashed up on the screen in his truck—Val—and Everly froze.

The air got sucked out of the truck, because Trace had frozen too. He made no move to answer the phone, and Everly reached over and touched his forearm. "Trace, baby," she said. "Your ex-wife is calling you."

21

Trace jabbed at the screen in his truck, praying the call would get dropped. Unfortunately, it didn't. In fact, the pad of his finger touched the right button, and the call stopped ringing and connected.

He said nothing, and he'd never had to say much when it came to Val. She was calling from halfway around the world, and her voice finally filled the cab as she said, "...are you guys?"

"You just came in," he said, flipping the truck into gear. He couldn't sit here in front of Everly's house and talk to his ex-wife. "Say that again."

"I was just asking how you guys are doing in Coral Canyon," Val said.

"We're fine," Trace said.

Val heaved a sigh, but he honestly didn't know what she expected from him. They hadn't spoken in years. The weight of Everly's gaze on the side of his face increased, and Trace's neck began to heat.

"I'm coming through the States," she said. "And I thought I'd stop by Coral Canyon and see you two."

"No," Trace said. No thought whatsoever; he simply wasn't going to consider letting Harry see Val. No way.

"Trace," Val said with a hint of darkness in her voice.

"No," Trace said again. He squeezed the wheel with all the strength he had. "My son doesn't deserve to be jerked around by his mother. I'm not sure if the proper documents reached you in Prague or Brussels or wherever you went after you *abandoned* my son at my parents' house, but I have full, sole custody of Harry. I do not have to let you see him."

"Trace," she said, and now she carried disdain in her voice. Like *he* was the one being ridiculous.

"No, Val," he said again. His chest heaved and his pulse pounded. "Go to LA and do your shoot, and then go back to Florence."

"I'm not in Florence," she said.

"I don't care."

"He's my son too."

"Not according to the law," Trace said. "Call my brother. Gabe will tell you what you can and can't do. But we submitted paperwork to the state that said you abandoned the boy. The judge gave me full and complete custody. As far as the state of Wyoming goes, you don't exist."

"That is unbelievable," she said. "I never saw that paperwork."

"Like, I said, it was sent to you. Or the attempt was made to notify you." Gabe had told him it wasn't his problem that Val was unreachable. *She'd* gone to Europe without telling him where or how to get in touch with her.

"I just want to see him for a few minutes."

"Well, I just want him to heal from his mother abandoning him," Trace said. "So you will not be seeing him."

Val sighed again, and Trace's anger reared. He was the type to bottle everything up until it was too hard and too heavy for him to carry alone. Then he had to take a solo vacation to get away from all the chaos in his soul, or he acted rashly and snuck away with Everly and kissed her spontaneously.

"I'm the one who's had to pick up all those pieces," he said. "I'm the one who's paying for his therapy. I'm the one who's put his life on hold so Harry knows how loved he is and how he'll always have at least one person in his corner."

"I raised that boy for ten years," Val shot back. "Basically without you."

"That is so not true," Trace said. "I paid for everything even then. Have you sent me any child support in the past two years?" She hadn't. "I paid for your ticket to Europe, which was how I knew you'd landed in Paris. I took my son every time I was home from Nashville, and every single summer—all summer long. We had shared custody, and you *abandoned* him, and I will not let you waltz back in here like you just went away for a weekend."

He couldn't breathe properly, and he didn't like the side of him that had come out. He took a long, deep breath and reached to turn down the volume on the call. Everly caught his hand as he pulled it back, and her gentle touch soothed him.

Her skin was cool, and it grounded Trace. He looked over to her, and while she wore anxiety in her bright blue eyes, she also exuded compassion. She grounded him, and Trace had absolutely told the truth earlier—he was falling in love with her.

He had been since the very first day he'd chatted with her on Christian Pool, and those feelings had only accelerated the more time he spent with her. Real, in-person, going-to-lunch time with her.

Harry liked her too, though Trace had not had a serious conversation with Harry about Everly yet. He would, but just not yet.

He reached to turn up the volume again, and to do that, he had to release Everly's hand. Val wasn't talking, and he said, "Sorry, I lost you," in a much quieter voice. One not so laced with danger and anger.

"I want him to know I love him," Val said.

Trace's jaw jumped as he pressed his teeth together. "Call Gabe," he said. "He'll tell you what I'm legally obligated to let you do."

"But we don't have to involve lawyers," Val said. "If you say it's okay."

Trace looked out his window, indecision raging through him. "Call Gabe," he said. "I'll talk to Harry, and if he decides we can do something different than what Gabe says, I'll let you know."

"Trace—"

"I have to go," he said, and he didn't feel bad as he touched the red phone icon to end the call. Awkwardness rained down around him, and he hated that he'd answered the phone with Everly in the truck. He didn't want her to see this ugly side of him, the messiness of his life with Val and Harry.

"Sorry about that," he grumbled.

"It's okay," she said. "She's his mother. I assumed you had to deal with her sometimes."

"I actually haven't," he said. "Val fell off the face of the earth over two years ago, and that's the first time I've actually spoken to her on the phone."

"What about Harry?" Everly asked. "Has she talked to him?"

"A card on his birthday," Trace said. "That's about it. If she's calling or texting him, he doesn't tell me." He tilted his head. "Actually, we got him a new phone when I moved back here permanently, and she doesn't have his number." He cut a look over to Everly. "So no. No contact."

"Wow. And she's calling now, out of the blue?"

"That's about how Val operates," Trace said dryly. "Everything is on Val-time. Val's schedule. She's very busy, and she'll squeeze anything she can into five minutes —if it's to her advantage." He shook his head. "I'm sorry. I'm not one to gossip about or speak ill of my ex." He exhaled heavily. "Tell me where you want to go to lunch."

"Trace, you can't just brush this away."

"I'm not." He glanced over to her. "I just don't want to talk about it anymore. Gabe will handle it." He'd have to call his brother later, and he didn't think for a moment Val wouldn't call him again. He'd simply make sure he dealt with her in private next time.

"Also," he said with a smile. "Blaze is asking how we can get Steve again, so thanks for that."

Her face lit up, and Trace would much rather see that sunshine in her eyes than the storm clouds she'd been harboring. "I told you that puppy was a game-changer when it came to healing."

"I think Blaze just likes dogs," he said.

"No, Steve gave him someone to focus on besides himself and his pain."

Blaze was doing a lot better these days, though he still had weeks and months ahead of him on his road to recovery. Trace would be moving back to his place tomorrow, as Jem was back in town. Morris would be returning to Coral Canyon from Nashville on Saturday too. He'd been cagey and vague on the details of how the meetings with King Country had gone, and Trace's nerves had started to fray slightly. Val's phone call only added to that.

"Steve is not a person," Trace teased her, to which Everly rolled her eyes.

"But you love that dog," she said.

"Correction," Trace said. "*Blaze* loves that dog. Is he available for adoption?"

"No, he's a rental therapy dog," Everly said. "I can see if I can get him again."

"Maybe I should get him a dog." He'd have to walk it every day and taking care of the dog would bring Blaze and Cash together too. They'd been getting along really well over the past couple of weeks, but Trace knew Cash disliked school a whole lot. With summer in full swing, Cash didn't have anything pulling on him negatively.

He pulled into a salad bar place Everly liked, and as he opened her door for her, he slid his hand up her hip to her waist. "We're singing at the Fourth of July picnic and fireworks this year. Will you be my date after the concert?"

Everly ran her hands up his chest. "So I have to go to the picnic alone, watch you perform up on the stage, and then once it's all over, and all of your fangirls have screamed and begged you for signatures, you'll come find me and we can watch the fireworks together?"

Trace started grinning after her first few words. "You, uh, forgot the part where you'll be babysitting my son during the concert."

Everly laughed, and Trace joined her. "I'd love to," she

said, and Trace did fall in love with her a little bit more right then. He touched his lips to hers, but he kept the kiss chaste and simple. "Thank you for not judging me about Val," he whispered.

"Thank you for sharing your son with me," she whispered back.

Trace wanted to share everything with this woman, but for now, he'd settle for lunch. Then more time with her. Picnics. Fireworks. He had another tour to complete, and with her life so rooted here, he didn't think she'd be able to come with him. Harry either, depending on whether Morris had been able to negotiate a summer-only tour the way the members of Country Quad hoped.

Trace felt like he'd thrown a dozen balls up into the air, and they were all coming down. Some were glass, and he had to figure out which ones those were and catch them before they shattered.

No matter what, he couldn't let Harry hit the ground, and he didn't want to ruin anything with Everly either.

When Trace got nervous before a performance, he plucked his way through chords he'd known for almost four decades. Luke bounced up and down on the tips of his toes like he was a champion boxer about to take on his biggest competitor.

Tex scrolled through his phone like he was looking for

the perfect picture to post on social media before the set, and Otis stood next to Trace, his sunglasses securely in place, his mouth a flat line. Usually, Trace could count on Otis to be the one to pump them all up and reassure them that the concert they were about to give would be the best one they'd done to date. He'd done so plenty of times in the past—once when Tex had walking pneumonia and still gave one of the most memorable performances of his life.

Trace knew the moment they stepped from backstage to stage, all four of them would flip whatever switch needed to be flipped so they wouldn't disappoint those who'd come to this year's picnic in the park.

Coral Canyon always did a concert in conjunction with the picnic, and families set up shades, umbrellas, and tables and made a whole evening of it.

Fireworks would blast off at full dark, which happened about ten, and Country Quad had a set of patriotic songs already recorded for the celebration. That way, they could join their families for the fireworks.

Trace had sat with his large family, which at things like this, included the Whittakers and the Hammonds.

They too had large families full of brothers, spouses, and kids. Trace especially liked Graham Whittaker and Ames Hammond, but tonight, he and Everly had sat with Cy Hammond and his wife.

Apparently Everly's younger brother loved motorcycles, and Cy built custom bikes for a living. Trace had enjoyed getting to know them better, and then he'd left

Harry with Everly, his parents, and Bryce and come to warm up for this concert.

"Ready?" Luke asked him, drumming his sticks in mid-air.

Trace smiled and nodded, his fingers still moving through the chords. "You?"

"Definitely." Luke grinned, and Trace had never met someone who loved the spotlight more than Luke did.

"Here we go, boys," Tex said, finally lifting his eyes from his device. "They're announcing us."

Trace stopped plucking and reached for his sunglasses too. They'd bought matching pairs for tonight, and they were going out as country rock stars for the beginning number. The crowd started to crow and whoop and holler, and Trace took his place behind Tex. His brother always led them out, and Trace always went second. Otis followed him, and Luke came last. He had no idea what his younger brother would do tonight, but Luke had done backflips, aerials, and the worm on stage before. Then he'd take his place behind the drums and keep them all in time for the duration of their concert.

Tonight, they were only playing for an hour, and nothing from their new album, as it wasn't even out yet.

Tex usually did something wild with small, local crowds, like take requests from the audience, though they hadn't played for one like this in a decade now. Before they'd signed their lucrative deal with King Country, these small-town festivals were how they paid their bills and kept making music.

They were how Country Quad had gotten off the ground.

Trace hoped that tonight's concert would reignite something inside Tex and Otis, though he suspected it would only be temporary even if it did.

Morris had returned from Nashville with good news— they could do a summer-only tour next year for the release of their album, but King Country wanted them to do TV interviews and shows too. Those were in-and-out events, so the band had agreed.

They still hadn't signed the offer for the next two albums, and Trace knew Tex wanted to talk to Bryce about perhaps joining the band. Harry would in a second, but the boy was fourteen, and Trace had put his foot down and said no, he wasn't going to bring his son into this business quite yet.

He'd always wanted the most normal childhood for Harry that he could provide, and as he'd not heard from Val again, he could only assume Gabe had scared her off sufficiently.

Trace had talked to his brother the next day and warned him that Val might call, and he'd said he'd handle it. That was that, and Trace believed in letting people do their jobs, so he hadn't followed up with Gabe at all. His brother ran a busy firm in Jackson, but he had brought

Liesl to Coral Canyon for the long Fourth of July weekend.

"Let's go boys!" Tex yelled, and he hippity-hopped out onto the stage. Trace pushed himself into a jog and followed him, one hand on the neck of his guitar and the other raised in a gesture of rock-dom, pinky and thumb out as he pumped his arm.

Otis had his guitars handed to him, so he came out in full jumping-jack mode, raising both hands above his head in a universal gesture of *get on your feet, people!*

Trace took his spot on the right-hand side of the stage and backed up a couple of feet to give Luke the room he needed to do whatever theatrics he'd perform tonight.

Otis went back to the left side of the stage, and Tex hovered near the piano while Luke ran onto the stage too.

He first tossed both of his drumsticks into the crowd, much to their delight, and then Luke caught the bottle of water Tex tossed to him, liquid splashing out of the open top, took a quick drink and then dumped the whole thing over his head as he screamed into the crowd. He threw the bottle too and ripped open his shirt, a couple of buttons flying into the front rows as well.

Oh my word, Trace thought as the female population of Coral Canyon went wild. That so wasn't the way to keep women from circling him, but Luke didn't always make two and two add up to four.

The whole crowd responded, and Trace shook his head, his smile genuine and real as Luke took the sunglasses from Otis and settled them on his nose. Adrenaline flowed through him, making his fingertips vibrate in anticipation.

Once Luke got behind the drums, Trace would start their first song. He looked down to check his connections to the amp and then he watched as a soaking wet Luke climbed the steps to his drum set.

Before his brother was completely set, Trace started the first notes of the song. It was their absolute best-seller, and he wanted to play through the opening twice to give people a chance to get excited and recognize it.

That only took about six notes, and then a fresh round of screams filled the park. He grinned out at everyone and took those steps forward again. His body moved naturally to the rhythm he'd set, and Trace could admit he liked the spotlight too—if only for a few seconds.

Then Otis joined him on the bass guitar, and Tex added the slap of the tambourine. Luke came in last, and Tex's smooth-as-still-water crooned out the first verse.

Trace lost himself inside the music, the way he did when he recorded and when he performed. He still knew how he was doing, if he hit the wrong note, or if his fingers walked along the bridge at the right tempo.

The crowd sang along with Tex, and Otis and Trace added their voices in the harmonies once the chorus started. Trace knew this song like his own face, and he migrated closer to Tex near the end of the song, so they could start the next one from the same mic.

Hardly a breath; no time for screaming and applause; they moved from the first song into the second, both of their voices twining together without any instruments for a few measures before Otis joined in with his fiddle.

This song came from their second album, which definitely had more country flair than the one before it or any since. Otis played the fiddle and ukulele in this song, and he sang as well. Luke used his voice too, but here at the beginning, it was all Trace and Tex.

Song by song, they played their set, and when they finally all stood in a line of four, Trace down on the end, then Luke, then Tex, then Otis, and bowed, it felt like the world had gotten to their feet and put their hands together.

Trace had given his guitar to a stage runner, and he lifted both hands above his head and waved his hands in silent applause. The crowd mimicked him, and his brothers joined in too.

All smiles, he finally left the stage. Without the bright lights shining on him from the stage, he realized how dusky the sky had become, and he took the water bottle from the stage manager and clapped the man on the back. He hurried down the steps, his feet hitting grass and sinking a little.

Fans back here screamed too, but Luke and Tex would handle them—at least for a few minutes.

Trace stuck with Otis, and the two of them wanted to get back to their families. He felt a little bit like a member of the marching band who'd just walked by in the parade, looking for his family along the route as he went, but no one intercepted him.

"There he is," he heard someone say, and then his son jumped to his feet.

"Dad." He threw himself at Trace, who caught him and hugged him hard. "That was *so good*. I haven't seen you perform like that in a while."

"Thanks." Trace grinned around at everyone and shook hands with his friends and family who'd stayed in this spot where they'd eaten dinner.

He kept his arm around his son, and they went back to their seats. Everly stood there, and she opened her arms to receive him too. He sank into her embrace and took a deep breath of her perfume, sweet and floral and wonderful as it was.

"That was the most incredible thing I've ever seen," she said. She stepped back and swatted at his chest playfully. "You can *dance*, cowboy. You've been holding out on me."

Trace grinned at her and grabbed both of her hands. "Let's go for a walk," he suggested.

"I'd go if I were you," Georgia said from a seat away.

Trace grinned at her while Everly asked, "Why?"

"Well, when Otis asked me to go for a walk at this event, it was to ask me to marry him. But I think Trace just wants to kiss you where we're not all watching."

Trace's pulse blipped, and he said, "Thanks a lot, Georgia."

"You're welcome." She smiled at him and lifted her bottle of Diet Coke to her lips. Trace loved her like a sister, and her news that she and Otis couldn't have children had hurt him deeply.

He and Everly hadn't talked too much about kids since the night of the dance, and Trace should probably bring it up again.

Maybe on their private walk—but Georgia had been right. He simply wanted to get her away from the crowd so he could kiss her with the same passion he poured into his music.

Unfortunately, the first strains of *My Country Tis of Thee* started to play, and the first display of bright red fireworks filled the sky.

"Missed your chance," he said to Everly, and then he sank into the camp chair he'd been sitting in before the concert and pulled her onto his lap so they could enjoy the fireworks show together.

22

Luke Young laughed as he tossed a box of Grape Nuts into the shopping cart Tex pushed. Of course, his older brother didn't think a version of football combined with Skeeball should be played in the small-town grocery store, but Luke hated errands with the fierceness of gravity, so he had to do something to make them fun.

Walking around and getting things for Blaze wasn't all that fun, and if he could count how many points he could "earn" by making baskets with the groceries, why not? He wasn't hurting anything or anyone.

Well, besides that dozen eggs that was down to ten after he'd tossed in a bag of frozen turkey steaks. Someone had to come clean up whites and yolks, but Luke had told Tex that he'd simply made sure someone's job was necessary.

Tex had rolled his eyes, but he hadn't chastised Luke either.

"Just get the hot dog buns," Tex said.

"I can't believe your wife put the list together based on where things are in the store." Luke started scanning the right side of the aisle for the buns.

"She says it makes shopping faster," Tex said.

Luke grabbed the bag of eight buns. "Do you think she'd do it for me?"

"Sure," Tex said. "But I forbid you to ask her. Abby's busy this summer."

"Maybe after she quits at the library." Luke grinned at Tex and tossed the buns into the basket from only three feet away. That was hardly worth any points at all.

They went around the corner to the frozen section together, and more than one Coral Canyon housewife looked in their direction. Luke supposed he shouldn't have ripped his shirt off on stage—while he was dripping wet—and then played most of the Fourth of July concert in the park half-naked.

His social media had blown up, and Trace said it wasn't in a good way. Luke maintained his own accounts, and he disagreed. For once, he hadn't argued relentlessly with Trace, but he'd quietly gone on his way with his posts, responding to messages, and commenting on any photos he'd been tagged in from the concert a couple of nights ago.

Tex pulled open one of the doors and got out

pepperoni and sausage pizzas. He added them to the cart without any tossing involved, and Luke frowned slightly.

"He wants orange sherbet," Tex said.

"All right." Luke went further down the aisle, searching the case for sherbet.

"Luke," a woman said, and the familiar voice drew him from his search.

He found Sterling Boyd only a few feet down the aisle. She held a basket over her forearm, and it only held things from the produce section.

"Hey," he said brightly. "How are you?" He stepped into her and gave her a quick hug, the grocery basket awkward between them. "Hot enough for you now?"

In their last massage, she'd complained about how it didn't get warm enough fast enough here in Coral Canyon, which existed in the shadows of the great Teton Mountains.

"Definitely." She gave a light laugh. Her eyes moved past him to Tex as he arrived with their basket. Sterling's eyes widened, and Luke recognized the look of someone who'd been starstruck.

Tex surely did too, but he smiled that country music smile anyway. "Howdy," he said.

"This is Sterling Boyd," Luke said. "She's my masseuse. Sterling, this is my oldest brother, Tex."

"It's great to meet you." Sterling extended her hand and shook Tex's.

"Likewise."

Sterling bumped Luke with her basket. "I saw you on stage the other night at the park. Great concert." She held his gaze for a few seconds and then looked at Tex. "Both of you."

"Thanks," Luke said with a grin.

"Caused quite the small-town gossip session," Sterling said.

Luke's grin vanished. "What do you mean?"

"You drenched yourself with water," Tex said dryly.

"And ripped off your shirt," Sterling added, as if the two of them had rehearsed this intervention in the ice cream section at the grocery store.

He looked at Tex and then back to Sterling. "Nothing you haven't seen before, though, right?" He laughed, and Sterling did too.

She shook her head, her pretty dark blonde hair swinging over her shoulders. "Good to see you, Luke. You haven't been in for a while." She moved past him and then paused to look over her shoulder. "Call and get an appointment, okay? Your shoulder looked...sore on stage." She walked away, and Luke found himself rotating his shoulder as she did. It didn't feel sore.

Tex whistled suggestively, which broke Luke's stare-fest. His eyes glinted with laughter too, and he leaned over the back of the cart, lifting the front wheels off the ground. "Oh, brother, she has a *crush* on you."

Luke's eyes widened, and he started shaking his head. "No. She's my masseuse."

"Yeah, who's seen you naked and likes it." Tex laughed then, and this time Luke's face heated.

"She was blushing so hard," Tex said. "Luke, that woman likes you."

Luke frowned, and his mind started to whir. Had she been blushing? *Yes*, he thought. Now that he thought about it, Sterling *had* blushed when he'd said she'd seen his body before. Well, she had. Maybe not head-to-toe naked all at once, and maybe not in some very specific places, but she'd definitely given him the best massages of his life.

Could she really have a crush on him?

He stared down the aisle where she'd gone, wondering why that didn't bother him the way it usually did when he saw women making eyes at him. He'd been back in Coral Canyon for a couple of years now, and he hadn't been on one date. Not one. He still didn't want to go out with anyone, but as he stood there, he didn't mind if Sterling had a crush on him.

Maybe he liked her too.

He scoffed, and Tex whistled at him again. This time, it meant, *hey, hurry up here.*

"Come on," Tex called from the end of the aisle. "We still have heaps of stuff to get, and the groceries don't jump into the cart on their own."

Luke turned away from the way Sterling had gone, his feelings settling right back where they'd been since Mandi had told him his daughter might not even be his.

No, he didn't like Sterling Boyd as more than a

masseuse, and if she had a crush on him, he'd have to find someone else to rub the soreness from his shoulders.

"So are you going to ask her out?" Tex asked, his voice far too suggestive.

"No." Luke scoffed again. "She doesn't have a crush on me. Don't be stupid."

"Because you're not dating, right?"

"That's right," Luke said. "I'm not dating." That had always been the end of the sentence, but as they went around the corner and got a bag of frozen strawberries for Blaze, the words *right now* sounded really loud inside Luke's head. He wasn't dating *right now*.

"Tex," he said as Tex consulted the list on his phone. He waited for his brother to look up. "Not a word about Sterling, okay? To anyone."

Tex sobered then, as he'd always done when he realized something meant something to Luke. "Of course not," he said.

They put in a few cans of frozen orange juice and then went on to cold cuts, hot dogs, and sliced cheese before Tex said, "And you know, Luke, if you like her too, it would be okay to ask her out."

Luke pressed his lips into a thin line, not sure what to say. The fact that he hadn't blown up already said a lot, and he looked at Tex. "What if she's a liar too?"

"They're not all liars, brother." Tex spoke with gentleness, and he gave Luke a kind smile. "I know why you feel that way, and I'm not saying you have to get out there right now. I'm just saying, no one is going to think badly of you if you do."

Luke nodded, his brain buzzing again. "Gabe's dating."

"Is he?" Tex asked. "I thought he broke it off with... whoever he was seeing."

"I can't remember her name either," Luke said. He thought of Leigh and Morris and how hard they'd worked in the past year. They'd overcome lies and deceit, and while Luke's ex wasn't anywhere on the horizon and he'd never ever go back to her, perhaps he could start to entertain the idea of going out with someone new again.

His next thought landed on the sweet girl the Good Lord had entrusted to his care, and his fiercely protective streak rose its vicious head. He would not allow anyone to hurt her—not even him. He wouldn't parade women through Corrine's life because he was lonely.

Besides, he told himself. *You're not lonely. You have a truckload of family here.* That was the truth, and Luke wasn't truly lonely. He did see Mav and Dani and their deep friendship, and now Trace was getting in deep with Everly, and he seemed a hundred times happier this year than he'd been last year.

Of course, Tex and Abby lived the fairy tale happily-ever-after life, and as Luke loaded groceries onto the belt so they could check out and get over to Blaze's and still have time to visit before band practice, Luke could admit he wanted the happily-ever-after too.

Whether that be with Sterling or not, Luke didn't know. What he knew was that yes, his shoulder was a bit sore, and as Tex drove them out of the grocery store parking lot, Luke texted the spa to get on Sterling's schedule for a massage.

23

Blaze looked up from the table as his front door opened. With how often people came and went at his very private, very out-of-the-way house, he'd deactivated the front cameras. The notifications drove him bananas, and it wasn't unusual for his mother to bring lunch and then Mav to stop by with dinner.

Harry and Bryce came over often, and they took Cash fishing, hiking, and camping with them. He'd also spent several nights out at Tex's, and he worked the farm in the mornings with Bryce and Tex when he did that.

Jem lived here with Blaze, and his kids came and went in both the front door and the back. Blaze himself had to leave the house to walk several times each day, and he'd actually started thanking the Lord above that he had the type of life he did that allowed him to focus solely on healing following his surgery.

Blaze adored his son in a way he hadn't known was possible, and he wasn't sure how much of that was the two of them learning more about each other, working together over the past couple of months since his surgery, or the fact that Blaze had started praying for him too.

He wasn't ready to go back to church or anything, but Blaze had definitely been reflecting on some of the things he'd been through in his life. Some he didn't dwell on, but others plagued him. Those ones, he knew he needed to repent of and repair as much as possible. Once he did that, maybe he'd be ready to enter a church and face God again.

Right now, Bryce's voice carried to Blaze at the table, and he and Harry came into the kitchen. Cash wasn't far behind, and neither was Joey.

She wore a bright pink plaid shirt, and Blaze grinned at her. "What're you lot doin' here?"

"My dad said you're not answering your phone," Harry said. "He sent us over to find out if you're coming to Otis's."

Blaze looked over to the double ovens in the kitchen, which he barely used. "I hadn't realized what time it was." He checked the computer in front of him, where he'd been writing an email to his ex-wife, apologizing for all the things he'd done wrong by her.

He decided it could keep, and he pushed the lid closed. "Let me get on some shoes."

He'd worn nothing but cowboy boots for the past thirty-seven years, but since his surgery, he'd traded them for a sensible pair of thick-soled running shoes. "Can you drive me?" he asked Bryce.

The boy was so different since he'd returned from his first year of college. He smiled and nodded, and Harry said, "Go get your bike, Cash. I'll ride with you and Joey."

The younger kids cheered, and Blaze grinned at them as they ran past him to the garage entrance behind him.

"They're riding bikes?"

"Yeah," Bryce said. "But I'll drive you."

"Great."

Ten minutes later, Blaze finally settled into Bryce's passenger seat. The kids had left to ride their bikes to Otis's several minutes ahead of them, and the radio played nearly silent country music.

"So," Blaze said, keeping his eyes out the window. Tex had come to see Blaze plenty of times, but he'd said nothing about his son. He didn't need to; Blaze had eyes and ears and opinions of his own. "What's eating at you?"

Bryce looked over to him, surprise in his eyes. "Nothing."

Blaze's eyebrows lifted. "Are you goin' back to school?"

His jaw hardened and he looked away. "No."

"Have you told your daddy that?"

Bryce shook his head.

"So is that the thing you're hiding from him?"

"Who says I'm hiding things from him?" Bryce asked.

"I do," Blaze said. He sighed, not sure how much to tell Bryce the things that would help him understand. He wasn't sure how much he knew about his rodeo life, or what Tex had told him. "Bryce, you're a great kid. One of the best, I've heard your daddy say. I'll admit I don't know you all that well, but I'm really good at reading people."

"I'm not that great," Bryce muttered.

So he'd definitely done something he wasn't proud of. Blaze would recognize that self-deprecation anywhere—and last summer, Bryce would've grinned and then shook his head. He wouldn't have verbally denied how amazing he was.

"You should talk to your parents," Blaze said. "I'm not one to give much advice, trust me. But I also know that all of my brothers gravitate to me...when they've done something they're not proud of."

Bryce looked over to him again, the drive to Otis's passing far too quickly. "Why's that?"

"Because I've done it all," Blaze said, gazing evenly back at Bryce. "I've done a lot of bad things in my life. I'm the black sheep brother, the one who doesn't believe in God, or at the very least turned my back on Him. I'm the one my momma cries about at night." He cocked his eyebrows. "Right? So when they're in trouble or they need someone to help them know how to make things right, they come to the person who's done a lot of things wrong."

Bryce swallowed and focused out the windshield again. When he said nothing, Blaze's assumptions that he'd done something at school he needed help with were confirmed even further.

"My best advice, though you didn't ask for it?" Blaze tried to speak kindly and slowly, like anything else would scare Bryce away. "Go talk to your daddy. He'll know what to do to help you."

"What if he doesn't?"

"That's even better," Blaze said breezily. "Then you get to figure it out together."

"I don't know how to tell him," Bryce said miserably. He reached up and ran his hand down the side of his face. "I've been thinking about it for months, and the words aren't there."

"Take it from someone who knows...they never come. You just have to open your mouth and start talking." He nodded though Bryce wasn't looking at him and stopped talking. Bryce would do what he wanted with the advice, and Blaze could maybe sleep better at night knowing that he helped his nephew, even if only a tiny bit.

"My dad is just so...*good*," Bryce said. "He'll be so disappointed."

"But he'll love you no matter what," Blaze said quietly. "That's something my momma and daddy are really good at. I always knew—*always*—that no matter what I did, my momma would fold me into her arms, hug me, and tell me she loved me."

Bryce met his gaze, such hope in his. Blaze gave him the best smile he could. "You put your daddy to the test and see if he doesn't do the same."

Bryce nodded, and Blaze immediately offered up a

prayer. *Lord, please help Tex to love his son unconditionally. Help Bryce to find the courage to open his mouth. Bless them both...and forgive them both for anything they've done.*

He couldn't think of anything else to add, so he thought, *Amen*, and left it there.

Then he reached over and patted Bryce's hand. The boy's shoulders shook, and Blaze wished he could take this burden from him.

But he knew better than most that he couldn't, and that Bryce had a path to walk that wouldn't be easy...but would most likely be worthwhile anyway.

THAT EVENING, BLAZE LAY IN HIS NEST OF BLANKETS, his phone held above his face. Faith Cromwell had texted, and he couldn't stop the smile that came whenever she sent him mundane news about her day.

She'd told him that truck that had very nearly caught on fire the night of the dance-off couldn't be salvaged. She'd sent several crying emojis with it, and Blaze had the very real feeling she'd actually shed real tears over the loss of the truck.

He would if he owned Hole in One, because that was how Faith made money in her business. One less truck for her was one-third less opportunity for her to sell doughnuts, as she'd also told him she was now down to two trucks.

So he'd sent flowers to Faith's listed business address. That had prompted a flurry of texts, and they became bright stars in Blaze's days, which were mostly a dark haze of pain, walking, therapy, and parenting through the pain.

He had not asked her out again. She hadn't suggested it either. They'd go days without speaking at all, and then he'd spend a couple of hours in a single evening chatting with her—like tonight.

He had no idea what he was doing. What he knew was that Faith made him smile. Faith made him want to be a better man. Faith made him want to try hard to be her friend before he asked her to be more.

Where will you be parked tomorrow? he asked her.

Why? she asked. *You aren't cleared to drive, are you?*

He hated being reminded of how dependent he was on others. *No*, he said. *But I could send someone to get me that roasted peanut one. I love that thing.*

I'm glad, she texted back. She didn't tell him where she'd be parked tomorrow, but he followed her on social media, and she posted the location of her two trucks every morning. *What did you eat for dinner tonight and who made it?*

He smiled as he thought about his simple dinner with his son. One of his brothers came over almost every single evening, but tonight Cash had texted everyone on the brothers' group string that he'd be making a ham and cheese omelet for dinner that night, so they didn't need any food.

Tex and Luke had stocked the fridge with everything Blaze had put on his list, and Cash actually liked cooking.

Cash made ham and cheese omelets, he sent to her. *They were actually good. Miss Georgia signed him up for some cooking classes at the community center, and he really likes them.*

That's amazing. Faith sent a few differently colored hearts with it. *I love baking. Cooking not so much, but baking, yes.*

How do you feel about driving through somewhere for dinner? he asked. *Or do you do delivery?*

I cook, she said. *If heating up soup or hot dogs counts.*

Blaze didn't like thinking of Faith eating something out of a can at home, alone. Of course, he'd lived that life, and he knew how lonely it could be even if his outward persona was anything but drab and lifeless.

No family in the area? he asked. This was delving into personal territory—he'd asked her if she cooked and about her family. She knew all about his, of course. Country Quad had been everywhere lately, as they'd played to a full park of people for Independence Day. He and Jem weren't exactly low profile either, and Morris had played in the NFL. Gabe ran the most successful father's rights law firm in the state, for which Blaze was personally grateful.

Not like you, she said back. *My sister and her family live here. Her name is Trinity.*

Are you close with her?

Yes, quite close.

Blaze wasn't sure what else to say to Faith, but he knew he didn't want to end the conversation there. He wanted Faith to come over to the house, but he was rarely alone, and he definitely didn't want to explain anything to Cash or any of his brothers.

Maybe she could come pick him up and they could go out. He could walk quite well, but something inside him bucked against having her come get him for a date.

She could bring food though....

Blaze's fingers flew across the screen, and he reminded himself that Faith had used his number of her own accord. She'd texted him after he'd put his number in her phone. It had only taken a week or so too, and Blaze suddenly had a brainwave. An inspiration. Maybe a thought from God.

He didn't know, but he quickly erased the message he'd been thumbing out and started a new one. *Will you let me pay to fix your food truck?*

He read over the message again and sent it without second-guessing too much. His shoulders and arms ached from holding his phone above his face, and he lowered his device to his chest while he waited for her to answer.

Faith sometimes clammed up when the conversation got a little too hard or a little too personal, but Blaze clung to the hope that he'd felt impressed to offer this.

"I can do it, Lord," he whispered. "It won't even be a sacrifice for me, and it would help her so much."

His phone chimed, and he lifted it to read her message.

Blaze, I really don't need you to do that.

Blaze took a deep breath and tapped the call button. He'd talked to her on the phone only once, and he figured now was a good time for a second conversation. His heartbeat flipped and blipped through his whole body as the line rang.

"Blaze," she said instead of saying hello.

"I broke your fryer," he said. "I want to make it right." He swallowed, thinking about everyone he'd been trying to make things right with. "See, Faith, I've been on this quest to make sure I'm right with those around me. I even wrote an email to my ex-wife, apologizing for all the things I've done wrong over the years."

He had done that, and several other emails had gone out too. Blaze didn't need responses. With every person and every thing he'd done wrong that he tried to make right, a burden lifted.

Faith remained quiet for several long seconds. "Is this part of some Alcoholics Anonymous program thing?" she asked.

"No, ma'am. This is me recognizing that your food truck means a lot to you, and I won't even miss the money it would take to fix it."

"I'll never be able to repay you," she said, her voice catching on the last word.

"I don't need you to repay me," he said. "I'll pay to fix the truck."

"I'll think of something to do for you," she said.

His spirits soared, and Blaze told himself not to ask her out. Her going out with him was not contingent on his ability and desire to fix her food truck.

"It's not necessary, Faith," he said. "You can just keep texting me. It makes me feel...less lonely."

She paused again, and then she said, "I don't believe you can be lonely with the number of brothers you have."

"Talking to a pretty woman is different than shooting the breeze with my brother," he said.

Faith laughed lightly, and oh, how Blaze liked the sound of her voice.

"At the risk of getting shot down yet again," he said. "Here's something I've been thinking about. I have a lot of people bringing food to my house. Sometimes, though, my son goes out to my brother's ranch and spends the night there. Usually, another brother will bring food and his family and stay for a while. But I'm pretty sure I can find a day where—" He cleared his throat and forged onward.

"You could bring some food, and we could spend the evening together."

"At your house?" she asked.

"Yes, ma'am. Right here at my house. You said you

don't cook, but I bet you can drive through somewhere. Maybe."

"I can drive through somewhere," she said, and that was as good as a yes in his opinion.

Blaze smiled up at the ceiling. "Great. Then I'll talk to my babysitters and see if I can find a night for us to get together. If you have any dates that won't work for you, will you text them to me?"

"Yes, sir," she whispered, and Blaze found himself calming even further. That was what this woman did for him, and he had no idea how she did it. But he liked that he wasn't so manic or so angry, and the moment he got off the phone with her, he'd text Trace to find out who was bringing what meals this week.

"All right," he said. "Now, talk to me about pets. Do you have any?"

24

Bryce Young faced the white farmhouse, his heartbeat floundering in his chest. "Today," he told himself. He'd made himself a promise, and he wasn't going to break any more of those. He left the shadowy recesses of the stables and headed down the sidewalk to the side steps. His father and Abby would likely be up by now, as they had been almost every other morning this summer when Bryce came in from caring for his four horses.

His palms felt wet inside his gloves, and he peeled them off and went back to the barn. Maybe he could talk to them tomorrow.

"No," he told himself. "Today." He took out his phone and tapped to get to Bailey's string, like she might have magically responded to one of his texts. She hadn't, just like she hadn't responded—not one single time—in the past three months.

Sadness dumped over his head, a swift, fast, icy drenching of regret and shame, and Bryce struggled to breathe through it.

He honestly had no idea what he'd been thinking when it had come to Bailey McAllister. In a lot of ways, he hadn't been using his brain at all.

He shuffled back to the house and up the steps. The scent of coffee and overly browned toast filled the top floor, and instead of scampering downstairs to shower and hide, Bryce went around the corner and into the kitchen.

Abby sat at the dining room table, spooning something mashed and orange into Bryce's half-sister's mouth. Melissa smiled and giggled and seemed to like whatever it was, and the little girl's spirit always brightened Bryce's day.

His dad turned toward him, his smile as equally as bright. "Hey," he said in his booming, fatherly voice. "How are the horses this morning? Did Yardley bite at his bandages?"

Bryce shook his head, his voice buried somewhere in the bottom of his stomach. His dad seemed to know it, and his smile dropped from his face too.

Bryce's face crumbled as he started to cry, and he hated the heat in his eyes, his nose, his throat. "Dad," he choked out. "I messed up."

"Okay," his dad said, and he folded Bryce into his

chest. Bryce clung to his father, halfway surprised that Uncle Blaze had been right. Even after last week's chat with his uncle, Bryce had put off talking to his parents. But he couldn't anymore. It was mid-July, and if he wasn't going back to school, things had to be sewn up.

"It's okay," Tex whispered. "Abs."

Bryce's step-mother arrived a moment later, and her firm hand patted Bryce's back. They said nothing, and Bryce wished they would. Perhaps if they asked enough questions, he could just nod or shake his head, and he wouldn't have to speak.

"Come sit down, baby," Abby said in her kindest voice. "Do you want some coffee?"

Bryce pulled away from his father and shook his head. He didn't move to go sit down. He hung his head and standing right there in the kitchen, he said, "I don't want to go back to school."

"Okay," Dad said. "That's fine."

"We figured," Abby said. Neither of them asked what he'd do instead.

Bryce took a deep breath and looked up into eyes that were so like his own. Only concern and compassion lived in his father's eyes, and Bryce didn't want to watch it change. "I want to run the horse rescue ranch. Maybe make it more into a ranch. Maybe go to Nashville and do something with music."

"I can help with both of those," Dad said.

Abby glued herself to his side, and she still wore her

nightgown. She folded her arms, her hazel eyes more penetrative than his father's. "Why don't you want to go back to school, Bryce?"

"Abby," Dad murmured.

"There's more here, Tex," she said, switching her gaze to him and then back to Bryce. "Whatever you say is fine, but I think there's something more here."

"I have...bad memories there," Bryce said. "I don't think I need a college degree." He swallowed, his brain screaming at him to say the real reason. He'd alluded to it, but he hadn't admitted anything.

He dropped his gaze to the floor again. "I...I slept with a woman a few months ago." Tears flowed freely from his eyes again, as they had every single time he'd allowed himself to think about his indiscretion.

Abby pulled in a breath, but Dad stood there, silent. Shoeless, and Bryce focused on his dad's toes.

"I told her it was a mistake, and well, that was a mistake too. I've texted her and called her lots of times since then, and she hasn't responded once." He hated himself, but he still said, "I miss her."

Dad finally cleared his throat, and that got Bryce to look up. He wore a shocked brightness in his eyes now, and Bryce didn't like it either. It was like his father had never believed he could do something wrong.

Well, he had.

The fury came, and Bryce didn't know how to deal

with it any more than he did the grief. The sadness. The regret. The unending knowledge that he'd sinned.

He'd heard of repentance, of course. Pastors from here to Boise to Bozeman talked about repentance, but Bryce had never had to seriously do it. He didn't know how to start. He didn't know how to know when he'd been forgiven.

In short, he felt stuck in purgatory. He was going through hell, and he didn't know how to move backward or forward.

"Okay." Dad reached for him and hugged him again, one hand up behind Bryce's head this time. "Okay."

Abby hugged him from behind, and Bryce became sandwiched between the two of them, the love they had for him unending and very, very real.

That only made Bryce weepy again, and he absolutely had to stop crying over Bailey McAllister.

In that moment, he realized he wasn't crying over his loss of her, though he had in the past. Today, standing in the kitchen with his parents, he was crying for himself. For the things he'd done wrong in Montana, and for the first time in months, a door opened in front of him and a tiny splash of light fell onto the ground.

"What do I do now?" he asked.

"Let's make an appointment with Pastor Daniels," Dad said. "He'll help you know some things to do."

Bryce nodded as the embrace broke up. "Abs?" He

looked at her. "Do you want me to make some banana bread French toast for breakfast?"

Tears filled her eyes and she took his face in both of her hands. "Yes, please," she whispered. "You're still a good boy, Bryce."

He shook his head, because he didn't feel like he was.

He wanted to talk to Bailey. He wanted to apologize for putting her in this situation too. For saying she was a mistake for him. She wasn't. But the truth was, he shouldn't have given in to his hormones, and he shouldn't have mistaken extreme physical attraction to manifest itself as love.

He didn't love her...but he thought if they could spend more time together, he could.

A COUPLE OF DAYS LATER, BRYCE WALKED OUT OF THE stables as the evening sun went behind the Tetons and bathed Coral Canyon in a gray dusk that would last for a while before true darkness took over. His phone rang, and he pulled it from his back pocket to check it.

He dropped the phone, a horrible cracking sound filling the sky around the ranch. Bryce scrambled after it and picked it up as it rang again.

He swiped on the call as quickly as he could. "Hello?"

"Bryce," Laney Whittaker said. It really was her voice. He'd called and texted Bailey's mother a few times since he'd come home from college, but she hadn't answered either.

His only assumption had been that Bailey had spoken ill of him, and she didn't like him any more than Bailey did. Which was that they didn't like him at all.

He hadn't seen them at the Fourth of July picnic last week, though Graham and Bailey's half-siblings had been there. "Yes," he said anxiously. "I'm sorry to badger you so much this summer, Mrs. Whittaker. I'm just real worried about Bailey."

She sighed. "I have been too, Bryce," she said. "I didn't call you or text you back because until an hour ago, I didn't know where my daughter was."

Bryce's mind blanked. "What? She's doing that internship in Butte." Bailey wanted to be a veterinarian, and she'd gotten on at the biggest practice for large animal care in the state.

"Right," Laney said. "I meant, I knew she was there doing that, and I wasn't sure why you didn't know that."

"I did," Bryce said. "I was just...worried about her. She hasn't spoken to me since she left school." And that had only been a week after he'd told her their relationship was a mistake.

Not the whole relationship, he knew now. Just the part where they'd gone too far. He understood on a fundamental level now why his father had preached to him about being married before being intimate with a woman. It meant so much more than Bryce had anticipated, and he'd been desperate to make Bailey understand what he'd really meant when he'd said it was a mistake.

Not her. He didn't regret the relationship they'd been cultivating for almost a year before they'd spent the night together. He simply wished he'd been strong enough to wait to be with her.

"She hasn't spoken to me much this summer either." Laney didn't sound very happy about that. "Bryce, I think you and your parents should come for dinner tomorrow."

"Oh." He frowned, though he wasn't sure why her invitation had confused him. "Okay."

What she'd said caught up to him. Him and his parents? Why?

"You know where the farm is?" Laney asked. "Go around the corner from Whiskey Mountain Lodge. We're the only other house out here."

"I've been there, ma'am." He'd picked up Bailey for dates last summer, before they'd both gone to Montana State for school. He'd been a freshman, she a senior.

"Tomorrow night?" Laney asked. "Six o'clock."

"Yes, ma'am," Bryce said. "We'll be there."

Laney didn't say anything else, and the call ended. Bryce looked from his phone to the farmhouse, another hard conversation about to happen. He'd spent the better part of the past two days with his father at his side.

He'd gone to both studio sessions with the band, only leaving to tend to his animals. They brought him so much joy that Bryce knew college wasn't for him. He loved teaching guitar lessons too, but he knew he needed more than that for a career, at least a real one.

He hadn't seen Pastor Daniels yet, but Bryce looked up into the still-lit sky. "Lord," he prayed. "Whatever it is, bless me with the mental and emotional strength to handle it."

He didn't know what else to ask for, and since he still stood on shaky ground with God as it was, he didn't dare ask for more.

THE FOLLOWING EVENING, HE STOOD IN FRONT OF Dad and Abby and rang the doorbell at the pretty farm at the bottom of the hill from Whiskey Mountain Lodge. He'd stood nervously on this stoop before, but tonight, he felt all of the anxiety possible, plus like a very tiny piece in a very big universe.

No one came to the door, and he, Dad, and Abby stood there and waited for what felt like a long time. "She said tonight, right?" Abby asked.

"Yes," Bryce answered. He looked at his dad, who nodded his dress cowboy hat toward the doorbell again. He'd been Bryce's biggest champion, despite the fact that Bryce had let him down so terribly.

He'd worried about Harry and Cash, because they looked up to him so much, and Dad had told him there was no reason they needed to know. His repentance could happen privately, and Dad just wanted Bryce to "get his light back."

Bryce wanted that too, and this dinner felt pivotal to doing that, so he reached to knock this time. Maybe the doorbell was broken.

Before he could knock or press the button again, the door swung open.

Bailey—his beautiful Bailey—McAllister stood there, and Bryce didn't even think. He moved immediately into the house and into her personal space. "Bailey," breathed out of his mouth, and Bryce wrapped her up into a tight, tight hug. "I've been so worried about you."

She hugged him back, but it didn't take him long to realize she was crying. Something also pressed against him strangely, and he pulled away, so many parts of him rejoicing at this reunion.

Another part of him told him something was very, very wrong.

His brain caught up to the things his body had felt, and his eyes widened as Bailey dropped one hand to her belly.

It wasn't as flat as it had been previously.

Bryce knew instantly that she was pregnant.

With tear-filled eyes, she looked at him and said, "The baby is yours, Bryce."

He had no idea what to say. Numbness spread through him, and all he could do was bring Bailey back into the circle of his arms as she said, "I'm sorry, Bryce."

"Sh," he whispered, because she wasn't the one who needed to apologize. "*I'm* the one who's sorry. I'm sorry, Bailey." Behind her, her mother and father appeared, and Bryce's instinct to bolt intensified.

"I'm sorry," he said again, and then again. "I'm so, so sorry."

But sorry didn't make a pregnancy go away, and sorry wouldn't help him to know what to do with a baby when he was only nineteen years old.

25

Tex stared up at the ceiling, his eyes wide open. The light from his wife's phone moved through blue to purple to pink to white and back to blue, and his peripheral vision caught on it from time to time.

Mostly, his mind took up all of his energy, leaving nothing for his eyes to see.

Abby lay at his side, one arm draped across his torso and the other pressed against his side. He had his arm around her, his hand holding lightly to her upper arm. He loved laying with her like this, in the middle of the night, and listening to her breathe.

"Are you asleep?" she whispered.

"No," he whispered back. He wasn't that surprised that she was awake too.

She didn't say anything else, however, because they

both had a lot to process. Abby definitely worked through things in a more verbal way than Tex did, but even she'd been fairly quiet since dinner with the Whittakers two nights ago.

His son's girlfriend was pregnant. If Bailey could even be called Bryce's girlfriend. They hadn't spoken in months previous to the dinner Bailey's mother had set up.

Laney Whittaker hadn't been terribly enthused by her daughter's behavior—what had gotten her in the delicate situation she and Bryce found themselves in, nor the fact that she'd gone dark for three months following it.

Bryce had obviously been trying to get in touch with her, and he'd been so worried and so unsuccessful, he'd involved Laney. Once Bailey had come home during a break in her internship, it hadn't taken a rocket scientist to put the pieces together and make a phone call to Bryce.

Just a mother.

Both Bailey and Bryce had cried at dinner. Tex himself felt like weeping right now. He'd never felt so stuck in his life, and it wasn't even him who'd made this mistake and now had to deal with very serious consequences.

In some ways, though, it was. He hadn't been very present in Bryce's early childhood. He'd done his best the past several years to be his son's father—the very best father he knew how to be—and it hadn't been enough.

"What are you thinking?" he asked Abby. She grounded him, and yesterday she'd taken him by the shoulders and told him this was not his fault. Bryce was an adult, and a human being who got to make his own choices. All they could do was help him deal with the fallout, and Tex had buried his head in his wife's neck and cried.

"I'm just trying to decide if we should talk to Bryce tomorrow about the baby."

Since dinner, they hadn't spoken about the pregnancy. Bryce had packed an overnight bag and gone to Blaze's house in the mountains. It sat far closer to Bailey's farm than Tex's house, and Bryce only came out east to feed his horses twice a day.

Tex had called Blaze and asked to be updated on anything Blaze found off or weird or noteworthy. He hadn't told his brother about the baby. Or anything Bryce had confessed to him. His brother hadn't called or texted once.

"We need to talk to him today," Tex said. "Those kids...they have options."

"Bryce might want the baby," she said. "I mean, Bailey doesn't, but he has rights too, doesn't he?"

"Gabe said he did," Tex said. She'd been there for the phone conversation Tex had had with his youngest brother. "When he gets here tonight, we'll talk to him too."

Tex hadn't told anyone else about Bryce's baby yet. It wasn't his news to tell, and he closed his eyes as a sudden wave of extreme exhaustion rolled over him.

"What if he wants to keep the baby?" Abby said. "He can live here with us, can't he?"

"He won't want to," Tex said.

"Keep the baby?" Abby asked. "Or live with us?"

"Live with us," Tex said. "We have money. We can help him while he figures things out." He honestly wasn't sure if Bryce would keep the baby when he couldn't keep Bailey with it.

Tex had seen the relief and adoration on his son's face. He might be in love with Bailey McAllister. He might not be; Bryce hadn't said.

He'd been shocked when she'd said she was pregnant, and then something like horror had crossed his face when she'd said she didn't want to keep the baby. She wanted to be a large animal veterinarian, and she'd gotten a full-ride scholarship to the best vet school in Montana.

She'd deferred to start the program until January, as the baby was due in December.

I want to put the baby up for adoption, she'd told them at dinner.

Bryce had sat there with his mouth hanging open and his eyes as wide as Tex had ever seen him. Neither he nor Abby had said anything. Graham and Laney had likewise remained silent.

Tex had never been in this situation before, and he didn't know what to do.

When Bryce had said, "What about us getting married?" Bailey had simply started to cry again. She'd shaken her head no, and that was when Bryce had gotten up and excused himself.

Tex pressed his eyes closed, but the images from dinner two nights ago would not go away. Bailey crumbling into her father's side.

Laney barking at her to pull herself together and go talk to Bryce. "Now," she'd said, and Bailey had done it. When the four of them—him and Abby and Graham and Laney—were alone, the true conversations had started.

There were no apologies made, though Tex had felt true sorrow while sitting at that dining room table. In the end, the four of them had agreed to let their adult children have some time to process, talk, and make some decisions.

At the same time, Tex needed to be there to guide his son. He wanted to know what he was thinking and make sure he understood all of the paths and options available to him.

He opened his eyes as he exhaled, and he rolled away from Abby slightly to reach for his phone on the nightstand.

"Are you texting him?" she asked.

"Yes." Tex put his legs over the side of the bed and sat up. "I'm not going to chance him coming while we're right in the middle of recording."

Country Quad was one song away from finishing this album, and then Morris would make another trip to Nashville. All of them would go with him this time, and they'd get the feedback from the music producers at King Country. If they needed to re-record parts of songs or whole songs, they'd do it there.

The trip was expected to take two weeks, and Tex was already dreading it.

Then, like a ray of heavenly light from God Himself, Tex had the very loud thought that he should take Bryce with him. To Nashville.

He twisted and half-looked over his shoulder at his wife. "I'm going to ask him to come for dinner tonight. Seven-thirty? Even if the band is going that late, I'll cut it off."

"I'll make corn on the cob and those pizza pockets he likes."

Tex nodded and went back to his phone, beyond grateful for his kind, good wife. She was a miracle for him, and he took a moment to breathe and thank the Lord for Abigail in his life. He couldn't do this without her at his side, that was for sure.

He started tapping to text his son, and he put everything in one big message.

Come for dinner tonight. 7:30. Abby's going to make all of your favorites. We need to talk about what you're thinking and what you want from your life.

The band is going to Nashville at the end of August, and I think you should come with me. I can introduce you around to the music execs again, and you can explore country music as a career choice, if you're still interested in that.

If you want to keep the baby, I'll support you. If you don't and want to put it up for adoption, I'll support you. If you want to live on this farm and get more horses, I'll help you do that. If you want to teach guitar lessons from a studio, I'll build you one right here on the farm.

I love you, son, and I will do whatever I can to help you through this period of your life. It's not the end of the world, that much I know. It might feel like it right now, but that's why you need to come home and let me and Abby help you.

Tears burned his eyes, and Tex looked up from the message. He just wanted Bryce to *come home.* He felt like his son was moving further and further from him, at a faster and faster rate, and Tex was desperately trying to catch up to him. Trying to let him know he didn't need to divorce himself from his support system simply because he'd made a mistake.

Bryce had example after example of that right in front of him in the form of his uncles. Morris and Leigh had made their relationship work—they'd made it stronger and better—after years of deceit. After a *very* big mistake one of them had made.

Tex himself had married the wrong woman for the wrong reasons, and he'd been living with the consequences of that—trying to fix it, do better, be better—for years.

Blaze had married the woman he'd gotten pregnant, and that had been a huge disaster. Tex didn't want that for his son any more than he'd enjoyed watching his brother go through it. Not only that, but Blaze was a completely different man now than he'd been when he'd moved to Coral Canyon last year. He understood the darker side of life, and Tex knew why Bryce had gone to him. He'd been praying that Blaze might have some insight into Bryce's situation, and that he'd say the right thing at the right time to influence his boy in the right way.

Another round of desperation clawed its way up Tex's throat, but he swallowed against it. He sent the long text and tapped out a much shorter one.

I love you. Please come home.

Home.

Tex wanted to provide the safest place for Bryce, and that was right here, at the farmhouse they'd worked on together two summers ago.

"Please, Lord," he whispered. "Bring him home."

He sent the text and lay back down, letting his tears track slowly down his face. Abby gathered him into her arms and stroked his hair back off his forehead. "I'm losing him, Abby," he whispered. "We're losing him."

Despite his prayer, Tex had the keen feeling that Bryce would not come home. He truly was losing him, and though Abby assured him they weren't, Tex couldn't help feeling like Bryce was already gone.

A meal, a text, the promise of help—none of it would bring him back until he was ready to come back of his own accord.

He cried, because he didn't want his son out in this

big, cruel world alone. He didn't want him to make more mistakes when he didn't have to. He didn't want the lessons he needed to learn to come at such a high cost.

He cried for himself, because he loved his son and would miss him terribly. He wept for Melissa, who wouldn't know how amazing her big brother was. He mourned for Cash and Harry, who looked up to and loved Bryce so much. Tex wouldn't be the only one who missed him and wished he'd come home.

His parents, Otis, Trace, Mav, Blaze, Morris, Luke, Jem, and even Gabe would miss him mightily. Bryce was one of them, and without him in the Young family, there would be a great big giant hole nothing and no one could fill.

Tex felt it start inside his heart, and as he eventually quieted and timed his breathing with his wife's, his heart broke that one bad decision could radiate out and affect so many lives.

Finally, he prayed for peace, and once he'd done that, he managed to fall asleep for a few hours. But when he woke, the situation still existed. The baby was still coming by Christmas. Bryce still needed to make some decisions.

SEVEN-THIRTY CAME, AND WITH IT, TEX ENTERED the farmhouse. He'd seen his son's truck in the driveway, and the first thing he did was toss the keys to the recording studio on the counter and pull his boy into a hug.

Bryce held onto Tex tightly too, and Tex thought perhaps his middle-of-the-night thoughts had been a touch irrational. Bryce would always be his, no matter where he went or what he did.

"I'm sorry, Dad," he whispered.

"Enough apologies," Tex said back. "You can't wallow in this forever." He stepped back and wiped his son's tears. "Okay?"

"Dinner is ready," Abby said quietly. "Let's talk at the table."

They did what she said, and after she'd said a quick prayer, Bryce seemed to realize what she'd made. He looked at her with wonder and said, "I don't deserve this."

"Of course you do," she said with a wave of her hand. "Bryce, we all make mistakes. That doesn't mean we have to punish ourselves for the rest of our lives." She put a big pizza pocket on his plate. "I think that's your dad's point. No more apologies. What's done is done. What we need to do now is figure out what the best thing is in order for both you and Bailey to move forward in your lives."

"And for that baby," Tex said quietly.

Bryce took a hot piece of corn as Abby held the plate in front of him, and then Tex took the plate from her. He buttered his corn and as he added an astronomical amount of salt to it—something Tex would've normally teased him about—he said, "I've been thinking."

He put the saltshaker down. "And talking to Bailey. And Uncle Blaze, believe it or not. And Uncle Gabe and Uncle Morris." He swallowed and met Tex's eyes. "I trust you, Dad. I do. I just needed...different eyes on this."

Tex swallowed and nodded. He did feel slightly left out, but then he reminded himself that God had given him this huge, loud family of various personalities for a reason. This was simply one of them.

"And?" Abby asked.

Tex appreciated his wife so much. She could prompt and prod and ask questions he couldn't. He didn't want to drive Bryce away, but when Abby asked, it didn't feel that way to him.

Bryce looked from Tex to her and back. He wore his nerves plainly in his face. "This might be a crazy idea, but I talked to Bailey about it, and she's okay with it."

He swallowed and looked over to Abby. "I need to talk to Uncle Gabe or someone about adoption, because I'm not even sure how that process all works."

Relief started to fill Tex. He thought the smartest option for Bryce was adoption, since that was what Bailey wanted, but he didn't want to pressure the boy. Bryce needed to learn and know he could make his own decisions. Plus, Tex didn't want the decision to come from him and have Bryce regret it—and resent Tex—later.

"I think I'd love that baby," Bryce said, his voice wobbly and pitching up. "But I'm nineteen years old, and I know way down deep inside me that I can't take care of it.

I can't give it the life it deserves. So." He took a long, deep breath and looked over to Melissa as she started to babble.

Abby put another chunk of pizza on the baby's tray, and she tried to grab it with her chunky fingers. Tex couldn't help smiling at his baby girl, but his life was completely different than Bryce's.

Tears filled his son's eyes as he looked at his baby half-sister too. "Like, I can't do what you guys do for Melissa. I see Uncle Luke and how good he is with Corrine. And Uncle Trace and Harry." He shook his head. "I can't do it. I'm not ready. I don't want to go to college, but I don't want to live in your basement and have you raise my kid for me."

"You're welcome here anytime," Abby said. "This is your home."

Bryce nodded. "I was thinking...Uncle Otis and Aunt Georgia want a baby, and maybe...they could have mine and Bailey's."

The words filled the kitchen, then the whole house. Tex gaped at his son, because that option had not existed inside his mind.

Abby burst into tears and wrapped her arms around Bryce's shoulders.

"Bad idea?" he asked, his eyes reading only Tex's reaction. "I read online that sometimes family members adopt babies, and I mean, I look a lot like Otis. That baby would never know it didn't belong to him and Aunt Georgia."

"*You* would know," Tex pointed out. "Every time we

get together for a family function, how are you going to feel?"

How was Tex supposed to feel, having his brother raise his grandchild?

Everything blurred and became so confusing inside his head, and Tex didn't know how to make everything line up right.

"I think I'd be okay," Bryce said. He swiped at his eyes. "I don't think Bailey wants to marry me, and I can't raise the baby on my own. So we both agree that adoption is the best choice for us and the baby. And Uncle Gabe said Uncle Otis has already started the registration process with an adoption agency in Jackson Hole."

He finally picked up his pizza pocket and took a bite. Tex hadn't been able to start eating yet, and Abby hadn't either.

She'd composed herself, and Tex met her eyes. He raised his eyebrows, silent questions flying between them. He already knew how his wife felt. She wanted her best friend to have a baby with her whole heart.

And this baby would be a Young in every way.

"Abby?" Tex asked anyway.

"I think you should at least talk to Otis and Georgia," she said, glancing over to Bryce. "Let's do it the right way. Let's talk to Gabe when he gets here, and then we'll know more if it's even a possibility."

Bryce nodded, and finally a smile came to his face. "Thanks, Abby." He met Tex's eyes again, more tears welling in his. He didn't let them fall, but he did add, "Thanks, Dad. I love you. I'm real sorry about this. Honestly, I am."

Tex leaned toward him and slid his hand around to the back of Bryce's neck. "I know you are. I think this is a good solution." He pressed a kiss to his son's temple. "I love you, boy. More and more every day."

Tex did eat then, and the conversation moved through what Bryce had been thinking and talking about with various people over the past couple of days.

"So have you told all the uncles?" Tex asked.

He shook his head, and the scared little boy Tex had rescued from his mother's house in Boise two summers ago shone on Bryce's face. "Will you? And ask them to tell their kids. I don't think—I can't do it."

"They'll learn that you're human," Tex said. "They won't think badly of you."

"I'm worried about Harry, especially," Bryce said, and he shook his head. "I hate that I can't be the person he thinks I am." Pure sadness emanated from him, and neither Tex nor Abby told him it was okay.

It wasn't okay. What he'd done was not okay, and yes, there would be long-lasting and far-reaching consequences from it.

But Tex knew Harry was his own person too, and how he chose to react would not be something Bryce had to shoulder.

Family relationships lasted a long time, and Tex

prayed that everyone in the Young family would have a forgiving heart, and that even if it took years like it had for his brothers, that the cousins would have the close bonds that Tex currently did with his brothers.

That was all he could do.

26

Trace saw Tex waiting in his truck as he pulled into the barbecue joint. It wasn't hard on a weekday in the summer, away from the lake and pretty much all civilization. Jurassic Tacos ran an amazing stand near Tex's house, actually, and they were more of a delivery or pick-up joint.

Today, however, Trace and Tex were going to order and then sit at one of the wooden picnic tables to talk and eat. Tex had called Trace late last night and said he needed "to consult" with him on something.

Trace hadn't asked too many questions. As the two oldest brothers, he and Tex had always been close. They often spoke one-on-one and then took issues to the rest of the family. Not so much in recent years, but especially when the family had been divided over the band.

Tex looked like he hadn't been sleeping, and Trace's

concern for his brother spiked. He did have a baby who was almost four months old, but he'd bragged on the family text last week that Melissa slept through the night. So there had to be something else.

Trace parked and got out of his truck too, saying, "Hey, brother," as he rounded the tailgate. Tex drew him into a hug, no words necessary.

Trace held him close, trying to determine the cause of the storm inside his brother's soul. He couldn't; he could only feel it seeping into him through osmosis and sinking all the way to the soles of his feet.

"What's goin' on?" Trace asked when Tex finally released him.

"So much." He turned toward the window, which was shaded by a single overhanging roof made of canvas. Tex ordered the chorizo chomper, and Trace held up two fingers to indicate he'd take that too.

They got sodas and chips and salsa, and Trace let Tex lead them over to a table with a big, red umbrella shading it.

Not many people drove this road, as the police dog academy that Ames Hammond ran sat out here. It wasn't a main road connecting the east side of Coral Canyon to the west, but it did lead up to the southern part of Dog Valley, so an occasional truck went by.

Trace unwrapped his straw and poked it into his lid. He took a drink of his diet cola and looked at Tex, waiting.

Tex fiddled with his wrapper and wouldn't look at Trace. "I feel like my life is falling apart," he said.

If Trace were Luke or Gabe or even Mav, he'd jump in with questions. *Is it Abby? Is she okay? The baby? What's going on, Tex?*

Trace simply put his drink on the rough wood and waited some more. He'd taken Harry to Hunter Hammond's that morning, and the boy was helping Hunter and his wife with their small child at the lake that day. Harry loved fishing, as did Hunter, and they'd bonded over that at the Fourth of July picnic.

Tex balled up his straw wrapper and took a drink of his soda pop too. "Bryce's girlfriend is pregnant," he said. "We just found out this week."

Whatever Trace had been expecting Tex to say, it was not that. The air whooshed out of his lungs, and his brain just sat there, blank.

Tex squinted past Trace, though he wore a cowboy hat that provided plenty of shade from the noon-day sun. "They're thinking they'll put the baby up for adoption, and Trace." He shook his head. When he looked up this time, his eyes locked right onto Trace's. "Gabe came into town last night, and he's got contacts and knowledge about adoption, right? He said there shouldn't be any issues with this, but I don't know. I feel...I don't know."

"You don't want him to put the baby up for adoption?" Bryce was a great kid, but that was the operative word:

Kid. Bryce was legally an adult, but still very much a kid in Trace's mind. "They won't get married?"

Tex shook his head. "I think Bryce would, if that's what the girl wanted. It's not."

"Ouch." Trace sighed and looked left and then right. For what, he wasn't sure. Someone to jump out and tell him this was a joke? And a bad one at that.

"Yeah." Tex sighed too. "He's worried about how Harry will react."

"Yeah, me too." Trace reached up and pushed his cowboy hat back so he could rub his hands through his hair. "My son idolizes yours. He's been talking about the horse rescue ranch and maybe starting a second family band once he's graduated, all of it."

"I know." Tex looked absolutely miserable, and Trace reached over and covered his hand.

"They'll figure it out. We all did."

Tex nodded, and Trace didn't have to specify that he and his brothers had worked past hurt feelings and through difficult situations to be where they were today. Harry and Bryce could do the same. Or they wouldn't. There wasn't anything Trace or Tex could do about it.

"He wants to give the baby to Otis and Georgia," Tex said next.

That sent a shockwave through Trace, and he once again fell silent and started to go numb. "That's...." He didn't know how to finish.

"That was my reaction," Tex said. "Abby was thrilled,

of course. Gabe was very matter-of-fact." He shook his head again and pushed his cowboy hat down lower over his eyes. "I don't know. It feels weird to me. Like, my brother is going to raise my grandson? Why shouldn't I just do it? Abby and I could do it. We have a baby right now."

"When's this new baby due?"

"Right before Christmas," Tex said. "The twenty-fourth."

Trace nodded. "Your kids wouldn't quite be nine months apart, Tex. Everyone would know it wasn't yours."

"So what?" Tex asked. "It'll be my grandbaby."

"And Otis and Georgia can't have kids." Trace shrugged. "I don't know, brother. This one is tough."

"What would you do?"

There sat the question. Tex had asked Trace this many times over the past forty years, and Trace sometimes had good advice to give. Or at least an opinion. This time, he had no idea what to say.

"Chorizo chomper," a woman said, and she put an enormous plate in front of Tex with more meat than Trace had seen in a taco ever. "Times two."

She put the same meal in front of Trace, smiled, and said, "If y'all need anything, just holler," before she walked away.

Trace stared at his food. "I'm going to need a gurney so someone can wheel me to my truck once I eat all of this." The spicy chorizo made his mouth water, and Trace started to fold his flour tortilla in half so he could take a monster-sized bite of the dinosaur-sized taco.

He moaned when the deliciousness hit his taste buds, and Tex's face did crack into a smile. After chewing and swallowing, Trace wiped his mouth and looked at Tex.

"You'll just have to rely on your gut with this one, Tex," he said. "Pray about it, and listen, and then do what you think is right."

"Abby doesn't want a baby who could go to her BFF," Tex said. "And honestly, I'm barely surviving with Melissa as it is."

Trace grinned and started to lift his taco to his mouth again. "That's the answer then."

Tex took a bite of his taco too, and once they'd both eaten, he said, "Bryce is requesting that I tell all the uncles and that they handle how and when they tell their children."

Trace nodded. "I can talk to Harry." He wiped his hands on his napkin. "Who's the mother? Are you telling that?"

"Bailey McAllister," Tex said, looking west, toward the hills where Graham and Laney Whittaker lived.

"Wow." Trace pictured Bryce and Bailey together, holding hands at last year's Independence Day picnic. Bryce had been made of smiles and laughter last summer, and he'd definitely changed once he'd gone to college. "Is he going back to Montana State?"

Tex shook his head no. "He's coming with me to Nashville when we all go with Country Quad. He'll keep teaching guitar lessons and doing the farm until he figures out what he wants his life to be. Bailey is going to work at the vet where she did her internship these past few months, and then once she delivers the baby, she's planning to start her doctorate in veterinary medicine."

No wonder she didn't want to keep the baby. She had career goals and plans, and Bryce was nineteen years old.

Trace and Tex had both had their sons when they were fairly young—all of their brothers had too. But not nineteen, and not when they weren't married.

"What do you need from me?" Trace asked. He put the last bite of his taco in his mouth.

Tex dusted his hands together and his shoulders slumped. "I hate to ask you, but I'm going to anyway. Will you tell all the brothers and Momma and Daddy? I don't have the energy, and I need to spend what I do have on my son." Tex wore worry in his eyes, and Trace cocked his head.

"What else are you worried about?"

"I'm honestly afraid I'm going to lose him," Tex whispered. "I think he wants to keep this baby close, but not as close as me, so he can see it if he wants to. But he doesn't think he can be a dad right now."

Tex shook his head, and this was the most confused Trace had ever seen him. "I'm scared to let him out of my sight. It's stupid, I know. He's been at Blaze's for the past couple of days, but he came home last night, and I don't know. I feel like I can't let him get too far from me, that he needs me."

"He probably does," Trace said. "I'll handle it. People might have questions. What do you want me to say?"

"Anything I just told you," he said.

"They're okay with everyone knowing it's Bailey?"

Tex nodded. "Bryce said he's not going to hide anything from anyone, not anymore."

Trace could admire and respect that. "Okay. I'll handle it."

"Thank you, Trace," Tex said. They finished lunch, and Trace picked up their trays and trash. He wanted to send a text right now, but he forced himself to wait until he'd hugged his brother good-bye, promised him everything would work out, and drove home.

Once he pulled into the driveway, he backed right back out again. This wasn't where he was supposed to be; Everly was waiting for him at the studio, and they were headed to Rusk today for a hot air balloon parade and evening festival that night.

Cursing himself for forgetting, he made the drive downtown. Sure enough, Everly sat on the curb, her feet in the gutter while she texted on her phone. She looked up at the grumble of his engine, and Trace dropped to the ground.

He suddenly didn't want to make the hour-long drive to Rusk. He just wanted to be with Everly and talk everything through with her. "Hey," he said in a rush. "I'm so sorry. My mind is moving in a thousand different directions right now."

She stood, and she wore the prettiest pale pink dress he'd ever seen. "So not a great lunch with Tex."

He'd already told her he was worried about what his brother would have to say. He shook his head, and there were so many things inside it, he swore he heard them knocking around.

Blaze still called on him first if he needed something.

Now Tex needed Trace to bear the burden of being the oldest brother.

He had Harry to worry about.

And Bryce and Bailey to pray for.

Not to mention Otis and Georgia and how they might react to being able to raise a near-blood relative as their own child.

He blinked and Everly stood in front of him. "You don't want to go to Rusk," she said. Disappointment carried in her voice.

He wrapped her in his arms and shook his head. "Will you let me come back to your place?" he asked. "I'll be nice to your cat this time."

She smiled up at him, but Trace didn't have the energy to return it. She sobered too. "Are you going to tell me what happened?"

"Yes," he said, but part of him wondered if he had room in his life for everything going on right now. It sure didn't feel like it, but as he led Everly to the passenger door and opened it for her, he told himself, *One thing at at time, Trace. Just handle one thing at a time.*

Right now, that thing was Everly, and he didn't want to be anywhere but with her. She could read over his text for the brothers, and she'd be at his side while he called his momma and daddy.

He needed her right now, and when he got behind the wheel, he said, "Ev, I need you right now, okay?"

She turned toward him with hope shining in her bright blue eyes. "You do?"

"Yeah." He sighed. "Wait'll I tell you what's going on with Tex...."

27

Everly took the phone from Trace, who got to his feet and started pacing again. Into the kitchen, pause at the back door, turn, and come back toward her in the living room. Mutant didn't like the nervous energy Trace had brought with him, and truth be told, Everly didn't either.

For a man who was usually so composed and cool and calm, this Anxious-Andy version of Trace unsettled her.

"I'm so worried about Harry," he said.

"We're not dealing with Harry quite yet," Everly reminded him. She focused on the text he'd typed out and which he'd asked her to read over and fix if necessary.

Hey, everyone, he'd said. *Tex asked me to send this to everyone and for you to direct your questions to me for now. He and Abby and Bryce would appreciate your prayers and love, but they don't have it in them to be on their phones all day right now.*

Bryce just found out that he's expecting a baby near Christmastime. The baby's mother is Bailey McAllister, and they aren't going to get married or keep the baby. They'll put it up for adoption, and they've already started that process with Gabe.

Trace had been on the phone with Gabe for a solid thirty minutes, and he'd called Tex again too, before typing out this text.

Tonight was supposed to be small-town festival fun, with hot air balloons, good weather, and trashy fair food. Instead, Everly had been sitting on her couch at Trace's side for the past couple of hours, silently waiting for him to need her.

She didn't want to complain—she wanted to be at his side when he needed her most. He simply felt...distant, and Everly had been with a version of Trace when he'd withdrawn from her. That was how this evening felt, and she told herself for the umpteenth time that he was allowed to have something this big consume him for a few days. Or longer.

She felt so selfish and needy, and she'd resolved to say nothing about it unless Trace continued to pull away from her. She knew what that felt like, looked like, sounded like, and she would not let him go without a fight. Not again.

I'm going to call Momma and Daddy right now, his text continued. *Please don't say anything to them yet.*

Please do tell your children when you feel it's appropriate for them to know, and again, offer up a prayer for all involved if you feel so inclined.

Everly looked up from the message. "It reads well," she said.

Trace reached for the phone, and she gave it to him. "Yeah?"

"Yes, sir." She tried to smile at him, but he didn't even look at her. Frustration built inside Everly, but she pushed it back.

"I wonder if Tex has talked to Otis yet." He tapped and lifted the phone to his ear again.

Everly curled her legs up under her body and watched him walk into her kitchen. His shoulders were up and boxy, tight and tense. He'd told her that Bryce and Bailey were going to talk to Otis and Georgia about adopting their baby, and she'd found that sweet and tender. Trace was worried others in the family wouldn't come to that conclusion on their own, but Everly thought they would. They'd be stunned that Bryce was responsible for creating a baby at all, the way she had been. The way Trace had been.

She hadn't changed when they'd come back to her place, holding onto the hope that once Trace got through his messages, they might be able to go out to dinner here in town. Now, though, as he spoke with his oldest brother again, Everly realized this would be their whole evening. Once he sent that text, he had to call his parents, and that would be another long conversation. Then he'd field the texts coming in from seven grown men, all of them intimately connected.

She went down the hall to her bedroom and shed her dress. She put on a pair of baggy sweat pants and a tank top the color of pink grapefruit and returned to the kitchen. She set a kettle on the burner, noting that Trace had left the room completely.

Everly found him on the back patio, pacing as he spoke on the phone, and she left him there as she ordered dinner for the two of them, fed Mutant his special supper, and went outside to the front driveway to keep working on her cabinet.

She'd stripped the lacquer from it finally, and she'd removed all the hardware. She'd then bleached the wood and left it to sit in the hot summer sun. Next, she needed to clean all of that off and paint it, and while it was probably too hot this afternoon to do that, she set up a shade to help cool down the dresser and got to work.

"Mama," she said. "There was no hidden compartment in this cabinet the way there was in yours." She sighed, her imagination always getting the best of her. "Trace is so busy with family stuff right now. I'm being selfish and bratty wanting all of his attention for myself."

She cleaned the wood without another word to her mother, because Everly knew what the problem was—it was her.

She should be at Trace's side and not upset they

couldn't go about their lives as planned. In fact, that was the definition of life—it happened.

It had twists, curves, steep drop-offs, and blindsides on a daily basis. It was how a person dealt with those unexpected hardships that defined them. And how a couple dealt with them that bonded them—or drove them apart.

Everly tossed down the rag she'd been using on the wood and went back inside. Trace sat on the back steps now, and she opened the door and went to his side.

"Did you talk to your momma?"

He nodded, his head barely moving. "She cried."

"I'm so sorry." Everly laced her arm through his and laid her head against his bicep. "I ordered dinner, and I think you should come inside and eat, and we can put on a movie, and you can fall asleep in my lap."

He looked at her then, and the zombified look in his eyes lessened. "Thank you, my Ev."

She smiled at him, because she *was* his, and it didn't matter how much they had going on. He'd always come back to her. "Come on," she said gently. "There's nothing more you can do today."

"Harry's going to walk down the road from Hunter's to Blaze's," he said. "So you're right. I don't have anything to do the rest of the night."

"Except sit by me and tell me how pretty I am in my sweats." She stood and cocked her hip, which nearly sent her pants down to her ankles.

Trace blinked, probably because he hadn't noticed

she'd changed. A slow smile curved his mouth. "You are the prettiest thing I've ever seen, definitely with the sweats." He reached for her and then pulled Everly into his lap.

She loved the way he held her, like he couldn't get close enough to her. He wrapped his hands around her waist and leaned his head into her chest. "Would you adopt my nephew's baby, Ev?"

She took a moment to consider her answer. "I would if I were Georgia," she said slowly.

"Why's that?"

"Because she can't have babies," Everly said. "And she probably really wants one that looks a lot like Otis. And Bryce's baby will look a lot like that, because he has Young genes."

Trace tightened his grip on her body but said nothing. Inside, the faint sound of her doorbell ringing met her ears, and Everly pulled back to look at him. "Dinner's here."

"We've talked a little about this before, but...do you want babies that look like your husband?" He made no move to get up and go with her into the house.

Everly gazed back at him, seeing his kind, wonderful soul through those deep, handsome eyes. "Yes," she said.

He nodded, his expression flickering ever so slightly.

"Have you changed your mind about having more kids, Mister Young?" She watched him closely, because she didn't want to pressure him to do something he didn't want to do. "Harry is so great, I can see why you wouldn't want to muddy the perfect kid pool."

Trace's face broke into a smile. "I think I could handle having more kids." His phone went off and instant exhaustion filled his face.

Everly held out her hand. "Give me your phone."

He looked like she'd asked him to split his head in half. "Now, Mister," she said. "It's stressing you out, and I want twenty minutes with my hot boyfriend to eat dinner without any stress."

His smile appeared again. "Hot boyfriend." He slapped his phone into her palm. "If Harry texts, you have to look at it."

"I can agree with that." She tucked his phone under her bra strap, right over her heartbeat. "Can you give me twenty minutes where we don't talk about your family?"

His eyes widened in mock shock. "Whatever will we talk about then?"

Everly had a few ideas. She leaned closer to him and with her lips almost on his, she whispered, "Where you're going to take me for a romantic birthday dinner next week. The band, my brothers, the studio, the corn harvest this year, literally anything, Mister Young, except Bryce and Tex and all the drama. You need it." She pulled back and looked into those eyes again. "*I* need it. I need you to be here, with me, right now, Trace."

"Yes, ma'am," he said, his voice hoarse. Then he kissed

her properly, and they both ignored the doorbell as it rang again.

An hour later, they'd eaten, had their easy talks about her birthday dinner and then nothing at all, and Trace had even started to joke when his phone made the twanging noise of a guitar.

He looked up at her from where his head lay in her lap. "That's Harry."

"I know." She pulled the phone from her shirt and looked at it. Oh, boy. He'd missed a lot of texts, and Harry's sat right above Bryce's.

Everly couldn't stop her eyes from reading the beginning of that message, and she pulled in a slow breath. "Honey," she said. "I think you should see this one first." She tapped on Bryce's text.

"It's from Bryce." Trace started to sit up, but Everly kept going. "It says, 'Uncle Trace, have you told Harry about me and everything? I hope not. If you haven't, will you please hold off on saying anything? I've been thinking about it, and I need to tell him myself.'"

Everly looked at Trace with wide eyes. "It came in about a half-hour ago." She handed him the phone, and Trace read the message himself. He frowned and tapped a couple of times.

"Harry said he's at Blaze's," Trace said. "He and Cash are having a hot chocolate and caramel popcorn bar." He turned the phone toward her and showed her a picture of the two of them.

Everly smiled at them, at the goodness of a fourteen-year-old boy hanging out with his twelve-year-old cousin and watching movies and drinking hot chocolate and noshing on popcorn.

It was the kind of thing she used to do with Reggie and Shawn, and a pang of nostalgia hit her squarely in the gut.

"I'm going to call Bryce," Trace said. "Is that okay?" He looked at her with that anxious edge in his eyes.

Everly nodded and leaned forward to kiss him. "Be quick. You're going to miss the part where Edward sparkles in the sun."

He grinned at her and got to his feet. While he headed outside again, Everly took out her phone and texted her brothers.

We need a movie night, just the three of us. Brownies, lemonade, hot coffee, and Shawn can bring all the burnt ends.

I'm in, Reggie said almost instantly. *I'll be there next week to get all that crap out of Shawn's garage.*

Name the night, Shawn said. *My place or yours?*

Everly wanted to do it here, because then she could lay out the treats the way she wanted. *Here,* she said. *Next Wednesday? When are you done that day, Shawn?*

I can get someone to cover dinner, he said. *I can't be out late. Start at six? Eat and par-tay?*

She giggled at her older brother's misuse of the word. Or maybe it simply dated him. Either way, she loved him for it, and she sent a thumbs up. Quickly, she added, *Reg, tell me when you're coming and I'll have my boyfriend and his huge, muscly brothers come help you pack up.*

She wasn't surprised when her phone rang, and she wasn't hiding her feelings for Trace, so she answered her younger brother's call with, "Heya, Reg."

"So you like this man."

Everly sighed, the kind of happy sigh a woman does when they've had an amazing first kiss with an amazing man. "No, Reggie," she said. "I don't like him. I'm falling in love with him."

28

Trace's headlights cut a path through the darkness as he drove home. Things with Bryce and Tex had calmed over the past week, thankfully. There had been an hour or two—or three—where he'd thought this would break him, break their whole family.

But the day after he'd called his parents, Momma had come to the house and talked through everything with Trace personally. She'd apologized for crying, said of course she loved Bryce to the ends of the earth, and that she'd do whatever Trace told her to do to support Tex, Abby, and their family.

Everyone had said that. They all wanted to know what they could or should do. Tex and Bryce had asked for some privacy; they didn't want to handle a bunch of texts, even well-wishes and shows of support and love.

The problem was, Trace wasn't used to being the oldest brother. He didn't have to know what to do. Tex had always filled that role—he was literally born to do it.

But right now, Tex was hurting too, and Trace would do whatever he could to protect him. He'd been in constant contact with Tex, and of course he saw the band every weekday, just like tonight.

The difference was, tonight, Bryce had taken Harry to dinner, and then dropped him off at Sarah's. Then, because the water in the Endman's house had suddenly had to be turned off, Sarah's mother had brought the teens to Trace's house.

Or she was on her way. Trace had left Tex's the moment Harry had called to say Mrs. Endman was driving him and Sarah to Trace's house. Trace didn't want them to be there alone, but Mrs. Endman had to deal with the leak in her basement and the water in her house being off this late at night. That was an emergency plumbing situation, and Trace didn't envy the Endmans tonight. In fact, he should call Sarah's mom and offer to let her bring the kids over here to use the water, showers, toilets, whatever they needed.

He would, once he got home and made sure his son was okay. When he'd called, he hadn't sounded upset, but Trace hadn't been focused on asking him what he thought of Bryce and their dinner.

He might have been worrying about nothing. Or Harry might not have wanted to show too much emotion in front of Bryce and then Sarah. Trace honestly didn't know, because Harry was a lot like him and could shutter his emotions behind a mask.

He made the final turn to get to his house and then he swung the truck into the driveway. He cut the engine and reached for his music bag, though he likely wouldn't even look at it before band practice tomorrow. It was the thought that counted, wasn't it?

He wasn't sure, but he collected the bag and got out of the truck. He went up the steps and into the house, where he immediately froze.

Harry stood on the other side of the island, one hand pressing into it as he leaned into it. Into Sarah.

His other hand had cradled her face, and he stood there, kissing her.

Trace's mind went on vacation for a moment, and then he took another step into the house and let the garage door slam closed behind him.

His heart slammed in the exact same way as the door, but Harry and Sarah jumped apart. Well, Harry jumped back. Sarah couldn't really go anywhere, pinned between Harry and the counter as she was.

"I'm home," Trace said needlessly. "Sarah, do you want me to give you a ride back to your place?"

She turned and faced him, her hand actually coming up to wipe her face. Trace almost shook his head. She should never wipe her mouth after getting caught kissing a boy. That was a pure admission of guilt.

"She just got here, Dad," Harry said.

Trace lifted his eyebrows. "You clearly wasted no time welcoming her to our home."

"Dad," Harry warned. He wore a storm in his eyes, and Trace felt it blow through his soul. His goal wasn't to embarrass his son, and a quiet voice in his head whispered, *It's just kissing, Trace.*

But kissing led to *more* than kissing, and Trace wanted to take Harry by the shoulders and lean into his face. He wanted to remind him of the situation Bryce found himself in—and that had started with kissing too.

Trace hefted his bag onto the dining room table. "All right," he said. "You guys hungry? Have you eaten dinner?" He looked from Sarah to Harry, and they looked at one another too.

"That's it?" Harry asked. "You're gonna make dinner now?"

"It's dinnertime, isn't it?" Trace asked.

"No." Harry's eyebrows drew down. "I went to dinner with Bryce a couple of hours ago."

"Yeah, well, Tex wouldn't let us quit in the studio until we had *Blue and White Dress* perfect."

Sarah hadn't moved, but Harry had come closer to Trace. He reached for his son and drew him into a hug. He wanted to say more to him, whisper something wise and sage-like, but nothing came to mind. In truth, he wanted to let his son know he loved him, and that he'd always love him, the way Tex had been doing for Bryce.

He released his son and asked, "How was dinner with Bryce?" He swept his cowboy hat off his head and tossed it next to the bag on the table. "Sarah, for real. Are you hungry?"

"Harry said he could pour me a bowl of cereal," she said.

"And you kissed this clown?" Trace shook his head, his smile filling his whole face. "Harry, you have to impress the girl *before* you kiss her." He scoffed. "Cold cereal? We've got to talk about your dating game."

He turned his back on the stunned teens and went into the kitchen. "I'm thinking something easy, like eggs and pancakes." He opened the fridge and got out the carton of eggs. "Sarah? Last chance."

"Yes, sir," she said. "I'd take a pancake and some eggs."

Trace faced her and Harry again. He wasn't sure how Harry was feeling by the expression on his face, but he hadn't yelled or stormed out of the room yet. "Great," he said. "Harry, I want to know all about your chat with Bryce."

What he really meant was *pull up a barstool, son, and start talking.*

Harry had learned Trace's hidden speech, and he sighed as he did what Trace wanted him to do. "I don't know, Dad. I don't know what to think."

Trace started cracking eggs. "He's still a good man."

"Yeah, I know." But Harry sounded pretty dejected.

Trace watched him for a moment, cataloging the

slump of his shoulders. "It all comes down to choices," he said. "You'll find yourself in similar situations." He pointed an unbroken egg at his kid and then Sarah. "Both of you. It comes down to what you decide to do in that moment. Your choices define who you are." He cracked the egg and dropped it into the bowl. "Scrambled eggs okay?"

"Yes, sir," Sarah said.

Trace wanted to talk more about Bryce, but he sensed that Harry needed some alone-time to process before that conversation. He'd gone straight from the dinner with his cousin to Sarah's, to kissing in his kitchen—which Trace also wanted to talk more about.

He glanced over to his boy, who wore a confused expression before he looked up and caught Trace watching him. "Go put something on the TV," he said. "I'll call you over when the food is ready."

Harry got up and gave Trace a quick smile. "Come on, Sarah."

She joined him, her hand slipping into Harry's easily. They looked at each other, and Trace liked how concerned Sarah looked. He couldn't keep his mouth shut, though, so he said, "Sarah?"

She turned back to him, and Trace pointed the fork he'd use to scramble the eggs at Harry. "Have you kissed him before, or was that the first time?"

"Dad," Harry said, his voice heavy with disdain.

Sarah's face turned the color of Santa's suit, and she muttered, "That was the first time, sir."

"Mm." Trace started scrambling. "Are you going to tell your mother, or will I have to?" He looked up in time to see the horror on the girl's face.

"I have a reputation to maintain," Trace said. "Your mother trusts me to keep an eye on you—on both of you. I can't be letting her down."

"No, sir," she mumbled. "I'll tell her."

"Okay," Trace said. "That'll probably be a better conversation than me tattling on you."

Harry rolled his eyes, and Trace wanted to tell him kissing was fine. It was probably exciting, even. He still got excited when Everly let him kiss her.

But they weren't fourteen, and he didn't want to ever call his mother and tell her that another of her grandsons had gotten himself into a predicament the way Bryce had. No, thank you.

So he'd keep his eye on his son and Sarah, and he'd keep himself in check too. He'd help Tex, and work on the music for the band, and do everything he could to love and support Bryce.

Don't forget about Everly, he told himself, and Trace didn't want to admit he had. Of course he hadn't. She was the one shining, bright spot in his life. They didn't argue, and he could relax and find comfort in her arms. She'd planned a movie night for that night with her siblings, and she'd likely call him first thing in the morning to tell him all about it. Her birthday dinner was coming up too.

No, he hadn't forgotten her. There was just a lot to juggle right now, and Trace had tossed her ball really high so he didn't have to think about catching it for a while.

"LET'S TAKE TEN," TEX SAID, AND TRACE immediately hung his guitar and reached for his phone. It had vibrated a couple of times in the past ten minutes, but everyone knew he was in the recording studio.

He expected to see Harry's name on his screen, but it was Bryce. He'd texted a couple of times, and as Trace tapped to read the messages, his phone rang.

Bryce's name sat there, and something in Trace's gut squirmed. He quickly swiped on the call. "Hey, bud," he said. "What's up?"

"Your ex-wife is here," Bryce said.

Trace's blood ran cold, and while Bryce kept talking, Trace didn't hear him. He couldn't see anything but his ex standing outside his house, trying to get to Harry while Trace was recording.

"...sure what you—" Bryce was saying.

"Do not let her in," Trace barked, coming back to himself. "Where are you? Where's Harry?"

He met Luke's eyes, and his brother's eyebrows eyes went up as he offered Trace a water bottle.

He shook his head. "Val's in town. I have to go."

"Go." Luke indicated the door.

Trace didn't waste another moment.

Bryce said, "Harry's in the backyard. He said he didn't want to see her. She's in her car in the driveway. I'm standing at the front window to make sure she doesn't do anything."

"I'm on my way," Trace said as he burst out of the studio. The sun had started to set, but there was still plenty of daylight left. He couldn't *believe* Val had ignored him and Gabe and come to Coral Canyon anyway.

He broke into a jog and said, "If she tries to come into my house or engage my son, call the cops."

"Trace?" Abby called.

He waved her off and kept going. Thankfully, he'd arrived close to last and could get out of his brother's driveway without having to go back to the studio and get someone to move their vehicle.

"See you soon," he said to Bryce, and he ended the call and swung himself into his truck. He backed out and drove off, not bothering to buckle up.

He did as he drove, and then he said, "Hey, Lola, call Gabe Young."

"Calling Gabe Young," his truck echoed back to him.

Gabe's line rang twice before he picked up. "Trace, I need five minutes," he said.

"I don't have five minutes," Trace practically yelled. "Val is at my house right now."

Gabe took a moment and then he said, "Call the police."

"Bryce is there with him."

Gabe sighed, and Trace added, "I'm on my way from the studio."

"I will call her right now," Gabe said. "Do I need to come to Coral Canyon?"

"I don't know," Trace said. "Do you? What can you do?"

"I'll call her and talk to her about a possible restraining order if she violates her custody agreement."

A hint of relief shot through Trace, but he could not relax yet. The call ended, and Trace just drove.

When he finally arrived at his house, a sleek, shiny, black car sat in the driveway. Trace pulled in beside it, but he couldn't see through the tinted windows.

He got out of the truck and moved to open the passenger-side door.

It was locked, and he knocked loudly on the window. His heartbeat banged in the same loud, obnoxious, anxious way.

A door opened, but it wasn't the driver's door. The back door near him opened, and his ex-wife unfolded herself from the vehicle.

"What are you doing here?" He very nearly rolled his eyes at the form-fitting gown she wore. Didn't she know there were no cameras in this town? And did she seriously have a driver?

Trace's phone rang, and he checked it while Val gazed at him, mute. Gabe's name sat there, and he swiped on the call. He did not turn away from his ex. He tapped the speakerphone icon and said, "You're on with me and Val."

"Great," Gabe said breezily. "Then she won't confuse you or herself with the terms of the custody agreement."

"I have a right to see my son," Val finally said.

Trace hadn't heard her voice in such a long time, at least not in person. He glared at her, but Val wasn't a pushover. He should've known she'd come no matter what he or Gabe said.

"You do," Gabe conceded. "But the terms of the agreement specify that you must make arrangements with Trace at least seven days in advance, and Val, you clearly haven't done that."

"I called him last month."

"But you didn't work out a date and time and place," Gabe said. He was so unemotional, and Trace marveled at his calmness in this storm. He himself felt like throwing the phone and then calling the cops.

"Let's work it out now, then."

"Where will you be in seven days?" Trace asked.

Val raised her chin, and that meant she wouldn't be on this continent in seven days. She probably had an hour or two to spare for Harry, and that made Trace want to deny her even more. "My son does not need you to drop by for an hour and grace him with your presence," he growled.

"He is my son too," Val shot back.

"Barely," Trace said. "You *abandoned* him here, Val."

"Trace," Gabe said quietly, and Trace took a deep breath in through his nose. He needed to calm down. He had never confronted Val face-to-face about what she'd done to their child. A human being. One with a good memory and plenty of feelings and emotions.

He'd called her and bawled her out until she'd hung up on him, and that had been that. Until today.

"Why can't you just ask him if I can take him to dinner?"

"If you don't set something up in advance," Gabe said. "Trace has to go along. Or another suitable chaperone."

"This is ridiculous," Val said, a slight accent in her voice Trace had not heard before. "I'm his mother. I'm not going to hurt him."

"You *have* hurt him," Trace said. "Badly, Val. He's in therapy now, and I've been picking up pieces and patching that boy back together since the day you walked out on him."

"I regret some of the things I've done," Val said. "I can't change them. I just want to tell him that."

"Well, too bad," Trace said.

"Dad."

He spun to find Harry coming toward him from the sidewalk that went around the side of the garage.

"Harry, go in the house with Bryce."

His son paused and looked at Trace, and then past him to his mother. "Hey, Mom."

Trace caught the brightness of her smile as he faced her again. She stepped past him, and Trace lost the fight.

She minced across the concrete in her four-inch heels and hugged Harry—who hugged her back. Trace watched them, so many emotions streaming through him.

"Give her an hour," Gabe said, though he couldn't see what was going on. "Maybe she'll leave him alone after that."

"Fine Thanks, Gabe. Sorry to blow up your afternoon."

"It's fine," Gabe said. "Call me if you need me."

Trace would, and he let Gabe end the call before he gripped his phone like he wanted to smash it with his bare hands.

Val stepped away from Harry, and she swiped at her eyes. Harry did not. He looked at Trace, and Trace honestly didn't know what to do. His mental slots were completely full with all he had going on in his life, and Val didn't get to descend on them and demand more from him. An alarm sounded on his phone, and he swiped it away without looking at it.

Val then faced him too. "Will you take us to dinner, Trace?"

He shook his head. "No. But you can come inside, and I'll put a pizza in the oven."

Val hated pizza, but to her credit, she pressed her lips into a fine line and nodded. "Very well."

She turned back to Harry, looped her arm through his,

and they headed for the front door. Trace followed, because he didn't know what else to do.

Harry still hadn't said much about Bryce and how he felt about that situation, and Trace had been giving him space and time to work through things before he forced him to talk about it.

Now, Trace would have to figure out what his son wanted and how he felt about his mother too. Mentally and emotionally, he was exhausted, but he could make it through the next couple of hours. He could, and he would —for Harry.

He spoke little as he fed his son and ex, and thankfully, Val didn't say anything terrible. She told great tales about Europe, things she'd seen and done in the course of her job over the past couple of years.

Harry played and sang for her, for which she applauded loudly and wore sunshine in her face when she hugged him.

She stayed for three hours, then hugged and kissed Harry, nodded to Trace, and left.

As he closed and locked the door behind her, he sagged into the wood and sighed.

It was then that he realized he'd forgotten about the birthday dinner date with Everly.

29

Everly extended her right arm, feeling the movement all the way through the tips of her fingers. The music flowed through her, and she got reminded how much she loved dancing.

She didn't teach competitive dance at her studio, but she'd done it growing up. She'd studied ballet in college, so she did teach little children the ballet basics. After that, she taught swing dancing with partners, and line dancing.

The lights burned brightly in the small studio where she moved through the choreography she'd put together for herself tonight, on her birthday.

Trace had not come to get her for dinner. She'd called and texted him, and he hadn't picked up. She knew he had a lot going on with his son, his brothers, and his band, but it hurt that he hadn't even been able to send a text.

She'd spent the morning at breakfast with Shawn, and

Reggie had come into town this afternoon. In fact, she'd sent him to Shawn's so she could get ready for her hot birthday date with the man she was steadily falling in love with.

Everly turned, her breath coming quicker as she continued to move and feel with her whole body. She loved trying to feel the music and movement with her entire soul, every cell, all of her.

Anything was better than thinking Trace had forgotten about her. About her birthday. About the reservation he'd made at Elements, the new, upscale restaurant that catered to romantic evenings for couples. They didn't take groups bigger than four, and they were an adults-only dining establishment.

Everly had really been looking forward to tonight, and not just for the restaurant. It felt like a pivotal moment in her relationship with Trace. She wasn't sure she could say the words "I love you," out loud to him yet, but she was really, really close.

She wanted to believe he was too, but then he hadn't shown up.

So she'd changed out of her little black dress and heels. She'd come to The Stomp with the goal of choreographing something that would bleed these negative emotions out of her life. Out of her mind. Out of of her body.

Darkness started to take over, and Everly danced. She finished the choreography, and still she danced. She went through it and over it until she felt spent and sweat ran down the side of her face.

Only then did she walk over to the bench and sit down. She lifted the water bottle to her lips and took a long draw on it, her lungs crying for air.

She swallowed and set the bottle down, the absence of the music making the clanking sound of the metal bottle on the wood so loud. Everly bent to pick up her bag, because while she danced without shoes, she needed them to drive home.

She noticed her phone vibrate when she jostled it in the bag, and that meant she'd gotten a text or phone call. She almost didn't want to read it. Trace would have the perfect excuse, and Everly sort of wanted to be upset with him.

The moment he started talking, she'd forgive him. She wasn't sure what that said about her, or about them.

"It says you'll do anything to be with him." Everly reached up and pulled out her ponytail. Her hair fell down around her shoulders and spilled down her back, and her chest tightened as she bent to pull out her sandals.

"You will not cry over him," she told herself. "Mama, I don't want to cry over him."

But you're in love with him, she thought. *It's okay to cry over losing something you love.*

She immediately refuted that thought by telling herself she hadn't lost Trace. Not yet anyway.

"Ev."

She turned at the sound of his voice, her pulse flailing in the vein in her neck. It sent shockwaves through her whole body, and sure enough, her Trace stood there, his cowboy hat in his hands.

He massaged the brim of the hat, the anxiety pouring from him filling the small back room of the studio in less time than it took for Everly's surprise to register inside her.

"What are you doing here?" she asked.

"Well, you weren't home," he said. "I called Shawn, and he said you weren't there." He shrugged one shoulder. "I figured you'd be here." He scanned her from head to toe and back, and Everly stood there, waiting for more.

She clearly wasn't dressed for a date at an exclusive restaurant in town, but Trace was. She loved his dark wash jeans and that navy blue polo that pulled across those sexy shoulders and chest. He wore cowboy boots and still mangled that hat with his big hands.

Everly finally sighed and looked down at the floor. She didn't want to start the conversation; he was the one who'd stood her up. He said nothing, so she asked, "Do you want to break-up?"

"No," he said.

She looked up and straight at him. "You stood me up on my birthday, Trace." He couldn't "my Ev" his way out of this one. "Where were you?"

"Val showed up," he said. "At my house."

The ex-wife. Now Everly felt like an idiot for being

mad at him, just like she'd known she would. "And you couldn't have texted me?"

His jaw jumped, and Everly wanted to rage at him. Tell him to *speak already. Say something!*

She'd take anything but him gazing back at her with that dangerous glint in his eyes. "She's on her way back to Milan tonight," he said. "I swear I won't miss anything with you again."

Everly put one hand on her hip and cocked it. "Trace, you tell me the truth now."

"Yes, ma'am."

"You forgot about our date. True or false?"

He hung his head, so she didn't need him to say it out loud, but he said, "True," anyway.

A stab went through her, and another round of tears filled her eyes.

"Have your feelings for me changed?" she asked, her voice pinched and tinny.

He looked at her. "Not even a little."

Her left eye couldn't hold all the tears, and a thin line of water streaked down her cheek. She made no move to wipe it. "Am I always going to come last in your life?"

"Everly." He moved toward her then, almost like he'd been afraid to before. He tossed his hat onto the bench and cradled her face in one hand. He wiped the tears from the left side of her face and stroked his fingers up and into her hair. "You are on my mind all the time. Every minute. Every hour."

"Except for tonight," she murmured.

"I'll admit I had a lot of other things on my mind tonight," he said. "I'm not going to go into all of them, because I did that on the way here—I ran a red light, I'll have you know—and it all sounded like excuses, even to me." He looked over and watched the motion of his hand as it moved through her hair and came back to her neck, then up to her cheek again.

She loved the touch of this man. She loved the way he looked at her. She loved how he'd driven here tonight to make it right. He hadn't called or texted his excuses. He'd shown up to own them.

"But Ev, tell me I didn't ruin everything. I'll take you to dinner every night for a solid year until we get to this night again, I swear."

"Don't you dare make that promise," she said. "For one, you're going to Nashville in a few weeks, so you won't even be able to keep it."

"I'm going to die in Nashville without you." He leaned his forehead against hers, the moment tender and quiet. Everly forgave him then, just as she'd known she would.

She still said, "My birthdays are very important to me, Trace. I told you that."

"I know," he whispered. "I'm sorry. I'm so sorry. Let me make it up to you."

She didn't want to ask him how he'd do that. The man had endless resources, and she wanted to see what he'd come up with on his own.

"You never answered my question," she said.

"No," he said. "You're not going to come last all the time." He pulled back and looked at her. "I promise you that, Everly."

She nodded and asked, "How do you know?"

"Because," he said. "I'm falling in love with you, and I want you to be the top priority in my life."

"After Harry," she said.

"Sometimes, yes," he said. "Like tonight, which was super poor timing on my ex-wife's part. I just.... Truthfully, I got lost tonight. I was so angry she was here, and trying to make sure Harry was protected, and then he came outside, and the night just imploded."

Everly wrapped her arms around him and held him. "Dance with me, cowboy," she whispered, and they started to sway back and forth together. The silence draped over them, and Everly could admit she wanted him in her life, even if she didn't always come first.

His phone chimed, and he said, "Come on, my Ev. Dinner's ready."

"Dinner?" She stepped out of his arms, and he bent to pick up her bag for her.

"Yep." He gave her a smile. "Did you eat without me?"

She tilted her head and gave him her best *Really?* look. Trace chuckled, and Everly adored the sound of that too.

"Where are we going?"

"We're stopping by somewhere to pick up the food, and then we're going to my place," he said. "Harry's there,

341

but he said he wouldn't mind seeing you." Trace gave her a winning smile then. "He even has a gift for you for your birthday."

"At least someone does," she said dryly.

Trace brought her flush against his body, and heat filled her instantly. She wanted to kiss him and hold him and tell him she was falling in love with him too.

"Who says I don't have something for you?" he asked.

"Do you?"

"Yeah," he said. "It's in the truck." He started to turn, but Everly grabbed onto his arm.

He turned back to her, and her heartbeat started to throb in the back of her throat. "Trace," she said. "I don't care about birthday gifts."

His eyebrows went up. That sparkle entered his eyes. "Oh?"

"I just want you," she said, the words nearly catching on themselves. "I want you to kiss me and hold me and dance with me. I want you to play your guitar for me, and call me when you have to travel for work. I want you to tell me everything about Harry, Tex, Otis, all of them. I want to tell you about my family too. I want us to be okay."

He took her into his arms again. "We're okay, Ev."

"Good." She looked up at him and wrapped her arms around the back of his neck. "Because I'm falling in love with you too."

His smile spread slowly across his face. He didn't say anything else before he leaned down and kissed her, and

Everly knew in that moment that she didn't need fancy dinners or perfect dates to fall in love.

She wanted them, but she didn't need them. Trace was who and what she needed, and she kissed him back with the same passion she felt coming from him.

He didn't kiss her too long, much to her disappointment. When he pulled away, he said, "Elements isn't going to hold our food for long, sweetheart. Let's get dinner and we can pick this up at my place, okay?"

Everly nodded, the taste of him still on her lips. "You ordered from Elements? I didn't think you could do that."

"You can't," he said. "I called in a favor."

"To who?"

"You don't want to know," he said with an edge of darkness in his tone.

"Oh, now I really do," Everly said. She stepped into her sandals and went with him toward the back exit.

He glanced over to her. "Blaze, actually. He's sort of been texting your friend, Faith, and she knows the new chef at Elements. She called him, and he agreed to do the meals for pick-up."

Everly shook her head, her eyes wide. She flipped off the lights and locked the door on the way out. "Let's back up to the part where your brother is texting one of my friends."

Faith hadn't dated in a while, at least according to Everly's knowledge. She'd been pouring everything she had—all her time, energy, and money—into Hole in One.

"What? You don't think Blaze is good enough for Faith?"

"I think they're complete opposites," Everly said.

"Yeah, that's what he said too." Trace opened her door and when she sat in his passenger seat, he added, "I don't much care who he dates or doesn't date. I know it's not the same, but I got you some great food, and we're going to eat it together."

"You're missing out on my little black dress."

He licked his lips. "There's always tomorrow night."

"Hm, you might be jumping the gun, cowboy. Let's see how tonight goes before I agree to another date."

He smiled and pulled open the glove compartment. He reached inside and took out a rectangular package. "Happy birthday, my Ev."

She took the gold-foil wrapped package and beamed at it and then him. She tore off the paper to find a box containing a digital picture frame.

She looked up at him, and he took it from her wordlessly. He opened it and pulled out the frame, which was a deep, dark wood. He pressed the button on the side, and the frame brightened.

He turned it toward her, and Everly's gasp filled the whole sky. Tears came instantly again. She grabbed the frame from him and brought it closer to her, as if the shining, smiling faces of her parents weren't real.

"I called Reg and Shawn," Trace said quietly. "Collected some pictures from them."

The picture of her mama and daddy dissolved into another one, this time of Trace and Harry, the two of them wearing backpacks as they hiked somewhere here in the Tetons.

"This is amazing," she whispered, and she pressed the picture frame to her chest and leaned forward to kiss him again. "Thank you," she whispered against his lips.

"Happy birthday," he said again. While it hadn't gone exactly as she'd hoped, Everly realized that it had gone exactly right.

30

Blaze entered the kitchen to find Harry and Cash had already made breakfast.

"Waffles," Harry said with a smile. Blaze marveled that the boy could actually make waffles, as Blaze wasn't sure he could accomplish such a feat.

"Coffee too, Dad," Cash said. "I made it, and Harry said it tasted okay."

Blaze's eyebrows went up as he turned to get a mug out of the cupboard. He'd pour himself a cup of coffee to be nice, but if it wasn't good, he wouldn't drink it.

"You drink coffee?" he asked Harry as he faced the boys again. Trace had gone to Nashville with Country Quad, and the band had timed the trip so that they could return with a week before school started.

Blaze had Harry staying with him and Cash, and Luke had left Corrine with Momma. Tex and Otis had wives to look after their children, and Blaze's heart shrunk one size as he thought of Faith.

He shoved her out of his mind, knowing she wouldn't go very far for very long. He cocked his eyebrows at Harry.

"No," Harry said. "I just tasted it to make sure he wasn't going to poison you. It tastes like what my daddy makes."

Blaze nodded and poured the dark liquid into his mug. It smelled normal, and he took his time stirring in sugar. "Therapy today for both of you," he said, not really asking.

"Can we go get that ham and egg French toast thing after?" Cash asked.

"You're eatin' breakfast right now," Blaze said. It wasn't the money he didn't want to spend, but the time. Everyone in Coral Canyon stared at him whenever he went out to restaurants or stores, and he'd milked his back surgery to the point of embarrassment. After all, he didn't need Tex to do his grocery shopping anymore.

Once the news of Bryce had come out, Blaze had asked Luke and Mav to do it, as Tex had a lot going on in his personal life. So did Otis and Trace, who was trying to keep their oldest brother comforted and sane, run the family and the band, and deal with Everly.

He'd forgotten her birthday when his ex-wife had shown up in town, and while Trace had been doing a lot for Blaze, he hadn't gone to him to add more to his plate.

It was ridiculous that Blaze couldn't do his own grocery shopping; he could. He simply didn't want to.

Everyone stared, and he supposed his online fame fueled that. Having Jem in town hadn't helped, as the man didn't have nearly the forked tongue Blaze did, nor the dark-eyed look that warned people away from him. In fact, Jem laughed, talked, and took pictures with anyone and everyone in town, and he'd set a precedent Blaze would not and could not keep up with.

"But we could have it for lunch," Cash said. "My appointment is done at twelve-thirty."

"I'm done before that," Harry said. "Is it the Croque Madame at Breakfast Brothers? Aunt Dani says that place is awesome, but my dad won't go there."

"Why's that?" Blaze lifted his mug to his lips and sipped his coffee. It was good, and he smiled at Cash as he lowered the drink. "This is good, son."

Cash beamed, and Blaze wished his praise wasn't so important to his son. At the same time, he was thrilled his twelve-year-old—who'd be thirteen in a couple of weeks— was still interested in what his father thought.

Harry shrugged. "He says it's frou-frou food."

Blaze burst out laughing, because that sounded like something Trace would say. He liked red meat and pota- toes, but he suspected Trace would take Everly to Break- fast Brothers if she wanted him to. Blaze *knew* he would.

Just like you would take Faith there if she wanted to go.

Well, that thought wasn't quite true. Blaze didn't want to go *out* with Faith. He wanted her to bring dinner to him. She'd seemed on-board with the idea when he'd texted her about it. They'd talked on the phone about it too. Faith had seemed excited about the forthcoming date, even if working out the schedule had been a bit tenuous in the beginning.

Then, the night she was supposed to stop by the Mexican restaurant where Blaze had called in the order and paid for it, Faith had texted to say she couldn't make it.

Blaze had asked her why not, and she hadn't answered. The next night, he'd asked her if they could reschedule, and she hadn't answered.

Last night, he'd finally texted her again, asking her what he'd done wrong. And she hadn't answered yet again.

Three strikes, and Blaze felt like Faith had struck him out. It had happened to him before, and he'd never cared all that much.

With Faith, though, Blaze cared. He wanted to know what he'd done wrong and how he could fix it. He had a plan in mind, but it required him to move outside his comfort zone and confront the woman, and he wasn't sure she was in a place where she'd appreciate him doing that.

"Please, Dad?" Cash asked. "You're always talking about how awesome French toast is with all this extra stuff, and now we have a place here like that."

Blaze smiled at his son. "All right. Harry and I will be waiting right outside for you when you're done with Miss Hannah today."

Cash cheered, and Blaze herded his kid into the shower after he finished breakfast. Harry retreated to the couch, his fingers flying over his phone, and Blaze wondered for a brief moment if he could talk to his nephew about Faith.

He quickly rejected the idea, as hardly anyone knew about his covert cellphone affair with the gorgeous food truck owner. Really only Trace and Everly, and Blaze considered calling his brother's girlfriend. He'd done her a favor by being her dance partner during her demo a couple of months ago, the least she could do was help him understand Faith Cromwell a little bit more.

He waited until he'd dropped Harry at his counselor's office, then driven down the block to Cash's. He walked his son inside and waited with him until the boy got called back.

Then Blaze did his exercise duty by heading out for a walk. He'd simply go up and down Main Street until Harry finished.

With his heartbeat throbbing in his temples, he dialed Everly.

"Blaze Young," she said in a playful voice that made Blaze smile. "What are you doing, calling me?"

"I have a favor," he said.

"All right."

"It's about a friend of yours." His throat felt like he'd swallowed sand. "Uh, Faith Cromwell?"

"Yeah," Everly prompted, obviously not keen on making this conversation easier for him.

"I guess I just need some insight," he said. "We, uh, had a date set, and she backed out last minute. I've texted her a few times since, but I've gotten only silence back. We'd talked about me paying to fix that food truck she lost at your event, and I know she took it into the shop last week."

He took a big breath, once again trying to reason through his plan. "I guess I'm wondering if I can stop by the shop and pay for it now, before she won't let me, and if I do, if she'll be upset with me for doing that."

Everly exhaled, and Blaze didn't think that was a good sign. "I don't know, Blaze."

"That makes two of us."

"She didn't say why she couldn't make the date?"

"She said something had come up at work."

"Hmm."

"Yeah." Blaze had felt like the reason was an excuse, and it was as bad as Faith saying she couldn't stop by a restaurant and get dinner and bring it to him because she had to wash her hair.

"Do I just stop by one of her trucks and pray she's the one running it?" He'd do that too. He had thirty-five minutes before Harry finished his appointment, and he could wait a few extra minutes if he had to.

"I can tell you which one she's at," Everly said. "She

runs the social media, so the most recent pictures are from the truck she's manning."

"Okay," Blaze said. "I can look it up."

"She's at the Canyon View Trailhead," Everly said, obviously already looking. "Her last picture was from seven minutes ago."

"All right," he said. "Thanks, Everly."

"Can I still bring dinner tonight?" she asked. "Harry and I have a date, and I wanted you and Cash to double with us."

He grinned at the way Everly wanted to spend time with Trace's son. He could only hope that the woman he found would find a way to love Cash too.

The boy was getting easier and easier to parent, as they both got to know each other better and better. As Blaze figured out how to be a father, and Cash learned that he had better ways to deal with his feelings other than fighting and anger.

Blaze had even been praying for the past week or so that Cash would get a just-right teacher for him this year, and that seventh grade wouldn't be as difficult as sixth had been. And if it was, Blaze felt more equipped to handle it this year.

"We're expecting you tonight, yes," Blaze said. "I appreciate it, Everly."

"Of course," she said as if she was family already. Blaze suspected she would be soon enough, as Trace had liked her for a good long time now. From what Blaze knew and had seen of the two of them, they got along really well, and Trace definitely looked at her with pure adoration in his eyes.

"Blaze," she said. "Faith is...."

He waited, because he really wanted to know what Everly would say about her.

"She sometimes gets in her own way when she's scared," Everly said. "And I love you to death—you know I do—but you're a little terrifying in the beginning."

Blaze's teeth pressed together as he nodded. "Yeah, I know." He did know. He'd spent a lifetime perfecting his bad boy persona, being the dark horse on the rodeo circuit, the party cowboy, the wild child of the Young family.

He *knew* that part.

The problem was, he didn't want to be that man anymore. He didn't want to play that part.

He wanted to find himself and be that man. Maybe that was part of his problem—he didn't quite know who he was yet. So he didn't quite know how to talk to Faith or how to present himself to her.

"Thanks, Ev," he said. "I'll see you tonight, okay?"

"Will I get a report on how it goes? You're going to the trailhead, right?"

Blaze had already turned around to head back to his truck. He didn't know where Canyon View Trailhead was, but he had a map app that could get him there. "Depends on how it goes," he said.

"I'll say a quick prayer for you," she said.

Blaze's throat narrowed, and he nodded. She couldn't see him, so he forced out another, "Thank you," and let her end the call.

The trailhead was up the canyon from his house, and he made the drive as quickly as he could. By the time he got there, he had less than ten minutes before he needed to turn around and get back to town in order to pick up the boys.

The Hole in One truck sat near the trailhead, and a handful of people milled about. The bright pink vehicle with lots of colored sprinkles wasn't the same one he'd seen at The Stomp, and this truck looked much newer and in much better condition. That made his heart take courage as he approached the ordering window.

He caught sight of Faith, and he suddenly wanted to high-tail it back to his truck. When she saw him, she wouldn't be happy.

She finished with the couple at the window, stepped to the side to put their order slip up, and returned, her smile already fixed in place.

Someone must be working the truck with her, Blaze thought, and he told himself he wouldn't be going into the narrow area inside the truck to offer his help.

Her eyes landed on him, and the chattering of the birds fell away. The people around him disappeared. The scent of hot oil and sugary doughnuts faded into the background.

There was only Faith and her wide, gorgeous, hazel

eyes. That pretty red hair. The high cheekbones and perfectly pink lips.

Oh, he'd lost hours thinking about those lips.

He forced himself to step up to the truck. "Howdy, Faith."

She said nothing, the pen she'd had poised now almost hanging out of her hand.

"I'll take the salty cowboy," he said. "And I'd love to know why you won't text me back." He swallowed, wishing he had something he could play with to keep his hands busy. "If I did something to upset you, I apologize. I miss you already, and I just want to make things right between us."

A man stepped to her side at that moment, and Blaze switched his gaze to him.

"Sorry," the man said. "Faith, we're out of bacon." He cut a look to Blaze. "We have to take the salty cowboy off the menu."

"Thanks, Joe," she murmured.

Joe nodded and looked at Blaze for another moment before he retreated back to the fryers.

"So no salty cowboy," Blaze said with an over-exaggerated sigh. "What would you suggest instead?" He backed up a little and looked at her menu. He didn't care about getting a doughnut. He might not even eat it. He just wanted the woman to talk to him. He noted, regrettably, that she still hadn't done that.

"The Elvis Presley is similar," she said. "It's salted peanuts, caramel, and banana."

"I'll take that," he said. He reached into his back pocket and extracted his wallet. "I can drive now. I'll come pick you up all Wyoming-proper and take you to dinner anywhere you want."

He tossed his credit card on the slim counter in front of him. Faith didn't move to pick it up. He met her eyes, and Blaze had seen women look at him like she was.

She liked him. At the very least, she was attracted to him. Before, his chest would swell and his pride got fed.

Now, he simply wanted her to agree to a date, though he knew now that was only half the battle.

"I have to say, though," he continued. *Bless her to talk to me*, he prayed. *Please, Lord. What do I say here? Why won't she talk to me?*

She'd had no issue texting and talking on the phone with him.

"I'm not sure my heart can handle it if this stunningly smart and gorgeous business owner I have this *massive* crush on stands me up again."

Faith ducked her head, but Blaze still caught a glimmer of a smile on her face.

"I will have to know why this beautiful girl backed out last minute." He nudged his card closer to her, and she finally picked it up. "It might not be easy for her to talk to me, but I think I'm a pretty nice guy. I'll just listen and try to do better if I did something wrong."

Faith ran his card and while it processed, she looked at him. "You didn't do anything wrong."

Blaze's eyebrows went up. "No?"

She shook her head. "I let my mind run away from me."

"Mm." He took his card back when she extended it to him. "I wonder how we can make sure that doesn't happen again. Maybe you can just text me what's going through your mind, and I'll tell you if you're right or wrong about me."

"Maybe." She turned around and picked up the doughnuts sitting there. Blaze moved out of the way a step so she could hand out the orders, but he wasn't leaving until he had a date on the calendar with this woman. Once she'd done that, since there weren't more customers waiting to order, he took the spot in front of the window again. "Tonight?" he asked. "I mean, I've got another woman coming over, but I can cancel that date."

Faith's face went blank, and she blinked. Blaze laughed. "It's Trace's girlfriend. She's bringing dinner for the boys. She's trying to spend more time with Harry and all that."

Faith relaxed and rolled her eyes. "You think you're so funny."

"I am," Blaze said, his grin wide and genuine. "But if you don't like these jokes, I have others."

She slid her hands out onto the shelf, and Blaze automatically lifted his to cover hers. "Blaze," she said. "You don't have to change who you are for me."

"Good," he said. "Because I'm still figuring out who I am now that I'm not in the rodeo." He squeezed her hands. "Everly's coming by about six. I can leave when she arrives and be at your place five minutes later. I really will take you anywhere you want."

She nodded, a hint of a blush making her sexy freckles stand out across her face. "All right, cowboy," she said. "I'll see you just after six."

Blaze floated away from the doughnut truck, and he was all the way back to the office building where Harry waited on the curb before he remembered he hadn't even picked up the Elvis Presley doughnut he'd paid for.

31

Everly snapped a picture of Harry's new shoes, her smile as wide as the Teton Mountain Range. "Your daddy is going to love those."

Harry wore the brightest smile on his face, but Trace would definitely not love the shoes. Everly did though, and she couldn't erase the grin as she tapped out a quick message to her boyfriend, who was currently in Nashville with his band.

Your son is going to break hearts this year.

She looked up from the phone to find Harry sitting down, taking off the shoes. "You want them, right?"

"I mean, kinda."

Everly pocketed her phone and went to sit by him. "What does that mean? Kinda?"

He gave her a look out of the corner of his eye. "I mean, I like them. I think they're cool, but I don't actually see myself wearing them." He started to pull on his cowboy boots. "They don't feel like me."

Everly nodded, not sure what to say. "What do you wear? Boots all the time?"

"I like cowboy boots," he said. He looked fully at her. "What's wrong with my cowboy boots?"

She smiled at him and reached up and brushed his long hair out of his face. "Nothing," she said. "They're perfect for you."

"I wear running shoes to school sometimes," he said.

Everly shook her head, her smile fading. "No, you don't. And you don't have to."

He dropped his head and tugged on the other boot. "I know I'm not a real cowboy, but I sure do like goin' out to Uncle Tex's and taking care of the horses. I like the line dancing, and we all wear cowboy boots to that. And I don't know." He stood up and picked up the box of shoes, already looking around for the clerk who'd pulled them from the back room.

Everly joined him and hitched her purse up higher on her shoulder. "You don't know what?"

"I like playing the guitar," he mumbled. "My dad's this big country music star, and while he hangs up his hat sometimes, he never wears anything but cowboy boots."

Everly smiled again, the image of Trace in her mind so clear and so perfect. "That he does not."

After Harry had given back the shoes, Everly herded

him toward the exit. "So we should be over at Bob's Boots. Why didn't you just tell me?"

"I wanted to try them on," Harry said. "We have time, right? My haircut isn't until this afternoon."

She linked her arm through his. "We have all the time in the world, Harry. But Bob's is over here." She led him down the row of shops, as Coral Canyon didn't have a mall. Just lots of little shops scattered along what Everly would label downtown. Thankfully, Bob's sat on the same block as the more athletic shoe store, and it was right next to Millicent's, which was where Everly was hoping to convince Harry to stop for lunch.

Since Trace had been so busy finalizing the album before his trip to Nashville, he hadn't taken Harry to do anything he needed to do before school started next week. When Everly had learned that the boy needed a few new pairs of jeans, some new boots, and a haircut, she'd volunteered to take him.

She wasn't the only "mom" out with her kids that Saturday, and one step inside Bob's Boots had her second-guessing their plan. "Oh."

"Welcome," a woman drawled at them. "We're a bit full this morning, so we're calling numbers." She handed one to Everly. "Once your number gets called, then you can enter the aisles. This will help us serve our customers in the fastest, best way possible."

"Okay," Everly said, looking down at the number. It was sixty-four. The door behind them opened as another customer wanted to come in, and Everly grabbed onto Harry and moved further into the store. "Maybe Saturday wasn't such a great idea."

"They have pocketknives here," Harry said. "I'm gonna go look at those, okay?"

"Okay." She didn't know Trace's personal stance on knives, but she figured it didn't hurt to look. She hovered near the boot aisles, which took up seventy percent of the store, waiting for a number to be called so she'd know how long she had to wait.

"Fifty-nine," a man finally said, and she relaxed slightly. The next few numbers got called almost in succession, and Everly turned to find Harry as they only had one number ahead of theirs now. She had no idea where the pocketknives were, but she found the tall, dark-haired boy easily enough.

He stood with a couple of other teens—boys his age for sure. She recognized a couple of them from her line dancing classes, and then she recognized the deep flush crawling up Harry's neck.

Since there wasn't a line, and Everly didn't need to stand here, she headed in his direction.

"...just saying," one of the boys said. "It took you months to kiss Sarah." He laughed like taking a while to kiss a girl was uncommon or stupid.

Everly's maternal instincts rose within her, but she paused out of Harry's sight.

"Shut up, Dave," Harry said. "Not all of us go around kissin' everyone."

"What about Miss Trebel?" Dave said as if Harry hadn't even spoken. "I wouldn't mind kissing her."

"Gross," another boy said. "She's our English teacher, man."

"Yeah, and I wonder if she knows any French." Dave laughed like he was the funniest boy in the world. Everly wanted to wrap her slim fingers around his throat and tell him to stop talking.

"Or our line dance teacher," another boy—Randall —said.

Everly's heartbeat started to pounce up her throat until it throbbed against the back of her tongue.

"No," Harry practically growled. He put the knife in his hand back on the display. "Don't say anything about Miss Everly."

"Miss Everly?" Dave laughed again, and the other boys joined in.

"She's really nice," Harry said. "And my dad's girl-friend, and I don't want to listen to you talk about kissing her. It's demeaning."

"Whatever, man." Dave laughed. "You're just jealous your old man got her before you."

"She's a real person," Harry said, his fingers curling into fists. "Not some fantasy object for meatheads like you."

Everly started moving again just as Harry turned around. One of the boys put his hand on Harry's shoulder, but he shrugged him off about the time he saw her coming his way. Panic filled his eyes as they widened, but Everly did not care. She'd heard rumors that some of her junior high students had crushes on her. She'd thought it cute...until now.

This was not cute. They were sexualizing her—and other women.

She handed him the slip of paper with the number on it. "It's almost our turn," she said, trying to communicate with him with only her eyes. "Go wait over there so we don't miss it, okay?"

"Miss Everly," he said.

"Go on," she said with a smile. "I'll be fine."

Harry had taken the paper, but he didn't "go on." He turned to watch her as she walked past him, her goal to put these boys in their place. They'd all seen her talk to Harry just now, and to their credit, they each looked like they might throw up.

"Boys," she said pleasantly as she stopped a couple of paces from them. "Getting new boots for school?" None of them had parents with them, so she doubted it.

No one said a word, and Everly closed the distance between her and them. "You should be ashamed of yourselves, talking about girls like they just exist to please you."

"Miss Everly," Randall started.

She silenced him with a sharp look. "I've heard enough from you, Randall. You have your mama call me if you want to sign up for classes again." She nodded at him, noting that he'd turned the color of a boiled lobster and hung his head. "In fact." She shook her hair over her shoulders and stood as tall as she could—which was not taller than any of these boys.

"None of you are allowed to re-enroll in any of my classes without your parents coming in to see me first. My studio is a safe place—for me and others—and you've broken that rule."

"You can't—" Dave started, but Everly gave him a look that muted his voice.

"I hope to see you all in class again," she said. "But not with this current attitude." She took one more step toward them and hoped they could feel the fire on her breath when she said, "And if you give that boy any more grief about kissing his girlfriend, you'll have to answer to me. Just. Don't."

She pointed at Dave, nearly striking him in the chest, before she turned and walked away. She didn't care if they liked her. She didn't care if she'd just lost four or five spots in her teen line dancing class.

"Come on, baby." She linked her arm through Harry's as she went by him. "I hope we didn't miss our number."

"You didn't have to do that," he said, stumbling along beside her for a moment. "I handled it."

She looked up at him. "Yes, you did. You did really well." She refused to look over her shoulder. "Are they really your friends?"

"No," he said. "The one boy is Sarah's brother though."

Everly blinked at him. "Oh, well, that's awkward then."

"Nah, he's okay," Harry said. "It's mostly Dave, and then Randall can't help himself. He has to have Dave think he's cool. The others...I don't know why they laugh when he does."

"Was it Dave who gave you a hard time the first time your dad and I went out?"

Harry nodded, his jaw clenching.

"Well." She didn't know what else to say. "Let's just hope you can get the boots you like here."

"Sixty-four," the man called, and Harry held up the slip.

"I will," he said. "I love everything they have here."

Everly followed along after that, letting Harry pick out the things he liked and try them on. In the end, it came down to two pairs, and when he couldn't decide, she said they should get them both.

"Both?" Harry acted like he didn't understand the concept.

"Yeah," Everly said, picking up the second box of boots. "Both. You have more than one pair of boots, don't you?"

"No," Harry said.

"No?"

"Why would I need more than one pair?" he asked. "If I'm not wearin' them, I don't need them."

"Oh, honey." She placed one palm against his chest. "You know your daddy has money, right?" She grinned at him while he rolled his eyes. "I can't wait to see how having two pairs of boots changes your life."

She glanced over to the check-out line, and it wasn't short either. "Now, come on," she said. "It's a busy shopping day, and by the time we get out of here, I want to go to Millicent's to hopefully beat the lunch rush. Then we'll go get the jeans you want before your haircut."

At lunch, she took a selfie of her and Harry and sent that to Trace too, and this time, he answered.

Hate the shoes.

Love that one with you and Harry. Are you having fun?

Having fun didn't accurately describe the day for Everly, but she typed out, *So much fun,* anyway. She wasn't doing him a favor or pretending at a role. To Everly, she wanted to be part of this family—part of Harry and Trace's family—and this shopping trip was her first experience truly doing that.

It was way more than fun.

It was crucial. It was beautiful. It was everything she'd ever wanted—just like Trace was, and she smiled quietly at her phone while she asked him how things were going in Nashville.

32

Otis frowned as he pulled up to Mav's house. There were far too many trucks here for this to be a simple family dinner with the two of them, as Mav had led him to believe. "We're not the only ones here," he said to his wife.

Georgia looked over to him, the weariness already in her face. "Do you want to stay?"

Otis looked in the rearview mirror at Joey. His beautiful daughter. Guilt cut through him that he wanted another child, as if she wasn't enough for him.

She was, and Otis pushed the damaging thoughts away. "I'm okay to stay." He put the truck in park. "You? I'm sure Dani would keep Roo if we want to slip out." He wasn't having as hard of a time with things as Georgia, and he'd like to spend time with his brothers and their significant others today.

Thankfully, Georgia shook her head. "I'm okay to go in."

Otis would keep an eye on her. She'd likely glue herself to Abby and Dani anyway, and if Trace had brought Everly, her too. She and Georgia were friends, as they both owned and ran businesses on Main Street. Not only that, but Georgia was actually very good at telling Otis what she wanted and needed, and they'd skipped a few family things this summer simply by her looking at him a certain way.

He'd hated being in Nashville for the past couple of weeks, but Country Quad had needed to meet in person with the music executives at King Country.

The album had been finalized. Finally.

The songs were locked in. Finally.

Cover art was in progress. Finally.

The summer tour would start next Memorial Day and last through Labor Day, and the marketing team would keep Morris and ultimately the band in the loop as far as stops, travel schedules, and more. Otis was already planning to bring Joey and Georgia on tour with him for the whole summer, and that would require his wife to make arrangements for someone else to run her bookshop here in Coral Canyon.

Bryce came out onto the porch, his phone up at his ear. He raised his hand to Otis and Georgia, and Joey said, "I'm going in, Daddy."

"Okay, Roo," he said brightly. "We're right behind

you." He smiled his nine-year-old out of the truck, noting that both Tex and Bryce had their vehicles here. Mav's family would be inside, of course, and Trace's big black beast was parked down the row a bit.

Another truck Otis didn't recognize sat beside it, and then a shiny, dark blue SUV—which totally didn't fit in here. At the same time, Otis knew the vehicle. "Gabe's here," he said, quickly switching his gaze back to the house and frowning. "Why would Gabe be here?"

"He talks to Mav a lot," Georgia said.

"But Morris isn't here." The twins rarely did anything without the other, especially now that Morris and Leigh were remarried and living happily here in Coral Canyon.

"Let's go in, baby," she said. "They're going to think we're going to bolt if we sit out here for much longer."

"Yeah." Otis got out of the truck and went around to join his wife. He took her hand with a smile and said, "You're the most beautiful woman in the world."

She grinned back at him, and Otis caught a glimmer of the woman who laughed with him. Who bought the most perfect birthday gifts for everyone in his family and inner circle, almost effortlessly. Who knew the precise book for every patron who walked into her bookshop, and who loved to watch the cows graze in fields after church every single Sunday.

Otis loved her deeply, and he hated it when she hurt. He hurt too, but he'd been rising up and up and up lately, feeling like the Lord knew him and Georgia and their situation, and that He had everything in His hands.

Georgia was recovering more slowly, but she talked to him about everything, and to Otis, that was all that mattered. A silent Georgia was not good, and thankfully, she hadn't gone quiet on him.

No one came out to greet them, and Bryce had gone inside with Joey. Otis didn't bother knocking, and he found plenty of people crowded into Mav and Dani's gourmet kitchen, trays of appetizers and finger foods out on the countertop and the big dining room table.

"Otis," Trace said, and a few of the conversations stopped. Not all of them, but enough for it to be noticeable. Trace took Otis into a hug, and Otis pounded his older brother on the back.

"What's goin' on?" he asked. He found Mav watching him, his just-younger-than-him brother coming forward already. "You said this would be a quiet dinner with our families."

"Well, it's a dinner with our families," Mav said as he hugged Otis. "It got a little out of hand, that's all."

"I'll say." Otis smiled as he pulled out of Mav's embrace. He didn't mind the extras. It felt good to be here with a lot of his family. "Where's Morris and Leigh?"

"Oh, Eric has a cough," Mav said. "They didn't want to come get all the kids sick before school starts." He leaned closer to Otis, who bent toward him. "Which I can't wait for. The kids are driving me nuts this year."

Otis chuckled, because nothing every really ruffled Mav. In fact, if he got upset, something *serious* had gone down.

Tex laughed from the other side of the kitchen, and that did Otis's heart some real good. His oldest brother had been so melancholy in recent weeks, and that put a damper on everything. It was interesting to see how much influence Tex had over the rest of the family, and while Trace had stepped up and handled a lot with the band, and a lot with Bryce, with grace and power—just like Tex would've—he simply wasn't Tex.

In some ways, Trace was more powerful than Tex in how he didn't say everything, but only exactly what had to be said. In other ways, Trace would always be a prince while Tex was born to be king. Otis knew he was way down the line as far as royalty went, but he loved his role in his family.

"How's Georgia?" Trace asked, and Otis blinked away from Tex and Gabe.

"Good," he said, finding her over by Abby, Georgia, and Everly, as he'd predicted. "I assume Joey went downstairs?" He didn't see any of the kids up here in the kitchen area, not even Harry.

"Yep," Mav said. "Skipped right on down, as usual."

Tex shifted to his right, and another woman stepped into the space he'd created for her. Otis pulled in a breath. "Whoa. Bailey McAllister is here?" He looked at Trace with wide eyes, then switched his gaze to Mav. "Are she and Bryce getting back together?"

"They're not really apart," Mav said.

"But they're not really together either," Trace said.

"That makes no sense," Otis said. He frowned at the woman across the room, and she looked up and right at him. He instantly tried to clear the confusion from his face and offer her a smile. If she was to be part of the family, he didn't want to be the one to scare her away.

It wouldn't be him anyway. Luke or Blaze or even Jem had a much darker look about them than Otis, that was for sure. And none of them were here, he noted.

Still, Bailey looked at him with plenty of apprehension in her gaze, as did Tex and Abby. In that moment, Otis realized that everyone here knew something he didn't. This was no friendly family dinner.

This was an intervention.

Bryce stepped up to Bailey and said something. She ducked her head to hear him, and that broke the connection between her and Otis.

He instantly stepped in front of Trace. "Tell me what's happening right now," he said.

Trace swallowed, and that didn't ease Otis's worries. "It's not bad, Otis."

"It better not be," Otis said. "Or I'm taking my amazing wife, and we're leaving." He glared at Trace and then Mav. "Tell me. Now."

"Bryce wants to talk to you about the baby," Mav said.

His words made no sense, especially spoken as gently as they were. He put his hand on Otis's shoulder and pushed him around to face the rest of the family. They'd all fallen silent.

"Let's sit down and eat," Dani said. "Everyone, come on. Mav, get over here and say grace, and everyone grab a plate, fill it up, and find a place to sit."

General commotion started then, but Otis didn't move a muscle. Trace stayed right at his side, and no one from Tex's family would look at him. Not Tex or Abby, not Bryce or Bailey.

Bryce wants to talk to you about the baby.

What did that mean?

Otis bowed his head while Mav prayed; he let others go through the line to get food before him, and he only went when Trace nudged him to do so. He was one of the last, and it was once again clear that he was being set up. Well, him and Georgia.

She sat right in the middle of the big table, with an empty spot on her right and Abby on her left. Bryce and Bailey sat directly across from her and where Otis would obviously sit, and Gabe had taken the chair next to Otis.

Conversations peppered the silence until everyone had their food and had sat down. Otis looked at Georgia, and she seemed perfectly at-ease. How, he didn't know. Something stunk here, and he wasn't going to take a single bite until he knew what it was.

"You're not going to eat?" Gabe asked. "These are

pepper jack mac and cheese bites from Halifax in Jackson." He popped one crispy bite into his mouth. "You love these."

"What's happening here, Gabe?" Otis asked. Sure enough, Gabe's eyes flew across the table to Bryce, and Otis followed his gaze. "Bryce?"

Silence draped over the table now, with only the occasional scrape of a utensil against a plate. Bryce wiped his mouth and looked first at Bailey at his side, who nodded, and his father, who did the same. Tex wore the fiercest look of determination Otis had ever seen, and the left side of his jaw jumped with tension.

"Someone better tell me what's going on," Otis said. "Like, right now."

"Otis, honey," Georgia said.

"No," he said. "They're up to something, and I don't like it." He glared at everyone on the opposite side of the table. Everly, Trace, Bailey, Bryce, and Tex.

He and Georgia, Abby, Mav and Dani, and Gabe sat on this side of the table.

No one under the age of eighteen had joined them, besides baby Melissa, and Otis should've scented something was off earlier.

"Uncle Otis," Bryce said, his voice rusty and too quiet. He cleared his throat. "There's not an easy way to say this, and it's not a bad thing anyway. I'm just nervous." He looked at his dad again, and Tex covered Bryce's hand with his own and squeezed.

Watching Tex parent Bryce through this hard time had been an extraordinary experience for Otis. His older brother had shown him what unconditional love looked like, and forgiveness, and acceptance, and strength.

Bryce's eyes burned with a fire Otis had only seen when he was passionate about something—his horse rescue ranch and playing the guitar. "Uncle Otis, Bailey and I aren't going to keep the baby. We want you and Georgia to adopt it."

Georgia sucked in a gasp of air at his side, her hand suddenly clawing at his arm. Otis could barely feel it. He hadn't heard right. Surely he hadn't heard his nephew say he wanted to *give his baby* to him and Georgia.

"Can you do that?" he asked. He looked at Gabe, his eyes taking in more than they ever had before. He suddenly knew why Gabe was there. How he'd missed the manila folder under his brother's plate, he'd never know.

Gabe slid it out and handed it to Otis. "Of course we can do that, Otis. It would be an open adoption, and people give babies to whoever they want all the time." He glanced over to the other side of the table. "I've advised everyone to draw up the legal documents and make sure all parties involved know who can do what, and when. You don't want Bryce and Bailey coming back to you in six months or a year and saying they want their baby back, right? And Bryce and Bailey need to understand what they're doing."

"*Tex and Abby* need to understand what they're

doing," Tex said. "I mean, that baby is my grandchild. And I want you and Georgia to raise him."

"Or her," Abby said, tears already wetting her face.

Otis had no idea how to process this. He looked at the manila folder in his hand and then at his wife. Georgia had started to cry too, and Otis wanted to wipe all of that away. "Is this happy or sad crying?" he asked.

Someone chuckled, but Otis felt outside his body. He knew Bryce and Bailey's story. He knew they weren't going to get married, that they had other pursuits in their lives they wanted to do, and that a baby didn't fit into those things right now. He thought Bryce had acted as maturely as he could, given his age, experience, and the situation, but this was just beyond anything Otis had ever imagined.

"What about your mom and dad?" He looked at Bailey, who sat up straight and wiped her tears.

"I'm almost twenty-five years old," she said. "They said they'll support whatever I decide." She looked at Bryce. "Whatever *we* decide. We've talked to them about this, and they're okay with it."

He looked at Tex, so many questions flying across the table. Tex only smiled, his eyes crinkling as he broke down too. That only made hot tears prick Otis's eyes, and he ducked his head. He was the strong one out of him and Georgia. He had his private moments with her, where he could be sad and grief-stricken and vulnerable. But he'd shown that to no one else.

"What about the other brothers?" he asked.

"What about them?" Gabe asked.

"Do they know?"

Bryce shook his head. "No, Uncle Otis. I've only been talking to everyone here."

"And Blaze," Trace said. "I think Blaze knows."

"I didn't tell him," Bryce said.

"I'm over there a lot," Trace said. "So are you. I think he's heard some things, and he's not a stupid man."

No, he wasn't. In the family, Blaze was also quiet, so Otis didn't worry about gossip flying too far if Blaze knew it.

"Well, I don't know what to say," Otis said. He reached up and wiped his eyes. "Baby?"

Georgia looped her arm through his and leaned further into the table. "I think Otis and I would love to talk more about it before we give a final yes or no."

"That's fair," Bryce said, his face falling. He looked over to Tex again, who put his arm around his son.

"But," Georgia added quickly. "I can also say that we're honored you thought of us." Her voice broke, and Otis wanted to come to her rescue too. He didn't, because Georgia was strong in her own right, and she could speak her mind when she wanted to. "We would love your baby as our own, and you could come see him any time you wanted."

"We'd do it all legally," Gabe said again. "Then there's no confusion, and no chance of hurt feelings in the future."

Otis watched his wife weep, her head down. He looked over to Bailey and Bryce, and he couldn't stay in his seat for another moment. He got up and went around the table. Bryce and Bailey stood too, and Otis gathered both of them right into his chest, one in each arm.

"The baby will look like you," Bryce said, his voice far too high.

"We both feel strongly about this," Bailey whispered.

"I will do anything to make my wife happy," Otis whispered back. "And I already know she wants this baby." He did too, but he needed some time to come to terms with it. He'd always heard it said that families were messy, and he and his brothers already had a million branches in their family tress.

Ex-wives times nine. *Nine* of them. Ten kids just in their direct line. Now Tex had a new baby, and Dani had a son from her first marriage, and Otis was going to raise his brother's grandbaby.... Things got tangled in his mind at that point, and all he could do was close his eyes against the burning tears and pray.

Lord, he thought. *I'll do what You want me to do. I'll go where You want me to go. If it's Thy will that we raise this baby, I'll do it.*

The sweetest feeling of peace came over him, and as Georgia joined the hug, all of the stupor and disbelief drained out of him. Adopting Bryce's baby was the right thing to do, and he'd go over whatever papers Gabe had in that folder to make it happen.

"See?" Mav asked as the foursome broke up. "Aren't you glad you came to family dinner tonight?"

Otis chuckled and wiped his face clean of the tears he'd shed. "What about Momma and Daddy? Has anyone told them?" He looked at Bryce, who shook his head.

"We can," Bailey said, her hand slipping into Bryce's. Otis wasn't sure why they couldn't be together. Why they couldn't get married and become the family they'd already created. "Or you can. We'll let you decide that. It's kind of your news to tell, we think."

Otis looked at Georgia, who simply shook her head. "I don't know," she said. "I'm too full of thoughts and emotions right now to decide."

"You don't have to decide right now." Tex hugged Otis and Georgia at the same time. "And I am coming over all the time to see that baby."

Otis understood his brother's turmoil on a deeper level now. He hadn't truly known the burden Tex was carrying in and out of the studio, day after day, until now. "I love you, brother," he said, for this was a sacrifice for Tex too. A big one.

His first grandchild—and he was going to give it up so Otis and Georgia could have their prayers answered.

"Come over any time," Georgia said, and Otis knew then that they didn't really need to talk. They both wanted a baby, and this one was a Young and needed parents.

"Daddy," Joey said. "Do we not get to eat too?" She stood at the end of the dining room table with her hands on her hips. "You guys started without us." Beth and Boston crowded in behind her, and Liesl came toddling over too, with Lars several steps behind her.

Several people laughed, and Otis swooped toward his daughter and lifted her into his arms. She giggled as he said, "We sure did, Roo. Come on, I'll help you get some food."

33

"Yeah, I'm packing up right now," Bryce said into his phone as he shoved his backpack into the last available spot on the passenger seat. From there, he'd be able to get the snacks Abby had packed for him and keep driving.

It would take him six hours to get to Butte, and if he didn't have to stop, he'd arrive by midnight. He had an apartment waiting for him, but he hadn't stepped foot inside it yet. For all he knew, it could be rodent-infested, and he'd sleep in his truck tonight.

Problem was, there was no room.

"Okay," Bailey said. "Well, let me know when you're here."

"You don't need to stay up." Bryce backed out of the doorway and looked toward the house. Dad came down the steps with the microwave, and Bryce's heart filled with love for his father. At the same time, such shame still assaulted him. He didn't really deserve a dad like the one he had—who could be so forgiving and so loving, even after Bryce had done so many things wrong. "I have to go," he said. "I'll call you back when I'm on the road."

He hung up and went to take the box from his father. "Dad, you shouldn't be carrying stuff. The chiropractor said nothing heavier than Melissa." He took the box, noting his father's frown.

"You sure you have to go?" he asked.

"Yes, Dad." Bryce turned away from his dad to go put the box in the bed of the truck. That was dangerously full too, but there couldn't be too much more inside the house. The uncles weren't coming to practice right now in the barn-studio, but Uncle Mav, Uncle Luke, and Uncle Trace had still shown up to help Bryce pack up. They, thankfully, had stayed inside.

His dad joined him at the tailgate. "I'm going to miss you."

Bryce sighed as he shoved the microwave forward. "Dad." He faced his father. They'd had several conversations about his decisions, but this one had sort of been skated over. "I feel more strongly about going with her than anything else I've had to decide and do this summer, okay?" He threw his hands up in frustration, because he was frustrated. "I know it makes no sense. I can't even figure out why it feels right. I only know it does."

"You're not going to get back together with her, are you?" Dad asked.

Bryce gritted his teeth and shook his head. "No. She's moved in with her roommates. I have my place. We're not dating. But when I was counseling with Pastor Daniels, it was like God opened a door between me and Him. He told me I have to be in Montana with her, so I'm going to Montana with her. Just until the baby's born."

His father nodded, the shape of his set jaw exactly like what Bryce had seen in the mirror that morning when he'd made the same face. "Then what?"

"I'm still waiting for an answer on that one," Bryce said. He lifted the tailgate and slammed it closed. "We're going to come back here to deliver the baby. And then honestly, Dad, you know what I want to do?"

His chest tightened and collapsed, but he had to start prepping his father now. Dad would try to talk him out of this for the next four months, and Bryce hadn't lied. He didn't know what he'd do after his baby was born and he gave it to Otis and Georgia to raise.

Papers had been signed. Everything was set. All that needed to happen now was for time to pass.

"What?" Dad asked.

"I want to run," Bryce said, his desperation surging up and clogging his throat. "Maybe I'll go to Canada or Mexico—or I know. Greenland. Siberia. Somewhere where no one knows me, and I don't have to look the people I love in the eye and wonder what they think of me." Tears splashed his cheeks, but he didn't care. He'd cried tons of times in front of his father this summer.

Just like he always did, Dad grabbed onto him and dragged him into his chest for a hug. "No," he said firmly. "You're not going to run."

"I know I won't stay here, Dad." Bryce clung to his father. "I can't, okay?"

"You'll feel differently one day," Dad said, his voice as anguished as Bryce's. "I know you will."

"I'm not there yet," Bryce said. "Maybe I will be by Christmas, I don't know. Right now, I want to run. I want to hide. I want to make new friends and never see anyone I knew ever again."

"Uncle Jem feels that way."

Bryce gave a choked laugh. "Funny, for the man who's literally snapping photos with every person in town." He sniffled and pulled away from his father. He wiped his eyes and looked his dad in the eye. "I'm working on getting better, okay? I am. But it's so slow, and I feel like I'm moving backward half the time."

He shook his head and blew out his breath. "I think once the baby comes, I'll be able to move forward. Bailey and I were talking about it the other day; we feel like we're in limbo."

Dad nodded. "I know, and you hate that."

Bryce did hate that. "I've got two students tomorrow," he said. "Bailey's got a job at the vet clinic before she starts her program." Another sigh escaped his lips. "I don't know what every day of the next four months looks like, Dad. I don't know what the day after the baby is born will look like or feel like."

He honestly felt like he and Bailey were doing right by their baby. It wasn't really theirs, and they both seemed to know it. At the same time, Bryce had very real emotions surrounding Bailey and the baby she carried. She was five months along now, and noticeably pregnant to everyone who saw her, no matter what she wore. Being tall and thin would do that for a woman.

On some level, Bryce loved her. Young as he was, he'd learned that he could feel love for a woman, and he did love her. Maybe not the way she was meant to be loved. Maybe not the way Dad loved Abby, or Otis loved Georgia. But Bryce loved her, and he wanted her to be happy. He wanted her dreams to come true. He didn't want her to be alone for the next four months.

Heck, *he* didn't want to be alone for the next four months either. Here in Coral Canyon, he'd never have to be alone, what with the sheer number of uncles and cousins he had. But it was precisely those uncles and cousins Bryce needed relief from.

No, what he needed relief from was his own guilt. He was working on it, but Pastor Daniels had told him repentance was a process. It wasn't something that happened overnight, simply because Bryce felt a little bit bad.

"Feel how you feel," Dad said, and Bryce nodded.

"I love you, Dad." He grabbed onto his father again.

"I'm going to call you every day, okay? I'm going to be okay; I lived in Montana all of last year, and I didn't starve or get hit by a bus or anything."

Dad chuckled, his voice low in his chest. "I love you so much, Bryce." They held one another tightly for several long seconds, and then the babbling of baby Melissa had Dad stepping back. Abby approached from next door, and she carried the baby girl in one arm and a brown paper bag in the other.

She lifted it and said, "Cheryl brought peach puffs from the fair."

"I love those," Tex said.

Abby swooped the bag out of his reach, her smile only for Bryce. "They're for Bryce, baby."

"What?" Dad stared as Abby handed the bag to Bryce and then hugged him, sandwiching the baby between them. She squawked and flailed her arms, but Bryce held his stepmother fast.

"I love you, Abby," he told her. He loved his biological mother too, but she'd checked out a long time ago. Abby never checked out. Ever. Even when things got hard, and she hadn't slept, and she'd been horribly busy this summer with the reading programs, she didn't check out.

She was there, all the time, for both Tex and Bryce, and he loved her so very much for that.

"Oh, I love you too, you dear boy." She smiled a wobbly, emotional smile as she stepped back. She transferred Melissa to Dad, who bounced the fussy girl in his arms. "Come with me for a minute." She looped her arm through his and led him back toward the house.

"He has everything," Dad called after them. "He's supposed to be leaving in two minutes."

"I only need one," Abby said back to him. She gave Bryce a warm smile in the next moment. "Your dad. Do you really think he cares if you leave in two minutes or twenty?" She shook her head.

Bryce grinned. "No, ma'am." In fact, he knew his father didn't want Bryce to leave at all.

Abby took him to the back patio, where she picked up a long, slender package. She'd wrapped it in plain kraft paper and decorated it with his name in brightly colored magic markers. "We had a gift-wrapping class at the library yesterday." She extended the present to him. "I don't want you to open it until you get to your new place." Her smile wobbled again. "You better text your daddy tonight, or he won't sleep."

Bryce studied the package, because looking at her was too painful. "Yes, ma'am," he whispered. "I will."

"All right." Abby slid her hand up the side of his face, and Bryce lifted his eyes to hers. "You better go now, baby. You have a long way in front of you."

Truer words had never been spoken, by anyone, and Bryce felt them deep in his core. The drive to Butte wasn't that long, but as far as the path he had to trod in his life... he definitely had a long way to go.

"No mice," he reported to Dad and Abby the next day. "No spiders. No roaches. No rats. It was sparkling clean." He glanced over to Bailey as she set her bowl of cereal down on the table and then sat beside him. "Lessons went well. I interviewed for a job at a menswear store today."

No, he didn't want to sell men's clothing. But he needed a full-time job, so he didn't have to take his daddy's money for the rest of his life. "I applied at three ranches today too," he said. "Haven't heard anything back on those."

"Ranching in Montana in the winter," Dad said. "Sounds like fun. I hope you get the menswear job." He grinned at Bryce from the screen, and he added, "If you need anything, shoot me a text. We're headed to the movies, but I can order some forks or whatever from my phone."

"I bought forks already, Dad." He smiled back at his father. "Talk to you later. Have fun at the movies."

They signed off, and Bryce laid his phone face-down. "We could go to a movie."

Bailey looked at him, her pretty blue eyes filled with exhaustion. "I nearly got trampled by an angry mama pig today," she said. "I'm not going to a movie."

He grinned at her and covered her hand with his. "All right." The moment sobered between them. The fact that he'd bought her favorite cereal on his way home from his job interview screamed into the silence between them. She hadn't specifically said she'd be coming over after work, but he hadn't been surprised to see her.

She lived with three other women, all of them in college, and one of her roommates had night terrors. Bailey's first text to him that morning had been about how the girl had been "screaming all night long," and she hoped she'd make it through her shift at the veterinary clinic where she'd done her internship.

Their eyes met again, and the thrill and spark between them burned as hotly as it ever had. In any other situation, Bryce would've leaned forward to kiss her. He stopped himself after he'd moved an inch or two, and he said, "I'd marry you, you know. We could be a family."

Sadness filled her beautiful eyes. "I know you would, Bryce."

"I love you, Bailey."

Her eyes widened now. "Bryce."

"I do," he said. "It might not be this deep, deep love yet, but I'd always choose you, and I'd choose to love you."

"I don't want you to *have* to *choose* to love me," she said.

"That's not what I meant." He pulled his hand away from hers. "I meant, we can grow and change and deepen our relationship over time. It doesn't have to be this massive, huge thing right now."

She nodded and focused on her cereal. "Bryce, I...I

think you're an amazing guy. I always have. I just...I feel like I'm not ready, and I know you're not ready, and I think we're young. Maybe we'll be ready next year, or in three years, or six, or ten." Hope filled her eyes, and she practically shone. "You have so much to do in your life, and I never, ever want you to wake up one day and go, 'Dang. I've missed so much because I had to marry that Bailey McAllister.'"

"Bay." He shook his head, not sure what else to say. They'd talked about marriage before. He wasn't even sure why he'd brought it up again.

"Just...keep buying this Cap'n Crunch," she said. "And letting me stop by after work. And we'll deliver this baby to your uncle, and then...then we'll see where life takes us."

"My life isn't taking me anywhere," he said. Just as he'd said, he got to choose. That was one thing his father had taught him. His choices made up what his life would be.

"But it could," she said. "I know it could. I've seen the emails you've gotten from Marv at King Country. You have to go to Nashville in the New Year. You'll hate yourself if you don't, and then you'll hate me." She spoke with such earnestness that Bryce nodded.

"Did you tell your parents that's where you'll go after the baby is born?" she asked.

He shook his head. "I haven't decided yet."

She finished her cereal and stood up. "I think you

have." She walked her dishes into the kitchen and put them in the sink. "Come help me put a movie on here. Then, can you rub this spot out on my shoulder? I'm pretty sure that pig stepped on me there...."

Bryce did exactly that, and Bailey stayed well past dark. She slept in his arms on the couch while he stared at the flickering TV, and when she woke, he walked her out to her car and said, "See you tomorrow, Bay," before returning to his apartment.

He didn't kiss her. He didn't tell her he loved her again. As she smiled, waved, and backed out, Bryce hoped he could handle having his heart ripped out when they finally parted ways. Because they would, once the baby came, and he knew it.

34

Morris Young stepped over a pile of lumber as he entered the storefront. Or what would become a storefront once all the electrical wires were put in the right place, sheetrock hung, textured, and painted, and appliances installed.

"It's huge," Leighann said, but Morris wasn't looking at how big it was. All he could see was dust hanging in the daylight—and dollar signs.

But Leigh wanted a bakery, and seeing as how she'd had to sell the one she'd spent the better part of a year setting up so she could come help Denzel after his car accident, Morris was keen to get her one. Or do whatever it took to help her open another bakery.

He'd played professional football for three years before he'd been injured, and he had plenty of money in the bank. Maybe not to the level as the band members or his billionaire bull-riding brothers, but enough. Enough to buy this whole building, knock it down for no reason, and then rebuild it.

"Careful," he said to Eric as the boy started skipping along the concrete. There were too many buckets, tools, and miscellaneous items lying around for skipping. "Hey, bud, come over here." He went to get his son, and he swooped the boy up onto his shoulders. "It's a construction zone, so we have to be careful."

"Okay, Daddy," Eric chirped above him. "Where Uncle Denzel and Scout?"

Morris turned back to the entrance they'd come through. "He should be here soon, okay?" He turned to follow Leigh further into the space, which had been advertised as suitable for a restaurant. It was zoned properly, and all they had to do was sign a lease, and the builder would finish it to her specifications. She'd have to invest in specialized equipment for the bakery, as she'd sold everything she'd purchased in Lake Point with the business.

They spent mornings together looking at industrial ovens and mixers, and even Morris knew all the names of them now. He'd gone back to volunteering at the hospital on Mondays, and doing camps up at Whiskey Mountain Lodge.

Leigh had quit at the lodge only a week ago, and she stayed home to take care of Eric full-time. The boy had turned four about two months ago now, and Morris loved him more and more with every passing day.

"So I love it," she said, facing him with a smile on her face that looked like she'd been caught with her hand in the cookie jar.

Morris nodded. "I figured you would."

"It's by far the best place in town," she said, rushing toward him. She put her palms against his chest as if pleading with him. "It's a great location. I know what I'm doing, Morris. It'll be so great, you'll see."

"Getting up at three a.m. to come to work doesn't sound like my definition of 'great,'" he said, grinning at her.

She smiled back at him. They'd come such a long way in the past thirteen months. From finding out he had a son he didn't know about, to falling for Leighann all over again, to getting remarried, to starting a bakery together.

She still went to counseling every week, and they went together as a couple twice a month. Things weren't perfect, but as his therapist had said a few months ago, if he waited for perfect, he'd be waiting forever.

"Do you still want to go look at that place in Jackson?" he asked. "It looked nice." And it wasn't under construction. In fact, the space for lease in Jackson was a functioning bakery right now, but the owner had just learned of a family member's illness and needed to move back East to attend to that. Leigh and Morris had an appointment to see it later that week.

"I mean, we might as well, right?" she asked.

"It's an hour drive to Jackson Hole," he reminded her.

"No," she said with a grin. "It's an hour drive to Coral Canyon from Jackson Hole."

He rolled his eyes, but he knew that if she wanted the bakery space in Jackson, they'd move there. Morris could make the drive here for anything band-related that came up. The album was done now and going into mastering and finishing at King Country. He should have a mock-up of the cover any day now, and he honestly spent more time in online meetings and on the phone than he did in person.

He loved working as Country Quad's band manager, and they paid pretty dang good too. He'd set the tour for next summer, and Leigh and Eric would simply come with him and the band as they traveled around the country. She'd have to have someone cover her bakery if it was open by then, but she could do so. They'd already talked about it.

The clicking of claws on concrete met his ears, and Morris turned to see Denzel standing in the doorway. He'd let Scout come in first, and the dog froze and whined.

"I'm not comin' in," Denzel said. "Stop whining."

Scout returned to him and stood directly in front of him, almost as if blocking Denzel from entering any further. The German shepherd kept his head low, and his tail almost tucked.

"Hey, Den," Morris said, picking his way past a couple of plastic garbage cans filled with who-knew-what. He arrived in front of Leigh's brother and gave him a quick hug. "Slide on down, Eric. You take Uncle Denzel over to the park."

"We just came from the park," Denzel said. He gave Morris a quick grin, which was the only type Denzel ever offered. "Is she in love with this place?"

"About," Morris said in an equally quiet voice. "I'll try to hurry her along. Do you and Eric want to head down to the restaurant? That should help me get her out of here faster."

"I don't need you two conspiring against me," Leigh said from out of nowhere.

Morris jumped and turned to face his wife. "We're not," he said with plenty of confidence in his voice. "Right, Den? We're just hungry." He slung his arm around her and pulled her into his side.

"Mm hm." She gave him a knowing look and then switched her gaze to her brother. "Denzel, what is wrong with your face?"

"What?" Morris asked at the same time Denzel made a swift turn to exit.

"Nothin'," he said gruffly.

"Denzel," Leigh warned, already going after him. "What did you do? Did you let that dog maul you?" Out the door they went, and Scout hurried after his master. He was a highly-trained police dog, who happened to fail his final test. Scout didn't know how to maul unless someone spoke to him in German and the bad guy he was attacking smelled like gunpowder.

Since Denzel could only speak English and didn't own a gun, Scout had definitely not mauled him. Morris hadn't even seen anything wrong with the man's face.

"Leigh sees so much more than everyone," he reminded himself as he stepped out of the construction zone and pulled the glass door closed behind him. It clicked in a satisfying way, and he took Eric's hand and said, "Come on, bud. We're eating pizza tonight."

LATER THAT WEEK, LEIGH SAT ON THE BED, HER BACK ramrod straight. "I can't go to Jackson this morning."

Morris looked up at her from his position on the pillow. He hadn't gotten up and showered yet, and Leigh had only been in the bathroom for a few minutes too. She hadn't showered either. "Why not?" He reached out and stroked his hand down her back. He loved being married to her, sleeping in the same bed as her, raising their son together. It all held a special kind of magic he was addicted to.

She twisted slightly toward him. "I'm sick."

"Again?" She'd thrown up most of the night before last, and he'd thought it was because of the rolled chicken she'd had at Bricks and Birds, a new restaurant in town.

She nodded, the misery rolling off her and punching him in the face. He tugged on her elbow to get her to lay back down, which she did. He gathered her into his arms and stroked her hair. "More throwing up?"

She nodded and sniffled into his chest. "I hate throwing up. It ruins my whole day." She'd done very little yesterday, true. She'd sucked on ice until she'd felt well enough to take a few bites of toast, and when she'd kept that down, Morris had let her eat a little more. They'd stayed home and watched movies, which had fit in really well with the cooler autumn weather that had arrived in Coral Canyon.

He'd made coffee and hot apple cider, but she hadn't had even one sip of either. She claimed her stomach "revolted" at the thought, and she'd stuck to weak tea and water.

"I can get you some ginger ale," he said.

"I want you to go to Jackson and check out the space," she said. "Would you? You can video-chat me, and I'll be able to see it."

Morris didn't want to leave her here with Eric alone if she was sick. He considered what to say, and in that pause, she said, "You can still go to lunch with Gabe, and it'll be the twin-thing you always want if I'm not there."

"You don't bother me or get in the way of me and Gabe," he said.

"I know," she said. "But I think I bother *Gabe*."

"You don't," he told her for the umpteenth time. "Gabe's just grumpy *all* the time, with everyone. You're not special."

"Gee, thanks."

"You know what I mean." Morris laid on his back and looked up to the ceiling. "I can ask Dani if Eric can come over." She had a son who loved Eric, and most of the other littles had started school already.

"I'm okay here alone with him, you know. I did it for a while before we got back together."

Morris nodded, not enjoying the thoughts of what she'd had to do alone. They left quickly though, because he had an excellent therapist who'd helped him recognize and banish irrational thoughts. "All right," he said with a sigh. "I better get in the shower and get going if I'm going alone."

He did that, and after he'd kissed Leigh and Eric good-bye, he made the drive to Jackson. It wasn't a terrible drive, and the roads between the two places were well-maintained, even in the winter. He arrived at the bakery a few minutes early, but got out of the truck anyway. The bakery was open, and he could definitely go for a chocolate croissant before he met the real estate agent.

He'd taken two steps toward the entrance when a version of himself exited it. He and Gabe were identical twins—at least in looks. Gabe went very few places without wearing a suit and tie, as he was today. He also glowered a lot more than Morris, but he loved just as fiercely and deeply as Morris did.

He opened his mouth to call out his twin's name when Gabe turned back to the bakery, his hand extended. A woman slipped her hand into his, and Morris stared as the dark-haired beauty grinned up at his brother.

Morris didn't recognize her, but it was clear she and Gabe weren't on their first date. His brother hadn't said a single word to him about it, when he'd been an open book about the woman he'd dated last winter.

Shock waved through him, starting to pulse in time with his heartbeat when Gabe leaned down and *kissed* the brunette right there on the sidewalk in front of the bakery. For the whole world to see.

He's a grown man, Morris told himself. Gabe certainly didn't need Morris's permission to date and kiss a woman. He fought for father's rights at his self-ran and established law firm here in Jackson Hole, and he wouldn't do anything that would shed a bad light on himself.

Unless a very public display of affection counted, because he was still kissing that woman. The length of the kiss spurred Morris to action, and he crossed the parking lot quickly and stepped up onto the sidewalk.

He cleared his throat loudly, as if he were Gabe's father, and tapped the toe of his cowboy boot. His brother finally pulled away from the woman and looked up.

Gabe froze in the next moment, and the flush that had already stained his cheeks deepened by double.

"Well," Morris said. "Want to introduce me?"

The woman turned to look at him too, and she gasped. Morris did too, because he *did* know this woman.

"Shelly?" he asked. She'd been his press manager in

the NFL. What in the world was she doing here? In Jackson Hole? With Gabe?

"How—?" She backed up, her eyes flying between him and Gabe, Gabe and him. A fierce look entered her eye, and she cocked on skirted hip and put her palm there. "All right. There are two of you." She pointed at Gabe—the one who'd been kissing her. "Morris, tell me what's going on. Right. Now."

"Morris?" Morris asked, and he too faced his brother. "She called *you* Morris," he hissed between his nearly-closed lips.

If anything, Gabe's face turned a deeper shade of red, and Morris got the message without his twin having to say a word. Oh, Gabe *had* been being naughty, and suddenly the stakes were higher than when they'd traded places in junior high.

So very much higher.

35

Luke couldn't relax on the massage table, despite the aromatherapy Sterling had wafted toward him at the beginning of the session. He couldn't stop thinking about what Sterling would be like out in the wild. He'd run into her at the grocery store a while ago, and he'd been back twice now.

He had no idea how to ask her out on a date while he lay naked on the massage table, and he didn't see her much before or after the session.

"You've forgotten how to be a candle," she said, a smile in her voice. "You're so tense. You have to *melt* into the table."

"I can't," he said, a groan following the words as she really leaned into his hip. "You're killing me. How am I supposed to relax?"

Sterling said nothing, and Luke did take in a long,

deep breath, and he forced his shoulders down. He felt them sink into the table, but that release only went about halfway down his back. Certainly not all the way to his hip, where she continued to jab her elbow.

At least he assumed it was her elbow. Luke didn't actually know, as he currently had his eyes closed, and his face aimed at the floor.

"How did things go in Nashville?" she asked.

"Good," he said. "We got what we wanted."

"Summer tour next year then," she said.

"Yeah," he said, groaning again. "I need those things to squeeze so I can pretend you're hurting as much as I am."

"If you would relax, it wouldn't be so bad," she said. She stopped with the hot poker in his hip, and she slipped a squishy ball into each one of his hands. "Your hands are cold," she murmured. "Is the table okay?"

"Fine," he said.

"I can turn it up."

"Whatever," he said, his tone definitely on the grouchy side. He didn't care about the table, but that wasn't why he had irritation firing through him. That all belonged to his complete inability to talk to a woman on a personal level. Not about his tour or his family or the first day of first grade for Corrine. Surface crap he'd talked to everyone about.

He wanted to ask Sterling about herself and find out what her favorite restaurant was and if he could take her there on Friday night. The moment he thought that, he rebelled against the very idea. He'd have to find someone to babysit Corrine for a Friday night date, and that would require him to tell them he had a Friday night date.

Sterling's hand landed in the middle of his back, and he flinched. "Luke."

"Yeah, I'm here."

"I lost you," she said.

"The table's fine," he said. "Honestly."

"I asked if the calf was still hurting you."

"Oh, uh." Luke honestly wasn't sure where his calf was right now. "Yeah, it's tight when I run."

"You're running? That's new."

"Now that we're done recording, all of us go into training mode."

"What does that look like?" She slid her hands down to his right calf, and Luke was suddenly hyper-aware of where his legs were. The right one, at least.

"A lot of working out," he said. "It's exhausting really."

"If you're putting more stress on your body, you should come more often."

"All right." He pushed his breath out slowly, hoping he wasn't being a huge wimp. But holy cow, the way she touched that hot spot in his calf and wouldn't leave it alone?

"It's right there," she murmured. "How far are you running?"

"My trainer started me at a mile."

"You sound upset about that."

"I usually go five or six," he said.

"Not right out of the gate."

Luke didn't respond. Most of what he did, he did explosively. He did do things fast, and he was still learning how to slow down, think through things, and come to informed, intelligent decisions. Having to parent Corrine by himself had helped a lot with that, but when it came to his dating life, he had no one to help him slow the heck down.

He had no dating life. Period. The end.

He still didn't want a dating life, and he finally relaxed.

"There you go," Sterling said. "Go to sleep, Luke. I'll take care of you."

He chuckled, because he wasn't going to go to sleep. Although, he had dozed off once or twice during previous massages. "Do you have clients who actually go to sleep?"

"Sure," she said. "If you book me for a relaxation and rejuvenation massage, you're encouraged to go to sleep."

"How do I do that?"

"Just talk to Cindy out front when you go," she said.

"I can't book directly with you?"

Sterling took a moment to answer. "What do you mean?"

Luke had no idea what he meant. Humiliation filled him, and he said, "I don't know. I'll talk to Cindy on the way out." He had to stop and pay her anyway, and he started obsessing over how big of a tip he should give Sterling. More than usual, and she'd know something was off about him—like she didn't already.

She did.

Sterling could read energy—according to her. She could touch his shoulder and feel "heat," she said, in the spots where his body was angry with him.

The massage continued, and as she had him roll to his back, she said, "Luke, I know you're this fit guy, but you have to stretch more before you start running, okay? Your calves are super angry with you."

"Yes, ma'am," he said. "I'll talk to Kate about it."

"Is she your trainer?"

"Yeah," he said.

"Kate Viridium?"

"Yeah." He opened his eyes and looked at her. "Do you know her?"

"Yeah, sure." Sterling's voice was a little too forced, but a smile came to her face. "She's a great trainer."

Luke wanted to roll his eyes. "She started me at a mile on the treadmill."

Sterling laughed lightly, and that buoyed up Luke's spirits. He still had no idea how to talk to her about more personal things, and he closed his eyes and let her work her magic on his hands, shoulders, neck, and feet.

He wasn't going to ask her out. He didn't even know how to do that, and Tex was wrong anyway. Sterling didn't like him for more than a client who tipped her really well.

A WEEK LATER, LUKE CURSED HIMSELF FOR BEING upset that his personal trainer had started him at a mile run. She'd increased him to five within a week, and he struggled to breathe and keep up with the speed of the treadmill at the same time.

Just like he'd told Sterling last week when she'd pressed on that hot spot in his hip, he was once again dying. He jabbed at the stop button on the machine, but he couldn't quite get to it.

"Luke," Kate Viridium barked at him. "Don't you dare turn that off."

"I'm...." He couldn't finish the sentence. His legs felt weak, and he was seriously going to lose his breakfast at any moment. If he didn't get off this thing, he was going to pass out. Then he'd be sliding off it while everyone in the gym stared at him. Kate would feel bad then.

He yanked on the red emergency cord, and the treadmill stopped instantly. His body was still moving, and the whole world spun. He groaned, and Kate said something in a voice that was less barky.

Luke wasn't sure how he got to the ground, only that he found himself there. So many people talked, but he couldn't distinguish any words or voices. He felt a rumble in his throat, indicating that he was groaning, but honestly, his body was outside of his control.

The next time Luke woke up, he wasn't in the gym at

all. An uncomfortable surface held him up, and the steady beeping of a machine told him he hadn't fallen asleep on the couch either. He sat straight up, but Trace said, "Whoa, don't do that."

"What is happening?" Luke asked, still struggling to sit all the way up. His back hurt. His abs throbbed. His shoulder screamed at him not to stay like this for long. Trace wouldn't let him sit up, and he couldn't stay in the half-up half-down position, so he settled back into the hospital bed. "Why in the world am I in a hospital?"

"You passed out at the gym," Trace said. "And you've been out for over an hour." His hand didn't let up from Luke's chest. "Stay down. I'm gonna get the doctor." He strode out of the room, and once he was alone, foolishness filled Luke all the way to the top.

He'd passed out while working out? How embarrassing.

He'd run half-marathons before. Before every album release, he and his brothers worked out to be ready for tour. They had to look their best for live performances, for one, and for another, the tour schedule was grueling. New cities every night, driving, dancing, singing, all of it.

Luke seriously wanted to bring Sterling with him on tour, if only so she could work her magic on his tired muscles every day.

Sure, he told himself with plenty of sarcasm in his mental voice. *That's the only reason.*

He couldn't believe how much he'd been thinking

about Sterling Boyd, and his irritation grew. He had to get out of here.

"You're right," a woman said as she entered the room. "He's awake."

Trace followed her, but Luke only had eyes for the gorgeous blonde looping a stethoscope around her neck. She wore a black dress that flowed around her legs like moving water, with a white doctor's coat over that. Her smile could've healed the most withered of hearts, Luke's included.

He sat up a little straighter, and he wished he'd just finished an amazing concert under bright lights, with screaming fans in the audience. He'd be riding a high, dressed in dark jeans and a black and white plaid shirt. Luke only ever wore black and white plaid on stage. Only.

Cowboy boots. Dark hat. Sometimes sunglasses, and sometimes he ripped open his shirt before he started.

If this woman had seen any of that, he'd feel more confident. As it was, he lay in a hospital bed, and she picked up his chart from the holder on the end of it. "Lucas Young."

"I go by Luke," he said.

She beamed at him. "You know your name."

He frowned and flicked a glance over to Trace. "Of course I know my name."

"You've been unconscious for a while, Mister Young." The doctor flipped a page, read for a moment, and looked up. She drew in a sharp breath. "All right. Let me take a look at you." She did just that, and Luke gazed back.

She smelled like red berries and cream, and he wanted a taste of her.

"I'm Doctor Gerry," she said. "Have you had fainting spells before?"

"No," Luke said.

"How long have you been working out?"

"Couple of weeks," he said. "This time. I work out all the time, though. This was just an increase lately, now that the album is done."

She nodded and used the stethoscope to listen to his heart. Her head tilted down as she listened, and then she turned to the computer. "Oxygen level is back to normal. Pulse is steady and strong. I see no reason why you need to stay here."

"Thank the Good Lord above," he said dryly.

She laughed, and Luke actually smiled. "I can spring you, cowboy. But I don't want you on a treadmill again if you feel sick. If you're lightheaded, you need to make an appointment with your doctor and do some follow-up care."

Trace's phone rang, and he said, "Excuse me," and ducked out of the room.

Dr. Gerry plucked his chart from the end of the bed again. "Who's your primary care physician?"

"Uh, I don't have one."

She looked at him. "You don't go to the doctor?"

"No, ma'am," he said. "My daughter has a pediatrician, but I don't suppose I can go to him for fainting spells."

Dr. Gerry smiled. "No, I don't think so." She reached into one of her oversized pockets. "You come see me if you have any more issues, okay, Luke?"

"Yes, ma'am." He took the card she held toward him, glanced at it, and then looked at her. "What if I want to see you outside of the office?"

Her eyebrows went up, and her blue eyes filled with surprise...and delight. Luke congratulated himself for being flirtatious with a woman, as he hadn't done anything like that in years. In fact, he'd put on scary faces and ducked his hat over and over to keep the women in this town away from him.

This one, however...to Luke, it felt like a good idea to bring her closer. He realized he'd had this same initial reaction to Sterling too, when he'd met her earlier this year. He hadn't wanted a female masseuse until she'd come out. He remembered thinking she was gorgeous, and a flutter of attraction he'd quickly tamped down.

Stuffed away, because he hadn't been ready to start thinking about dating.

He was now, and for some reason, he didn't want to cut his teeth on Sterling Boyd. But Dr. Gerry....

"Can I see you outside of the doctor's office?" he asked. "Or the hospital? Preferably when I'm not in a bed or wearing a see-through gown?"

She grinned at him and reached up to tuck her hair behind her ear. "All right," she said. "You have my card."

He looked at it. "Trudy Gerry," he said. "This is your work card."

She plucked it from his fingers and started writing on the back of it. When she gave it back, she said, "Now it has my personal cell on it." She started for the door. "And Luke? Never call me Trudy. It's my given name, but I've properly chastised my parents for burdening me with such a horrible name."

Dr. Gerry reached the door and turned back to him. "I go by Tea. Like sweet tea."

"Yes, ma'am." He lifted her card almost like a salute, and Tea's smile widened even further.

"I'll get your discharge processing," she said. "Don't wait too long to use that number." She flirted openly with him, and Luke wondered how old she was. He wondered if she did this with all of her male patients, or if he'd sparked something inside her too.

"No, ma'am," he said, and the moment she left the room, Luke started looking for his clothes and his phone. He'd just found a plastic bag with his things when Trace came back in. Luke didn't care if his brother saw him in his boxers, but he did wonder who'd undressed him.

He didn't ask as he pulled on his gym shorts. "She said I can go home." He started searching for his phone. "What time is it?"

"Mav's getting Corrine," Trace said. "Though you have hours yet until school is out."

Luke's mania started to subside, and when he found his phone at the bottom of the bag, more relief filled him. He flipped over the card Dr. Gerry had given him and started entering her number.

"What are you doing?" Trace came closer, and Luke decided in a split second he wasn't going to hide this.

"I got Doctor Gerry's number," he said. "I'm texting her to find out when we can go to dinner." He finished the text, sent it, and looked up into his brother's shocked eyes. They both started to smile at the same time, but Trace laughed first, the sound full and loud.

"I can't believe it," he said through his chuckles. "Luke is finally dating again."

Luke couldn't believe it either, but he laughed with his brother. And when Tea texted him back that they could go out that weekend, he showed Trace the phone and said, "Better pray for me, brother. I haven't been on a date in so long, I don't even know what to do."

"Hey, you *got* a date," Trace said. "That's like ninety percent of the battle right there."

36

Blaze glanced up as the waitress arrived with the desserts. A smile split his face, and he watched Faith light up across from him too.

"Mm," she said as the waitress set the peach cobbler right in the middle of the table. She'd already brought two spoons for the vanilla bean ice cream piled high on top of the cobbler, and Blaze reached for one of them.

"Let me know if you need anything," the waitress said, knocking on the end of the table.

"Thanks, Diane," Blaze said. He knew her, because he and Cash came to The Burger Barn a lot, and she worked evenings.

A loud round of laughter—only one male voice amidst several females—filled the immediate vicinity, and Blaze pressed his eyes closed in a long blink.

"Can you do something about your brother?" Diane asked. "He's flagging me down *again*."

He opened his eyes to answer, but Diane stalked off in the direction of Jem's table. Blaze refused to turn and look.

Faith leaned out of the booth slightly, and her eyes widened. "He's something else, isn't he?" Her eyes met his, and Blaze gave her a tight smile. He honestly didn't know what Jem was doing right now.

Truth be told, Jem didn't know what Jem was doing right now. He should be at home with his two kids, and yet Harry currently babysat at Blaze's house. Cash was old enough to sit with Rosie and Cole for a couple of hours too, but Jem was always out longer than a couple of hours.

He staggered home in the middle of the night—if then —usually laughing too loudly at his own thoughts inside his head. He'd told Blaze several times that he'd simply drunk too much and "had to crash" somewhere until it was safe to drive.

Blaze had told him he needed to sober up and shape up. More than once. Jem only laughed, slept until noon, and repeated his days on what felt like an endless loop.

"I think I'm going to have to ask him to move out," Blaze said darkly. Once he got Jem alone, at home, without any women around. It wouldn't go well, Blaze knew that. He and Jem had been best friends their whole lives. No one knew Blaze better than Jem—at least the version of Blaze he'd been on the rodeo circuit.

He'd assumed their friendship and brotherhood would transfer to Coral Canyon, but it hadn't. Jem and his kids lived with Blaze, and that was about it. Blaze got Cole ready for school every morning, and Luke came by to get him. Even when Luke had fainted, he hadn't missed the school pick-up.

Jem, on the other hand, seemed to have forgotten that he was a father at all. Blaze bathed Rosie most mornings, and he let her toddle alongside him as he did his walking therapy in the morning. He'd order lunch and feed everyone, as Jem was up by then, and then he had a couple of hours to rest, walk some more, or deal with family issues before Cash got home.

Now there was homework, therapy appointments in the late afternoons, dinner to be made, laundry to be done, and then Cash had joined a flag football team. So practices and games had landed on their schedule.

He pushed Jem and his partying ways out of his mind. This date with Faith had been their best yet, and he wanted to see her again. Soon. "I heard there's a Harvest Celebration here in town." He scooped up a bite of steaming peaches and melting ice cream. He put the bite in his mouth and looked at Faith. "We should go tomorrow."

"Tomorrow?" Her eyes rounded, and Blaze watched as the light in them got snuffed right out. She'd gone from warm to cold instantly, and Blaze had no idea why.

His eyebrows went up. "Yeah," he said. "It only goes

through the weekend, and I've got that family thing on Saturday. You could come to that too, of course."

Faith paled. "You want me to come to your family thing in two days." Her spoon hovered in mid-air, a bit of vanilla ice cream dripping from it.

"Sure," he said. "Why not?"

Her horrified expression was why not. Blaze frowned as he peered at her. They'd been out twice—tonight was date number three—since he'd shown up at her doughnut truck. He liked her more and more, and he couldn't fathom what he'd done wrong by asking her out for another date. Men did that, right? Women *wanted* men to do that, right?

"Blaze." She shook her head. "I don't know. I don't... think we're working."

Blaze could only blink at her. "Are you kidding?" He hadn't kissed her yet. He'd held her hand on the last date, as they'd gone up to the apple orchards for the last good weekend of picking. A chill had hit Coral Canyon, and Blaze had been reminded of why he'd enjoyed Vegas so much. Winters.

"No." Her voice ghosted from her mouth. "We're just...so different." She looked up at him, apprehension and regret in her eyes. "I just feel like we'll never be on the same page."

"You like me, though, right?"

The tiny smile she gave him when he said something

humorous flickered against her lips. "Yes," she whispered. "But Blaze, we might be better off as friends."

He rejected that idea most wholeheartedly. "No," he said. "I don't want to just be friends." She had to feel the same things he did. The crackles. The lightning in his bloodstream. The way her smile made him happy. He'd seen it all in her face in the past couple of weeks.

Maybe you saw wrong. The voice of doubt spread through his mind until it screamed in his ears.

"I'm sorry," she said. "I was still working through it, but I don't see how I can keep going out with you when I'm so unsure." She gestured with her spoon, sending droplets of ice cream through the air. "I mean, your family party?" Once again, the horror washed across her face. He saw that plainly enough.

Blaze had no idea what to say. He'd broken up with plenty of women, and they'd broken up with him. None of those had felt like this.

Jem's obnoxious voice boomed laughter into the air, adding another layer to Blaze's frustration. It turned into irritation, and he did turn and glare at his brother. Jem didn't notice at all, and he had an arm around two different women. They gazed up at him with stars in their eyes, and while Blaze had seen this type of behavior—heck, he'd participated in this type of behavior—in Vegas, it didn't fit here in Coral Canyon.

At all.

He didn't fit here either. He thought he had, but with

Faith telling him they were just too different, he wondered if he did or not.

"I'm going to go," she said.

Blaze swung back to her and found her already standing at the end of the booth. "Go?" He'd picked her up. "How are you going to get home?"

"I called my sister." She held up her phone. "Really, Blaze, I'm sorry. I just think this...will be for the best." She took a tiny step toward him, almost like she'd lean down and hug him goodbye. She jerked, then turned and fled.

Blaze didn't have a spare second to call her back or tell her to wait. He sat there, numb, and watched Faith hurry toward the exit. Out the door she went, leaving him alone with the entire peach cobbler dessert.

"Jem," a woman whined. "It's my turn for a dance."

Blaze couldn't sit here for another moment and listen to his stupid brother's annoying voice. He certainly couldn't watch him flirt with six women, one of whom he'd probably go home with that night.

He set down his spoon calmly, the raging storm inside him gaining speed. He wiped his face and stood, looking for Diane. He didn't see her for a moment, and then she appeared, carrying a huge tray of drinks.

"Be right there, Blaze," she said as she hurried past him to the group booth two away from him. He followed her and waited while she passed out the next round of drinks.

She turned and nearly ran into him, and he said, "My bill goes on his tab." He nodded to his brother, who didn't seem to even see Blaze standing there. He was tall and broad, and very difficult to miss. Which meant Jem was purposely avoiding making eye contact, or he was already too drunk to do it.

"Oh, uh, okay," Diane said.

"If he doesn't pay, I'm good for it," he said, pulling out his wallet. He took out a fifty-dollar bill and gave it to her. "For the tip."

Her smile bloomed. "Blaze, you're too good to me." She didn't flirt with him. Didn't touch him. Didn't spark anything inside him, not the way Faith did. "Come back with Cash or Faith anytime, okay?" She bustled away, and Blaze leveled his gaze at Jem.

His brother finally looked over to him, and his face burst into a smile. "Blaze!" he yelled. "There's room for you, brother." He started gesturing wildly, saying, "Scoot over. Scoot, scoot. Blaze needs to sit because of his back."

"I'm not staying," he said gruffly. "You should come home with me."

Jem met his eyes again, his watery and too wide. "The party's just starting, bro."

"The party should be over," he said. "You have two kids, Jem. Two. *Kids.* Waiting for you at home." He ignored the simpering women at the table, all of whom had gone silent.

Jem's expression turned angry, and that only fueled Blaze's irritation with him. "I know I have two kids, Blaze."

"Do you?" He indicated the drinks, the fried cheese,

the little purses in the middle of the table. "Why are you here, then?"

"It's Karaoke Night." Jem leaned back in the booth, his arms spread wide along the back of the seat.

"That's actually on...Saturday," one of the women said, her expression now worried as she looked from Jem to Blaze.

Blaze nodded toward the door. "Come on."

"No," Jem said. "I'm not ready to go." He picked up an eggroll that had been cut on the bias. "But you go on without me."

"This isn't going to replace Chanel," Blaze said. "And she's not here to pick up everything you break, Jem. I am, and I'm sick of it. Come on."

Jem came over the table then, a roar coming out of his mouth. Blaze backed up, because he couldn't afford to be thrown to the ground. His back surgery was a summer old now, but he was still fragile.

"Hey!" someone yelled, and Blaze had never been happier to see a big, burly bartender with black tattoos on his arms. "You boys are gonna have to leave. We're a family establishment."

"I was on my way out," Blaze said coolly. He ran his hands down the front of his shirt. "He's got his tabs to settle." He walked away from Jem then, and every eye at every table between the group booth and the door watched him leave The Burger Barn.

Hot humiliation streamed through Blaze. This was

why Faith didn't want to go out with him. She considered him just like Jem. How many times had he said he and Jem had been inseparable in Las Vegas?

"Too many," he muttered as he finally gained the freedom of the restaurant. Cooler air slapped him in the face, but it didn't ice his emotions. He wasn't really angry at Jem. He wasn't angry at Faith either, though the reason he felt like punching a brick wall stemmed from her break-up.

He was angry at himself. For the man he'd spent so long being.

"I was doing so good!" he bellowed into the sky. He felt closer to his parents and brothers. He and Cash were getting along better, and Cash had had a strong start to the school year. He'd survived his back surgery, and he'd even been praying for the past several months.

He hadn't gone to church yet, and he honestly wasn't sure if he ever would. He didn't think faith and belief had to be exercised only on Sundays, or only within the walls of a chapel. He did feel closer to God now that he was back in Coral Canyon, and he didn't hate that. In fact, he liked it.

But tonight, he felt like he'd just been shipped back in time to the day he'd arrived here in town. Nothing made sense, and he hadn't been this angry in a long, long time.

"Blaze," Jem yelled from behind him. He turned to face his brother, and Jem threw both hands up into the air as he strode forward. "What was that, man? Come on."

Blaze stayed right where he was, only a few feet from his pick-up truck. "That was a reality check, *man*."

Jem stopped a pace or two away, his anger simmering in the glower on his face. "You said I'd pay for you and Faith's dinner?"

"Yeah," he said. "You ruined it enough times with your loud laughter."

Jem shook his head and rolled his eyes. "You know, not that long ago, you were the one bringing over all the women and causing the scene."

"Yeah," Blaze said again. "But I grew up, Jem. I have sole custody of my son now, and I can't act like that anymore." He took a step closer and swatted his brother's chest. "It's time to grow up."

"Don't you dare tell me what to do," Jem spat. "Everything I do, I learned from *you*."

Blaze didn't doubt that, and it only caused a tidal wave of grief to drown him. *This is why Faith broke up with you,* a voice in his head whispered. *Deep down, at your core, you're no good.*

And she was.

So they'd always exist on opposite ends of the spectrum. He should be glad she could feel it now, but he wasn't. He so wasn't.

"I'm going home," Blaze said. "And you need to find somewhere else to live if you're going to keep living like this." He turned away from his brother and opened the driver's door.

"Fine," Jem called after him. "Fine! I don't need you and your fancy, overblown, mansion house! You think I can't find somewhere to live? You're wrong!"

"I hope I am," Blaze said under his breath as he got behind the wheel. He started the truck and glanced in the rearview mirror. Jem marched away, and he didn't look too unsteady yet. Maybe he'd been putting on a show and hadn't really drunk that much.

Regret lanced through Blaze. He'd always been Jem's safe place to fall, and Jem had always been Blaze's. When they lost in the rodeo. When they were hurt. When their marriages didn't work out. When they needed help with their kids.

He didn't truly want Jem and his kids to move out, because then who would take care of Rosie? She deserved a good dad, and even if Blaze was a stand-in, the four-year-old who'd been ripped away from her mother needed stability. Even if it didn't come from Jem.

He sighed, put the truck in reverse, and called his momma. She answered with, "Blaze, baby, how are you?"

"Bad," he said, letting all the darkness inside him bleed into his voice. "Momma, I think I just made a huge mistake with Jem...."

37

Trace looked up from the ice cream cake Everly had brought him for an early birthday celebration in his behalf. Harry had just gotten home—and he shouldn't be here.

His son wore absolute fury on his face, and Trace dropped the knife instantly. "Hey, bud," he said. "What's goin' on?" He approached like Harry was a wounded dog and would snap if touched. He just might.

"I can't believe Bryce," he said. *Yelled* might've been a more accurate term. "He has the gall to call me up and bawl me out for having a girlfriend? Is he kidding?"

Trace threw a panicked look to Everly, who sat at the bar with a surprised look on her face. Shocked, actually. Trace knew, because he felt the waves of surprise rolling through him.

"Hey, come sit down," he said to Harry, but his son didn't even hear him.

"So then I got all defensive with him," Harry said, pacing toward the couch. He turned and faced Trace. "And he said I should break up with her."

"With Sarah?"

"Yeah, with Sarah. Who else am I going out with, Dad?" He spoke with pure venom in his voice, and Trace cocked his head, like, *Did you really just say that to me?*

Harry once again did not even see him. "So I tell Sarah, and you know what she says? She says, 'maybe he's right.'" He flung his hands out three times on the last three words. "And then we started talking about breaking up, and the next thing I know, she's broken up with me." He threw his hands into the air. "For no reason! Because stupid Bryce got his girlfriend pregnant—and I have to take advice from *him*? Really?"

Trace had no idea what to say or do. Harry had been stunned to learn about Bryce's baby and all that entailed, but when Trace had first talked to him about it, there was no vitriol. They'd talked about repentance actually, and how God wanted all of His children to return to Him, no matter what they'd done. To Trace's knowledge, Bryce was trying to do that.

Maybe telling Harry not to have a girlfriend was a bit of a stretch, but Trace honestly wasn't sure what had transpired between the two cousins.

Trace's phone chimed, but he ignored it. "How'd you get home?" he asked.

"Mrs. Endman drove me," he said. "It was so stupid, Dad. Like, I'm just sitting there holding her hand, and Bryce calls out of nowhere. Says he's 'worried about me,' and he 'wants to protect me.' BS."

"Hey," Trace said, his voice a bark. "Language." He glanced at Everly. "Sweetheart, we probably need to reschedule."

She got to her feet and joined him on his side of the island. "Do we?" she asked.

Trace looked at her, not sure what language she was speaking with her eyes. It was clear she wasn't leaving.

"If we get married," she said. "I won't run away every time you need to deal with something with Harry."

"Whoa," Harry said, holding up both hands. "You're getting *married*? My life just keeps getting better and better!" He glared at the pair of them, huffed loudly, and spun on his heel.

"Harry," Trace called after him.

"I need to be alone!" Harry kept going, disappeared down the hall, and slammed his bedroom door closed a moment later.

Trace flinched and shuttered with the echoing sound of it, and then he sighed. His eyes landed on the ice cream cake, but he didn't want it anymore. How could he just go back to his intimate evening in with Everly now?

He braced himself with both palms against the countertop. "That wasn't how I imagined I'd approach him about the two of us getting married," he said.

"You have to stop pussy-footing around your son," Everly said.

That brought Trace's head up. "I'm sorry. What?"

Everly wore a hint of irritation in her eyes too. In fact, they shone like sapphires with the angry kind of glinting. "Sweetheart, we probably need to reschedule." She mimicked him by talking in a lower voice. She lifted one hand in a *what-was-that?* gesture. "No, we're not rescheduling us anymore, Trace."

"Harry is...a good kid," Trace said slowly. "I know how and when to talk to him."

"This would've set you back two months," she said. "Admit it."

Trace wouldn't admit to anything. "I don't know the future, Ev." He picked up the knife. "Do you want some cake?"

Silence filled the gap between them, and he hated that one even existed. His phone rang, and he put down the knife in favor of this device. "It's Sarah's mom." He quickly swiped on the call with, "Jamie, hey."

"Trace," she said. "I just dropped off Harry at your place. I wasn't sure if you were home or not."

"I'm home," he said. "Thank you."

"He's real upset," Jamie said, and she sounded nervous.

"Yeah, he is." He sighed and turned to face Everly.

She lifted her eyebrows, but he couldn't understand that language either, so he frowned at her.

"Put it on speaker," she said. "I want to hear what she's saying."

"...Sarah's crying," Jaime said. "Anyway, I wanted you to know."

"I know," Trace said. "I guess...good luck with Sarah?"

Jamie gave a mirthless laugh. "Yeah, and good luck with Harry."

The call ended, and Trace set his phone down. "She just wanted to make sure I was home."

"You could've put it on speaker."

"I just told you what she said."

Everly picked up the knife and sliced off a round of cake. She took a fork from his utensil drawer and put a delicate bite in her mouth. When she brought her gaze back to his, she said, "Trace, you be honest with me now."

He swallowed, because she'd started sentences like that before. "Yes, ma'am," he said.

"I've told you what I want—and that's to be that boy's mother figure. I took him shoe shopping, and we had a great time. He's not embarrassed we're dating anymore. But it feels like you're cutting me out when it comes to parenting him."

"Because you're not his parent," he said. "Not yet." They had been talking about marriage. So much that Trace had suggested they go look at rings together in the coming weeks. He wanted to be a good boyfriend and get Everly something she'd like.

"I have to get some experience," she said. "You can't just shoo me on home when things get hard." She forked off another bite. "Besides, *we* had plans tonight, and you're going to let him ruin them. Again."

Trace shook his head, his own frustration growing. "You know what, Ev? I think you're doin' that just fine on your own."

She sucked in a breath. "What does that mean?"

"It means you're being difficult about this, and it feels like you're doing it on purpose."

She clamped her mouth closed and very slowly and deliberately set her plate on the counter. "I'm going home now," she said. "Have a good time with your family for your birthday. Tell Harry I'm real sorry about Sarah."

"Come on, Ev." Trace didn't want her to leave. Not like this. "I just—"

"Good night, Mister Young." She held her head high as she went to get her jacket from where she'd tossed it over the back of the armchair. She didn't pause to shrug into it but headed for the front door without breaking her stride.

Only when that door had very quietly clicked closed did Trace realize she didn't have a car here. He'd picked her up at the studio after her last class. "Everly," he said, moving to follow her.

When he reached the front porch, she wasn't there.

She wasn't in the driveway or crossing the front lawn. The night had swallowed her whole, and Trace exhaled mightily again. Then he looked up into the eaves of the roof over the porch. "Lord," he said. "Can't one night go right? Can't I get a little peace and quiet in my life?"

Things had been insanely loud since Tex had taken him to lunch and told him about Bryce and Bailey. If Trace had learned anything from this summer it was this: He wasn't meant to be the oldest brother.

He constantly disappointed everyone, himself included. Harry. Now Everly.

He hurried back inside to get his phone, and he called Everly. She didn't answer. He immediately tried again.

"What?" she asked when she answered.

"You can't walk home from here," he said. "It's dark and cold and there's probably coyotes."

"I need to be alone," she said. "You give that courtesy to Harry, so I know you'll give it to me."

"But not at the risk of your personal safety."

"Don't worry about me, Trace," she said. "Shawn's almost here."

"Call me when you get home," he said in a rush, feeling like she'd hang up on him at any moment. "I know I messed up, Ev. I'm sorry."

She let several beats of silence fill the phone line, fill his head, fill his soul. "I need to be alone for a minute," she repeated. "I'll talk to you later, Trace."

Everly ended the call before he could say anything

else, and he wanted to throw his phone through the sliding glass door. But if he did that, he'd need a new phone and a new door to go with his very broken life.

He set his phone on the counter and faced the hallway. Harry had been alone for a good twenty minutes, and it was time for him to talk.

Trace went to the door and knocked before he tried the knob. Harry hadn't locked the door, which was a good thing, or Trace might have dismantled the whole house to get inside. He entered the room and closed the door, as if he had to seal them inside for privacy.

From whom, he had no clue. It just felt like the right thing to do, because his own father used to come to his room when Trace was upset. He'd say, "Tex, give us a minute, son," and then he'd close the door once they were alone.

Channeling all of his father's calm energy, Trace approached Harry's bed. His son lay on it, curled into a ball, his chest rising and falling far too fast to be normal.

Trace didn't say anything, because his father wouldn't have. He always let Trace lead their conversations, but Harry was too much like Trace. He wouldn't start, and Trace would have to prompt him.

He reached out and placed one palm against his son's back and simply held it there. He hoped Harry could feel the love moving through him, along his palm, and right into his body. This was the absolute worst part of being a father, and no one had told Trace he'd want to take his son's pain as his own simply so Harry didn't have to carry it.

In that moment, Trace understood his Savior on a much deeper level than ever before, and the words he should say flowed into his mind. "Harry," he whispered. "I love you so much. I'm so sorry you're going through this, but I'm right here."

His son rolled over, and Trace gave him a weak smile. "God knows how you feel right now. But I don't, not exactly, so you're gonna have to tell me."

Harry had been crying, but he currently wasn't shedding tears. He sighed and rolled onto his side facing Trace and put his hand on Trace's thigh. "I like her a lot, Dad."

"Yeah."

"I thought she liked me."

"Mm hm." Trace didn't believe for a moment that Sarah Endman didn't like Harry. She did; he'd seen them together; he'd caught them kissing. The girl definitely liked Harry.

"I've only kissed her three times," Harry said. "And Bryce has no right to lecture me, as if I'm going to do every single thing he did."

"No." Trace kept his eyes on the plaid pattern of his son's bedspread. Harry lay on top of it, testifying of just how good he was—he'd made his bed before school that day. Without being asked.

Of course, Val had been a neat-freak, so Harry had

learned from a young age how to stay out of trouble with his mom.

"Do you think she meant it?" Trace asked. He thought of Everly and how angry she'd been when he'd suggested they reschedule. He'd done it to give Harry some privacy. But life was messy, and if he and Everly got married, she'd be exposed to his chaos every single day.

She already had been, and his mind flowed over all of the dates he'd broken or ruined because of his family drama.

"I don't know." Harry sighed and clutched a stuffed football to his chest. "I don't know, Dad."

"Maybe you should call her," he said.

"Nah." Harry switched his gaze to Trace's. "Maybe tomorrow. Mom used to say that about her dates. Even if you really want to, you don't call until the next day."

Trace's eyebrows went up. "Is that what your mother said?" For some reason, he smiled. "She gave you dating advice as a six-year-old?"

Harry cracked a tiny smile. "I think I was seven."

Trace chuckled, but Harry's face fell again. "I didn't mean to freak out about you and Everly getting married."

"Yeah." Trace cleared his throat. "About that."

Harry sat up now, and Trace scooted back to make room. He took the football from his son and squeezed it. "Is she still here?" he asked.

Trace shook his head, unable to verbally confirm that

she'd walked out on him, leaving behind the immaculate ice cream cake she'd special-ordered just for his birthday. "She's mad at me too. I'll be lucky if she calls me tomorrow."

"Dad." Harry peered closer at him. "What did you do?"

Trace's teeth ached, because he pressed them so tightly together. "I think I keep trying to make you perfect in her eyes," he said slowly. "My life is so messy, Harry. So loud. There's a million moving pieces all the time, with Tex, the band, you, Luke fainting, Blaze's surgery." He sighed, his mind moving a million miles per hour. "It's a lot. I can't even manage my life, and I guess I didn't want her to see that."

"Dad." Harry gave a half-laugh. "She's already seen it. From day one, she saw it."

Trace looked at his son, and Harry laughed right out loud. "I mean, what about how I practically screamed at her at her own dance at the beginning of the summer?" He shook his head. "Dad, she knows exactly what she's getting when she gets you. Us. When she gets us."

Trace's heart warmed. "You like Miss Everly, son?"

"Yeah," Harry admitted, dropping his chin and nodding a couple of times. "I like Miss Everly, Dad, and I wouldn't be upset if you married her." He looked up and Trace couldn't believe the wisdom in his boy's eyes. "She calms you, Dad. She's the steadying force in your chaotic life."

"I'm very calm, I'll have you know," Trace said. "My momma says I'm the calmest of all the brothers."

Harry laughed again, and Trace figured that was better than crying. Or angry outbursts. "You are calm on the surface, Dad," he said. "But it's what you hide underneath that boils and boils."

Trace drew his son into a hug. "How'd you get so smart?" he whispered.

"I have a really good dad," Harry whispered back.

Trace closed his eyes and held his son tightly. "And I have the best son in the world."

When he pulled back, Harry wiped his eyes, and Trace asked, "Now, what are we gonna do about Bryce?"

Harry rolled his eyes and lay back down. "Right now, I'm mad at him. That's what I'm gonna do."

"But you'll forgive him," Trace said. "Because that's what families do."

"Yeah, like when Uncle Luke took a swing at Uncle Gabe before Uncle Mav's wedding." Harry spoke with a tone that mirrored the desert, and rolled over again. "Is there any ice cream cake left?"

"You saw that when you couldn't hear or see me?" Trace asked.

"It's ice cream cake."

"Yeah, that my maybe-ex-girlfriend brought for an early birthday celebration. For *me*." He stood and headed for the door. "But let me get you some, son."

"Dad."

Trace turned back to him, another sigh growing in his chest.

"I'm sorry," Harry said. "I know I ruined things for you tonight, and I'm sorry."

His whole heart melted, and Trace waved him off. "It's okay. I'll call her tonight *and* in the morning, and it probably wouldn't hurt if you apologized too."

Harry nodded, but then he simply rolled back toward the wall, leaving his phone on the nightstand.

Trace went to get him some cake, and when he returned to the kitchen after delivering it, he wrapped up the cake and put it in the freezer. It had melted quite a bit, but it would solidify again.

Then he picked up his phone and stared at it. "Here we go," he said. "Some inspiration like I had a few minutes ago would be nice."

Then he dialed his Ev.

38

Everly had given her phone to Shawn the moment he'd rolled up to the curb where she'd been standing. She'd asked him to turn it off and not give it back to her until he dropped her off at home.

Since he'd opened a restaurant in addition to his catering, her brother worked long hours. Very long hours. She'd gone back to Pork and Beans with him, and she currently had soap suds up to her elbows as she scrubbed a pot that had held baked beans. Really baked on, baked in, baked beans.

She didn't mind the manual labor. It gave her hands something to do while her mind whirred. And around and around it went right now. She didn't want to push Trace away, and she didn't want to break-up with him. She did want to be involved in his life, whether that included a storming, angry teenager, or that meant a quiet evening with ice cream cake and movies on the TV that neither of them watched.

Honestly, she thought she'd be laying in his arms on his couch right now, perfectly content and falling more and more in love with Trace Young with every breath she took. The fact that she wasn't had her scrubbing the pot harder and harder, until she realized how achy her knuckles were.

She tossed the steel wool into the sink and straightened with a grunt. She'd pulled her hair up into a ponytail the moment Shawn had pulled away from the curb, and she pushed the end of it over her shoulder now. "Maybe you could just get your phone and call him."

She should at least tell him she was safe, right? He *had* called, concerned about her. Tears pressed into her eyes, but she sucked in a breath when the plastic door swung into the dish room and her brother entered.

He finished laughing as he turned toward her, the last of his laughter falling into silence instantly. "I'm exhausted."

"Pots are almost done for the night," she said brightly. She couldn't meet his eye, so she bent over the sink again to finish up. "I can sweep and mop after that."

"Ev." Shawn came toward her, and when she wouldn't look at him, he took the steel wool right out of her hands. "What happened tonight?"

"Nothing." She flipped on the sink and started to rinse the pot.

"Yeah, because I pick you up in some random neighborhood on a nightly basis." He turned the water off.

Everly sighed and leaned into the sink. "Trace and I just got into a little...thing." She skimmed her gaze past her brother's. "It's fine. I'll call him tomorrow, and it'll be fine."

Shawn gazed at her for several long moments. "You love him."

"Sort of," Everly said, because she didn't want to admit it outright. Not yet.

Her brother grinned at her. "How do you 'sort of' love someone?" He looked up to the top of her head and ran his fingers down the side of her face. "Mom would've loved to see you dance with him at your wedding."

Her tears came fast then, and she couldn't hold them back. She collapsed into Shawn's arms and started blubbering. "What if he won't take me back?" she asked. "I said so many mean things to him."

"Like what?" Her brother held her close and spoke softly, so much like their dad.

"I said he was trying to keep me out of the family, and that he was letting his son ruin our night together." It had felt like that, but she knew by now that she couldn't rope the Young family and make them play to her schedule. Harry could've just as easily had an amazing night at his girlfriend's house, and she wouldn't even be standing here.

"And I hardly ever talk to Mama anymore, because I'm talking to Trace and telling him everything. He probably thinks I never shut up, and I'm so tired this week, and I just wanted to have ice cream cake and maybe whisper to him that I love him after he falls asleep on the couch."

Shawn rocked with her, and Everly's sniffles filled the dish room now that the water had been silenced. After maybe a full minute, he asked, "So you two are to the point where you're falling asleep together on the couch?"

"Sometimes," she whispered. She needed to pull herself together, and she straightened and reached up to tighten her ponytail. She drew in a long breath, wiped her face, and dared to look up at her brother. "I'm in love with him."

Shawn gave her the kindest smile, the kind only a loving, understanding older brother could give to his younger sister. "I know you are, Ev. Sounds like he doesn't, though."

She shook her head and turned back to the pot. "He has a lot going on in his life." All the time, it seemed. She wondered if they'd ever catch a break, and part of her ached for it. Another part liked the vibrancy of his life, how all of his brothers' lives intertwined with his, and that he knew what to do with his irate son on a night like tonight.

"Yeah," Shawn said. "And you're one of those things."

"Sometimes," she said again, a new measure of sadness filling her. "I don't want to talk about it anymore, okay? Let me help you get out of here sooner, and I'll see how I feel in the morning."

Her brother nodded and went back out into the

kitchen. More and more dishes got brought back as they closed and the cooks cleaned up for the evening. Everly didn't care. She washed and washed and washed and washed, and when Shawn finally dropped her off at home near midnight, she didn't have any energy left to turn on her phone and text Trace.

"You haven't spoken to him since?" Georgia stopped on the path in the cemetery and gaped at Everly.

She shook her head, glad she'd left her hair down this morning. She needed it as a shield against Georgia's lasery glare.

"This was Wednesday?"

She nodded, her voice apparently on vacation now that they'd arrived at the cemetery. Her parents weren't buried here, but Georgia's sister was. When Everly had heard that she'd be coming here today, she hadn't wanted her to go alone. That, and she'd wanted to visit the cemetery and feel closer to her parents.

Stupid, she knew, but she swore she could feel the spirits of those who'd already passed no matter what cemetery she visited. She'd come to the one here in Coral Canyon often and just wandered up and down the rows of resting places for loved ones lost.

"Honey, it's been three days." Georgia started walking again. "He's called and texted?"

"Both," Everly said. She looked up from the path beneath her feet and blew her breath out into the blue sky. The weather wasn't exactly warm, but the sun shone brightly. Her breath didn't steam in front of her, and her eyes ached from the brightness of the light.

"I don't know, Georgia."

"You don't know what?"

"I think maybe I broke us," she said.

"I doubt it," Georgia said.

"He's just so busy," she said. "And I'm demanding. I want him to put me first, and he doesn't. Sometimes I get it. I do. But sometimes it's just annoying."

Georgia smiled softly at the ground. "That it is."

Everly heaved another sigh. "I think I've always had this picture in my head, you know? Of how my husband will treat me, and I'm the queen." She could see herself with the golden crown and everything. "We don't always agree, of course, but in the end, he sees I'm right, or he says things like, 'if it's between the dog and you, I pick you,' or 'whatever you want, Miss Everly, as long as I can dance with you every night.'"

Her words hung in the still silence at the cemetery until Georgia started to giggle. Everly looked over to her. They walked slower than snails, and Everly enjoyed the pace of this day.

"What?" she asked.

"You sounded a lot like him right then." Georgia grinned at her. "He's got a bit deeper voice though."

Everly rolled her eyes, but she stepped over to Georgia and laced her arm through hers. "Thanks for letting me crash your cemetery visit."

"You're welcome," Georgia said simply. "Otis is taking Joey to Dog Valley, and I don't know. With the weather changing, it felt like a good time to come visit her."

"Do you come a lot?" Everly asked.

"Not really," Georgia said. "My family and I come on the anniversary of her death every year. That kind of thing."

"Do you miss her?"

"All the time." She looked at Everly, but she kept her eyes forward. "You?"

"Like crazy," she whispered. "I can't help feeling like my mama would know what to do."

"Honey, I can tell you what to do."

Everly did turn to meet Georgia's eye now. "Then tell me."

"You should be on the phone with him as soon as possible," Georgia said. "I get it, Everly. I do. I dated Otis while they were in the middle of song-writing and band stuff. He has a daughter too. All of it. I had a lot of family stuff going on as well, and then with the bookshop...you have to find a way to put each other first."

"I feel like I do that for him," she said. "But he doesn't do that for me."

"I think he does," Georgia said. "You're just not *seeing* it all."

Everly took a couple of steps while she thought about what Georgia had said. "What do you mean?" she asked. "What do you see?"

"Well, like last week during his momma's Sunday dinner, Trace got up after everyone had gotten food and was sitting down. We're all eating, right? And he gets up and goes back into the kitchen and opens the fridge. Why'd he do that?"

Everly's mind blanked. "I don't know."

"He got you the sweet pickle relish," she said. "His mother hates it. She doesn't own it. *Trace* brought it. For you."

Everly blinked, trying to remember the Sunday dinner they'd had last week. He had gotten up and brought her the relish from the fridge. She hadn't known he'd bought it specifically for her.

"He arranges for his son to get rides, so he doesn't have to leave you to pick up or drop off," Georgia said. "Luke or Otis take Harry home with them so Trace can pick you up at the studio and drive through to get hamburgers." Georgia smiled at that one. "I'm not complaining, because when we get Harry, he makes dinner. All my dogs love him, because he's a pushover and will give them bites of everything."

She couldn't seem to stop smiling, but everything she said made Everly feel worse and worse. "So you're saying he's done all these things, and because I'm such a hag, I didn't see them."

"No, of course not." Georgia squeezed her arm tighter to her side. "I'm saying, Ev, that you're looking for these great, big, life-changing moments. You want him to yell at his son to go to his room, that he'll deal with him later, because right now, it's all about *you*."

Everly said nothing, because that sounded about right.

"When really, the man has been catering to you since Day One in little ways. Ways it's hard to see when he's so handsome, and so talented, and so perfect for you. You overlook those things, and I'm saying...you shouldn't."

"I shouldn't," Everly repeated.

"He puts you first, Everly," Georgia said. "In the way he knows how, and I think it would be a real shame if you didn't call him in the next five minutes and tell him you love him and want to marry him tomorrow."

Everly smiled and shook her head. "I'm not marrying him tomorrow."

"No," Georgia said. "But it's the *sentiment*, Ev. You have to tell him you would, if he wanted to." Their eyes met, and all the dots connected for Everly. "Right?"

"Right," she said. "You're right."

"Of course I am," Georgia said. "These Young brothers aren't all the same, but if there's two that are similar enough, it's Otis and Trace. They're almost attached at the hip when they song-write."

"I think I missed most of that," Everly said.

"Lucky you," Georgia said dryly. She followed that with a laugh, and this time, Everly joined in. She drew in a deep breath and nodded ahead of her. "She's right up there, and I'd like to talk to her alone for a minute."

"Oh, sure," Everly said, immediately stopping and withdrawing her arm from Georgia's.

"You call Trace," Georgia said, her eyes still trained up ahead. "I can't wait to hear all about it once I'm done talking to Lindsey about the new baby I'm getting for Christmas." She smiled a smile made of a million watts and walked on, leaving Everly to marvel at her strength and resiliency.

Now, if she could summon even an ounce of what Georgia possessed, she'd be able to call Trace and tell him everything...and trust that he'd still want her in his life.

39

Trace watched his son's fingers as they moved up and down the bridge of his guitar. They didn't stutter or skip, and every note came out beautifully. Harry looked up and met Trace's eyes, and they smiled in tandem.

They'd already finished the lyrics, and Trace's guitar sang with Harry's over the last few notes. As the ending chord hung in the air, love filled Trace over and over again, spilling out and filling the house next.

"That was it," he said, almost reluctant to add his voice to the hum of music still vibrating in the air.

"When is she going to be here?" Harry asked as he let his guitar lay in his lap.

"I have to call her first." Trace hadn't even done that yet, because his last few calls to Everly had only resulted in hearing her voice on the recorded message. She wouldn't pick up, and she hadn't answered his texts, and her "minute" felt like an eternity.

His palms started to sweat, and he unlooped the strap from around his shoulder and balanced his guitar on the couch. "I'll go try again."

Harry said nothing, and his phone provided a great distraction for him as Trace opened the sliding glass door and went into the backyard. The weekend had brought another wave of cooler weather, and Trace didn't hate it. He didn't much enjoy the snow, but autumn might be his favorite season.

"Dear Lord," he started. "I'm in love with Everly Avery. Can you somehow let her know that, and help her heart be softened toward me? Just enough to get her to answer the phone. I think I can take it from there."

He and Harry had been playing together for the boy's entire life, but after the disaster that had been Wednesday night, their guitars had become instruments of healing too. Trace had written a song with Harry in a couple of hours on Thursday afternoon, and they'd been practicing it in every spare moment either of them had.

Sarah had come over last night, despite that being the designated night Trace was supposed to go out with his brothers for his birthday. Instead, on the day he'd turned forty, he'd served his son and his once-again girlfriend a delicious dinner of chicken pot pie buns—a recipe he'd called his mother to get. He may have even gone over to his parents' condo during the day while his son was at school to get a demonstration and a lesson on how to make the buns.

They'd eaten the refrozen ice cream cake, and Trace's heart had wailed for Everly.

He looked down at his phone, ready to tell Everly's voicemail he loved her if he had to. He really didn't want to say those words to a machine, but maybe they'd get the woman to call him back. He'd known Everly could be stubborn about some things; he just hadn't expected it to be him.

As he swiped to get to her name to call her, his phone rang. Her name appeared on the screen, and his heartbeat boomed like a gong in his ears. He couldn't answer fast enough, and his voice sounded full of air as he said, "Everly."

"Hey, Trace." She sounded resigned, and he hated that.

He spun on his heel, ready to go get her right now. "Where are you?" he asked. "Harry and I have something for you."

"You and Harry have something for me?"

"Yeah," he said. "Can I come get you? Or can you come over, like, right now?"

"Right now?"

"Yeah," he said. "I miss you so much. I'm so sorry. I'm already getting my keys. Just tell me where you are."

"I'm at the cemetery with Georgia," she said.

"Oh, right," he said. "I'd forgotten about that." He

opened the sliding glass door, and Harry looked up, his eyebrows high. "Did you drive together?" He didn't want to seem like an overeager golden retriever, but he sort of was.

"I miss you too," she whispered. "I'm the one who's sorry for not seeing everything."

He frowned, his feet taking him toward the hooks beside the garage door. "Seeing everything?"

"It's nothing." She sighed. "I don't think Georgia will mind if I ditch her. She picked me up, so I don't have my car."

"I'm on my way," he said. "Don't hang up. I like the sound of your voice. Tell me what you've been doing the past few days."

"Staring at the TV," she said. "Feeding Mutant too many times, because I can't remember if I've done it or not. He's probably gained six pounds."

Trace chuckled, because Mutant probably weighed six pounds total. "What's got you all shook up?"

"You, Mister Young," she said. "This was how I was last year when you said we couldn't go out again, and then again after Christmas when my plan to get your son to love me backfired."

Trace sobered as he got behind the wheel. "My Ev, my son loves you." He swallowed, his throat turning into a drinking straw. *Wait*, he told himself. *Don't tell her you love her for the first time over the phone.*

She said nothing either, and then he heard her sniffling. "I hate that I'm not there," he said. "I changed my mind. I'm going to hang up, so I don't make you cry, and I don't say something I don't want to say."

"What don't you want to say?"

He swallowed again and dang near backed into his still-closed garage door. He reached up to hit the button to open it, his nerves firing like cannons. "I'll tell you when I get there."

"Okay," she said. "See you soon."

"Yep." He ended the call, and he gripped the steering wheel. "This is okay," he lectured himself. "She's going to say it back. She loves you too, Trace." He wasn't sure if he'd ever been loved by a woman, as he and Val hadn't really taken the time to fall in love. Their romance had been so whirlwind, and so fast, and so full of passion. Trace still wanted all of that, but he wanted depth too.

"You have that with Ev," he told himself. They'd known each other for longer than he and Val had been married, and telling her he loved her wasn't the same as a proposal. He had more time for that too. More time to fall deeper in love with her, to make sure she and Harry had the experiences she wanted them to have, and to talk about what their family life should look like.

He drove as quickly as possible, arriving at the cemetery on the south side of Coral Canyon only a few minutes later. The branches in the tall trees here swayed in the wind, and Trace liked how peaceful they were.

He spotted Everly wearing a dark brown jacket and

those jeans that seemed glued to her skin. She'd tucked her hands in her pockets, and she walked slowly toward him. He pulled up to the curb and jammed the truck into park, already unbuckling and swinging out of the vehicle.

He left his door open as he strode toward her, breaking into a jog after only a few steps. "My Ev," he said, and as he reached her only a second or two later, he swept her into his arms. "I have hated the past couple of days without you. I didn't even know who I was without you, and I never want to go through that again."

She clung to him too, and Trace wanted to shield her from anything and everything. The weather. Tense situations with his son. His family and all their drama. Everything. If the two of them could simply be together forever, Trace would be happy.

Everly stepped back and wiped her eyes. Trace's hands followed hers, the softness of her skin sending a thrill through his body. "I love you," he said, the words making him smile. "You're the first and only woman I've ever loved." He chuckled and ducked his head. "Wow, it feels amazing to say that."

He looked at her, and let the tree branches whisper around them as she studied his face, her eyes wide. "You love me?"

"I'm catastrophically in love with you," he whispered. "I can't live without you." He leaned down and touched his forehead to hers, his eyes falling closed. "Tell me I won't ever have to live without you."

They breathed in together, and as Everly exhaled, she said, "I can't promise you that, Trace."

He pulled back and looked at her, a vein of shock striking through his bloodstream. He had no idea what to say, and he wished he'd played the song for her first.

"Things happen sometimes," she said next. "I mean, Georgia's here visiting her sister, and I came, because I love visiting cemeteries, as it helps me feel closer to my parents. They were taken from earth far too soon."

He nodded, trying to work the muscles in his throat enough to swallow.

"I never want to live without you," she said, and his eyes flew back to hers. A tiny smile pulled at the corners of his mouth. "But I can't promise anything."

"Can you promise to be mine?"

"Is this a proposal?"

"No," he said quickly. "This is me telling you I love you, and I sometimes do stupid things that make you mad, and I don't want us to ever go an hour without talking to each other again. The past couple of days weren't okay with me."

"They weren't okay with me either," she whispered. She tipped up onto her toes and invaded his personal space. "Because I love you too."

Joy burst through Trace, and a smile formed on his face. "Oh, you've been holding that back for a while."

"So have you," she said, settling back onto her feet.

She grinned up at him. "Are you going to stand there grinning, or are you going to kiss me?"

"I'm going to kiss you." He brought her flush against him and held her face in his hands as he did exactly that, and while he'd kissed Everly many times in the past few months, none of them felt like this one. There was something special about kissing a soulmate, and Trace hadn't experienced it until this moment.

He moved slowly, stroking his mouth against hers and truly experiencing her for the first time, over and over again, until Georgia said, "I don't think you're supposed to kiss like that in a cemetery."

Only then did Everly pull away and bury her face in Trace's chest. He grinned at his brother's wife. "Hey, Georgia."

"Trace," she said with a knowing tone. "Ev, I guess you don't need a ride home?"

"No," she said. She stepped away from Trace and into Georgia's embrace. She said something to her that Trace didn't catch, and then she quickly returned to Trace's side.

"Come on," he said, lacing his fingers through hers. "Harry and I have something for you, and he's waiting for you before he goes over to Sarah's."

"Oh, did he and Sarah get back together?"

Trace shook his head at her, a teasing energy flowing between them. "Don't tell me you didn't know. I read my son's texts." He led her toward the truck and paused before opening her door for her. "And I'll have you know that it hurt that you'd text him back and not me."

Regret shot across her face. "Trace...." She put one hand against his chest. "I needed a minute to work through some things."

He nodded and looked away before coming back to focus on her. "Did you work through them?"

"Mostly," she said.

"Enough to know that we have to be together," he said.

"Yeah." She smiled at him and touched her lips to his sweetly. "Enough to know I'm madly in love with you, and I want to be with you as much as possible."

Trace grinned at her, all the pain and doubt from the past few days completely gone now. "We've talked about marriage, Ev, but what's my timeframe here?"

"Timeframe?"

"When's your dream wedding date? Season? Something. Then I can plan a proposal that will give you enough time to plan a wedding and have it when you want it to hit."

She slid her hands up his arms and around to the back of his neck. He encircled her in his arms, wanting to hold her forever and ever. "Trace, I don't care when we get married, as long as we do."

"Oh, we will," he said.

"And Harry's okay with it?"

"Like I said a few minutes ago, Harry loves you. He

was just frustrated and irate in that moment, and nothing was right in his head. He can't wait to see you."

She grinned up at him. "All right, well, I'll just say this. You turned forty yesterday, and I'm thirty-five. If you want more kids, we probably shouldn't date for another twenty months before we get married."

"I'm hearing sooner rather than later." He leaned down and kissed her again, and she didn't have to confirm what he'd said. Her kiss said it all.

40

Everly couldn't stop weeping. Watching Trace and Harry play and sing together was a truly spiritual experience. They looked like one another; they sounded like one another; they moved and played almost exactly like one another.

"Family," they sang together. "We want her to be our family." That last note undid her, and Everly buried her face in her hands as Harry continued to play. Trace stopped, the remnant of his notes still mingling with his son's.

"Hey, my Ev." Trace wrapped his arms around her, and Everly leaned into his touch. "I'm sorry. I didn't mean to make you cry."

"Yes, you did." She swatted at his chest, her tears still flowing down her face. "That's what you do when you write a song so perfect and then sing it with your son."

Harry set his guitar aside and came over too. She opened her arms to him, and he sank right into her. Trace held both of them then, and Everly had only felt this loved and this safe with her core family. Her parents and siblings.

"I love you guys," she whispered. She hadn't expected today to go like this, but she sure was glad it had. She'd known she needed to call Trace, but she honestly hadn't been sure how he'd react. It had never really been her style to ignore people when they called her, but the two days of pondering had only reinforced what she'd been feeling.

She loved Trace Young, and yes, she had for a while and had been holding it back. Maybe the moment he kissed her at his brother's wedding.

"Can I play at the wedding?" Harry asked. "And you'll come to my holiday recital, right, Miss Everly?"

"I wouldn't miss it." She looked at Trace. "I wouldn't be opposed to him playing at our wedding."

"Me either," Trace said with a smile. He got to his feet and turned back to his guitar. He took impeccable care of his instruments, and he put both his and Harry's guitars in their stands. "Let's go up to Dog Valley for dinner."

"Can you drop me off at Sarah's on your way?" Harry asked. "Her uncle is in town, and they're doing a *Star Wars* movie marathon."

"Yeah, that's the plan," Trace said. He grinned at his son and slung his arm around him as they moved into the kitchen. Everly wiped her eyes, glad she hadn't put on much makeup that morning. She'd done a partnering class before going to the cemetery with Georgia, and now she watched as Trace leaned closer to Harry and said something.

She got to her feet, curious. She got close enough at the end to hear Trace say, "...say thank you in the morning, okay?"

"I will, Dad." Harry glanced over to her.

"Where are you going in the morning?" she asked.

Trace faced her and blinked. "I asked Tex to pick him up from Sarah's tonight and have him sleep over. They're going to talk to Bryce in the morning, after breakfast."

Everly's eyes widened. "Wow." She looked from Trace to Harry. "How are things going with that?"

Harry shrugged one shoulder, but she'd seen him in full-on fury mode. "I have some things to say to him, and I'll say them as kindly as I can."

Everly nodded, marveling at how wise Harry sounded. "All right," she said. "I can't wait to hear how that goes."

"Yeah," Trace said. "Me either." He grinned at the pair of them. "Now, let's go."

"Why are you in such a hurry?" Everly asked. "Can I at least go make sure I don't have raccoon eyes?"

"You don't," Trace said. "But go on. I guess I can wait." He grinned at her, and she rolled her eyes as she turned to go into the guest bathroom down the hall. Once there, she looked at herself in the mirror. No, she didn't have black makeup smudged around her eyes. She didn't look too blotchy, and what mild patches she did have from the crying would fade before they got to Dog Valley.

A new glow rode in her expression now, and she knew exactly what it was. The look of a woman who was loved by a very, very good man.

She left the bathroom and hurried into the kitchen. "Harry, I have an idea," she said.

"Yeah?"

"Yeah." She indicated his guitar. "You should play at the next dance I do at The Stomp."

Harry's eyes widened. He looked at his father.

"You said you wanted more opportunities to play," Trace said. "There you go."

"Did you tell her that?"

"No, sir," Trace said, grinning. "I think Miss Everly knows a little bit about us, which is a good thing, since she's going to become such an integral part of our family." He beamed at her, and Everly swooped into his arms, hooking Harry in the process. The three of them stood there and embraced, and Everly hadn't known the Lord could answer prayers so perfectly until that moment.

"PUT THOSE ROLLS OVER THERE, DEAR," CECILY Young said to Everly. She did as Trace's momma said and then shot a glance over to her brothers. They'd stuck together, but they had been moving around the room.

The Young family had rented an enormous barn that functioned as an event center for their Thanksgiving Day dinner, and she wasn't the only person who'd brought her family. Abby's parents had come, as had her brother and his wife, Cheryl. She was due any day with a baby, and she hadn't moved from the chair her husband had put her in when they'd arrived.

Leigh's brother Denzel sat on one of the couches and chatted with Blaze, his German shepherd at his feet, and as the conversation Reggie and Shawn were having with Gabe wrapped up, they turned their attention in that direction too.

Everly went over to join them, as there were plenty of helping hands in the kitchen. "What's your dog's name again?" she asked Denzel.

"Scout," he said, smiling up at her. She sat next to him and scooted all the way over so her brothers could pile on the couch too.

Blaze only watched them squeeze four people onto a couch made for three, his dark eyes observant and assessing. She'd not spoken to him much in the past couple of months, but everyone knew Faith had broken up with him.

Her heart squeezed, but something in her head told her not to say anything. "How's the stocking stuffer thing coming?" she asked him.

"Good enough," Blaze said. "Believe it or not, a bunch of former bull riding champions isn't the most organized group on the planet." He grinned, and she giggled.

"You rode bulls?" Reggie asked.

Blaze looked at him. "For over two decades, give or take a year." He leaned closer. "Are you in rodeo? Because it takes a huge toll on your body."

"Reg plays professional baseball," Everly said, a hint of pride creeping into her voice. "He's already got physical therapy and chiropractor appointments all the time."

"Not all the time," Reg said, but Everly knew better. Sometimes she still texted him to make sure he was going to the appointments, as they shared a calendar as siblings.

"What team?" Blaze asked without missing a beat. Most people fawned over Reggie, and he claimed to love coming "home" to Coral Canyon, because it wasn't a huge baseball town. None of them had grown up here, but the small town did feel like home to all of them.

"The Mariners," Reggie said.

"Tell me about the program," Shawn said. "I feel like my military buddies could use an opportunity to serve in the community."

Blaze fixed his nearly-black eyes on her brother, and Everly looked back and forth between the two of them.

"As if the military hasn't served us enough," Blaze said quietly.

"It's always a good time to serve," Shawn said evenly, and Everly reached over and took her brother's hand in hers.

"Shawn is doing the free food truck rally later today,"

she said with more than a hint of pride in her voice. "He loves giving back to the community."

Blaze leaned back in his chair and watched them all. "Some of my friends in the rodeo—former champions— we're doing a Christmas gift program for families in need. It's called Santa's Stocking Stuffers, and we want to make sure there aren't any kids who go without this year."

"In Coral Canyon?" Shawn asked.

"Coral Canyon," Blaze confirmed. "Because I'm here, and another big star from a decade or so ago—Todd Christopherson. Wyatt Walker comes up here in the summers, but he's sponsoring Three Rivers, Texas. Todd and I are doing Rusk, Dog Valley, Coral Canyon, and even parts of Jackson Hole."

"That's amazing," Shawn said.

"There's a woman in Calgary," Blaze said. "Former barrel racer. She's taking part of the city up there. We've got guys in Montana, Texas, and Alabama too. We meet every week, and we're doing things in our local communities, but also on this global scale. It's a lot, is all."

"I can help," Everly and Shawn said at the same time.

"I can too," Denzel added.

Blaze looked at all of them with a hint of surprise in his eyes. "I might take y'all up on that," he said. "I feel like I'm in over my head."

"You need a coordinator," Everly said. "Someone to manage all the details, so you can just do the shopping and wrapping."

He grinned and shook his head. "Oh, I'm not wrapping."

"What?" she demanded. "Blaze, that's the best part."

"For who?" He gave her a mock glare, though his smile stayed in place.

"Who what?" Georgia asked as she arrived. Abby came with her, and Everly lifted up her hands so she could take Melissa from her. With the baby in her lap, Everly experienced more joy than she'd known previously.

"She can't hold the baby," Blaze said.

"What?" Abby asked. She looked from Everly to Blaze and back. "Oh, right."

"What? Why can't I hold her?" Everly asked as Abby whisked the nine-month-old away. "I want to hold her, and you're busy in the kitchen."

"No, dinner is almost set," Abby said. Melissa fussed on her hip, but she shushed her. She glanced over to the door, and Everly did too. In this huge hall, it wouldn't be hard to see someone come in, but she had no idea who Abby was looking for.

Everyone who was coming had arrived, at least according to Everly's knowledge. She glanced around, noting that Otis had disappeared. Luke wasn't here, though Corrine sat at the kids' table, a fat blue crayon in her hand. Someone had covered the table with a big sheet of paper, and both Cecily and Jerry sat with the littlest kids and colored with them.

If dinner was ready, why were they coloring?

"Where's Tex?" she asked when she didn't see him. Harry wasn't there, and neither was Trace. "Where are all the Youngs?"

None of them were there. Not Morris, or Gabe. Not Jem or Mav. Not Bryce, not even Blaze's son, Cash.

She looked over to Abby, then Georgia, then Blaze. Her heartbeat plummeted to the soles of her feet. "Where's Tex?" she asked again.

"Oh, I don't know," Abby said, about the worst lie on the planet. She eyed the door again, something fierce coming into her face, as if she could will it to open and her husband to walk through it.

Surprisingly, that was what happened.

Almost.

The door did open, but it wasn't Tex who entered first.

It was Trace—and he was carrying a guitar in his arms. His son came behind him and immediately went to his right-hand side.

Then came Tex, also with a guitar, and then Otis, and then Luke.

When the five of them had formed a line, Trace began to play. He walked toward Everly, who'd apparently positioned herself perfectly, and he didn't take his eyes from her.

He smiled, and Everly couldn't help returning the smile. He was so gorgeous and so good, and they'd been talking about marriage, weddings, and babies for over two months now. She wasn't impatient for him to ask her to marry him—until now.

Now she wanted him down on both knees, his whole family surrounding them, while he asked her to be his wife.

Morris fanned out to one side, while Gabe and Mav joined the other. Bryce and Jem went to the other side, and soon enough, Everly had the entire Young family of brothers and sons of brothers coming her way.

"Blaze," she said.

He only chuckled as he got to his feet. His daddy handed him a guitar, and the two of them joined the line that had now reached the edge of the rug in this sitting area.

"You don't think you'll find a true love," Trace started to sing, his voice smooth but oh-so-country. "In a small Wyoming town."

Tears pricked her eyes, and Everly pressed her palm over her heart as he sang a short, perfect love song for her.

Otis and Tex sang back-up, as did Bryce and Harry. The two cousins weren't standing next to each other, but as far as Everly knew, they'd made up.

All of the Youngs played, and if there were any missed or wrong notes, Everly would never know. She'd hear about it from Trace later, but right now, the serenade was exquisite.

When Reggie and Shawn got up, shock coursed through Everly. They joined the line, and while neither of them played, they'd obviously been looped into this, because they knew the lyrics to this original song.

We'd be so lucky to add her to our family.

Our family

Our family.

If she'll have us, we want her in our family.

Our family

Our family.

As the song ended, Trace handed his guitar to Shawn, dug in his pocket, and came toward Everly. He dropped to both knees and held out a massive diamond ring. She'd seen it before, because they'd gone shopping together.

Only one guitar talked now, and Everly knew enough to know it was Harry. The boy played beautifully, and he understood dynamics better than anyone. That was how Trace's hoarse, husky voice still lifted above the music as he said, "My Ev."

He dropped his head then, his throat working as he swallowed. When he looked up again, unshed tears glistened in his eyes. Everly reached out and cradled his face in one hand.

"I love you," he said. "I've been falling for you since that first date almost two years ago. I've always known I wanted you, and I've always hoped we could be together, that what I've been saying for months—my Ev—would come true."

Tears filled her eyes too, because she could remember

the very first time Trace had called her that. It had been life-changing, and she did want to be his.

"Will you marry me?"

"Yes," she said, no hesitation whatsoever. "Yes, I can't wait to marry you." Her hand shook as he slid the ring onto her fourth finger, and then he took her into his arms and kissed her while everyone who'd gathered for Thanksgiving dinner cheered, whooped, hollered, and whistled.

Everly laughed against his lips, because this was the big, huge, loud family she'd been craving—and he was giving it to her.

"I love you," she said.

"I love you too."

"All right, all right," someone yelled, and Everly looked over to the mass of men holding guitars. Trace got up off the floor and sat next to her on the couch while Morris handed his guitar to his twin and moved to the center of the group.

He wore a smile made of all the joy in the world. "I have an announcement too. Leigh and I are expecting another baby."

His mother gasped into the silence created by his statement. Then the room went wild again, and Everly whooped and applauded as loudly as she could. She didn't know Morris extremely well, though he was involved in the band, but she knew that he and Leighann had been married before, and that he hadn't known about his three-year-old son until last summer.

He wiped his eyes as his family descended on him, and Everly's heart felt like it might burst from happiness. He hadn't been able to make that announcement last time. He hadn't been here to feel this love and support and joy.

"You'd think *he* was the one growing another human inside his body."

Everly turned to find Leigh perched on the armrest near her brother. Their eyes met, and Everly burst out laughing. Leigh joined her, as did Denzel, and she reached over and squeezed Leigh's hand. "How's the bakery coming?"

Leigh's smile didn't slip even a little bit. "I decided to put it on the back burner," she said. "I'm going to have two children under the age of five soon enough, and the one I've got runs me ragged sometimes." She grinned all the while, and Everly knew she adored her son.

Morris came over and lifted his wife right up off her feet, the two of them so joyful and full of sunshine.

"Let's eat," Cecily yelled, and that got her sons to quiet down enough for a prayer. Everly tucked herself into Trace's side as his daddy said grace, thanking the Lord for all the many blessings they each brought with them to the table that morning.

Everly thought of her mom and dad, and how much they'd have loved to be here for this. Only a pinch of sadness entered her heart, and it only stayed for a moment.

Mama, she thought. *I love him, and he loves me, and we're going to be a family.*

She swore she heard a voice say, *That's wonderful, dear. Do us Averys proud.*

The prayer ended, and Everly didn't join in the "Amen" chorus. Cecily had obviously dealt with her huge brood of loud men before, because she got up on a chair quick as lightning and raised both hands above her head.

"All of the food is out," she yelled. "Eat dessert first, or mashed potatoes, or salad. It doesn't matter. There are no assigned seats, but be good to each other. After dinner, we'll do our gratitude journal for this year, and we'll go around and share what we're grateful for this year, so get ready for that."

She'd apparently given this speech before, because once she'd said that, voices filled the hall and men moved to get food from the buffet that had been created.

Everly looked up at Trace. "Gratitude journal?"

"We do one as a family every year," he said. "Well, there were a few lean years there, where some of us weren't talking to others of us." He shrugged one shoulder. "Or where there were very few of us actually in town...." He frowned. "We did it as kids, and Momma's revived it in the past couple of years, let's say that."

She went with him toward the buffet. "Does everyone have to say something they're grateful for?"

"No," he said. "Momma's goal is not to embarrass anyone. Just say pass." He handed her a plate, his eyes kind but still somewhat fiery. "You don't have anything you can say in front of my family?"

"You mean the whole town?" she teased.

He laughed, and that made her smile. He put a couple of slices of turkey on his fake china plate and leaned closer to her. "We're engaged, Miss Everly. You're my fiancée."

She looked down at her hand and gasped. "Oh, wow, cowboy. You're right." She beamed up at him, and he leaned down to kiss her again.

"There's no kissing in line," someone growled, and Everly pulled away from Trace as embarrassment heated her veins.

"Jem, leave 'em alone," Tex said. "They can kiss if they want to. In fact, where's my wife? Maybe I'll kiss her in this buffet line too." He gave Jem a pointed look, and the other cowboy rolled his eyes and walked away.

Tex stood next to Trace, and they both watched Jem. "He's not doin' good," Trace said.

"No," Tex agreed. "Have you been to his place?'

"Not since Halloween."

The two brothers exchanged a look, but Everly didn't get the message. Tex sighed and said, "I'll sit by him and see what I can find out, but I'm only doing it because you just got engaged."

"Thanks, brother."

"You owe me," Tex said as he walked away.

"What's wrong with his place?" Everly asked.

Trace's demeanor darkened, only to go back to shining white when he looked at her. "He's...not a great house-keeper, let's say that."

"He barely dresses his kids, you mean," Blaze said darkly. "They have no food in their fridge, and their father's drunk all the time. I think that's what you meant, right, Trace?"

"Blaze," Trace warned. "Do not do this. It's Thanksgiving, and Momma and the other ladies have worked real hard on dinner."

Blaze pressed his lips together and nodded. "Fine, I won't do this here. But someone better do something, or he's going to lose his kids." He too walked away, and all kinds of alarms rang through Everly.

"Is that true, baby? He'll lose his kids?"

"Well, he's not taking care of them," Trace muttered. "Blaze and Mav or I go over there every day to get Cole off to school and get Rosie dressed and fed. More often than not, Mav takes her home with him for the day and then to her afternoon preschool class."

"That's terrible."

"Jem's going through a hard time," Trace said.

"Someone always is," Everly agreed. "We can sit by him too. Might be less obvious."

"No," Trace said as he moved down the line and kept piling food on his plate. "Look at your brothers, Ev. They need you."

She found them sitting by Gabe and Morris, looking back and forth between the identical twins with pure confusion on their faces. "Oh, brother," she muttered.

"Am I going to have to tell those two to stop acting like they don't know which twin they are?"

"Yes," Trace said. "They're like big ten-year-olds. Please tell them."

"Miss Everly," Harry called as she and Trace left the food table. "I've got seats here for you." He indicated the two spots next to her brothers that he'd left open, and Everly went toward him.

She sat between Harry and Reggie, the two young men she adored, and she first swept a kiss along her brother's cheek and said, "I love you, Reg," and then turned to Harry.

His hair had grown long again, and she swooped it off his forehead. "I love you too, Harry. I can't wait to be your stepmom. I'll do the best I can, okay?"

"You'll be great, Ev," Harry said with a smile. She wrapped him in a hug too, smiling with tears in her eyes as he said, "I love you too, okay?"

She nodded and released him. Across from her, Trace watched her, questions in his eyes. She simply shook her head, which caused an errant tear to track down her face. She swiped it away quickly and said, "I'm going into full carb mode." She picked up her roll. "Bread first."

Trace smiled at her and reached across the table for her hand. She slid her fingers between his and squeezed. "Love you," he said.

"Love you too."

Read on for a sneak peek at **BLAZE**, featuring Blaze Young, the next brother in the Young Family who can't seem to...well, you better read the sneak peek chapters - keep tapping and scrolling to get to them! - to find out what Blaze is going to do about Faith...

Sneak Peek! BLAZE Chapter One:

Blaze Young left the family party while it was still in full swing. His son was not here with him this year for Thanksgiving, but he'd agreed to stop by his ex-wife's parents' house anyway. In truth, he'd done so just to be able to leave the Young family shindig early.

He paused outside, though the Wyoming winter had started early this year. Honestly, it started early every blasted year, and Blaze hated the cold. If he had a pretty redhead to keep him warm, he might not mind it too much.

He banished all thoughts of Faith Cromwell, noting that she marched out of his mind—with that gorgeous auburn hair and those unkissed lips—without much of a fight today. He disliked that too, but she'd broken up with him when they'd just been getting started, and he wasn't going to chase her.

That wasn't really Blaze's style and never had been.

"I thought you were leaving," one of his brothers said, and Blaze glanced casually over his shoulder. It wasn't Jem, as his brother hadn't spoken to him since the night Faith had broken up with him.

Blaze had tried to apologize, but Jem wouldn't come out of his bedroom. He'd texted him, and Jem hadn't responded. He'd moved out the very next day, and he hadn't asked anyone for help.

But Blaze had put their momma on the job, and she'd organized the brothers and wives to go help him get his house set up. Blaze had not gone, so he only knew about Jem's new place and the conditions of it second-hand.

Since then, though, he did go with Mav in the morning to help with Rosie and Cole. Mav always went in first, and if Jem wasn't up yet, he gestured to Blaze from the front door, and Blaze would go in. And Jem was never up in time to help his children get off to school, get break-fast, or show them he cared about them.

Blaze worried about him constantly, but faced with Luke in the near darkness though it was only three-thirty, he managed a smile. "I am," he said. "Just taking a minute to enjoy the silence."

"Right?" Luke practically growled the word.

"You goin' to Tea's?"

Luke nodded, but a big sigh accompanied the action.

"Brother, that doesn't sound like you want to go to Tea's."

"Her family is as big as ours," Luke said. "Last time I was at her house, it was like her front door was one of those revolving ones. You know, how they never lock and anyone can walk in anytime?"

Blaze watched the dislike roll across Luke's face and tense up his shoulders.

"Not only that, but I haven't introduced her to Corrine yet." He glared at the gray sky above them. "I haven't even *told* her about my kid yet, and a couple of days ago, Tea said she didn't want kids."

"Mm." Blaze wasn't in the business of offering unwanted advice. If Luke wanted to talk, he'd listen, but he wasn't going to tell Luke what he should do.

"I love my daughter," Luke said fiercely. "I love all the kids in our family, and maybe I'm stupid, but seeing Tex with his new baby, and Mav, and even Otis and Georgia, even if it's not biologically theirs...I want another baby."

He didn't say that he'd missed out on most of Corrine's first three years of life, but he didn't have to. Blaze had missed eleven years, so he got it without words being said. He also didn't want to say he wanted to try being a father to a baby too. A toddler. A five-year-old who got to go to kindergarten for the first time.

Blaze smiled just thinking about it. "So what are you going to do?"

"I don't see how I can keep going out with her."

"Mm." Blaze fisted his hands in his coat pockets. "And

yet, you're standing out here like you'll leave to go to her family party."

"I'm not a total jerk," Luke said. "I can't break-up with her on Thanksgiving." He glared at Blaze, but Blaze had faced two-ton bulls, and Luke was nothing compared to them. He shook his head. "Besides, she just said it to a friend, and I overheard. Maybe she didn't mean it."

"Maybe she didn't," Blaze said. "Go. Have fun."

Luke frowned. "But what if she means it?"

"Then, brother, you figure out what to do." Blaze put his arm around Luke. "Do you like her?"

"Yeah." He didn't sound like he did though.

"Yeah, I'm convinced," Blaze said.

"There's...." Luke shook his head, a personal war marching across his features now. Like Blaze, he was dark in every way. He had good reason to go slow with women, but Blaze didn't pry into Luke's private life. He knew his brother's paternity had been up in the air for a while there, and Blaze wouldn't wish that kind of betrayal on anyone.

He may not be proud of what he'd done in the past, but he'd never cheated. Luke hadn't either, at least that Blaze knew of.

"There's what?" Blaze asked.

"Nothing." Luke took a deep breath and coughed. "Wow, it's too cold to do that." He smiled at Blaze, and a tiny bit of it went up into his eyes. "Where are you headed? Home?"

"Over to the Peters'," he said.

Luke's eyebrows went up. "Really? Isn't Cash in Utah?"

"Yeah." Blaze nodded. "Yep. But Fiona doesn't talk to her parents hardly at all, and they need the lifeline to their grandson." He spoke softly and slowly, not wanting to say anything too badly about his ex-wife. He knew the reasons she couldn't come back to Coral Canyon, and he didn't blame her. Not one bit.

He'd even enjoyed getting to know his ex-in-laws, as messed up as that sounded. Cash had too, and his son had a massive, amazing support network here in Coral Canyon that he desperately needed.

"You're a good man, Blaze." Luke put his arm around Blaze too.

"I'm trying to fix a lot of things I broke," Blaze said. "That's all."

Luke nodded. "Yeah, I get that." And he probably did.

They stood there for another few seconds, and then Luke dropped his arm so Blaze did too. "I should go," his brother said.

"What am I going to do about Jem?" Blaze asked.

Luke had taken a couple of steps away, but he turned back instantly. His eyes widened, and he searched Blaze's face. "I don't know, Blaze. None of us know what to do about Jem."

"He didn't drink like this in Vegas," Blaze said. "I'm worried I forced him into retirement when he wasn't ready."

Luke stepped back up onto the curb. "No," he said. "Blaze, this isn't on you at all."

"I humiliated him in public."

"No, he did that himself with how much he'd drank." Luke shook his head. "Blaze, Jem loved Chanel, even if their marriage wasn't perfect. He's drinking to erase her." He spoke with enough power to make Blaze think he had personal experience with such things.

So Blaze nodded too. "I've apologized a dozen times." More, even. "He won't talk to me, and he's my best friend." Blaze's chest collapsed again, just like it did every time he thought about Jem and the state of their relationship.

"Tex is talking about an intervention," Luke said. "Rehab. Someone's gonna need to take his kids if he goes into an in-patient facility. Blaze, we all know that will be you."

"Could be Mav," he said. "He takes Rosie a lot."

"It'll be you." Luke was right, because Blaze didn't have a job, he didn't have a wife, and he didn't have small children the way Mav and Dani did.

"His house is a wreck," Blaze whispered. Every morning when he went inside, another layer of Blaze's heart shredded off. Honestly, someone should take Jem's kids right now, and the only reason Blaze hadn't done it yet was because he thought it would destroy his brother even further. At the very least, that directive couldn't come from Blaze.

Tex, maybe. Even Trace, who Jem loved and admired.

Blaze had once thought Jem loved and admired him, but they weren't the same men they'd been on the rodeo circuit. Things changed. Too many hard truths had been spoken.

Regret lanced through Blaze, though he thought he'd done the right thing. Maybe just not at the right time.

"Yeah, I've been over there," Luke said. "We'll talk more at Tex's on Sunday, okay?" He clapped Blaze on the shoulder, which sent a shock along his back, where he'd had surgery earlier this year.

He grunted, and Luke yanked his hand back. "Sorry. Shoot, Blaze, I'm sorry."

"It's fine." The discomfort faded as quickly as it had come. "I have to get going too." He smiled at Luke, pulled him into a hug, and they went to their trucks. He made the quick drive to Carrie and Marion's, parked in the driveway, which only held one other vehicle, and reached for the loaf of chocolate sourdough bread his momma had made for them.

On the front stoop, he rang the doorbell, so unlike what a true family member would do. But when Carrie Peters opened the front door, she wore a smile as big as Jupiter. "It's Blaze," she called into the back of the house, and then she wrapped him up in a tight, motherly hug. "Oh, it's so good to see you."

"Sorry I don't have Cash this year," he said as he hugged her back.

"We'll take you alone." She stepped back and grinned

at him, and Blaze saw all the fair features of his son in her face.

He smiled at her and offered the bread. "My momma made it."

"Thank you," she said. "Come in, come in. It's freezing out there." He entered and she closed the door behind him. "But it's a good thing you've got your coat."

He'd started to unzip it, because Carrie had the house heated to the level of Hades. Maybe hotter than that. He paused. "Why do I need a coat?"

"We're going to the food truck rally," Carrie said cheerfully. "They're taking donations if you can give it. Otherwise, you can eat anything out of any truck for free."

Blaze's heart sagged down to his stomach. "Oh, great," he said with zero enthusiasm. Marion came out of the kitchen, along with Fiona's brother and his wife, and Blaze hugged them all. "Ready?" Marion asked, and he reached for the winter coat that had been draped over the back of the couch.

"So ready," Blaze said, sweating already—and not only from the insane temperature inside this house.

"Do you want to ride with us?" Carrie positioned a scarf around the back of her neck and looked at him with raised eyebrows.

"I think the rally is downtown," he said. "That's almost back to the canyon, so I'll drive." That way, he could leave if he wanted to. When he wanted to. If he maybe ran into Faith.

Of course you're going to run into Faith, he told himself. She'd plastered all over the social media for Hole in One that she'd be at the free food truck rally today. Blaze might have gone otherwise, but he didn't need to make things awkward for either one of them. Not at a charity event.

He followed Carrie and Marion and McKenzie and Matt over to the food truck rally. Plenty of people had come out for this thing, and that lifted Blaze's spirits. Hopefully, this event would raise a lot of money for people in need. A voice in his head told him that he could help with that, and he should.

So after he parked, he reached over and opened the glove box to get out his checkbook. He quickly scrawled out a check, scribbled on his signature, and stuffed it in his back pocket as he slid from the truck.

He hadn't parked very close to the Peters', but he'd find them once he got to the massive circle of trucks. As he walked down the block toward the festivities, he scanned for the bright pink doughnut truck that would be covered in even more fluorescent sprinkles. He didn't see it.

Of course, there were more trucks on the other side. He approached the line to enter the big inner circle, and he found the Peters' waiting for him. He forced a smile to his face and joined them.

As they approached the donation box, he reached for his check.

"We're doing a raffle from the donation box," a man

kept saying. "Checks will have the info, but if you're donating cash, be sure to get a ticket." Over and over he said it, and two women worked the line, handing out tickets.

At the box finally, Blaze shoved his check inside and flashed the man a tight smile.

"All right!" someone yelled into a microphone—which never needed to happen in Blaze's opinion. "It's time for our four o'clock drawing. Owen, bring that box up here, would you?"

Blaze kept moving, because he was in now. He scanned all the trucks now, left to right, right to left. There was no bright pink one. Maybe she wasn't here. Concern spiked inside him. Could her truck have broken down again?

After they'd broken up, she hadn't contacted him again, though he'd tried to pay for her truck one more time. When she'd ignored him, he'd dropped the subject.

Maybe she'd never gotten it fixed. *But she has two other trucks*, he thought. He didn't care about the raffle, and he thought he really needed to find another dessert truck to get his Thanksgiving Day pumpkin pie fix. He stepped over to Matt, who'd gotten a complete list of all the trucks there.

"All right, we've got the lovely mistress of Hole in One drawing this hour," the announcer said, and Blaze jerked his attention back to the stage.

"Hole in One?" he asked right out loud.

"Yeah, they're here," Matt said, completely unaware of the way Blaze's heart had turned into a giant bass drum and was beating, beating, beating at him to find Faith and demand another chance.

He didn't have to find her, because she walked up on stage in the next moment. Her lovely red hair had been tied back, and she wore an apron that looked like a big tom turkey. She smiled out at the crowd, made a big show of looking away as she reached into the donation box, and withdrew a check with a flourish.

A check.

Blaze's mind went into frenzy, but he told himself lots of people still used checks.

No, they don't, his brain screamed at him. People over seventy-five and retired bull riders, apparently.

Faith grinned with all the happiness she possessed as she looked down at the check. He knew he'd won the moment all of her emotion slid behind a strong, tall, cement wall.

"Well?" the man on stage with her asked. "Who is it?" He peered over her forearm and let out a squeal. "My goodness!" He started searching the crowd. "Blaze Young, and he wrote a check for fifty thousand dollars!"

A collective gasp went through the crowd, and Blaze had never wanted the earth to open up and swallow him whole more than he did right now. *No,* he thought. *No, no, no.*

Had he really written a check for fifty grand? He honestly couldn't remember.

"Where's Blaze?" the man asked. "Let's get him up here!" He actually put his hand to his eyes as if he needed to shade them, when there wasn't a stitch of sunshine to be found.

Blaze stood at six-five and had shoulders like a linebacker. He couldn't hide in a crowd even if he wanted to. Plenty of people knew who he and Jem were, and all of those eyes landed on him.

He lifted one hand as if to wave off the announcer, but he would not be swayed. He actually waved back. "There he is!" He looked over to Faith. "Come on, Mister Young! Get up here and collect your prize."

Blaze saw no other choice, and he told himself with every step that if Faith were the prize, he'd have run up and accepted gladly. As it was, he climbed the steps on the side of the stage and moved on wooden legs to stand next to her.

She stared at him, that wonder and wide-eyed look so perfect on her pretty features, and Blaze stared right on back.

"Well, isn't Faith and Hole in One the lucky one today?" the man said, and Blaze wanted to shove the mic down his throat. "She'll get half of the donation for her business, and the other half goes right to residents here in Coral Canyon! Let's all thank Blaze for supporting small businesses and the community. Come on! Put your hands together!"

He didn't have to ask more than once. The crowd there whooped and hollered, but Blaze felt like he'd been hollowed out.

Faith got half the money?

Oh, she was going to kill him, and as he stood there with a forced smile on his face, he was actually looking forward to it.

Sneak Peek! BLAZE Chapter Two:

Faith Cromwell couldn't stay on this stage for much longer. The cameras kept going off, and she felt sure she and Blaze Young—blasted Blaze Young—would be on the front page of a dozen papers tomorrow. Online articles. Social media. The works.

So she kept her smile buttoned in place, and she even pinched the very tippy corner of the check on the right side of it while Blaze did the same on the left.

"All right!" Karl finally boomed into the microphone. "Wow, wasn't that exciting? Thank you for the donation, Mister Young, and those of you out there waiting for food? Don't forget to donate too!"

Faith needed to get off the stage. Now. She'd left Ricky and Walt in the truck alone, and while they were just fine, she was the one who sold the most doughnuts.

They worked like dogs, though, and she hoped she could give them some of this money.

She didn't even know what twenty-five thousand dollars looked like. Her eyes dropped to the check—it looked like half of that. She couldn't even imagine writing numbers like this and then signing her name on the line, but Blaze had done it—and sloppily too.

Looking up, she figured he'd be gone. Out of the spotlight, where he claimed he didn't like to be—at least not anymore. But he hadn't left the stage. He hadn't looked away from her. Her mind blanked at the sight of that rugged jawline, those full lips, the dark and dreamy eyes.

He watched her without speaking, and she half-heartedly lifted the check. "You had no idea what you were doing when you wrote this, did you?"

He shook his head, and Faith wanted to rip the check to shreds. At the same time, she absolutely would not do that. Guilt gutted her, and she wished she could rewind time seventy-one days. Then she'd be sitting at dinner with Blaze, his brother making too much noise with his rodeo bunnies, and they'd get up and walk out together.

He'd hold her hand and drive her home. He'd walk her to the door and kiss her good-night. Oh, how Faith had dreamed of kissing Blaze good-night. And for the past seventy-one days, she wouldn't have been alone. She wouldn't have struggled to get her third truck back in the rotation. She wouldn't have thought of Blaze every day, wondering if she'd hurt him too much for him to take her back.

One look into those black-as-coal eyes, and she knew she'd hurt him...but not so much that he wouldn't give her a third chance. He'd probably strike her out if she failed with him again, and Faith wasn't going to take that swing.

He wasn't right for her, plain and simple. That was why she'd ended things before.

She herded him toward the steps, and he went silently. Once she'd joined him at the bottom of them, she grabbed onto his forearm and took him around the back of the stage so they could have some more privacy.

"We do a raffle drawing every thirty minutes," she said. "One of the food truck owners gets to draw out of the donation box. The donator gets a bunch of free coupons for our truck, and we get half of the amount of money we pull."

"Did it cost you anything to get to do that?"

She nodded. "Yeah, I had to donate a certain amount to the general fund for Hunger No More." The food truck committee had named them as their receiving charity this year. "You realize we didn't even raise twenty-five thousand dollars last year, total?"

"I wasn't around much last year," he said coolly.

Faith sighed and reached up to push her newly-cut bangs off her forehead. She hated them and regretted cutting them. But she'd needed something to make her feel different. She hated getting up in the morning and looking at herself in the mirror. Seeing the same woman who'd broken up with this fine specimen of a man, walked out on him, and then refused to respond to any of his texts or calls.

Her pulse thrummed in her veins, setting her entire bloodstream on fire. "Yeah, well, we didn't even raise twenty-five thousand dollars last year, and now, with this —" She waved the slip of paper. It was crazy that something so insignificant could mean so much. "You've exceeded it single-handedly."

He swallowed and nodded. "It would've been nice to get a memo on what people usually donate."

"For comparison," she said, glancing over her shoulder. "Tony from Chicken-Chicken pulled out a twenty dollar bill a half-hour ago."

"Congratulations, Faith," someone said, and she turned to smile at another food truck owner.

"Thanks," she said with a laugh. As she turned back to Blaze, the façade fell away. "You see why this is shocking."

"I do now, yes," he said. He shifted his feet in the dirt, and she noticed he'd gone full cowboy for Thanksgiving. Blue jeans. Black wool coat that barely fell to his waist. Midnight-black cowboy boots. He even had a matching hat.

No wonder she was about to blurt out how stupid she'd been and beg him to take her to dinner tomorrow. She gritted her teeth and bit back the words.

"Well, I should go find my people," he said.

"Who did you come with?" she asked. "I didn't see any of your brothers."

"My ex's parents," he said.

That made Faith's eyebrows shoot up. "You hang out with them?"

"No." He smiled at her, and wow, he couldn't do that. Heat filled her face, and she had to look down so she wouldn't return the grin. "I visit them," he said. "They're my son's grandparents, so I try to stay in touch."

"That's...." Adorable. Perfect. Touching. Amazing.

Faith could've said all of those things. She didn't know how. Blaze himself was adorable, perfect, touching, and amazing, and she'd never felt so inadequate in her life.

Then his fingers stroked along the side of her neck to her jaw. Fire licked through her system, and she brought her eyes up as he gently nudged her to do the same with her head. "I miss you," he said quietly. "It's sure good to see you and talk to you."

Faith didn't know what to say. Nothing had changed between them. Had it?

They were still from two different worlds. He would always outshine her and be on another level than her. Always. She was his opposite in every way, including how he could say things so eloquently, and she stood there mute and unsure.

His gaze burned into hers. "Congratulations on winning the donation." He dropped his hand and moved by her to go back the way he'd come. Faith turned and watched him, go, every cell in her body urging her to call him back and tell him she missed him too.

Her mouth couldn't do it, and Blaze walked around the corner and past the steps that led up to the stage. Then he was gone.

"I miss you too," she whispered. "I may have been wrong to break up with you." A sigh fell from her lips, and she folded the check in half and put it in her front pocket. She had hours of work ahead of her, and her guys needed her in the truck.

Before she moved, though, Faith took her phone from the front of the turkey apron. She might not be able to say things right to Blaze's face, but she'd always been a pro at texting him. She hadn't erased any of his messages, and in fact, the man's name was still pinned to the top of her texting app.

That alone spoke how she really felt about him, and she quickly thumbed out a message and hit send.

I miss you too. I'm sorry I broke up with you in September. Do you think we could try again or am I insane?

She shoved her phone into the pocket again and told herself she would not check it until she made it to her truck. "Why can't you talk to him?" she muttered to herself. "What is this third try going to look like, Faith? You texting him day and night and never seeing him? You have to learn to *talk to him*."

She went around the corner of the stage, her stride as

long as she could make it. Irritation at herself burned through her veins. Her complete ineptitude was just another reason she shouldn't ever go out with another man.

"No," she said to herself. "Just not Blaze Young."

"Why not Blaze Young?"

She froze at the sound of his voice. He stood on the fringes of the crowd, obviously having just pushed through them. He held up his phone. "You're not insane."

Faith wanted to run and hide. "I don't think it'll work."

"You just asked if we could go out again." He frowned. "I'll take you right now."

She shook her head. "You're here with your in-laws."

"Ex-in-laws." He came closer to her. "Explain this to me." He looked at his phone and back to her. "And tell me what's going on in your head."

"The same stuff as before," she blurted out. "You're like, this mega-god of a man. You write checks for fifty thousand dollars, Blaze. You're like, perfect all the time. Perfectly dressed. You smell perfect. You say all the perfect things. And I don't know if you've noticed or not, but I'm a mess. A huge, hot mess, and perfection shouldn't get mixed up with hot mess."

Her chest ached because she'd spewed all of that in one breath. She wiped her hair back and drew in a deep breath. "I hate my bangs. I work fifteen hours a day. I think about you all the time and wonder if I did the right thing or if I was just scared."

He still said nothing, and Faith wasn't sure how long she should keep talking. "So I second-guess everything, you know? Everyone will look at us and go, 'wow, what's he doing with a loser like Faith Cromwell?' or 'Jeez, did she win him in some bachelor auction? That's the only reason a man like him would go out with her.'"

Blaze cocked his head and studied her, but blast him, he still said nothing.

"So then I focus on my truck and my employees, but I go home alone every night. No one texts me during the day. I'm *lonely*, and so then I wonder if I want to go out with you just so I won't be lonely, because you made me feel less lonely, and is that a good enough reason to want to go out with someone?" She shook her head. "I'm not making sense, I know."

She pressed her eyes closed and tried to think through the frenzy in her mind. It was impossible. "I'm not saying anything else until you say something."

"There's so many things wrong with what you just said."

Her eyes popped open. "How dare you?" She swatted at his chest with both hands.

Surprised filled his expression, and he stumbled backward. For one, two, three terrible moments, she thought he might fall, but he caught himself. Then he caught her around the wrists.

"I'm not wrong."

"Yes, you are," he growled at her. He brought his

hands toward him, and hers went with them. She followed, and they stood nearly chest-to-chest, both of them breathing hard. "One, I'm not perfect. I'm about as far from that as a person can get. I've just been hiding it all from you. Two, you're not a loser. Never once have I thought that, and no one else is thinking that. Three, you're not a hot mess. You're a medium mess, and I happen to like it. It makes my hot mess of a life seem more...normal."

She blinked at him, pure surprise running through her.

"Four," he said. "I'm lonely too, and yes, it's okay to go out with me so we can both be less lonely."

"You have a million brothers," she said, finding her voice again. "You can't be lonely."

"Faith, sweetheart," he said, his voice grinding through his throat. "A man needs more than brothers." His gaze burned into hers. "You're feisty, and I love that about you. You didn't hesitate to talk to me the first time we met; it's only been recently that you've withdrawn, and I hate that. I don't want the scared-rabbit version of Faith Cromwell. I want that gorgeous, sexy, redhead who barked at me to get out of her truck, called me arrogant, and said she wouldn't go out with me."

Faith couldn't believe this man. She pulled her wrists out of his grip and then straightened her apron. "Fine," she said.

"Fine."

"You're still arrogant."

"At least I didn't tell you how much money I have this time."

"No, you wrote a check for fifty grand," she said dryly.

Blaze took a step closer to her. "Have you taken five seconds to think that you being the one on stage to pull that check from the donation box wasn't a coincidence?" he asked. "Because I have—just five seconds—and I'm not even that religious, full disclaimer. But I feel like God is telling me to try again with you. And blast it all, I want to shake Him and ask, 'Why? This woman doesn't even like me.'" He sucked in a breath, held it, and then exhaled.

Her eyes flashed between his, trying to read the emotion in the dark depths. "There's so many things wrong with what you just said."

"Enlighten me," he said.

Faith had to get back to her truck. She could not stand here and do this with him right now. "I will," she said. "At dinner tomorrow."

Blaze looked like she'd thrown ice water in his face. The expression only stayed for two seconds, and then he smoothed it away. "All right," he said. "I'll pick you up at six."

"Fine," she said.

"Fine." He reached up and smoothed her bangs back down. "I like the bangs," he said quietly, showing her that Dr. Jekyll and Mr. Hyde personality he had. She supposed she did too, going from silent and scared to demanding and flirty.

"I really do have to get back to my truck," she said.

"Right." Blaze dropped his hand again and fell back another step. "You have the same number?"

"Yes."

He tipped his hat at her and said, "See you tomorrow, Faith Cromwell." Then he turned and melted into the crowd again. Several of them stared at her, and Faith lifted her chin and set her sights on her ugliest food truck, which sat parked right in the middle across from the entrance to the circle.

She hadn't had the funds to paint it pink like the others, but it didn't matter. A huge line of people waited outside the truck, and Faith pushed Blaze and all of his perfect glory from her mind—at least for a moment.

He wouldn't go so easily, and she found she didn't even want him to. She was even less lonely when he lingered in her mind, and as she worked the rest of the food truck rally, she practiced over and over talking to Blaze the way she did her customers.

Lord, she thought. *He might not be religious, but I am. Could you make me less insecure, please? Less tongue-tied, just for one evening.*

Faith could admit she hadn't prayed much in the past year or so. It seemed like no matter what she asked of the Lord, she didn't get it. She'd been learning, however, that it wasn't about getting what she wanted. Prayer was about maintaining an open conversation with the Lord.

And she needed to do the same thing with Blaze.

You did it with God by praying no matter what, she thought, and the answer to her prayer appeared in her mind.

She had to talk to Blaze, no matter what. No matter if she was nervous or scared. Insecure or weak. Full of self-doubt or not.

She simply needed to keep talking to him. After that... well, Faith would start their third try off with dinner—a dinner full of conversation—and then she'd go from there.

Preorder BLAZE today! He's coming soon!

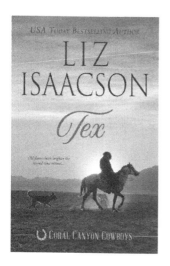

Tex (Book 1): He's back in town after a successful country music career. She owns a bordering farm to the family land he wants to buy...and she outbids him at the auction. Can Tex and Abigail rekindle their old flame, or will the issue of land ownership come between them?

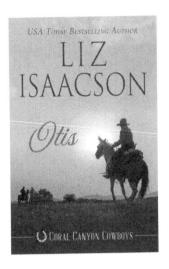

Otis (Book 2): He's finished with his last album and looking for a soft place to fall after a devastating break-up. She runs the small town bookshop in Coral Canyon and needs a new boyfriend to get her old one out of her life for good. Can Georgia convince Otis to take another shot at real love when their first kiss was fake?

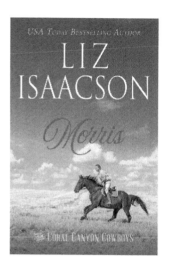

Morris (Book 3): Morris Young is just settling into his new life as the manager of Country Quad when he attends a wedding. He sees his ex-wife there—apparently Leighann is back in Coral Canyon—along with a little boy who can't be more or less than five years old... Could he be Morris's? And why is his heart hoping for that, and for a reconciliation with the woman who left him because he traveled too much?

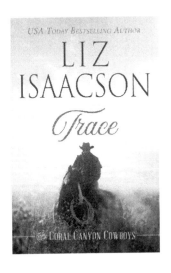

Trace (Book 4): He's been accused of only dating celebrities. She's a simple line dance instructor in small town Coral Canyon, with a soft spot for kids...and cowboys. Trace could use some dance lessons to go along with his love lessons... Can he and Everly fall in love with the beat, or will she dance her way right out of his arms?

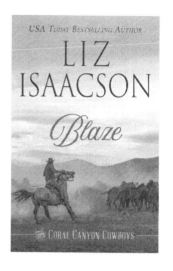

Blaze (Book 5): He's dark as night, a single dad, and a retired bull riding champion. With all his money, his rugged good looks, and his ability to say all the right things, Faith has no chance against Blaze Young's charms. But she's his complete opposite, and she just doesn't see how they can be together...

...so she ends things with him.

Her Cowboy Billionaire Birthday Wish (Book 1): All the maid at Whiskey Mountain Lodge wants for her birthday is a handsome cowboy billionaire. And Colton can make that wish come true—if only he hadn't escaped to Coral Canyon after being left at the altar...

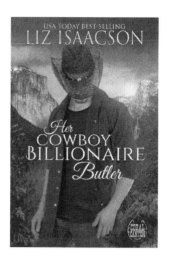

Her Cowboy Billionaire Butler (Book 2): She broke up with him to date another man...who broke her heart. He's a former CEO with nothing to do who can't get her out of his head. Can Wes and Bree find a way toward happily-ever-after at Whiskey Mountain Lodge?

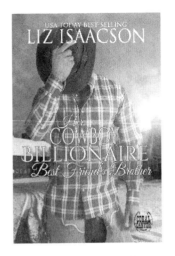

Her Cowboy Billionaire Best Friend's Brother (Book 3): She's best friends with the single dad cowboy's brother and has watched two friends find love with the sexy new cowboys in town. When Gray Hammond comes to Whiskey Mountain Lodge with his son, will Elise finally get her own happily-ever-after with one of the Hammond brothers?

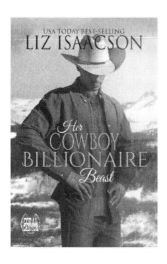

Her Cowboy Billionaire Beast (Book 4): A cowboy billionaire beast, his new manager, and the Christmas traditions that soften his heart and bring them together.

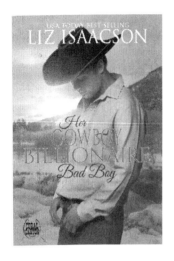

Her Cowboy Billionaire Bad Boy (Book 5): A cowboy billionaire cop who's a stickler for rules, the woman he pulls over when he's not even on duty, and the personal mandates he has to break to keep her in his life...

Books in the Christmas in Coral Canyon Romance series

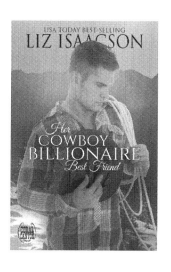

Her Cowboy Billionaire Best Friend (Book 1): Graham Whittaker returns to Coral Canyon a few days after Christmas—after the death of his father. He takes over the energy company his dad built from the ground up and buys a high-end lodge to live in—only a mile from the home of his once-best friend, Laney McAllister. They were best friends once, but Laney's always entertained feelings for him, and spending so much time with him while they make Christmas memories puts her heart in danger of getting broken again...

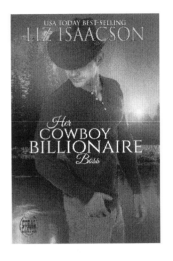

Her Cowboy Billionaire Boss (Book 2): Since the death of his wife a few years ago, Eli Whittaker has been running from one job to another, unable to find somewhere for him and his son to settle. Meg Palmer is Stockton's nanny, and she comes with her boss, Eli, to the lodge, her long-time crush on the man no different in Wyoming than it was on the beach. When she confesses her feelings for him and gets nothing in return, she's crushed, embarrassed, and unsure if she can stay in Coral Canyon for Christmas. Then Eli starts to show some feelings for her too...

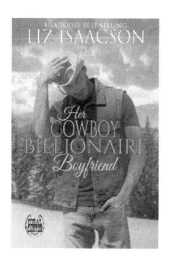

Her Cowboy Billionaire Boyfriend (Book 3): Andrew Whittaker is the public face for the Whittaker Brothers' family energy company, and with his older brother's robot about to be announced, he needs a press secretary to help him get everything ready and tour the state to make the announcements. When he's hit by a protest sign being carried by the company's biggest opponent, Rebecca Collings, he learns with a few clicks that she has the background they need. He offers her the job of press secretary when she thought she was going to be arrested, and not only because the spark between them in so hot Andrew can't see straight.

Can Becca and Andrew work together and keep their relationship a secret? Or will hearts break in this classic romance retelling reminiscent of *Two Weeks Notice*?

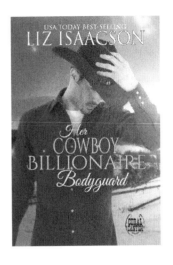

Her Cowboy Billionaire Bodyguard (Book 4): Beau Whittaker has watched his brothers find love one by one, but every attempt he's made has ended in disaster. Lily Everett has been in the spotlight since childhood and has half a dozen platinum records with her two sisters. She's taking a break from the brutal music industry and hiding out in Wyoming while her ex-husband continues to cause trouble for her. When she hears of Beau Whittaker and what he offers his clients, she wants to meet him. Beau is instantly attracted to Lily, but he tried a relationship with his last client that left a scar that still hasn't healed...

Can Lily use the spirit of Christmas to discover what matters most? Will Beau open his heart to the possibility of love with someone so different from him?

Her Cowboy Billionaire Bull Rider (Book 5): Todd Christopherson has just retired from the professional rodeo circuit and returned to his hometown of Coral Canyon. Problem is, he's got no family there anymore, no land, and no job. Not that he needs a job-- he's got plenty of money from his illustrious career riding bulls.

Then Todd gets thrown during a routine horseback ride up the canyon, and his only support as he recovers physically is the beautiful Violet Everett. She's no nurse, but she does the best she can for the handsome cowboy. **Will she lose her heart to the billionaire bull rider? Can Todd trust that God led him to Coral Canyon...and Vi?**

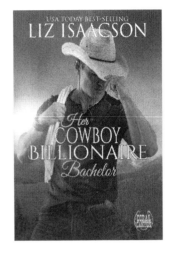

Her Cowboy Billionaire Bachelor (Book 6): Rose Everett isn't sure what to do with her life now that her country music career is on hold. After all, with both of her sisters in Coral Canyon, and one about to have a baby, they're not making albums anymore.

Liam Murphy has been working for Doctors Without Borders, but he's back in the US now, and looking to start a new clinic in Coral Canyon, where he spent his summers.

When Rose wins a date with Liam in a bachelor auction, their relationship blooms and grows quickly.

Can Liam and Rose find a solution to their problems that doesn't involve one of them leaving Coral Canyon with a broken heart?

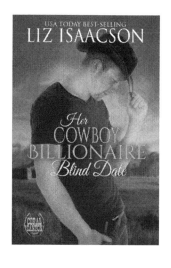

Her Cowboy Billionaire Blind Date (Book 7): Her sons want her to be happy, but she's too old to be set up on a blind date...isn't she?

Amanda Whittaker has been looking for a second chance at love since the death of her husband several years ago. Finley Barber is a cowboy in every sense of the word. Born and raised on a racehorse farm in Kentucky, he's since moved to Dog Valley and started his own breeding stable for champion horses. He hasn't dated in years, and everything about Amanda makes him nervous.

Will Amanda take the leap of faith required to be with Finn? Or will he become just another boyfriend who doesn't make the cut?

Her Cowboy Billionaire Best Man (Book 8): When Celia Abbott-Armstrong runs into a gorgeous cowboy at her best friend's wedding, she decides she's ready to start dating again.

But the cowboy is Zach Zuckerman, and the Zuckermans and Abbotts have been at war for generations.

Can Zach and Celia find a way to reconcile their family's differences so they can have a future together?

About Liz

Liz Isaacson writes inspirational romance, usually set in Texas, or Wyoming, or anywhere else horses and cowboys exist. She lives in Utah, where she writes full-time, takes her two dogs to the park everyday, and eats a lot of veggies while writing. Find her on her website at www.feelgoodfictionbooks.com.

Made in the USA
Middletown, DE
20 October 2022

13137751R00314